FORBIDDEN HARVEST

A Novel

by

PETER RIZZOLO

© Peter Rizzolo

Publisher: Create Space, a subsidiary of Amazon Publishing Group

Editor: Charlotte Hoffman

Cover design by Phil Daquila

This is a work of fiction. Any names, characters, or places are coincidental. However, several prominent nonfictional physicians and researchers are referenced in the recounting of organ research and transplant surgeries.

Dr. Bernie Siegel, well-known surgeon and best-selling author, makes a cameo appearance in this novel. He has graciously given the author permission.

FIRST EDITION 2013

Dedication

My best childhood friend, Mark Stillman, died of renal failure at age fourteen in 1942. A kidney transplant would have saved Marky's life, but that option was not a reality until 1954 when Doctor Joseph Murray and his colleagues at Peter Bent Brigham Hospital in Boston performed the first successful human-to-human kidney transplant. Marky wanted to be a scientist. He was a year ahead of me in school. I was in awe of how smart he was. To this day I wonder what he might have accomplished. I dedicate this novel to his memory and all children whose lives might be saved by the timely gift of a donor organ.

Acknowledgements

I would like to thank the members of my writing workshop, who critiqued my manuscript, page by page, chapter by chapter. Especially Charlotte Hoffman, workshop leader, whose editorial skill and creative insight were indispensable. Other workshop contributors included Orman Day, Chuck Hauser, Robin Kirk, Beverly Lemons, Carol Mann, Donald McKinney, Neal Paris, Lucia Peel Powe, Tom Shetley, and Frank Stallone.

Foreword

The protagonist of *Forbidden Harvest*, Dr. Kenneth Bernholtz, develops a method of preserving human organs by a complex freezing process. Although preservation of human organs by freezing is a method vigorously pursued by scientists, it has not passed the experimental stage.

Of the major organs, the heart is most sensitive to oxygen deprivation. This critical dependence of cardiac muscle on an adequate supply of oxygen makes the quest for expansion of preservation time a matter of life and death for children and adults awaiting a heart transplant.

Intense public interest and extensive experimentation followed the first successful human-to-human heart transplant by Dr. Christiaan Barnard in South Africa on December 3, 1967. One year later, Dr. Norman Shumway performed the first successful heart transplant in the United States. But the initial excitement among cardiac surgeons quickly subsided because of the high rate of post-operative deaths due to organ rejection.

Dr. Shumway and his team used newly introduced drugs, such as cyclosporin, to combat the problem of rejection of the implanted organ. His perseverance and successes in the use of such drugs encouraged other cardiac surgeons.

With improving survival, the number of candidates for transplant surgery expanded rapidly. But the limited availability of donor organs, coupled with the rapidity at which harvested organs deteriorate, made the viability of donor organs a matter of utmost importance. The time that major organs remain viable:

Heart: four hours
Kidney: eighteen to twenty-four hours
Lung: sixteen hours
Pancreas: eighteen hours

The freezing of major organs remains a promising approach to preservation, but scientists have not as yet been able to prevent tissue damage primarily caused by the crystallization of water within the organ.

Dr. Roger Gosden and his colleagues at Notre-

Dame Hospital in Montreal, Canada, in 2002 were the first to demonstrate that an entire organ can be safely frozen, stored and thawed. They transplanted rat ovaries that had been frozen in liquid nitrogen. More than half of the rats that received the implanted ovaries menstruated normally. One recipient became pregnant.

In this novel, Dr. Bernholtz's other approach to preservation, the subjecting of an organ to several atmospheres of pressure, is also an area of scientific research. And although progress is being made, researchers as yet have not solved the problem of avoiding the toxic effects of oxygen at elevated pressures.

Researchers are making progress in both areas, but have not as yet achieved Dr. Bernholtz's dream of stockpiling donor organs.

CHAPTER ONE

Waking at five each morning, Tom Bradshaw didn't have to look at the clock. It was as though an internal alarm had gone off. From his bed he glanced toward the window. The white oaks and sugar maples that crowded the northwest side of his home, having cast off most of their leaves, revealed patches of grey sky. He rolled to a sitting position on the side of the bed, head in his hands, staring at his feet. Part of him wanted to lie down, but he knew sleep wouldn't come. He got out of bed and went to his study. Standing at a window that overlooked Lake Washington, he could barely make out the distant shore. Early morning fog drifted in ghost-like clusters across the water. He turned from the window and walked to a massive mahogany desk that had been his father's. A stack of unread correspondence lay there. He picked up a photograph of Brenda and Link. He ran his fingers over her image. Why had he survived? He would have been driving if he hadn't been drinking. It was his fault she died. He thought of the last time they made love. He breathed deeply, drawing into himself her sweet essence. The sense of her being there in bed beside him never abated. But now when he moved his hand into that space, it was empty, cold.

Folding his arms on his desk, he rested his head. He was soon asleep. When he awakened, he looked at his watch. It was six-thirty. My God. Link'll be late for school, he thought.

Forbidden Harvest

He headed for Link's room, taking the steps two at a time. Link lay sprawled on his belly, sleeping quietly. Tom shook his shoulder. "Hey champ, it's time to get up."

Link rolled over and rubbed his eyes. "Dad, it's Saturday."

Later that day, Tom and Link sat on the floor of their family room watching a baseball game. The Mariners were in a tough race for first place in their division. Ken Griffey Jr., their star centerfielder, had recently won the 1990 Golden Glove Award. Link owned a baseball bat signed by Griffey. Link, sitting cross-legged, leaned back on his arms

"Dad, if the Mariners get in the World Series, can we go see them play?"

"Wouldn't that be great?" Tom said. "I've never been to a Series game." He sat with one leg flexed, his chin resting on his knee. "Tickets sell out fast."

"How can you buy tickets ahead when you don't know which teams are playing?" Link asked.

"Don't know. I'll check it out."

"Yeah. Don't forget."

Tom and Link were caught up in the excitement of the pennant race. Tom loved baseball, not only because he grew up with a passion for the game, but it was an interest he and his son shared.

Link moved behind his dad, pressing against him. Tom poked him in the ribs with his elbow. Link grabbed him around the chest, trying to wrestle him to the floor. It was getting so that if Tom let up even a little, Link might get the better of him. Rolling onto the plush carpeting, Tom wrestled Link onto his back and sat over him in a straddle position.

Forbidden Harvest

"This is getting harder all the time," Tom said.

Link was sweating profusely. He grimaced.

"What's the matter, champ?" Tom released Link's arms.

"Feels like somebody's sitting on me." Link rubbed his chest.

"Does it hurt?"

"No. Just a heavy feeling. It's hard to breathe."

Tom pressed Link's chest. "Is this where it's sore?"

"No."

"It's probably nothing to worry about, but I'm gonna call Dr. Boat. See what he says."

Dr. Boat insisted Tom bring Link to the emergency room at St. Joseph's Hospital. "I'll call ahead."

On the way to the hospital, Link lay quietly in the back seat of their Volvo. Tom adjusted his rear view mirror so he could see Link. "Feeling any better, son?"

"Do you think I'm having a heart attack, like Grandpa had before he died?"

Tom gripped the steering wheel as though someone were trying to take it from him. The muscles in his jaw tightened. He struggled to make his voice sound casual.

"I think you probably pulled a muscle. Happened to me playing football. I know that a pulled muscle can hurt a heck of a lot."

At the hospital entrance a uniformed attendant helped Link into a wheelchair and walked with them to emergency. There was a long line at the clerk's desk. Link held his hand over his chest. The color drained from his

Forbidden Harvest

face. Tom pushed to the front of the line. The receptionist was on the phone. As he approached, she swiveled her chair, so as not to face him.

"Pardon me, ma'am," he said.

She ignored him.

"Ma'am, this is an emergency, excuse me!"

"These are all emergencies."

"My son is having chest pain. I spoke with Dr. Boat...."

The clerk peered over her almond-shaped glasses. She pressed an intercom button. "Send out the triage nurse. We have a young boy here with chest pain."

A nurse came to the reception area. She wheeled Link to the rear. "Does your chest still hurt?" she asked.

"Yeah, kind of."

She bypassed the triage room, taking him directly to a curtained cubicle where she helped him onto a stretcher. He was given a gown and asked to take off all his clothes. Tom sat beside the stretcher. A young woman entered the cubicle and looked from Tom to Link. "Hi. I need to start an IV. Okay?"

"Has Dr. Boat called in?"

"Yes, he ordered lab work, a chest x-ray and EKG."

She set a tray on the stretcher. She took Link's blood pressure, pulse and temperature and then applied a tourniquet. She filled several glass vials with blood. Tom's heart raced. A wave of nausea sweep through him.

"Are you feeling okay, son?" he asked.

"It's not too bad. Where's Dr. Boat?"

"He should be here pretty soon."

After hooking up the cardiac electrodes, the nurse

looked at the monitor. Tom saw her startled expression. "Is anything wrong?" he asked.

"I need to get the EKG machine."

Tom watched as she rushed down the hall. Link tugged at his sleeve.

"Dad, what's the matter?"

"She didn't say. Maybe it was hooked up wrong or something."

When the nurse returned, she attached a maze of wires to Link and pushed some buttons on the machine. She tore off the EKG strip. "I want the doctor to look at this. She'll be back to examine you in a few minutes."

Link put his hand over the center of his chest and looked away from his dad.

"The pain coming back?"

He nodded. As he turned to face his dad, there were tears in his eyes. He moved his hand to his jaw. "Now it hurts here."

Tom leaned out of the curtained cubicle, scanning the area for the nurse. She and another woman approached him.

"I'm Dr. Sharma." After listening to his chest she said to Link, "We're going to have to keep you in the hospital for observation."

"Do I have to, Dad?"

Before Tom could respond, Dr. Sharma placed her hand on Link's shoulder.

"We need to do more tests." She motioned for Tom to follow her.

Tom and Dr. Sharma walked a few steps to the nurses'

station. The area was crowded with people in scrub suits and white coats. Phones, beepers, and the overhead pager were all going off at once.

Tom shouted, "How can anyone even think in this place? What's going on with my son?"

"Mr. Bradshaw, the EKG shows a pattern suggestive of an evolving heart attack."

"He's only twelve. That's impossible. Where the hell is Dr. Boat? I can't believe this."

Tom hurried back to the cubicle. He held Link's hand as an orderly wheeled him from the emergency room to the coronary care unit.

"You'll have to go to the family waiting area until the nurse says it's okay to come see him," the orderly said as they approached the CCU.

Tom pressed Link's hand against his lips. "I'll be right down the hall. Dr. Boat should be here soon."

Tom looked about the familiar CCU waiting room. He and his mom had spent many hours there after his father's heart attack. It's all a mistake, Tom thought. How the hell could Link be having a heart attack? Dr. Boat knows Link. Tom was certain he'd straighten them out.

A stack of *National Geographics* lay on a nearby table. Tom flipped through the magazines but couldn't concentrate. The image of his son's frightened face, as the door to the CCU closed between them, made it hard to resist the urge to race down the hall and force his way into Link's room. To be certain he was okay.

An elderly white-haired gentleman approached Tom. He extended his hand, "I'm Dr. Holmes, attending cardiologist in the CCU. You're Link's father?"

"Yes, doctor. What's wrong with him?"

Forbidden Harvest

Dr. Holmes pulled up a chair and sat next to Tom. "The EKG continues to be abnormal, suggesting evolving damage to the bottom wall of the heart. Initial blood tests are consistent with heart muscle injury."

"My God! Are you sure? I...I've never heard of such a thing!"

"We'll have to wait several hours to confirm the diagnosis, but I'm afraid he almost certainly has had a heart attack. We're starting a medication that will limit the amount of heart muscle damage by dissolving any clot that may be forming."

Dr. Holmes stood as though preparing to leave. Tom remained seated, gripping the arm rests of his chair.

"I don't understand how a perfectly healthy twelve-year-old boy can have a heart attack."

Dr. Holmes took a deep breath and let it out slowly. He looked at his watch before answering. "I can't say for sure at this time, but I suspect the vessels that carry blood to Link's heart muscle are abnormal. There is a test we can do after the situation has stabilized. It'll give us a clearer picture of the arteries that nourish the heart. Mr. Bradshaw, I really must leave now."

Tom's face flushed. "Dr. Holmes, I've just been told my son has had a heart attack, and I'm not ready to end this conversation!"

Several people sitting in the waiting area turned and stared at Tom.

"Mr. Bradshaw, I understand you're under a great deal of stress, given the situation. I can stay perhaps another ten minutes. I have a patient waiting in the Emergency Room."

"I don't understand why Link's heart condition wouldn't have bothered him until now," Tom said.

"The heart, over a period of years, can grow new arteries by extension of existing blood vessels. These are called collateral vessels. They can sustain the heart muscle for a long time."

"So why did he have a heart attack?"

"As the body continues to grow, the heart has to work harder," Dr. Holmes said. "The collateral vessels alone aren't enough to do the job. But without further tests, especially cardiac catheterization, we can't be certain of the diagnosis."

"His mother died in a car accident a year ago. Could the shock have caused something like this?" Tom asked.

"I'm very sorry to hear that, but I doubt that would explain your son's present heart problem."

Tom wasn't convinced. "Can I see him now?"

"Certainly. When I left, Dr. Boat was with him. I know he wants to speak with you. Do you know the way to the CCU?"

Tom was already moving toward the door. He turned. "Yes, I do. Thank you, Dr. Holmes."

Tom saw Dr. Boat walking toward him. They shook hands.

"Tom, he's stable and is in no imminent danger. Let's have a talk after you've had a chance to see him. I'll be at the nurses' station."

Tom had become accustomed to the maze of equipment in the CCU after his dad had his first heart attack. But he was not prepared for how small Link looked in that crowded room. Tom hugged him gently, as though Link was suddenly fragile.

"Don't worry, Dad, the doctors told me I'm doing okay. I

got a shot. My chest doesn't hurt anymore."

"You do look better."

"They got me wired up like an astronaut. The nurse at the desk can tell my pulse and blood pressure without even coming in the room. They got my heart hooked up to a computer. The doctor told me an alarm goes off if anything weird happens."

"Sounds like you've got this place pretty well figured out, champ." He leaned close to Link. "Dr. Boat says you're going to do just fine. I have to go talk with him now, but I'll be back."

Dr. Boat never appeared to know what to do with his long legs. At six feet four inches tall, he seemed ill suited to care for little people. Somehow, however, he always managed to get down to the child's level. His wisps of brown hair looked like feathers, and his long, narrow nose made it appear to be a beak. Link nicknamed him "Big Bird."

The nurses' station was muted compared to the Emergency Room. Dr. Boat ushered Tom into a room that looked like a storage area. The walls were covered with open shelves that held bottles and boxes of all sizes. There was a counter and sink on one wall. They sat at a small table.

"Tom, Dr. Holmes is a fine heart specialist. I've known him for years. But Link's going to need a pediatric cardiologist. I'd like to transfer Link to Children's Hospital."

"But you told me to bring him here."

"When you called I had no way of knowing how serious it might be. This hospital is much closer to your home."

The room was barely larger than a closet. It was warm and stuffy.

Forbidden Harvest

"Yes, of course," Tom said. He could feel perspiration running down the inside of his shirt.

"We can transfer him once he is over the acute risk. At Children's Hospital, the entire team is expert in caring for children with heart problems."

Tom's mouth was dry. He grabbed a paper cup from a wall dispenser and filled it with water.

"What do you mean by acute risk? I thought you just said he's not in any danger."

"In the first two to three days after a heart attack there is increased risk of developing abnormal heart rhythms."

He told Tom that he would make all the arrangements at Children's Hospital and would work with Dr. Holmes to determine when Link could be safely transferred.

After his conversation with Dr. Boat, Tom went to Link's room.

"I'll call your grandmother to tell her you're in the hospital."

"Yeah, tell her I'm okay. And don't forget to bring my glasses."

As Tom left the hospital he decided to drive to his mother's condominium instead of calling her.

"Tom, I've been calling the house all afternoon. No one answered the damn phone!"

"Mom, Saturday's Mrs. McAllister's day off. And you know how Albert likes to putter around outside."

They walked to the living room. Tom was wearing blue jeans and a tee shirt. He sat next to his mother on a brightly flowered chintz couch. He was silent for a few moments, not knowing where to begin.

"Tom, look at me. What's going on? Has something happened to Link?"

He went on to describe the events of the day, leaving out some of the details and stressing how well Link looked.

Lydia sat with her hands on her lap, her face ashen.

"You should've called me."

"Yes, but..."

"Damn it, you should've gotten some indication that Link wasn't doing well. How could he have a heart attack without problems showing up on all those check-ups with Dr. Boat?"

Tom stood. He tucked his hands in the front pockets of his jeans. "Mother, that's not fair. The doctors said there was no way to tell that anything was wrong with Link."

As he spoke he circled around the coffee table. He noticed a dish of cashews and realized that he hadn't eaten all day. He grabbed a handful and chewed as though he bore a personal grudge against each nut.

"Those doctors will close ranks to protect each other," Lydia snapped. "I'd fire Dr. Boat. I never did think much of him. Leaving Link's tonsils in after all those strep throats and Boat's hair looking like a bird's nest! I'll call Kenneth. He'll recommend someone. We need to get the very best doctors for Link. Even if it means transferring him to another hospital."

"Slow down, Mother. Link loves Dr. Boat. I'm sure Dr. Boat will bring in whomever he has to."

Lydia walked around the table and stood directly in front of Tom. "Very well, but I'm still going to call Kenneth to see what he thinks of the cardiologist Dr. Boat recommends."

Forbidden Harvest

Tom put his arms around his mother. At first she drew away but then embraced him tightly. She rested her head against his chest. "You're right, Tom, that wasn't a fair thing to say. I just go half crazy when I think of anything happening to Link."

"I know, Mother."

By this time, Tom had eaten all the cashews. She stared at the empty dish.

"Can I get you more cashews?" Lydia asked.

"I'm starved. What else do you have?"

CHAPTER TWO

As soon as Link's condition stabilized, Dr. Boat arranged for his transfer to Children's Memorial Hospital. At Dr. Boat's request, Dr. Cronce, Chief of Cardiology, agreed to care for Link.

Tom sat at Link's bedside, looking about the room. The walls had been transformed from hospital sick-green to a pale blue. The deep windowsill was crowded with columns of toy soldiers, boxes of baseball cards, a prized baseball signed by the entire Mariner team, and a brand new Louisville Slugger bat.

"I'm glad grandmother thought to bring your own stuff."

"Yeah, Dad, and turn off the lights. Look at that ceiling."

A star-filled night sky glowed above them.

"I hope they don't make us paint it over when you leave."

"That would be dumb," Link said. "Maybe Uncle Ken can fix it so they wouldn't. Grandma told me he's sort of a big-shot around here."

On the fifth hospital day Link was scheduled for cardiac catheterization. Tom had insisted he stay with Link during the procedure. They took Link on a stretcher to a small room, just outside of the cath lab. A cheerful nurse greeted them. An orderly handed her Link's hospital chart.

"Top of the mornin' to you, Master Bradshaw."

Link gave her a heavy-lidded weak smile.

Tom reached for the nurse's hand. "I'm his dad."

"Name's Maggie O'Brien. I'll be needin' to start an intravenous. The doctor should be here soon."

Tom liked the gentle way she spoke with Link, and how she explained everything she did ahead of time.

"It's kind of cold in here." Link drew his arms around his chest.

Maggie walked to a cabinet and returned with a flannel blanket. She tucked it around him. "There now, lad, is that better?"

"Yeah. It feels good."

A young man in a blue scrub suit came into the room, a stethoscope draped around his neck.

"Hi. I'm Dr. Fletcher." He turned toward a counter where the nurse had placed Link's chart. He stood with his back to Tom and Link. The room was quiet except for the sound of the pages of Link's chart being turned. Tom cleared his throat to remind the doctor they were there. After several minutes, the doctor turned to face Link.

"Well now, Tommy..."

"Everybody calls me Link, even though it's my middle name."

The doctor asked Link to sit up with his legs hanging over the side of the stretcher. He proceeded to do a physical examination. Tom noticed that Link's lips were blue. The doctor seemed oblivious of the shivering, frightened boy before him. Tom got another blanket and wrapped it around Link's shoulders.

"What exactly is your position here, doctor?" Tom asked.

"I'm a cardiology resident."

"Do you report to Dr. Cronce?"

By this time the doctor was entering the results of the examination on the chart. He looked up at Tom.

"He's chief of the cardiology service," the resident said.

Tom would like to have told him exactly what he thought of his bedside manner, but didn't want to unsettle Link.

"Will Dr. Cronce be doing the catheterization?" Tom asked.

"He'll be here, but the senior fellow will do the procedure."

Tom gave Link a quick smile. "How're you holding up?"

"That extra blanket helps."

The resident pulled a patient consent form from a wall rack. He started to read aloud from it, verbatim. Tom interrupted. "Dr. Cronce went through that with us yesterday. There should be a signed form on the chart."

Tom didn't want the resident to get to the part about complications. Dr. Cronce had said it was extremely unlikely, but in rare instances a blood clot could form in the femoral artery. And even less commonly the leg could be damaged beyond repair.

Link began to cry. "It sounds really scary, Dad."

Tom squeezed Link's hand. "Dr. Cronce said complications are extremely remote. He said you're more likely to be struck by lightning than have a serious complication."

"Okay. There is a signed consent form here," the resident said. He looked up. "Dr. Cronce is with another patient, but he should be ready to see Tommy soon."

Tom sat at the head of the table. Link grimaced as they injected numbing medicine in his upper right thigh. On the television monitor Tom watched the catheter rapidly make its way to Link's heart. When they injected the dye, it showed on the screen as dense white streaks that spread rapidly across Link's pulsating heart. The image came and went so fast, Tom couldn't understand how the doctors could see anything.

"How do you feel, Link?" Dr. Cronce asked.

"Hot all over."

"That's a normal reaction to the dye we just injected."

Tom's insides churned as he looked at his son's heart on the monitor. He felt lightheaded. He grasped the sides of the table to steady himself. He could hear the doctors talking, but he couldn't process all that was happening. The room began to spin. He closed his eyes.

"Mr. Bradshaw, are you okay?" the nurse asked.

When he didn't answer she went to him; he fell into her arms. She eased him off the stool onto the floor. He had no strength in his arms or legs. He was unable to speak.

"His pulse is slow but strong. His blood pressure's fine."

"That's why having a parent in the cath lab is not a good idea," Dr. Cronce said. "When he comes to, take him to the waiting area. I'll be there shortly to discuss the test results."

After the procedure, Dr. Cronce met with Tom. "As we suspected, Mr. Bradshaw, Link has a congenital abnormality resulting in insufficient circulation to parts of his heart muscle. That's what caused him to have what appears to have been a rather mild heart attack." He went on to explain that other tests were pending, and they would like Link to remain in the hospital a few days to make sure no further heart damage occurs.

Early the following morning, Lydia entered Link's room. He was holding an ice-bag over his right upper leg. His thigh below the bag was purple and swollen.

"My goodness. What happened to your leg?"

"It was swollen when I woke up this morning. The doctors saw it on rounds and ordered the ice-bag."

She lifted the bag. A bluish bulge extended half-way down his thigh. The overlaying skin was tense and shiny.

"It looks disgusting but it doesn't hurt," Link said. "The doctor said it wasn't anything serious. They said blood leaked out of the artery."

Her first impulse was to call Dr. Kenneth Bernholtz, chief pathologist at the hospital and long-time family friend. But she decided instead to call the hospital Medical Director. He agreed to see her immediately.

Dr. Krandell came from around his desk and shook Lydia's hand. He appeared to be her age, pushing very hard against sixty. His hair was jet black. She wondered if he colored it.

"Please have a seat, Mrs. Bradshaw. What can I do for you?"

"As you probably know, my grandson, Link Bradshaw, has had a heart attack."

"I have lunch frequently with Dr. Bernholtz."

"Dr. Krandell, you're a busy man so I'll get directly to the point. Since Link's been admitted to the hospital not a day goes by that there isn't some kind of disaster. Half the time his meal tray is left by the door to his room. It's only after they're sure it's stone cold, that someone eventually brings it to him."

Dr. Krandell listened attentively, nodding as she spoke.

Lydia leaned forward. "The medical students who draw blood don't seem to have any idea where the veins are located. And yesterday an intravenous leaked, and Link's hand blew up like a balloon. And now this awful swelling in his thigh from the catheter they inserted. Link looks like he's been in combat."

Dr. Krandell stood, sat on the corner of his desk, close to Lydia. "Mrs. Bradshaw, I'm sorry you and Link have had a bad experience here. You have every right to be upset. The quality of care you described is not up to our standards and is certainly not acceptable. I'll speak with the nursing supervisor and Dr. Cronce immediately. Is there anything else that concerns you?"

"Upset is not close to what I feel. I'm disappointed and angry and will not tolerate any more screw-ups. If we ran our company like this hospital, we would soon be out of business."

"Mrs. Bradshaw, we have a well-trained committed staff. I assure we can do better..."

"You will do better. Can isn't good enough!" She stood and turned toward the door. "My grandson, and every child in this hospital, deserves the best care possible. If you don't provide it, I'll find a hospital that will."

When Lydia got back to Link's room, a young doctor was standing next to his bed.

"Hi, Grandma. This is my new doctor."

He was a nice-looking man with thick wavy dark hair and a friendly smile. He wore white pants, a white coat, and his shoes were polished, not stained with blood. Thank God, she thought, not the crumpled scrub suit and scruffy stained shoes that seemed to be part of the hospital's dress code.

He extended his hand. "Hi, I'm Dr. Frank Tupelo. I'm Link's new intern. I started on the cardiology service today."

"I'm pleased to meet you. I'm Lydia Bradshaw."

"I know. The intern I replaced told me you spend a lot of time here."

She walked to a chair across the room. "You two can just ignore me." She removed a book from her purse and began to read.

"Link, my routine is to make rounds in the morning with the team of doctors. I'll check in on you around lunch-time. Then, if I have time in the late afternoon, I'll stop by, and we can talk about the test results and plans for the next day."

"What about the operation they did yesterday? I heard the doctors talking during the operation, but I was real sleepy and don't remember what they were saying."

"I can understand that. They use so many technical terms."

Dr. Tupelo opened Link's chart and showed him a drawing of the vessels that carry blood to the heart muscle.

"This is what your coronary arteries look like."

"I remember seeing something like that on the screen when they shot dye in my leg."

"The test showed what Dr. Cronce suspected. You were born with one less artery supplying your heart muscle."

Forbidden Harvest

"So why did I wait so long to have a heart attack?"

"When you were little you did okay with only one artery. But as you continued to grow, one artery couldn't deliver enough blood to your heart muscle."

Lydia liked the direct way he spoke to Link. Dr. Tupelo, she must remember his name. Dr. Krandell should also hear about the good ones.

After the first week, Lydia no longer stayed overnight and spent less time at the hospital during the day. She did try to be there late in the afternoon when Dr. Tupelo stopped by. One day while she was there, he brought a copy of an ultrasound picture of Link's heart. She sat in a chair by the window reading. She smiled at Dr. Tupelo; then continued to read.

"Link, this is called an echo-cardiogram. That's because the image is made by sound waves that bounce off the heart. Sort of like what your voice does when you hear an echo."

Link, who had been sitting in a chair beside his bed, stood next to Dr. Tupelo, leaned over to get a better look.

"I saw something like this that they did of my mother. It showed she was gonna have twins."

Lydia closed her book and looked at Dr. Tupelo.

"I read on your chart your mother died about a year ago in a car accident. I didn't realize you had any brothers or sisters."

Lydia was about to say something, but decided not to.

"My mom found out she was pregnant the same day she had the accident. Her and my father went to a party to celebrate. The accident happened on the way home. My dad almost died. He was in the hospital a long time."

Dr. Tupelo flushed. He placed an arm around Link's

shoulder.

"I'm real sorry what happened to your parents. I had no idea your mother was pregnant at the time."

Neither of them spoke for awhile. Link had tears in his eyes.

"If you would like, Link, sometime you could tell me more about your mom."

Toward the end of the second week, Dr. Tupelo told Lydia that Link would be ready for discharge in a couple of days. He said Dr. Cronce asked him to set up a family conference. They planned the meeting for the following day.

Lydia was first to arrive at the conference room, which was located down the hall from Link's room. As she waited, she thought of her first encounter with Dr. Cronce. If she were casting a play, she would never have chosen him for the part of a medical sub-specialist. He had a cherubic face and blond hair that hung well below his ears. He seemed distracted and disorganized most of the time.

Ken had told her that Dr. Cronce was the best cardiologist on the hospital staff. Despite her initial negative impression, she was pleased about his availability and responsiveness. On the other hand, she had to restrain herself from telling him to stop fidgeting so damn much.

Link and Tom arrived next, followed moments later by Dr. Cronce. He sat at the conference table, a coffee mug in his right hand. Link tilted his head to read what was printed on the oversized cup. Lydia smiled. The inscription read: *Metamucil...it's the way to go.*

"Good morning, folks. Would anyone care for some coffee?"

No one answered. "I'd love a cup," Link said.

Forbidden Harvest

Dr. Tupelo shook his head and winked at Link.

"He wasn't talking to you, champ," Tom said.

"I called this meeting," Dr. Cronce said, "to talk about what happens now that Link is ready to go home."

He took his stethoscope from his neck and laid it on the table. He absently tapped the end-piece on the tabletop. It was the only sound in the room except for a soft gurgle coming from the coffee maker.

"Within twelve weeks Link should be fully recovered from the heart attack. The heart muscle will have healed, and he'll be able to do most everything he did before. I'd advise, however, against engaging in strenuous physical activity. I believe Dr. Tupelo's already outlined a special exercise program for him."

"Yes, I went over that with them earlier this morning," Frank said.

Dr. Cronce continued. "Of course the basic heart problem we've talked about hasn't been resolved. Within a year or two Link's likely to require heart surgery to correct the defect."

"Why would you want to take that long?" Tom asked. "I understand there may be some risk in waiting."

Dr. Cronce continued to click the chest piece of his stethoscope. "Any correction we make at this time may not be adequate once Link is fully grown. By waiting as long as we can, we may avoid having to operate a second time."

When no one spoke, Dr. Cronce continued, "Link will go home with a medicine that'll dilate his coronary arteries and allow more blood to flow to the heart muscle. He will also have a prescription for Nitroglycerin."

"We're familiar with that," Tom said. "My father had to use Nitroglycerin after his heart attack."

Forbidden Harvest

Link looked at Dr. Tupelo and smiled. Lydia recalled Link joking about putting an explosive under his tongue. He had asked Frank Tupelo what if he put two tablets under his tongue at the same time. Would it blow off his ears?

Dr. Cronce explained, "He may never need to use it, but he does need to carry it with him at all times. The clinical pharmacologist will discuss both medicines with you before Link is discharged."

"How often will you have to see him?" Tom asked.

"Once a month initially; then every two months. Dr. Boat will of course continue to see Link for his routine medical care."

Lydia set her jaw. Not if it were up to me, she thought. She looked at Link, who was silently mouthing the words, "Big Bird."

As they left the conference room, three nurses who had been sitting at the nurses' station rushed over to say goodbye. They hugged and kissed Link, and thanked Tom for the flowers and candy he had delivered that morning. They gave Link a card they had all signed. One of the candy stripers had written her telephone number under her name.

As Lydia, Tom and Link walked through the hospital lobby Tom said, "You know, when I left the hospital the nurses' didn't make such a big fuss over me."

"It's called 'sex appeal,' Dad. Some guys got it; some guys don't."

Forbidden Harvest

CHAPTER THREE

It had been six months since Link's heart attack. He and his dad sat at a small table in a bay window just off their kitchen. Link stared in the direction of their swimming pool. The early morning sun cut a bright irregular path across the water. As Link turned to look at the sports pages, a jagged black image that slowly turned to red, then yellow appeared to burn through the page. He removed his glasses, rubbed his eyes and laid down the newspaper.

His dad, without looking up, poured himself a second cup of coffee as he glanced through the paper. Link rolled up the sports section and put it to his eye like a telescope.

"You know, I can see pretty well even without my glasses when I look through a tube like this."

His dad shrugged.

"I can't wait for the baseball season to start," Link said. "Does Bradshaw Industries still have box seats at King Stadium?"

That got his dad's attention. Tom put down the paper. He reached for another piece of toast.

"You bet, and I've reserved a pair of tickets for you and me on opening day," he said. He applied a glob of peach jam to his toast.

Forbidden Harvest

"Is it a school day?"

"Heck, one day of school more or less won't make that much difference."

His mother would never have allowed him to take a day off from school to see a baseball game. He wondered if his father had ever cut school when he was a kid.

"Can I invite Mike to come with us?"

Tom gulped the rest of his coffee. He grabbed his briefcase and stood as he looked at his watch.

"I'm afraid not," he said. He hurried toward the front door. "Aiding and abetting a truant minor! You don't want your dad to go to jail, do you?"

"What about me? I'm a minor." Link walked alongside him.

"I'll write a note saying you are suffering from seasonal melancholia. I'll say I determined you needed a break from the school routine."

Link tried on his father's Stetson before handing it to him.

"Sounds reasonable to me," Link said. "What about today? I feel a little on the sad side."

Tom wiggled his index finger at Link. "Don't push your luck, young man. Finish breakfast and get thyself to school."

Link watched as his dad hurried toward his car and stood transfixed as the car disappeared around the curve of their drive. He fought the urge to run after the car, to plead with his dad not to go. He looked at his watch. The school bus would be there soon. He'd better hurry.

Link always sat next to his friend Mike Stephano.

"You missed a lot of school this semester," Mike said. "You gonna be able to start eighth grade in September?"

"Yeah, I hope so." Link stared out of the window. He and Mike had been in classes together, ever since preschool.

Mike didn't live in the same neighborhood as Link. Most days the bus dropped Mike off at Link's house after school. Link and Mike would hang out until Mrs. McAllister drove Mike home just before dinner time. Now that Link couldn't participate in sports, Mike and some of his other friends didn't come around as much.

Mike gave Link a hard poke in the ribs.

"Hey, knock it off," Link said. But he was really glad Mike wasn't treating him like he was sick or something.

"If they keep you back, I should get demoted at least a couple of grades."

"The doctor said I can't play school sports until after I have the heart operation."

"Shit. That's a bummer," Mike said. "How come?"

"The heart muscle has to heal up. He said in another three months it'll be as good new."

"Speaking of heart attacks, I gotta tell Julie something."

Mike walked a few rows to where Julie was sitting. He leaned over and whispered something in her ear. She laughed.

The bus driver shouted, "Stephano, get back to your seat."

On the way back to his seat Mike held up his middle finger but positioned his hand so the driver couldn't see it. "Way to go Stephan-o," one of the kids shouted.

As Mike sat next to Link, Jennifer Cummings, who was

sitting across the aisle, leaned forward and smiled at Mike.

Mike smiled back. He said to Link, "Even before she leaned over, I could tell it was her, because her you know what, stick out so far."

Link didn't say anything. He could feel his ears starting to get warm just thinking of Jennifer. She had long straight blond hair that hung below her shoulders. She had a habit of holding a strand of hair and brushing it lightly against her ear while she read. The hairs on Link's neck stood at attention whenever he saw her do it.

Mike had told Link that the nun in home room sent a note home to Jennifer's mother saying she should wear looser-fitting clothes because Bradshaw was always looking at her and his grades were going down.

Link punched Mike in the arm.

"What was that for?" Mike asked.

"Because you're so full of bull, that's why."

"What about pick-up baseball games after school? That's not school sports."

"I could maybe umpire."

"Sounds like basketball's out."

"Yeah. I guess. I can shoot hoops if I don't run around."

In class that morning, as the teacher was writing an assignment on the blackboard, a girl sitting in front of Link handed him a folded piece of paper. Link read the note. He adjusted his glasses and read it a second time. Then he looked over at Jennifer. As he did, the girl sitting behind Jennifer poked her in the back and pointed to Link. When Jennifer looked at him she raised her eyebrows like she was asking him, "Well, how about it?" He could feel his cheeks get warm. He buried his head in his book. Before he left class he put the note in his pocket and didn't read it again until he got home. He went directly to his room. He kicked off his shoes and turned on the stereo extra loud; then sprawled on his bed. Kylie Minogue's remake of *Do the Locomotion* filled the room. Link glanced at a row of toy soldiers on a shelf opposite his bed. With the stereo volume up, the soldiers jiggled around like they were dancing. He jumped to his feet and picked up a baseball bat that was propped against the wall. Standing next to one of the stereo speakers, he held the bat across his upper thighs as though it were a guitar. He sang along with the music:

Everybody's doin' a brand new dance now

C'mon, Baby, Do the loco-motion

I know you'll like it if you give it a chance now

C'mon Baby, Do the loco-motion

My little baby sister can do it with ease

He dropped to his knees:

It's easier than learnin' your ABC's

So come on, Come on, Do the loco-motion with me.

He lay on the bed and removed the note from his pocket and read it again.

"Dear Link, I notice you looking at me a lot. I think you're the cutest guy in class. I would like to have a date with you. Come to my house after school tomorrow. We can listen to LPs and hang out. I can hardly wait, Jennifer."

Link went hot all over... exactly how he felt when they injected that dye into his leg. He had never gone on a date before except for birthday parties when he was little. He guessed all the girls thought he was kind of nerdish...having to wear glasses and being the smartest kid in class. Except for Jim Burns, who was a lot smarter. But Jim was a real nerd. Sometimes he played chess with him because everybody else avoided him.

At school the next day Link took Mike aside and showed him the note. Mike slapped him on the back.

"The girl is crazy for you, man. Do you know where she lives?"

"How should I know? All I ever said to her was 'Hi.'"

"Want me to ask her?"

"Why would anyone have the hots for me?"

Mike pounded his fist into his opposite hand. "Every guy in class would kill to be in your shoes," Mike said. "I can't wait to tell them."

"Just keep your mouth shut, okay? This is between you and me. And how do I know you didn't write the note?"

"I can't write that fancy."

"One of your girlfriends probably did."

"Tell you what, you go up to her and say you liked the note she wrote you. If she says, 'Hey man, what are you talking about?' You say, Oops. I guess it was some other Jennifer."

During lunch recess, Link mustered the courage to walk up to Jennifer. She was a couple of inches taller than he...he was glad she was sitting. As he approached, she leaned back, placing her elbows on the table behind her. He had to try extra hard not to look at her chest. "Hi, I'm Link Bradshaw."

"I'm sure glad you told me. I thought you were Tom Cruise."

The girls sitting around her began to laugh. Link's ears got red, but he remained determined. He looked from the other girls to Jennifer.

Forbidden Harvest

"Could we talk over there?"

"Sure, Link."

They walked to an unoccupied table.

"What's on your mind?" she asked.

"Somebody sent me a note with your name on it, but I don't think you sent it."

"Do you have to wear those glasses all the time?"

"Not when I'm sleeping."

"You notice you're dreaming out of focus?"

They both laughed. Link hoped Mike was watching.

After that, he and Jennifer talked almost every day, and she was beginning to be his best friend after Mike. Link started to spend more time fussing with his hair, and when an occasional zit appeared, he was mortified. Lydia took him shopping for clothes because his father didn't have the foggiest idea what kids were wearing. When he went for a new pair of glasses, Jennifer and his grandmother went with him to pick out frames.

Jennifer smiled. "You look seriously cool in those."

He looked at his grandmother. "You like them, Grandma?"

She pushed against the nose piece, elevating the glasses slightly. "I agree with Jennifer. I can't think of better words to describe you."

It wasn't until the next day that Link realized just how cool he was. Mike couldn't wait to tell Link the bad news.

"Hey man, I hear hot-shot Joe Romaine is taking Jennifer to the junior high dance."

Link thought he was kidding at first, but he did notice Jennifer was avoiding looking at him in home room. At recess he walked with her. They stopped in front of Jennifer's locker.

"Mike told me you're going to the dance with Joe."

She leaned against the locker, raising one knee. She pursed her lips before speaking. "Yeah, he's right, but I have no idea how he found out. I wanted to tell you myself."

"You and I talked about going..."

She turned and opened her locker. "Nothing was definite. We just kinda talked about it. And when Joe called me last night, I guess he caught me off-guard."

Link wanted to kick the locker, but bit his lip instead. "I don't care." He spun around and walked down the hall.

"Come on, Link, it's not like that."

Link kept walking. It was probably just a big joke, he thought, hanging out with me; then going to the dance with Joe.

Link moped around for a few days. He hated seeing Jennifer and Joe talking and laughing together. Mike tried to cheer him up.

"Hey buddy, you had her all to yourself for almost a month. You got a rep, man. Just wait and see. All the other cool chicks will be fighting over you."

Link didn't tell Mike that he was sort of relieved in a way, not to have to worry about what he wore, or whether or not he had a zit on his nose. And he really hated his new glasses.

CHAPTER FOUR

Tom read everything he could find about Link's condition, but there wasn't much available. He knew that without surgical correction, his son's life expectancy after a first heart attack was only two to three years. He learned to his relief that most surgery for coronary anomalies was highly successful, especially since advances made in the methods used to maintain circulation and oxygenation. During the operation, the patient's blood was bypassed through an external pump. Another device added oxygen to the blood.

Dr. Kenneth Bernholtz was a great source of information, and Tom called him frequently. Ken had told him it was pretty tricky to pick just the right time to operate. Tom had asked Ken if he thought Link might eventually need a heart transplant. Ken told him it was unlikely he would reach that stage until his late teens.

Each evening Lydia called Tom to ask how things were going and to say "hi" to Link. From Link's end of the conversation Tom could tell she was asking him about school.

Afterwards Link said, "Dad, Grandma wants to know every little detail about my day. It's getting so I'm thinking about what I'm going to tell her even before I do things. I wish you would ask her not to worry so much."

"I understand, son. If I had to check with her about everything that happened when I went to school, she would have had white hair by the time she was thirty."

Lydia continued to call despite Tom having asked her to lighten up. But after awhile, Tom noticed that Link didn't seem to mind so much. Tom even enjoyed eavesdropping on their conversations.

One night after speaking with his grandmother Link said, "Grandma is really pretty cool. She goes to the PTA meetings at school and knows most of my teachers. She's always cracking jokes about them."

Tom looked at the mileage gauge on his exercise bike. He had already ridden the equivalent of ten miles. As he wiped perspiration from his face he glanced at Link, who was now hunched over a small desk across the room, presumably doing his homework.

"Yeah, I heard you laughing tonight," Tom said. "What was that about?"

Link turned the desk chair around to face his dad. "She was talking about Sister Theresa, my math teacher who wears real thick glasses. Remember, I said when a kid comes to class late, that she has to ask who it is? And we always have to sit in the same seat so she knows who's there."

Tom walked over to where Link was sitting and looked at the materials spread out on the desk. "Are you almost finished with your homework?"

"Dad, I was trying to tell you about school."

"Sorry, son, the bike drains the blood from my brain." He sat on the floor close to Link's desk. He stretched both legs, and then leaned forward, stretching his lower back.

Link had a balled-up piece of paper on his desk. He threw it at his dad. Tom grabbed Link's foot and growled.

Forbidden Harvest

"Grandma...PTA...Sister Theresa, are you with me, Dad?"

"Fire away."

"Grandma saw Sister Theresa at the PTA meeting. You know how Grandma wears her hair pulled back and likes to wear slacks? Sister Theresa shook Grandma's hand and said, 'It's so nice to meet you, Mr. Bradshaw.'"

"Grandma said she was tempted to make her voice sound deep and go along with it."

Tom sat up. "I don't believe my mother would do that."

"She said she didn't because there were too many people standing around, and Sister is such a sweet person. She said next time she's going to have to wear a dress."

Tom noticed that Link had removed his glasses. He braced himself as Link charged toward him. Link dove for Tom, knocking him onto his back. He grabbed Tom's wrists and slammed them to the floor.

Tom offered very little resistance, fearful that Link might somehow hurt himself. Tom had always enjoyed wrestling with Link, but now he just couldn't. At one level he realized that Link's heart condition would have surfaced anyway, and yet, would he have had a heart attack if he had not been wrestling?

Tom lay firmly in Link's grasp. "You're picking on a post-exercise, out-of-shape, almost middle-aged man...who also happens to be your father."

Link let go of his dad's hands and got to his feet. He grabbed his glasses and walked toward the door.

Tom sat up. "Hey, what's going on?"

Link spun around. "I'm sick of you treating me like I'm some sort of damn Christmas tree ornament. I want us to be like we were." He ran to his room, slamming the door behind him.

Tom stood and slowly climbed the stairs to Link's room. He hesitated as he grasped the door knob. What would Brenda have said to him? What more does he expect from me, Tom thought. He knocked. "Can I come in?" Not waiting for an answer Tom stepped into the room.

Link was sitting on his bed, propped up against the headboard. Tom sat next to him.

"Link, my dad always said never go to bed mad at somebody."

Link didn't look up, as he flipped through a computer magazine. "It's just the whole darn situation. Kids at school don't horse around with me like they used to. Everybody is so nice to me, it makes me wanna puke. And even Mike doesn't come around that much."

"I can see why you're upset, champ."

Link slammed the magazine shut and threw it on the floor. "And don't call me 'champ'!" His eyes glistened. "I can't even take gym with the rest of the kids in my class." He reached over and grabbed a tissue from a table beside his bed and blew his nose. Tom took a couple of steps to Link's desk and grabbed the waste basket.

"I know your life has changed a lot these last few months. Let me know how I can help."

"Dad, I know you and Grandma mean well, but I feel like I'm being smothered."

"I never realized how differently we were treating you."

"It's little things. Like you putting my snot rag in the wastebasket. And I'm sick of always eating my favorite things. What about the icky stuff you like? It's like being on death row. Mrs. McAllister asks me every day what I want to eat the next day."

Forbidden Harvest

Tom shook his head, "Yeah, she told me what you said." Tom smiled. "Shit-burgers? She actually called me at the office and asked if I ever heard of such a thing."

Link swiped his nose with his forearm. "Just ignore me once in awhile and maybe even yell at me like you used to. I don't know how to say it...but you treat me like every day could be my last."

Tom took a tissue and absentmindedly grabbed Link's arm to dry it off. "I don't believe that..."

"It's real scary, Dad."

"I'm scared too, Link. I guess that's why I'm such a pain in the ass." Tom reached for Link and squeezed him against his chest. Link squeezed back as hard as he could.

"You're breaking all of my ribs, Dad. But it's okay...it's a good start....can I tell you one more thing?"

"Sure, son, what is it?"

"You smell really bad, Dad, after you use your exercise bike."

One evening a few weeks later, Lydia got Tom on the phone. "You must call Dr. Cronce first thing in the morning. Link said he was short of breath swimming at school today."

"Mom, he swims laps. I'm sure anyone would get a little short of breath."

"No, it's something new. Take him to the doctor in the morning. Promise me!"

Tom sighed. "Sure, Mother. It certainly won't hurt."

The following day Dr. Cronce examined Link and did an echocardiogram. Afterwards they went to Dr. Cronce's consultation room. Link sat in a chair next to his dad. Dr.

Cronce sat at his desk. It was piled high with journals and papers and empty coffee cups. Link stood and dragged his chair part-way around the desk so he could see the doctor.

"Mr. Bradshaw, in the area where Link had heart damage, the heart muscle is bulging out when his heart contracts. In other words, it's moving in the opposite direction of the rest of the heart muscle."

Tom moved to the edge of his seat. "What does that mean?"

"It's a sign that there has been weakening of the damaged area. We refer to this type of bulging as an aneurysm. But it's small and not of great significance at this time."

Tom looked at Link. He couldn't tell anything from Link's expression.

Tom took a deep breath. "He had all those tests in the hospital. How come the aneurysm wasn't discovered sooner?" Tom massaged the back of his neck. The soreness never seemed to go away.

"We didn't discover it because it wasn't present then. Apparently there wasn't enough healthy muscle in the damaged area to allow for complete healing."

Tom looked past Dr. Cronce. He stood, walked to the window and leaned on the sill. It was an overcast day and a light drizzle hung in the air. He breathed deeply; then turned to face Dr. Cronce. A large vein that covered an erratic path across Tom's forehead bulged as though he were lifting a heavy weight. "You've been checking Link once a month. How the hell could this thing just suddenly appear?"

Dr. Cronce swiveled around to face Tom. "Mr. Bradshaw, I've seen aneurysms develop within days of having a normal echo-cardiogram. Believe me. I'm also distressed by this development."

Tom crouched in front of Link. "Why didn't you tell me you were having symptoms? Damn it, Link. If you expect me and grandma to lay off you, we have to believe you'll tell us when you're not feeling right."

Link avoided his father's eyes.

Tom lifted Link's chin. "If you want me to not hound you all the time, I have to believe you'll come to me when something happens."

Link nodded. Tom asked Dr. Cronce, "Do you think we need to be talking about surgery?"

"Link should be entering a rapid-growth phase soon. I believe it's still safe to wait."

Two months passed without any change. Then Link began to notice that it was getting harder to climb the stairs at school. His friend Mike would race up the steps two at a time and wait for him at the top of the stairway. Link would stop on the landing, pretending to tie his shoes until his heavy breathing stopped.

Link figured he would need the operation soon. If he could only hold off until school was out, he could get the operation in the summer and be okay to start school in the fall.

After awhile, Link started putting a nitroglycerin under his tongue to make it easier to climb the stairs. It helped, but sometimes it gave him a bad headache.

After a few days, Mike got tired of waiting for Link. "Hey, I gotta look over the assignment. See you in class."

His best friend was getting sick of him. Link was even sick of himself. He wondered if he should get home tutoring and screw the whole school bit. Then one day the physical education teacher sent a note home with Link, expressing concern about his decreasing exercise tolerance. Link didn't show the note to his dad right away.

It was one thing to talk about the operation, but now that he was sure it was needed, he began to perspire whenever he thought of it. One night when his father had to work late, Link had seen an operation on television. It was a fifty-year-old man. They were grafting coronary arteries. Using a power tool, with a tiny round blade, they cut open his chest and cracked his ribs open like he was a walnut. They injected something to make the man's heart stop beating. That night Link dreamed a surgeon in a long white coat and mask was chasing him with a chain saw. He ran as fast as he could but his legs were too heavy. The doctor was gaining on him. Link fell and rolled onto his back. He extended his arms to keep the man from his chest. But the saw blade was so long he couldn't reach the guy. The blade pressed against him. The saw motor screeched as the chain teeth cut through Link's clothes and skin. He screamed and awakened to find he was in his dad's arms.

His father kept saying, "It's okay, son, it was just a bad dream....just a bad dream."

Even during the day Link couldn't stop thinking about the saw. He wondered if a person could still hear after being anesthetized.

By the end of the school week, his shortness of breath was worse. When Link finally told his father about his trouble breathing, his father called Dr. Cronce immediately. They met at the doctor's office that evening.

Link sat on the exam table. Although the room wasn't cold, he couldn't stop shaking. Dr. Cronce asked questions as he examined him. "Do you wake up at night short of breath?"

Link couldn't talk. His jaw muscles were tight. His tongue felt paralyzed.

Dr. Cronce placed Link's shirt across his shoulders. He put his hand on top of Link's hand. "I know this must be frightening for you..."

"My dad...he's going to be real mad."

"Why is that?"

"I didn't tell him about using nitroglycerin. And I'm scared to have the operation."

After the examination, Link, his dad, and Dr. Cronce sat in the doctor's consultation room. Dr. Cronce said to Link, "I want to recommend to your father that you come in the hospital for some tests. My examination indicates that you've built up fluid in your body."

"Can't you give me medicine to take at home? I could stay in bed."

"There are tests we can't do at home," Dr. Cronce said.

"Why is this happening so quickly?" Tom asked. "Could he have had another heart attack without us knowing it?"

"The electrocardiogram doesn't show evidence suggestive of recent heart damage. There's a condition that's called cardiomyopathy, which is basically a weakening of the heart muscle. In Link's case, it's probably related to poor coronary circulation. In-hospital tests should clarify the picture."

"Can I bring a computer to the hospital, Dr. Cronce?" Link asked.

"That shouldn't be a problem."

"How long will I be there?"

"We have no way of predicting that, but it's quite possible you will be discharged in about two weeks."

It was a week before Link's thirteenth birthday. He had campaigned for a laptop computer. His grandma insisted she buy it for him. She gave Link a state-of-the-art model with every feature he could have asked for.

"I don't want Grandma staying with me," Link said on the drive to the hospital. "None of the other kids my age have their family stay unless they're dying or something."

"You don't mind if we drop in once in a while?"

Link pursed his lips. "Well, I'll have to think about that."

Link was surprised when Dr. Tupelo walked into his room.

"Give me five, little buddy."

"Look what I got for my birthday." He reached for his computer and set it on the bed.

"Listen, Link, you can call all those guys with grey hair, 'Doctor.' Call me Doc Frank. Okay?"

"Sure. When do you get to leave the hospital and be a real doctor?"

"This year I'm a second-year resident. I even have students and interns working for me. But I still have one more year to go in my residency. After that I want to stay and train as a heart specialist. If you keep coming here you'll be stuck with me for a long time."

"Wow! You're gonna be a hundred years old before you get out of here."

Forbidden Harvest

Frank bent his knees and held out one arm as though he was using a cane. "Well, not quite that old," Frank said, smiling. He propped one leg on the edge of Link's bed. He looked serious all of a sudden.

"How are you handling all this stuff coming at you so fast?" Frank asked.

Link only wanted to think about his new computer. When he was using it, the sound of the bone saw in his mind wasn't so loud. He could forget that bloody quivering heart on television. He couldn't keep the lower part of his mouth from shaking. "I guess I'm sort of afraid of the operation. Do you think I gotta have it this time?"

Frank scooted farther up on the bed. "It's only natural to be anxious about a big operation. But they do it just about every day in this hospital. The doctors are really good. Would you like to talk to someone who had the operation already?"

"Yeah. I guess."

"It's important to talk about what you're afraid of. I appreciate you sharing your feelings with me."

"When are you coming back?" Link asked.

"I'll see you on rounds every morning and stop by in the afternoon."

The new medicine they gave Link made him urinate a lot, and after three or four days he was feeling much better. He began to think that maybe they wouldn't have to operate after all.

Dr. Tupelo explained that the fluid buildup in his lungs was what made him short of breath. He'd probably have to take medicine to keep the fluid from coming back.

Link asked about the echocardiogram. Dr. Tupelo didn't

say anything right away. Link could tell bad news was coming. He wished he hadn't asked.

"Well, your heart has enlarged quite a bit over the past few months. Even after losing all that fluid, your heart is still enlarged. Hold on, I'll run and get a plastic heart model."

Nobody had mentioned anything about his heart being enlarged until now. He wondered if his whole heart was turning into an aneurysm. He put his hand on his chest. He could feel his heart pounding against his ribs. It used to beat hard like that when he played basketball. Half the time he felt as though he couldn't get enough air. He walked to the window and tried to pull it up. It could only be opened a few inches. The sun was shining for the first time in days. He put his face close to the opening in the window and breathed deeply. Dr. Tupelo came back into the room.

"I know how you feel, Link. On a day like this I sometimes wish I built houses."

He walked over to where Link was standing and placed the heart model on the window sill. He took it apart so Link could see the inside.

"When your heart enlarges, these valves don't close all the way. That causes some of the blood to flow backward instead of forward. When that happens there's not enough blood going out to your muscles; that's why you tire so easily."

"Why can I feel my heart beating hard all the time?" Link asked.

"Because it's gotten bigger. When it fills with blood it's much closer to your ribs."

"Is it going to keep getting bigger and bigger?"

"Actually, it's gotten a little smaller since you got rid of all that fluid. With the right medicine we should be able to keep it from enlarging." Frank gathered up the parts of the plastic heart. "I have to run now, I'll see you later."

Link didn't want Dr. Tupelo to leave...he really liked talking with him. He helped Link understand what was happening to his heart. It was scary...but it was ever scarier not to understand why he felt as he did. But were Dr. Tupelo and all the others really being honest with him? He imagined his heart like a balloon stretched to the limit...on the verge of bursting with the next puff of air.

Forbidden Harvest

CHAPTER FIVE

Early the next morning, a young woman in a long white coat stood at the foot of Link's bed. A stethoscope hung from her neck. Her glasses were perched on the tip of her nose. She peered over them as she spoke.

"Mr. Bradshaw, I'm Dr. Watson, and how are we today?"

"You sure look young to be a doctor," Link said. He figured she couldn't be a real doctor. Besides, she looked kind of familiar.

"We all start out that way. Now, young man, I need to examine you."

"Okay," he said, deciding to go along.

"You're going to have to strip buck-naked."

"Wait a minute, you're no doctor."

She took off the glasses and wiggled a finger at him. "Had you scared for a few seconds, Bradshaw."

She wore a cap like the surgeons use in the operating room. Her eyes were made up as if she were going to a party. Link thought she looked kind of okay.

"Don't I know you from someplace?"

"I go to the same school as you. I'm in the tenth grade.

Forbidden Harvest

You came to drama club once. Remember?"

"Martha Lopinski! You were in the school play last year."

"Actually, Lopinski is my stage name. My real name's Barrymore. My friends call me Marty."

"What're you doing in the hospital?"

"I wanted to get out of school for a couple of weeks. I told them I had a tumor in my left leg. After they did some tests they said my leg would have to come off."

Link's eyes widened. Then he smiled. "You're crazy. You expect me to believe that?"

"If you think that's crazy, you don't know me very well."

"Okay. So you may be even crazier than I think," Link quipped.

She walked to the side of his bed and swung her left leg onto the mattress. She was wearing a green scrub suit. She pulled up the pants leg to her knee. Her lower leg was made of pink plastic with a hinge at the knee and ankle.

"My gosh. I'm sorry, I didn't..."

"Hey, you're cool. I freaked out for awhile. But they had to do it, or the cancer would have killed me. Ever hear of osteosarcoma?

"No."

"It's a mean bitchin' tumor."

"Does it hurt or anything?"

"Not anymore. But it's funny how the fake foot itches sometimes, and I have to scratch it just like it's real. I heard you have some kind of heart trouble, Bradshaw."

Some of the kids at school called him Bradshaw, but none of his close friends. It seemed okay though for her to call him that...it made him feel older. He decided to show off his medical knowledge. "I have a coronary artery anomaly that caused me to have a heart attack. After awhile I developed an aneurysm. And after that I went into congestive heart failure, and that's why I'm in the hospital." He sat back and smiled.

"No wonder Doc Frank calls you Little Doc."

"You know Dr. Tupelo?"

"Sure, when he realized we went to the same school he told me you liked older women...so here I am."

Before Marty came into his room, Link had been fooling around with his new laptop computer. Marty walked to the bedside and flipped up the screen. "Wow, this is really nice. Is it yours?"

"I got it for a birthday present. Let me show you something. Okay, say you could fly any place in the world. Where would you like to go?"

"Hawaii! I always wanted to go to Hawaii." She did a little hula imitation. She looked kind of shapeless in the oversized scrub suit but Link was still a little embarrassed when she swung her hips around.

He dialed into CompuServe, typed in 'Go-Air' and the screen listed a number of questions. Destination? Departure time? Staying over the weekend? First class? Coach? Excursion? Airline preference?

Looking over his shoulder she said, "Let's see, first class of course, window seat, departure tomorrow would be fine, I'll be staying two weeks."

"Smoking or non-smoking?"

Marty pressed close to Link as she peered at the screen. She put an arm around his waist. She squeezed the skin on his right side.

"Hey, that tickles."

"Non-smoking," Marty said.

"What? Oh yeah, Kosher, vegetarian or regular meal plan?"

"Gourmet vegetarian, please."

"Okay," Link said. He punched in a few commands. "That will cost you $1,695. Would you like to put that on your credit card?"

"That's incredible, Bradshaw. I love it. Gotta pick me up one of those."

She moved toward the door. "I'm in room 437." Fluttering her eyes she added, "Give me a call before you come by. I'll need time to change into something sexier."

CHAPTER SIX

Marty groaned as an aide banged into her room with an insulated food tray. She dropped it on her bedside stand. She took one look and decided she wasn't hungry. Soon the doctors would arrive, and she didn't want them to see her without her prosthesis. She placed a sock over her lower left thigh and strapped it on. The rounding doctors' voices grew louder as they drew nearer to her room. She quickly threw on a clean scrub suit. Her sparse hair required only a few strokes of her brush. She donned a Braves baseball cap, pulled over her bedside tray, flipped up the mirror section, and squinted at her morning-face. She quickly colored her lips with a swath of fire-engine red. As she applied eye-shadow, she heard Frank say, "Mark, here's a printout of recent journal articles about osteosarcoma. Pull these for grand rounds conference next week."

Later that morning, Marty asked Dr. Tupelo where he had gotten the references. She was interested in reading about her condition but didn't know where to start.

"There's a computer in the residents' on-call room that can make a connection with the National Library of Medicine. You ask a few questions, and it searches thousands of journals for articles. It took me only a few minutes. At the library it would have taken hours."

"That's fantastic. Can you show me how you do that?"

"I'll have some time right after rounds. I'll stop by."

As Marty waited for Dr. Tupelo, she walked to the window. She leaned on the sill, her chin cupped in her hands. From the sixth floor she could see a maze of buildings that made up the nearby University Medical Center. The early morning sun cast elongated shadows that hurried after people as they scurried past. A person takes up so little space in this world, she thought. And when you're gone, everything is just the same. It's like you were never here. The shadows linger...gray, featureless. Soon even that passes.

"Marty?"

She turned slowly to face him. "Hi, Doc Frank. I didn't expect you so soon." She grabbed her baseball cap. "Let's go."

She memorized the numbers as he punched in the combination on the door to the residents' on-call room. It might come in handy, she thought.

"Each doctor has his own logon name and password. Most people use their last name to login. Your secret password has to be a combination of letters and numbers."

"Why secret?"

"To protect patient confidentiality."

"What kinds of stuff can you look up?"

"Right now laboratory tests and pathology reports. Eventually we expect to have the patient's entire medical record computerized. That way if someone at another hospital needs to look at the record, we just push a button and the whole record can be reproduced at the other hospital."

As he spoke, she leaned close to him to get a better view of the computer screen. He smelled really good, she thought. Like one of those after-shave commercials. She wanted to run the back of her hand across his cheek and say, "Oooh, nice." Why do all the really cool guys have to be so old? She wondered.

He entered his last name. It showed up on the screen. Then he typed in his password. That didn't show on the screen, but because he typed using only his index fingers, she could easily see which keys he struck. It was just a bunch of letters and numbers. Marty wondered how he could remember a password that didn't make any sense.

"Pull up a chair. You're going to get tired leaning over me like that."

Gosh, he must be almost thirty years old. He doesn't look that old, though. Let me think, twenty one when he got out of college, twenty-five when he got out of medical school and now a second-year resident. So even if he went straight through, he's gotta be a least twenty-seven.

"You don't look that old," Marty said.

"Who said I looked old?"

"I was just thinking about all that school you've been through."

"You know, I always thought learning was more fun than just about anything. With a few exceptions."

"Like what?" Marty asked.

"Like playing baseball or reading a good book. My mother's cooking is pretty high on that list."

Marty grimaced. "Learning is hard though...but I understand what you mean. If it was easy everyone would be as smart as you."

"Flattery will get you everywhere, young lady."

Forbidden Harvest

"My mom says the same thing about learning. Can you show me how to use the computer to look up medical stuff?"

"The basics of searching are simple but it does take practice." He looked at his watch, "Darn, I have only a half hour to spare. That's not enough time to make you an expert, but I can teach you enough to be able to play around with it."

He showed her a database called Cancerlit.

"It's just about dummy proof," he said. "There are menus that list categories such as diagnosis, prognosis, staging, treatments, and so on. You choose one, and it gives you the latest information available on the subject. It's updated once a month."

"What's that category---research protocols?"

"It tells about treatments that are still being evaluated. It also lists the hospitals where the treatment is available."

Frank's beeper went off. He went to the phone.

"I've got to run, Marty. I have to log off."

"I'd like to fool around with it if that's okay?"

"Okay. Just type *logoff* at the blinking prompt."

After he left, she wrote down his password, K1N9A8R8F.

I get it, she thought. It's his name spelled backwards with 1988 between each letter.

She typed *logoff* and the computer screen went blank except for the blinking prompt in the upper left-hand corner. She went through the logon steps and the main menu appeared on the screen.

"Great, I got it on the first try!"

Forbidden Harvest

But Cancerlit wasn't on the main menu. *How did he do that?* She played around for a few minutes and was soon hopelessly lost. So much for dummy proof. She decided to come back every day until she figured it out.

Over the next few days Marty looked forward to her visits to Link's room. He was kind of shy and smarter than the guys she knew at school. She especially liked to see him blush when she said something outrageous. She'd pretend she was the leading lady in a school play, writing the script as she went along. He made her forget the bitchin' tumor and chemo. Right now, most of the pain was in her head, because she knew the cancer had come back, and as the spot in her lung got bigger it was probably going to hurt a lot. Judy, a girl in a room down the hall from Marty, had to take shots for pain and was always spitting up blood. Marty checked her own spit often to see if there was any blood. That morning as she took a shower she had a coughing spell. She got a sharp pain in her chest. Later that morning she told Dr. Tupelo.

"I can hear a kind of rough sound right over here," he said as he listened to her chest.

"That's just where it hurts. And it's a lot worse when I breathe deep."

"We'll have to get a chest x-ray to be sure what's going on. That's about where you have the spot on your lung. It's probably irritating the covering of the lung."

He tried to look cool, but she could tell he was worried that it could be really bad.

"You think the chemo will help?" she asked.

"Probably. In the meantime I'll order a medicine to cut down the inflammation."

After her physical therapy, Marty headed for Link's

room. Instead of going past Judy's room she walked down the stairway at the end of the hall. She didn't want Judy to see her go by without coming in. She couldn't this morning. Maybe later, she thought.

"Hi, Little Doc. You ready for another exciting guided tour?"

"Sure. But I have to be back in an hour. My grandmother's coming to see me."

"You ever been to R.T., L D?"

"Is that rehab?"

"Nope. You'll see."

Link got into his wheelchair. They took the elevator to the eighth floor. The sign on a door said Recreational Therapy.

It was a large room, with a ping pong table at one end and a pool table in the middle of the room. There were tables with checkers and chess boards and puzzles. There was a soda machine against the one wall and an old-fashioned juke box on the opposite wall. Two older guys were playing ping pong. The juke box was blaring Van Halen's *Feels So Good*.

"You want to shoot a little pool?" Marty asked. "I'm warning you ahead of time, I'm pretty good."

"Okay."

She picked up a cue stick and held the fat end by her mouth, as though it were a mike. She sang along with the record:

Yesterday---I saw my love light shine

Straight ahead in front of me

You never really know...When love will come or go

She racked up the balls and handed the cue stick to Link. "All right. Show me your stuff."

The guys playing ping pong stopped and stared at them. Marty ignored them, but she could see that Link was embarrassed because his ears were getting red. He lined up his shot and gave the stick an extra hard push. The q-ball flew into the air and landed on the rubber bumper at the far end of the table, then bounced across the floor.

"Neat trick. You wanna play for money?" she asked.

Marty had been in the hospital so many times most everyone knew her. They let her roam and even allowed her to go to the snack bar as long as she told the nurse where she was going. Link could walk short distances without having to work hard to breathe. On longer trips he used a wheelchair. When he got tired Marty pushed.

In the basement where the snack bar was located, the hallway was slightly uphill. She could see Link struggling to get the wheelchair up the incline. "Let me nudge you along here. We'll get there quicker."

"You don't seem very sick to me," he said. "Why do you have to stay in the hospital?"

When they had reached the top of the incline, Link resumed wheeling the chair. Marty held the door open as he moved into the snack bar. She ordered two sodas and one bag of chips. It was close to noon. The room was crowded with visitors. There was no place to sit.

Marty gave Link his soda. She tore open her chips. She sat on the armrest of his wheelchair. "You sure you don't want some chips?"

"No. Thanks. I asked why you have to stay in the hospital."

"I came back to the hospital for chemo, which I hate

worse than anything. It starts next week after they do a bunch of tests."

"What's chemo?" He asked.

"Well, I'll be. There's actually something you don't know. Chemo is short for chemotherapy. Hey, those guys are leaving. Let's grab their table." She continued..."They call it medicine, but actually it's poison."

"That's nuts. Why would they give you something lethal?"

"They give you a little less than what they think will kill you. Then you cross your fingers and pray it kills the cancer cells."

Why would she want to have it again? Link wondered. "You had it before?" he asked.

"Yeah, once. It made me puke my guts out. And then I got bruises all over. Then my hair brush started to fill up with my golden locks."

He turned and looked at her baseball cap, his nose all scrunched up like he smelled something bad.

She grabbed the brim of her cap. "You wanna see?"

"No. That's okay. How'd you find out about the cancer?" Link asked.

"I was running track and figured I was just having shin-splints. I would ice it after I ran. Then one day it hurt so bad I couldn't run anymore. The coach made me get an x-ray."

"My legs hurt sometimes when I run," he said.

"That's why I waited. It was good that I didn't stop running," Marty said"

"How come?"

"With bone cancer it almost always spreads other

places by the time you know you have it. Because I kept running, I got a stress fracture, and that's how come they found the cancer."

"Was it anywhere else besides your leg?" he asked.

"No. But they gave me chemo just in case."

"So why do you have to get the chemo again?"

"Since the last treatment I got this spot on my lung. They're pretty sure it's the same bitchin' tumor," Marty answered.

Link looked at his watch. "We'd better head back. My grandmother's probably already here."

The following afternoon Marty suggested they go to the snack bar for lemonade and a chips-fix.

Link was still in his pajamas. He slipped on a navy blue bathrobe. "I'm not supposed to eat chips, remember," he said. "But lemonade sounds good."

"Hey, I'm not gonna tell anybody what you buy in the snack bar," she said as she wheeled him along.

"It's the salt, it makes me swell up."

"That's a drag. Chips are the ninth wonder of the world."

"What's the eighth?" Link asked.

"You are, LD You always do exactly what you're told."

"No, I don't."

Marty laughed. "Yeah, I bet you have bad thoughts. The nuns say that's just the same as doing something bad."

He didn't say anything for awhile. "You know, you can be a real pain sometimes."

When they reached the snack bar, Link parked his

wheelchair by the door and walked in with Marty.

"Find us a booth and I'll get our stuff," she said. "And don't pout. I was just kidding."

Marty soon returned with their sodas and a bag of chips. "Hey, Little Doc, you ever been in a real live morgue?" she asked.

"No, but I've seen them plenty of times on television."

"Well, unless you have smell-o-vision you have missed the real experience." She held her nose and stuck her tongue out so far it almost touched her chin.

Link laughed. "If it's that bad, let's skip it."

"I got this weird thing about smelling things," she said. "Like erasers and gasoline and stinky cheese. You ever pick out stuff from between your toes? No matter what, you gotta smell it."

He grimaced. "That's really disgusting."

"Come on. Admit it. I bet you do the same when nobody's looking," she insisted.

"Sometimes I stick my finger in my ear and smell it."

"Hey, there's hope for you yet!"

After they left the snack bar, she wheeled him down a long corridor. On the walls on either side were large color photographs.

"The pictures were taken by people who work here," Marty said. "It's supposed to make the place more cheerful."

"It won't make that much difference when they're wheeling <u>me</u> to the morgue," he said half aloud.

She was quiet for awhile. "Yeah, I think about dying sometimes, but like my mom says, you gotta think positive.

You know, some kinds of butterflies only live a few days. You don't see them moping around. The morgue's down that way. I'll park you here and go ahead to make sure there's nobody in there."

"Wouldn't they keep the door locked?" Link asked.

"I'll huff and I'll puff and blow the door down."

Marty stopped in front of doors. She took a piece of paper from the breast pocket of her scrub suit. She punched in some numbers. She slowly opened the door and peeked in. The room was empty. She motioned for Link to come ahead.

"How come you have the combination?" he asked as he wheeled his chair through the open door.

"I'll tell you sometime." She had read somewhere that you shouldn't tell a guy too much about yourself. A little mystery makes you more interesting. "Just look at this place."

It was a cavernous room with a small office area in one corner separated by partitions that went part-way toward the ceiling. A stainless steel table dominated the center of the room. A massive operating lamp hung directly over the table. Also hanging from the ceiling were a microphone and scale. On a smaller table nearby was a collection of intimidating steel instruments, including saws of varying size. Link glanced at Marty's artificial leg. She guessed what he might be thinking.

"I bet they used a saw like that big one to cut off my leg."

"The smell is sickening." He crossed his arms and shivered. "I'm glad there are no dead people. Let's go."

"Don't be so sure." She walked to a side wall. "You see these drawers? You want to see one?" she asked.

Forbidden Harvest

"Maybe some other time."

"Let's just take a peek." She pulled a drawer part-way open.

Link wheeled his chair closer. A white sheet was draped over the body. Marty turned down the sheet so that only the head was visible.

Link opened his mouth as though to speak, but nothing came out.

"My God. It's a baby," Marty said. "I wonder what it died of." She peeked under the sheet. "It's a girl."

When she looked at Link there were tears in her eyes. "I thought it would be an old person."

"What did you expect?" Link said. "This is a children's hospital." He glanced at the other drawers. His arms and legs began to shake.

She covered the baby, slid the drawer shut, and turned toward Link. "I don't get it. It's freezing in here, and you're all sweaty. I'd better take you back to your room."

After they left the morgue and headed down the hall, a tall bearded man walked past. Marty thought he looked like Abe Lincoln.

"Hey, Uncle Ken," Link said.

Ken stopped and turned. "Link, what are you doing down this way?"

"I was taking him to the snack bar, and I guess we sort of got lost," she said before Link had a chance to answer.

"Uncle Ken, this here is Marty Lopinski. She goes to the same school as me."

Ken knelt next to the wheel chair. He took Link's hand. "My God. You're covered in perspiration. Do you feel all right?"

Forbidden Harvest

"I'm just cold..."

"I'm taking him back to his room. I was going to ask the nurse to check him," Marty said.

"Absolutely. Now Link, be sure to go directly to your room."

As Marty rolled Link's wheelchair toward the elevators, she was unusually quiet. "Dr. Bernholtz is your uncle?" she asked.

"No. He's a really good friend of the family. He's my godfather though. He used to play golf with my grandfather before he died."

"He sure didn't look dead. Somebody better tell him."

"Aren't you ever serious?"

"Not if I can help it." She pushed the wheelchair into the elevator and punched the button for the fifth floor.

"I wonder if Uncle Ken was just now going to do an autopsy on that little baby," Link said.

"I guess so. It's not exactly a place he'd go to just hang out."

By the time they got off the elevator on Link's floor, he looked as though he had just run a quarter mile flat-out. She wheeled him into his room and helped him into a chair.

"Does anything hurt?"

"No, it's just really hard to breathe."

"I'll stop by the nurses' station and tell them they need to check you right away," Marty said. "My mom's waiting for me, so I'd better be getting back to my room."

Marty hurried to the nurses' station. She told Link's nurse that he was shaking like he was cold and sweating at the same time. And that maybe he needed oxygen or something.

Moments later Link's grandmother walked into his room. "Link, where have you been? I went to the snack bar looking for you."

"I was with Marty," he whispered.

"Good lord. Look at you." She helped him into bed. "I'm getting the nurse." She ran from the room.

Link pressed a button in the side-rail of his bed, raising the back as high as it would go. When he took a deep breath it felt like a million tiny bubbles busting deep in his chest. Is this what it feels like when a person is drowning? He looked at his hands. His fingernails were blue. Jeez, *am I having another heart attack*? He closed his eyes and could see the table in the morgue and all those weird instruments.

He could hear people running down the hall. A nurse and his grandmother came into the room. The nurse put a thermometer in his mouth. She checked his pulse and blood pressure. She ran an oxygen line from the wall into his nose. She picked up the phone. "Room 425, *Code White*."

"Hold on Link, hold on," Lydia pleaded as she squeezed his hand.

Frank Tupelo was sitting at the nurses' station on the third floor, reviewing an admission with his intern, when the overhead pager went off. "Code White, room 425. Repeat, Code White, room 425."

He jumped to his feet. "That's Link's room. Let's go." He and the intern raced for the stairway and up one flight to the fourth floor. Link's room was at the opposite end of the hall. As he passed the nurses' station he shouted, "Bring the crash-cart!"

Forbidden Harvest

"Dr. Tupelo, for God's sake do something!" Lydia pleaded.

Frank and the intern listened to Link's chest. He coughed up frothy sputum. Despite his strenuous efforts to breathe, his color remained a dusky grey. His eyes were closed.

"Sounds like pulmonary edema," the intern said.

Frank nodded. He turned to Lydia, who was standing next to the bed, her mouth gaping, her face ashen.

"It would be best if you waited at the nurses' station, Mrs. Bradshaw," Frank said.

"I must call Link's father." She hurried off.

A nurse pushed a crash-cart into the room.

"Link, I have to start an IV. You'll feel a needle stick right here," the nurse said. Link did not respond.

She hooked up cardiac electrodes and ran a rhythm strip. Dr. Tupelo studied the tracing. He asked the intern, "What's your diagnosis?"

"It looks like SVT (supra-ventricular tachycardia)."

"Right. How would you treat it?"

"You could try carotid massage?"

"Miss Conte, prepare an amp of verapamil."

Frank vigorously massaged an area in the right side of Link's neck, while observing the monitor. "There's no change. Inject the verapamil." He continued to observe the monitor.

"Miss Conte, prepare the defibrillator for synchronized cardioversion. Set at 25." He turned to Link. "Hold on, Link. You're going to be okay."

Frank took the paddles from the nurse. "Link, I have to

put paddles on your chest, and give your heart a small electric shock. It'll hurt, but just for a split second."

"Stand back," he shouted. Link's body shuddered. Frank glanced at the printout. "He's still in SVT." He ordered the nurse to double the charge. "Dear God, make this work," he said half aloud. He applied a second electrical shock.

"Great," the intern shouted. "He's in normal sinus rhythm."

After a minute or two, Link opened his eyes for a moment and gave Frank a weak smile. Frank listened to his chest.

"He's not wheezing nearly as much," the intern said.

"I agree," Frank said. "Although his heart rate's down we're going to have to watch him carefully. If the wheezing returns, he may need a bolus of furosemide. Call me if he goes back into pulmonary edema. I'm going to call the attending."

"Link, you feel okay?" Frank asked.

"Yeah," Link whispered. "I can breathe a lot better."

"We have to transfer you to the CCU so we can monitor you more closely. I have to call Dr. Cronce...I'll be back."

Link watched Dr. Frank's back and broad shoulders as he hurried from the room. He reminded Link of a wide-receiver headed down the football field, the defense nowhere in sight. He wondered how it must feel to save someone's life.

CHAPTER SEVEN

Lydia called Tom's work number. "Tom, Link's having some kind of breathing problem. Dr. Tupelo's with him."

"God almighty! What more can happen?"

"They've given him oxygen. He's a little better. But come as soon as you can, and for God's sake, drive carefully."

"I'm on my way."

It was obvious to Lydia, as she watched Dr. Tupelo approach the nurses' station, something was terribly wrong.

"What on earth happened?" she asked.

"He developed an abnormal heart rhythm. Fluid built up in his lungs."

"Is he breathing easier?"

"He's much better. I can tell you more after I speak with Dr. Cronce."

"Can I see him now?" Lydia asked.

"Yes. He's been asking for you. I'll join you in a few minutes."

"Hello, Dr. Cronce here."

Forbidden Harvest

Frank quickly recounted what had happened.

"It sounds like the tachycardia threw him into heart failure and pulmonary edema. Nice work, Frank. I want him transferred to the CCU."

"I've already arranged for that."

"I'll be at the hospital in about a half hour. Tell the Bradshaws I want to meet with them after I've had a chance to examine Link."

Frank hurried to Link's room. "I spoke with Dr. Cronce. He'll be coming in soon to see you."

Link's eyes were as round as Raggedy Andy's. His voice trembled. "Do I have to go to the CCU?"

"It's just a precaution," Frank said. He didn't want to let on how serious the situation had been. What if Link's heart hadn't slowed in response to the electric shock treatment? Might he have suffered another heart attack? Would he survive a second heart attack?

Lydia reached for Link's hand. "He's freezing." She went to the closet for a blanket.

"Dr. Cronce wants to meet with you and Link's dad after he's had a chance to examine Link," Frank said.

"Tom's on the way," Lydia said. She snuggled the blanket about Link. He smiled his thanks.

The call from Lydia reinforced Tom's fear that the doctors waited too long to do something definitive about Link's heart condition. Now he's developed some kind of breathing problem. Was there no hope for recovery? And if he did, would he be a cardiac invalid? Lydia had said not to drive recklessly. That Link was stable, according to Dr. Tupelo. But Tom had no faith in such an inexperienced young doctor. Was that the best Children's Hospital could offer? Tom pressed the accelerator to the floor.

As Tom stepped into Link's room his heart constricted. The bed had been stripped. Then he recalled his mother saying they would probably take Link to the CCU He raced up two flights to the sixth floor. Lydia was standing by the door. As he approached, she rushed toward him. Her face was drawn. She had been crying.

She grabbed both his hands. "Dr. Cronce and Dr. Tupelo are with him. They said to meet in the room next to the nurses' station."

Dr. Cronce and Frank joined Tom and Lydia. Dr. Cronce sat opposite Tom, and as he did, he removed his stethoscope from around his neck and placed it on the table.

"I asked Dr. Tupelo to call this meeting," Dr. Cronce said. "We can't be sure yet why Link developed an abnormal heart rhythm. It usually means there's an irritable area in the upper heart that breaks free of the rate-control mechanism."

"Why?" Tom asked. "Was he too active? Could it have been a reaction to his medicine? Could he have had another heart attack?"

Dr. Cronce removed his glasses. He drummed the table top.

"We can't be sure exactly what caused it," Dr. Cronce said. "It may have been triggered by increased demand on the upper heart chamber caused by his enlarging heart. A drug that commonly causes this type of abnormal heart rhythm is digitalis, but we stopped that a week ago. Low potassium can be a problem, especially in people taking strong diuretics. But he's taking a potassium supplement...we've been monitoring his levels closely. In most people a rapid heart rhythm is not a serious problem, and in fact often resolves spontaneously," Dr. Cronce said. "But because Link's cardiac output is barely adequate, the rapid rate resulted in a back pressure that caused a buildup of fluid in his lungs."

Lydia looked ashen. "Is this likely to happen again? What if it should happen when he's at home?" she asked.

Dr. Cronce began to clean the lenses with his tie. Lydia reached into her purse and handed him a tissue.

"Yes, this could happen again. Talk of going home is premature," Dr. Cronce said. "We need to do more tests, but I believe we are rapidly exhausting the extent to which we can control Link's condition medically. Right now the weakening of the heart muscle is even more serious than the coronary circulation problem. I believe it's time we brought in the thoracic surgery team."

"But if his heart is so weak, isn't this the worst time to be talking about surgery?" Tom asked.

"I'm not saying he needs surgery now, but I believe it's time to involve the surgical team."

Tom hit the table with his fist. "Damn it. I don't understand why you waited so long to consider surgery. You told us from the beginning that the success of surgery depends on the heart being strong."

"Mr. Bradshaw, we've monitored Link carefully. The deterioration we've seen these past four weeks has been totally unexpected and unpredictable."

Lydia's eyes flashed in anger. "Please set up the meeting with the surgeons as soon as possible. At the meeting I expect to get a better answer to Tom's question."

After the Bradshaws left, Frank and Dr. Cronce remained in the conference room.

"I need another cup of coffee," Dr. Cronce said, He walked to a table in a corner of the room. He poured a cup and tasted it. "God. This stuff is vile. Can I pour you a cup, Frank?"

Frank shook his head. "No. Thanks."

"The Bradshaws are absolutely right to be angry. I waited too damn long," Dr. Cronce admitted. He sat opposite Frank. He removed his glasses and rubbed the sides of his nose. "Tom Bradshaw raised the question of surgery when Link developed that small aneurysm," Dr. Cronce said. "Frank, are you sure you want to be a pediatric cardiologist?"

"All the studies showed excellent cardiac reserve," Frank said. "If we had gone ahead with surgery, he might still have deteriorated. Then our only choice would have been a transplant."

"I'm afraid that's where we are now," Dr. Cronce said. "There's very little chance simple coronary artery reconstruction is going to solve Link's problems."

Frank dreaded the meeting with the surgical team. It was one thing talking about the possibility of a heart transplant. Now the medical team would be virtually helpless as they searched for a compatible donor. How was he going to tell Link that their chance to do coronary artery grafting had passed? Now Link and his family must face the prospect of a heart transplant. Getting through the operation was bad enough. He'd be looking forward to a lifetime of taking strong medicines, living in constant fear that his body would reject the new heart. And what could he expect five or ten years down the road? No one really knew.

CHAPTER EIGHT

Marty headed for Link's room. He had looked so pale and frightened the day before, she wondered if going to the morgue could have caused him to have a panic attack or something. The door to his room was open. When she saw that his bed was stripped, and none of his things were there, she turned and ran to the nurses' station. Frank was sitting at a desk looking through a patient's chart.

"Doc Frank, what's happened to Link?" she asked breathlessly.

"Hey, he's okay. He's been transferred to the CCU."

She flopped into a stool next to Frank.

"It's my fault. I shouldn't have taken him to the morgue. He looked so scared." She began to cry. Her mascara ran down her cheeks. "Shit, it's my fault."

"He developed a rapid heart rate. It had nothing to do with you."

She blotted tears with the sleeves of her scrub suit. "Can I go see him?"

"Only immediate family can visit in the CCU." He stood and walked a short distance from the nurses' station. He motioned for her to come to him. "You and Link went to the morgue?"

"We were passing by. The door was open so we went in. We were only there a couple of minutes."

"Is that when you noticed something was wrong with him?"

"Yeah. He got real pale and sweaty. I thought he was just scared, I didn't think it was anything serious. As soon as I got him back to his room I told the nurse to check him right away."

"Like I said, it could've happened anywhere."

"Does Link have a phone in his room?" she asked.

"No."

"Does he have his computer with him?"

"Yes. I just left him. He was fooling around with it."

"Can I use the computer in the residents' room to send him a message?"

"Okay, there's probably nobody sleeping in there this time of day. The door might be locked. You'll need to know the combination."

"That's okay. I know it already."

He smiled shaking his head, "For some reason I'm not surprised. And you better look in the mirror before you do anything else. It sort of looks like you're on the warpath."

Link had shown Marty how to hook up to CompuServe using his password. She hoped she would remember all the steps. After a few tries she got through and typed in, *Go-Bulletin Board.* She entered the following message: *Dear LD, get your little butt out of the CCU. We got places to go and things to do. Your friend, Madam Butterfly.*

She knew Link browsed the computer bulletin board to

read the weird messages people left. She would check tomorrow to see if he had picked up hers.

The next day she looked through messages. There it was: *Dear Madam Butterfly, It's not so bad here; lots of gadgets. I hope I'm out before your chemo starts. Your friend, LD.*

Marty was due to start chemotherapy the following week. She was curious about her blood type. Why not look it up myself? She wondered. She was glad she had memorized Frank's password. *It would be fun to be a spy...even though the thought of it makes me jumpy.*

It took a little fumbling around, but she eventually was able to gain access to the laboratory data bank. She figured they would have checked her blood type along with her other admission labs. She looked up the date.

"Bingo," she said aloud, tickled that she had been able to find it so easily.

She decided to find out what Link's blood type was. She punched in his name. Only one *Thomas Lincoln Bradshaw* was listed. A piece of cake. She looked up his laboratory tests. She couldn't believe how many were listed. Finally she went to the admission date. There it was...type O negative, the same as hers! Does Doc Frank realize that she and Link have the same blood type? If he does, why hasn't he said anything to her?

Marty and her mother had been asked on each hospital admission if they wanted to participate in the organ-donor program. Marty didn't like to think about it. She could tell her mother didn't either. But when Dr. Tupelo told her that Link might eventually need a heart transplant, she began to wonder about actually being an organ donor. She reached her right hand up under her shirt top. She placed her palm against her chest just below her breast. At first she couldn't feel her heart beating. She blew out and held her breath like the medical students made her do when they listened. She could feel it beating. Lub-dub, lub-dub, lub-dub. *Geez, it's really creepy how that small muscle starts to beat even before a person's born and just keeps going.*

She logged-off the computer and left the residents' room. She wanted to talk with Dr. Tupelo about becoming an organ donor. She wondered if the cancer or the chemotherapy had damaged her heart. Dr. Tupelo would know.

Later that afternoon he stopped by her room. Piled on the bed were school books and stacks of papers. She was sitting in a chair beside her bed, an open book on her lap. She was gently brushing her sparse hair as he entered.

"Hi," Dr. Tupelo said, "the nurse said you were looking for me."

She closed her political science book and tossed it on the bed. She reached for her Braves baseball cap.

"Who brought in the homework?" he asked.

"They have no mercy at the Mount. My homeroom teacher had my mom pick up all this stuff yesterday."

Marty was wearing her usual scrub suit bottoms. But today she wore a red silk blouse with needlepoint embroidery of dragons and butterflies.

"Nice top," Frank said.

"Doc Frank, did you know that Link and I have the same blood type?"

"I did notice...it's quite a coincidence, because it's not a very common one."

"Link heard one of the doctors saying it was just a matter of time that he was gonna need a new heart."

"I know you and Link are good friends. But unless he

gives me permission, I can't talk about his medical condition."

"Everyone around here knows everything about everybody." She raised both palms to the sky. "So what's the big deal?"

He smiled and shook his head. "Yes, like the fact that your blood types are the same."

Frank pushed some papers aside to make a place to sit. He lifted himself onto the foot of her bed.

"And besides," Marty said, "I heard you, Dr. Manning, Dr. Cronce, and the Bradshaws, excepting Link, are meeting this afternoon. And everybody knows Dr. Manning's the transplant doctor."

"I won't confirm or deny that rumor." He looked at his watch. "But I'm supposed to be there in ten minutes."

He reached over and pulled the peak of her cap down to her eyebrow level.

"So what's really on your mind, young lady?"

"Could I be a heart donor, what with me having cancer and chemo a couple of times?"

"I don't think the chemo would be a problem. But it's not recommended for someone with cancer to be a donor."

"Why is that? Cancer's not catching, is it?"

"Actually the risk of passing cancer to the person getting the organ is extremely small."

Marty removed her baseball cap and slapped it against her school book. "The risk of dying without the operation is like a hundred percent. Why not take a chance?"

He stood and stooped to smell a bouquet of roses on her bedside stand. "I'll talk about this with Dr. Bernholtz as soon as I get a chance. Okay?"

"Thanks. No rush. Tomorrow's soon enough."

Marty knocked on the door to the residents' on-call room. When there was no answer she punched in the door lock combination and let herself in. She booted the computer, logged into CompuServe, and typed in a message on the bulletin board:

"Dear LD, Meeting in question to commence at 1600 Pacific Time. Will keep you informed as the situation evolves. Your friend, Madame Butterfly."

She sat in the darkened room, unsure as to whether to add a post script telling him that she had decided to be an organ donor, and to name him as the person to get her heart. No, she'd better wait until she hears from Dr. Tupelo, she thought. Besides, it'd be like saying he had to have a heart transplant no matter what. She didn't want him to quit trying to get better and not need a stupid operation.

Forbidden Harvest

CHAPTER NINE

Alison Simmons, Tom Bradshaw's executive assistant, sat next to Tom's desk as he stood at the window watching a car circle a man-made pond that glistened in the afternoon sun. A flock of Canada geese honked in unison as they darted across the water.

"Your afternoon's shoulder-to-shoulder meetings," she said. "And Fred Nance says he needs you to sign off on the pricing of our bid for the Japanese contract. He's leaving town early in the morning."

Tom's heart ached as he thought of the terror, pain and uncertain future his young son had to face. He strode to his desk and began loading papers into a briefcase. "Mother and I are meeting with Link's doctors. I have to swing by to pick her up on the way." He headed for the door.

"What about the retirement banquet tonight? You're supposed to hand out the awards."

"I'll be a little late. Make sure they eat slowly, and ask Fred to stop by my house tonight around ten. Have him bring all the papers with him."

As he drove to Lydia's townhouse, he tried desperately not to think of what lay ahead for Link. At the fringes of his peripheral vision, flame-like flashes of light shimmered. He knew that soon severe pain over his forehead would bring tears to his eyes. The migraine headaches had started after the car crash. The doctors called the shimmering light an aura, warning of the severe headache to come. He reached into his pocket and removed a small plastic medicine bottle. He placed the tip in his nostril and squeezed. Sometimes the medicine prevented the headaches, sometimes not. He recalled that night in agonizing detail.

Tom loosened his tie, unbuttoned his shirt collar, and glanced at the leather briefcase on the seat beside him. It was packed with financial reports, clippings from the Wall Street Journal, and the text of a speech he was to deliver to the Seattle Chamber of Commerce the next day. He sighed and rolled down the window, letting in a gust of cool air, as he sped past a wall of leafless hardwoods, their lacework of branches lit by the pink evening sky. Beyond a clearing, the heavy-lidded sun was ready to call it a day.

A car in front of him swerved, plunging into a leaf pile. As the car accelerated, leaves filled the air. Tom smiled, wondering how old the driver might be. He still had the urge, but now he worried about what might be hidden underneath.

At Tom Bradshaw Industries, he was in charge of a multi-million-dollar company that manufactured aircraft navigation equipment for Boeing. He enjoyed being in control, of guiding the destiny of the company his father had founded. He anticipated preparing his son, Link, to take over the job someday. At home Brenda, tall, slender, soft spoken, with eyes as brown as chestnuts and hair to match, and a smile that could melt a stone, was uncontested CEO.

On the evening news, he learned that Sony had purchased Columbia pictures for 3.4 billion dollars. Noriega was said to be in the pay of the CIA, even as he blatantly carried out a massive drug-smuggling operation in Panama. Sadam Hussain, armed with American weapons, was threatening to annex his small oil-rich neighbor to the south.

He turned onto route 90, drove over the Lacey Murrow Floating Bridge, and headed for Mercer Island. Once on the island, he turned south on West Mercer Highway, minutes from home.

As Tom stepped into the front hall, he heard Brenda call. Before he could answer, she leaped into his arms. Dropping his briefcase, he spun her in a full circle. His feet and the briefcase competed for the same space, and Tom lost his balance. He and Brenda fell to the floor.

"Sweetheart, if this is how you're going to greet me, we'd better get thicker carpet."

She lay on top of him, her hair falling about his face. "Tom, I went to the doctor's office today."

Wrapping his arms about her, he rolled her onto her back. "He told you to make love to your husband in the front hall?"

"The fertility pill worked."

"You're pregnant? Oh, my God. That's great."

Link came into the front hall. "Dad, brace yourself."

Tom searched Brenda's face. He knew the pill sometimes caused triplets or more. "Don't tell me we're having a litter?"

"Not quite a litter."

"Mom has a copy of the ultrasound," Link said.

Link walked ahead of Tom as they went to the kitchen. His legs seemed longer in proportion to the rest of his body, and his walk was a bit awkward. Tom could remember being a teenager, when parts of his body grew faster than others. He banged into things and his nose seemed to become adult-sized long before the rest of him. But Link was still baby-faced, with full cheeks and a softness about his nose and eyes.

Hopefully, someday he would have the Bradshaw nose, straight, imposing; but Link's brown hair, fair skin and freckles were straight from his mother. Link picked up the ultrasound picture from the kitchen table.

He handed it to his dad. The doctor had drawn arrows to show the fetuses. Tom studied the black and white images.

"There're two of them, all right. Could the doctor tell the sex?"

"I told him I didn't want to know."

"Mom, did you have one of those pictures when I was inside you?" Link asked.

"No. Twelve years ago they didn't do ultrasounds."

Tom made a fist and gently tapped Link's chin. "Listen, champ, you're going to be a big brother. Think you can handle it?"

"I can't believe how little they are." Link stared at the fuzzy images.

"Maybe we can figure out the sex," Tom said. "Look here, there's something sticking out on this one. I bet it's a boy."

"I see what you mean." Brenda pushed between Tom and Link, bending to study the picture. "I believe those are called legs."

"What do you think, Link?"

Link had just poured himself a glass of milk. He took a sip before answering. "I think you're both right."

"Now this young man will go far in the world." Tom grabbed a chocolate chip cookie, and reached for Link's unfinished glass of milk. Link walked to the refrigerator to pour himself another.

"Let's do something special tonight. We need to celebrate."

"Have you forgotten we're going to Jill and Brad's for dinner?" Brenda asked.

"Shh...oot. I've had this ominous feeling."

Tom liked Jill well enough, but he and Brad were definitely out of sync. Everything Brad wore had someone's name on it, and that British accent...

"What about Link?" Tom roughed up Link's hair. "Shouldn't he be part of our celebration?"

"Nice try," Brenda said.

"Let's go to see Field of Dreams," Link suggested.

Tom guessed that Brenda was probably eager to tell Jill and some of her other friends the good news. He gave up. "All settled."

Link sat at the table munching cookies. "Dad, why don't I order a pizza?"

Tom checked his watch. "Anchovies and mushrooms on my half. You call it in while I shave."

Sixteen guests pressed elbow to elbow at Jill's dinner-table. Brenda sat opposite Tom. To her right, a plump, bearded man leaned forward, addressing a woman on Tom's left.

"How could you stand to take another course from that old mutton head?"

She said, "Oh, I don't know." She pushed the food in her

plate as though checking to see if it might move on its own. Her straight blond hair hung to her shoulders. Tom thought she was pretty, in an undernourished way. He looked at the index finger of her right hand and wondered how many meals it had re-directed.

"I could tolerate his lisp," she said. "If only he knew what the hell he was talking about."

The man roared with laughter, spraying droplets of digestive juices half way across the table. Tom looked at Brenda, who rolled her eyes. As they waited for dessert, Brenda leaned over and whispered to Tom, "I'll bust if I don't tell someone soon."

"Then let's liven things up a bit," Tom said.

He jumped to his feet, but the conversational frenzy around the table continued. Brenda reached for a fork and banged her water glass. The room quieted.

Tom looked about the table, holding his glass high. "I want to toast our gracious hosts, Jill and Brad." *After everyone raised their glass, Tom continued,* "And I want to make an announcement. Today, we learned that my darling wife, Brenda, is pregnant." *There were shouts of approval*

Jill, coming in from the kitchen, rushed to Brenda. She knew how long the Bradshaws had tried for another child. "Oh, honey, I'm so happy for you. I thought you looked especially radiant tonight."

Tom remained standing. "Another announcement, folks. It took us so long to make a second baby we decided to have a couple while we were at it."

Brenda's friends crowded around her. Someone came up behind Tom and slapped him on the back, causing wine to spill from his glass. Holding the half-empty glass he turned and saw Brad grinning at him. Brad was wearing a white silk dinner jacket with a shawl collar faced in green satin, white flannel pants and matching green satin slippers. Tom had avoided him the entire evening, but now he was trapped.

"Congrats," Brad said, "Didn't think you had it in you."

Tom smiled. He thought how pleasant it would be to pour the rest of his drink over Brad's head and watch the burgundy rivulets run down his jacket. He glanced at Brenda, who was standing nearby. She gave Tom a disapproving frown, as though anticipating what he might say. He noticed a slight dimpling at the corners of her mouth.

He looked Brad over deliberately before speaking. "Fantastic outfit. I especially like the emerald earring...great touch." Before Brad had a chance to respond, Tom said, "Excuse me, Brad, old boy, I need another drink."

The wine being served was a 1976 vintage Bordeaux, one of Tom's favorites.

He had had several glasses. As they prepared to leave, he handed Brenda his car keys. "You drive, sweetheart. My brain's been wined and Bradded...it's thoroughly numbed."

"I noticed."

Tom tilted back the passenger seat. "I'm going to rest my eyes. Are you okay?"

"Relax. I'm fine."

They wound their way toward the highway. What had been a light rain suddenly turned into a downpour, pelting the windshield with such force that the drops burst and coalesced in an unending cycle.

Brenda reduced her speed and moved into the right lane.

Forbidden Harvest

Tom sat up, wide awake. "Hey, maybe we should pull over and wait this out. It can't keep up like this very long."

"I'm okay." She glanced at the gas gauge. "I can't understand why your gas tank is always on empty. We'll never find an open station."

"This engine is used to running on fumes."

"Alcohol or gasoline?"

Tom placed his hand over her lower abdomen. "I still can't believe there are a couple of little Bradshaws in there. Do you think they would mind if Daddy came knocking tonight?"

She squeezed his hand. "The last I heard, you had unrestricted visitation."

Tom struggled to keep his eyes open.

"Besides," Brenda said, "You'll be in the arms of Somnus before your head hits the pillow."

"What a price I pay for having married an English major."

"Damn, the wipers are going full speed," Brenda said. "But I can barely see twenty feet ahead."

Tom leaned toward the windshield. "The shoulder's too narrow here. But pull over the first chance you get."

He checked the speedometer. He glanced behind them. Brenda was driving well below the speed limit. A line of cars was following her.

"God almighty," she muttered as she leaned forward.

He glanced back. "Put on your flashers, honey, and keep driving at a steady speed."

She glanced in the rear-view mirror.

"Oh, my God," Tom shouted.

Forbidden Harvest

To their left he could make out a truck heading across the median toward them. Brenda flashed her high beams on and off as Tom pressed the horn.

A terrifying screech filled the night as the truck's tires skidded over the wet pavement. Brenda swerved to the right. Their car slammed into a metal guard rail. Tom was thrown violently against the passenger door.

When the front end of the truck slammed into them, Tom jack-knifed forward, striking his head against the dashboard. Brenda screamed. Her air bag exploded, filling the space between her and the steering wheel. The truck crashed through the windshield and ripped along the driver's side of their car.

The car tumbled down an embankment. It came to rest with a violent jolt. Tom, who had been knocked unconscious at impact, was suddenly awake. He could feel his weight pressed against the door. They were in total darkness. He could sense Brenda, suspended above him.

"Sweetheart, are you okay? Brenda? Oh, my God, say something!"

Rain poured through the shattered windshield. He struggled to free his arms and legs from the crumpled dash. Blood from a scalp laceration covered his face. He grew light-headed.

The faint wail of a siren grew louder and louder. Soon, the blackness was lit by flashes of red and blue lights. He looked toward Brenda...her silhouette appeared to move toward him with each flash of light.

Someone reached into the windshield and wiped Tom's face.

"He's still alive!"

Tom, unable to speak, struggled to remain conscious. They placed something over his eyes, but he could still see flashes of light and felt intense heat against his skin. He wanted to tell them to stop. They were burning him.

"Make them stop!" he tried to say.

Voices shouted to one another.

"She's bleeding badly."

"I can't get a pulse."

"No way can we get her out in time."

"Dear God," Tom prayed, "They must save her...they must not let her die."

Tom opened his eyes. He was on his back on a stretcher, a bright light above him. He couldn't move his arms or legs. Was he paralyzed? Where was he, what was happening to him? Someone leaned over him.

"Mr. Bradshaw, I'm Dr. Mason. You were in a very bad crash, and you need to have an emergency operation...can you understand me?"

He had trouble focusing on the doctor's face. "What...what operation?"

"You had a severe head injury that caused a blood clot on your brain. We have to operate immediately."

"My wife...where is she?"

"I'm terribly sorry, Mr. Bradshaw. Your wife was...she had very severe injuries. We can talk after the operation."

Tom turned his head away from the doctor. He closed his eyes. "I just want to see her."

A nurse standing on the other side of the stretcher was adjusting an infusion of blood. "Mr. Bradshaw, there's no time. We need to take you to the operating room now."

He knew then she was gone. "Oh God," he cried silently, "it should've been me! It should've been me."

Forbidden Harvest

Tom glanced at Lydia as they sat. He could tell by the set of her jaw that she was angry, prepared not to like this new doctor, who had been suddenly forced upon them. His oversized desk and high-back chair accentuated the slightness of Dr. Manning. He was clean-shaven except for a pencil-line mustache. Intense slate blue eyes stared at them from behind thick horn-rimmed glasses.

Dr. Cronce introduced the Bradshaws to Dr. Manning and went directly to the issues. "We're approaching a critical time in the management of Link's heart condition. His cardiac reserve has diminished to the point where he can maintain basic metabolic needs. But any excess demand, such as simply walking, could cause a worsening of his heart failure."

"Have you done everything possible?" Lydia asked.

"I believe we have, Mrs. Bradshaw."

"That may be so, but I want to bring in outside consultants."

"Yes," Tom affirmed, "We know that surgery may be necessary. But I'm sure you can understand our need to be sure nothing else can be done."

"Of course, Tom," Dr. Cronce said. "I'll arrange to have all of Link's records sent to whomever you choose. If you would like I can recommend physicians with the most experience in dealing with Link's condition."

"Not just look at the records. I want them to come to Seattle to evaluate Link!"

"That may be difficult to arrange on such short notice," Dr. Cronce said. "But we will certainly do our best to get them here. However, I would still like Dr. Manning to discuss the surgical options with you."

Dr. Manning leaned back in his chair. "I've examined Link and have reviewed his angiogram and other studies.

Dr. Cronce is quite correct in saying they're doing medically as much as is humanly possible. At bed rest, Link has no pain or other symptoms, except for nausea related to his medications."

There was absolute silence in the room as Dr. Manning paused for a few moments. He continued, "Just walking across the room to the bathroom causes Link to become short of breath. Even after bathing himself he has to use the nasal oxygen to ease his breathing. Without surgical intervention, in my opinion, Link's life expectancy is less than six months."

Again no one spoke. Lydia leaned against Tom. He reached around her shoulder. They had read about the poor prognosis and Dr. Cronce had told them as much, but somehow in this setting it took on a degree of certainty they had not felt before. Lydia's hand trembled as she reached into her purse.

"Yes, Dr. Manning, you were saying?" she said.

"Heart transplant in children has only been done for the past few years. Initially surgical mortality was very high, and organ rejection and other complications were discouraging. But improved techniques and drugs, such as Cyclosporine and Prograf, are used to prevent rejection and have contributed to much better results."

Tom thought of how close he and Link had become since Brenda's death. The thought of losing Link too was unbearable.

"What about physical activity after transplant surgery?" Tom asked...his voice tense with emotion.

"Many transplant recipients today are back in school and even able to engage in sports activities. It's imperative that we don't wait so long that other organs such as the kidneys and liver begin to fail. Good kidney function is vital"

Forbidden Harvest

Lydia stared across the room without speaking.

"I understand there aren't enough organs for everyone who needs a transplant," Tom said. "How do you decide?"

"The system for organ procurement and distribution is very complicated," Dr. Manning said. "There are over a hundred centers in the United States doing heart transplant surgery, and probably more than one hundred organ procurement agencies referred to as O.P.A.s."

Tom stood, took his jacket and hung it over the back of his chair. He removed a memo pad from the inside breast pocket.

"Who controls these agencies?" he asked.

"They're non-profit corporations, organized and managed locally. Their purpose is to meet the needs of organ recipients in their geographic areas. There is also a voluntary national organ-sharing network that is federally supported and referred to as *U.N.O.S.*"

Dr. Manning continued, "Most *O.P.A.*s use this computerized network. Many problems exist with the network, the most serious of which is a lack of any universally agreed-on set of criteria governing prioritization and distribution."

"What kinds of criteria?" Lydia demanded.

Tom marveled at his mother's resilience. A few moments ago she was petrified with fear. Now she seemed ready to take charge of the meeting.

"The prognosis is the most critical," Dr. Manning said. "If the child is considered to have less than a year to live, he or she would meet the basic requirement. They do not accept children with life-threatening conditions such as cancer, severe renal disease, leukemia ... conditions of that sort."

"I recall hearing about a private procurement program here at Children's Hospital," Lydia said.

"Yes," Dr. Manning said. "We're fortunate here in that we have one of the most successful organ-procurement programs in the country, thanks to Dr. Bernholtz. He's established a network of volunteers throughout the state who make presentations to various groups signing up organ donors."

"So the donor can indicate a specific individual?" Lydia asked.

"Yes," Dr. Manning said, "that person will receive the heart assuming they meet all of the criteria I mentioned. Otherwise, they go to the waiting list."

"Is the ability to pay one of the criteria?" Tom asked.

"Unfortunately in most *O.P.A.s*, unless persons have insurance coverage or are prepared to pay in cash, they're not considered for organ transplantation," Dr. Manning said. "At Children's Hospital we have an endowed foundation that funds uninsured and needy children. Several years ago Dr. Bernholtz organized the foundation. Now income from the fund can support as many as four transplant surgeries each year."

"I recall my dad talking about that," Tom said.

"Yes, now that you mention it," Lydia added, "Link's grandfather was an early sponsor of the foundation."

"Is there a long waiting list?" Tom asked.

"Yes, but that's somewhat deceptive," Dr. Manning said. "The blood type of the donor must match that of the recipient. They test for ABO and Rh factor as well as other criteria that could make the tissue incompatible. Incompatibility of blood type would lead to immediate rejection."

"I've read about that, but I'm not sure I understand it," Tom said.

"Antibodies in the recipient search out foreign cells and try to destroy them. After surgery we give medicines to block the immune system from doing that."

"What other criteria are considered?" Lydia asked.

"In children, the size of the donor and recipient organ is a limiting factor. They must be fairly closely matched."

After a pause he continued, "They often go quite far down the list to find a compatible recipient." Dr. Manning rose and walked around to the front of his desk. He leaned back, resting on the edge. "I'd urge you to move as expeditiously as possible. The sooner we get Link on the waiting list, the better his chances of getting a donor heart."

Forbidden Harvest

CHAPTER TEN

Ken was on the phone when Lydia entered his office. She sat opposite his desk. He rose with a start, striking his knee against the desk drawer. He winced in pain. Lydia shook her head ever so slightly. Dear Kenneth, she thought, I can still bring out the clumsy boy in him.

"What a nice surprise," he said as he hung up.

Lydia spoke in a whisper, "Kenneth..."

He came from around his desk and crouched next to her. "Lydia, what is it?"

"Link's condition's gotten so much worse."

"What's happened?"

She told him about the meeting with Dr. Manning.

"He wants us to place Link on a waiting list for a heart transplant."

"I've been worried it might come to this."

"But, Kenneth, how can we be sure they've done all they possibly can? Tom and I want to get a second and third opinion. Could you help?"

Ken stood. He began pacing in the small office.

"I'll start on it immediately. I know pediatric pathologists at a number of hospitals. I'll ask them to give me the names of the most outstanding clinical cardiologists they know."

Lydia stood and embraced Ken. "I knew you would." She pressed her cheek against his. "You have no idea how much that means to me."

Ken spent the remainder of the afternoon tracking down pediatric cardiologists. He called Tom, giving him the two most highly recommended. Tom asked Ken to make arrangements for them to come to Seattle.

Within a week the doctors arrived. They reviewed the records and talked with Link's doctors. They examined Link and reviewed his x-rays and other laboratory studies. Both consultants concluded that Link was receiving outstanding care. One suggested the use of a drug still under investigation that worked in some children. He said that it reportedly improved left-ventricular function beyond the range of available medications. The other consultant laid out a precise set of criteria for the use of a mechanical device to support circulation, if and when Link's condition became desperate while he awaited a donor heart.

Lydia stopped by Ken's office. "My head's swimming with all the things consultants told us. Can you come to dinner tonight? Tom's coming over. I really need your help in sorting things out."

"Yes, of course."

"Come around seven." She took Ken's hand. He stood awkwardly as she rose on her toes and kissed him on the cheek.

After she left, Ken felt his cheek where she had kissed him. The rest of the afternoon he had difficulty concentrating on his work. As he sat at his desk, he leaned back in his chair and closed his eyes. *My God. Where have the years gone?* He recalled their first meeting, when they were students. Ken was a pathology resident at Massachusetts General. She was in a master's program at Vassar.

She was standing next to him at the dining-room table pouring a drink. She looked up just as he noticed her. Her long straight auburn hair rested lightly on her shoulders. She wore a close-fitting knit dress with a single string of pearls.

As their eyes met, his right arm involuntarily jerked, catapulting his drink over the front of her dress.

He stared at her in disbelief. "I...."

She smiled and said, "Apologies accepted. I'm Lydia Lincoln."

She extended her right hand. He was still clutching his empty glass as he reached for her hand.

She stared at the wine glass he had thrust in her direction.

He placed his glass on the table and shook her hand vigorously.

"I'm Ken Bernholtz. Nice to meet you, Miss Lincoln."

They parted after a few awkward minutes, but throughout the evening he couldn't help staring at her. He also noticed her glancing at him from time to time. Finally as the party began to break up, he headed for her, drink in hand.

As he approached her, she said, "If you spill another drink on me, Ken, you're going to have to take me to dinner."

Three whiskey sours had bolstered his courage. He held

the glass between them. "Now that's a tempting proposition." They chatted a few minutes as the crowd dissolved around them.

The hostess approached them, "I'm so glad you've managed to meet each other. Please feel free to stay as long as you like. Tomorrow's Sunday; we can all sleep late."

Lydia looked at her watch, "Oh my, it's almost midnight. I must be getting back to my hovel."

"Can I walk you to your car?" Ken asked

"That would be nice."

They saw each other for several months before she met Tom Bradshaw Sr. Tom was a brash young engineer doing postgraduate work at MIT. He already owned two patents related to submarine navigation equipment. Lydia and Tom were married after a six-month perpetual motion courtship. Tom was eagerly recruited by several corporations, and when Lydia was offered a job as assistant curator of the Seattle Museum of Natural History, Tom accepted an offer from Boeing Aircraft, also located in Seattle.

After Lydia and Tom were married, Ken did not fade from the picture, but instead became part of their inner circle. Tom and Lydia had tried to play matchmaker by inviting single women to their social functions, but Ken would lose interest after a few dates. After awhile they stopped trying.

On completing his fellowship, Ken had his pick of academic positions. When offered a faculty appointment at the Children's Memorial Hospital in Seattle, he jumped at the chance to be close to Lydia and Tom.

Through the years Tom and Ken developed a friendship of their own. Tom was an ardent golfer and Ken, who was not athletically inclined, applied himself with great determination to the sport. He surprised himself how quickly he learned to *play a respectable, consistent game. Golf after all is a game of precision and repetition of a learned skill; and Ken was certainly precise in his approach.*

Tom often said that Ken would have made a great brain surgeon judging by the meticulous way he addressed a golf ball. Tom, on the other hand, would attack the course as though it were a war zone. He never took a practice swing, and always pounded the ball as hard as he could. Two very different men became golfing buddies, but they also had something else in common...they were both in love with Lydia.

Forbidden Harvest

CHAPTER ELEVEN

As Gladys Lopinski prepared to visit her daughter at the hospital, she thought of Marty's father.

She had dropped out of Barnard College the summer after her freshman year. She became caught up in the anti-Vietnam student protests, even went with a bus-load of students to Chicago to join the protests from around the country at the Democratic Convention in 1968. There she met Cleve. He was one of the protest organizers. He had also been involved in the riots at Columbia University earlier that year.

He was a charismatic, passionate, romantic figure. He raced about with a megaphone, pushing over police barriers and stoking up the protesters. She was at his side when the police gathered them up and hauled them off to jail. They talked through the night about the war and where the country was headed. They were released the next day without being charged. Gladys was besotted. After that, she accompanied Cleve as he traveled to college campuses around the country, inspiring and organizing student protests.

It was an exciting, carefree time, but unfortunately, he introduced Gladys to pot and LSD. In 1970 she was arrested for possession of thirty grams of marijuana. She faced a possible five years in jail. But since it was her first offense, she was given the option of going into a rehab program, followed by two-years probation. She chose rehab. After her release, she pleaded with Cleve to enter detox.

On the drive to their apartment, Cleve offered her a joint.

"Damnit, Cleve. I just spent a month of my life getting sober. I'm on probation. They'll test my urine for drugs. Do you want me to end up in jail?"

Cleve was driving their canary-yellow Volkswagen Beetle. "There's ways of beating those tests. I know some guys."

"I saw men and women in there for the third and fourth time! Their lives were in shambles. They couldn't put two coherent sentences together. Damn it! I don't want to end up like that. I don't want you to end up like that."

"I have things under control. So layoff, okay."

He lit a joint and smiled. "You sure you don't want one?"

The war in Vietnam was over. She got a job as a secretary. Cleve never held a job for very long; she blamed his drug and alcohol abuse. She had hoped that after Marty was born, he would change...but he didn't. Over the next two years, he sank deeper and deeper into dependency. They separated when Marty was in kindergarten.

Cleve's parents took no interest in the baby, who they referred to as "their supposed grandchild." When Gladys called to see if Cleve's mother knew of his whereabouts, she said she had no idea where her son was and didn't really care.

"My dear," she said, "are you sure he's the daddy? Ii don't for the life of me know how you hippies figure out who has fathered who."

Whenever the subject of her father came up, Marty

would brush it off, saying she really didn't care. Gladys didn't believe that for a minute.

Gladys jumped when the phone rang. "Hi, Marty. I was just getting ready to leave."

"I wanted to make sure you're coming. There's something I really gotta talk with you about."

"What is it?"

"I want to wait for you to be here."

"Sure, sweetheart. I'll be there in about thirty minutes."

Dr. Tupelo had mentioned to Gladys that Marty was asking about being an organ donor. She wasn't opposed to organ donation in general, but was appalled at the thought of a surgeon cutting into her daughter's body, removing life-sustaining organs.

At the hospital, Gladys sat in a chair next to Marty's bed. Marty sat on the edge of the bed with her good leg tucked under her. Gladys braced herself to prepare for some major manipulation.

"Mom, I've never seen that dress before. You look really great tonight."

"I know. And I'm the best mom in the world, right?"

"Yeah, and I really mean it." Marty leaned back on her arms and smiled. "I never could fool you. You've had fifteen years and six months to totally figure me out."

"So you've been thinking about the organ donor program?"

Marty leaned toward her mother, resting her elbows on her knees. She nodded her head slowly. "Mom, when Doc Frank told me Link might eventually need a heart transplant, I began to think about it a lot. There are probably lots of kids like him waiting to get a heart."

"I'm sorry Link's getting worse."

"I'd like you to meet him."

"I'd love to...you've talked about him so much...but isn't he in intensive care?"

"No, he came out a couple of days ago. Let's go see him right now."

"We can't just barge in on him."

"I already told him we might come by."

When they entered his room, Link was propped in bed with his computer on his lap.

"Hi, LD, this is my mom."

"I'm sure glad to meet you, Mrs. Lopinski." He smiled and reached to shake her hand. "Marty says she gets her acting talent from you."

"It's nice to meet you. Did you see *Taming of the Shrew*?"

"I did. She looked a lot older on stage. When I first saw her here I didn't recognize her."

Marty picked up a get-well card from his bedside table. She flipped it open.

"Is this from one of your many lady friends?"

"She's just a kid in my class." Link blushed. "Give me that."

She danced away from him. "Oh listen to this, 'J.S. turned out to be a real jerk. I hope you're not still mad at me. I did write that note in class and I meant it too. Your friend, Jennifer.'"

"Marty! Give that back to Link."

"Okay," Marty said. "I got carried away. Jealousy is an ugly thing."

An orderly entered the room.

"You gotta go to PT now," he said to Link.

"Sorry I have to go. Maybe you can come again sometime, Mrs. Lopinski?"

"Yes. I'd love to," Gladys said.

"Yeah. Next time we'll make an appointment," Marty said.

On the way back to her room, Marty asked, "Well, what do you think, Mom, should I marry him?"

"He's a real charmer, and I know how fond you are of him, but I'd say he's a tad young right now. Give him eight to ten years before you commit."

"Remember when they asked about organ donation in case I were to die?"

"Honey, you're going to live a long time. I don't want to think about that right now."

They stopped in front of a row of elevator doors. Gladys removed Marty's baseball cap and brushed the hair back from her forehead. How devastated Gladys had felt after the first bout of chemotherapy when Marty lost all her hair. It had since grown back but was much thinner. Marty had her father's aristocratic nose and blond hair. But her prominent cheek bones, full lips and hazel eyes were so much like her own.

"Mom, there's no way I want to die. But if I do, I want to help Link. We can name him as the person to get my heart. That way he won't die waiting for some stranger's heart. It won't do me any good, after I'm dead and maybe I could save his life?"

Forbidden Harvest

Gladys embraced her tightly, still not responding.

The elevator doors opened and several people exited.

"I guess we'd better go to your room if we want some private squeezing time," Gladys whispered.

Marty didn't let go. People hurried around them.

"I want to do this more than anything. Please, Mom."

"He seems like a wonderful boy and a good friend. It's your decision."

The following day they met with the hospital organ procurement coordinator. Gladys told her that Marty wanted to join the donor program to name a specific person to receive the donor organ.

"Thomas Lincoln Bradshaw," Marty said. "That's who I want to get my heart."

The woman looked up from a summary of Marty's hospital record. She removed her reading glasses. "I'm sorry, my dear, but with your diagnosis the only tissues we could accept are your corneas."

"Dr. Tupelo said if he's gonna die because they can't find a heart, his family is willing to accept the risk."

"Mrs. Lopinski, your daughter has disseminated cancer. There's no way we could even consider this."

Marty stood and leaned toward the woman. "Who are you to say? Who's your boss? I want to talk to your boss. Dr. Bernholtz told my doctor we could do it."

"Dr. Bernholtz? Mrs. Lopinski, did you speak with him?"

"No, not directly, my daughter told me."

"I see. I'll need a statement in writing from Dr. Bernholtz, saying that an exception can be made in this case. I'm sorry, but until then, my position is unchanged."

Forbidden Harvest

Marty's chemotherapy started two days later. The protocol called for five days of intravenous treatment. They placed a catheter in her right upper chest, passing it into a major vessel returning blood to the heart. The medicine was too toxic to give through ordinary intravenous routes because it could cause serious damage to smaller blood vessels.

She couldn't leave her room. She was too sick to think about anything. Everything she tried to eat came right back up. They fed her a mixture of fat, protein and carbohydrate through a second catheter placed in her upper thigh. Gladys took a week off from work and stayed at her bedside the entire time. Because of the constant severe nausea, Marty required frequent injections of anti-nausea drugs and narcotics. In a state of delirium she screamed at imagined attackers. Gladys, constantly at her bedside, held her in her arms until she quieted.

When her white blood count dropped to under a thousand, the doctors gave her large doses of antibiotics to prevent infection. She broke out in quarter-sized weeping sores over her arms and legs.

Several days after the therapy was completed, Marty was finally able to regain her strength and appetite. She still had deep dark circles about her eyes and had lost several pounds. When she was finally given permission to leave her room, the first thing she did was to ask Dr. Tupelo about Link.

"He's out of the CCU. He's in a telemetry bed."

"What's that?" Marty asked.

"They have a monitor attached to his chest, and it sends a radio signal to a control room where someone checks on it twenty-four hours a day. If they detect something unexpected they call the doctor right away."

"Does he have to stay in bed?"

"No, he can move around some. But the nurse has to know where he is, in case something unusual comes up on the monitor. You can visit him. He's on the sixth floor, next to the CCU."

She changed into a clean scrub suit and put on lipstick, cheek coloring, and mascara. Her hair was a mess...that morning a large clump had fallen out as she brushed it. She donned her Braves baseball cap and a long-sleeved blouse. She still had scabs on both arms and she didn't want to gross Link out. She was nervous about seeing him because she figured that by now he knew she was trying to be an organ donor, naming him specifically. Would he even want her heart, with her cancer and all? She didn't want that to change things between them.

CHAPTER TWELVE

Ken stood in the operating room, several feet from where the surgeons were huddled around a small figure on the operating table. As he prepared to hand a donor heart to one of the masked surgeons, he suddenly realized it was Lydia reaching for the heart. He turned and saw that Link was wide awake; his chest cavity spread open by large retractors.

Lydia screamed, "For God's sake, Kenneth, give me the heart!"

He couldn't get his legs to carry him the short distance to Lydia's outstretched hands. He leaned forward as far as he could, when suddenly the heart leaped from his hands. It struck the floor with such force that it burst. Blood flooded the area covering Ken's shoes.

He awakened with a start, flicked on a bedside lamp. He was drenched in perspiration. He propped a pillow against the headboard and picked up a journal he had been reading. As his eyes glided over the printed page, his thoughts drifted back to a bright, sunny Saturday morning four years ago.

At the quarterly meeting of the Washington State Board

of Medical Examiners, Ken was on the agenda to discuss an unprecedented proposal. He looked around. The dark, ornately paneled room added to the formality of the proceedings. It was ten after nine and Dr. Mark Sears, chairman, looked at his watch, impatiently waiting for a quorum.

Twelve board members sat at a massive mahogany table, quietly scanning the minutes of the previous meeting.

Dr. Sears called the meeting to order and skillfully guided them through the early agenda items. Finally he turned to Ken.

"Ken, I'm sure our board members are curious about this next agenda item, simply listed as Saudi proposal."

Ken tugged at his beard as he glanced about the table, "Mr. Chairman, Dr. Gamal Faysal, a physician representing Saudi interests, wants to purchase a small hospital in Puyallup, Washington. The hospital is on the verge of bankruptcy and is interested in selling the property."

The chairman's face had an over-inflated look, his skin color ranging somewhere between pink and crimson. If the button of his shirt collar were ever to come off, Ken feared it would catapult with considerable velocity across the room.

"By Saudi interests do you mean government or private?"

"A Saudi prince, whose first-born son died of kidney failure, is putting up the capital. The hospital will be named in the boy's honor. It will be called the Hakim Medical Center."

"I see. Obviously a private Saudi citizen can buy a hospital in the State of Washington, just as they've bought hotels and other businesses," Dr. Sears said.

"They would also like to staff the hospital with Saudi physicians, whose only purpose here would be to treat Saudi children sent to the States for transplant surgery."

Dr. Sears leaned back and clasped his hands behind his head. Ken thought, my God, here comes the button!

"I don't understand," Dr. Sears asked. "Why not just admit the children to one of our hospitals?"

"There are several reasons," Ken said. "The Saudis have many well-trained transplant surgeons, who in their own country are idle because of lack of donor organs."

"Why is that?" Dr. Sears asked.

"In Muslim countries most Islamic religious scholars teach that organ transplantation is somehow unclean. Wealthy Saudi families are forced to send their children here where they have to wait weeks, even months for an organ. It would be desirable for them to be in an environment with other Saudi children and to have doctors who speak their language."

A board member said, "We have many foreign physicians trained both here and abroad, practicing here. But they are part of our system of care. Are you suggesting we allow a hospital staffed by foreign doctors to function independently?"

"Of course not," Ken said. "The professional activities of any hospital staff member in this State would come under the jurisdiction of the State Board."

"I wouldn't even consider this proposal unless it were clearly understood that a Saudi-owned hospital be subject to all the state and federal regulations that pertain to American hospitals," Dr. Sears said. "Ken, no one on the board questions your expertise in the area of organ transplantation. But I believe there are broader issues here. They'd be competing for transplant surgery at a time when many of our own children are dying because of a lack of donors. I'd anticipate an uproar from transplant surgeons at ours and other hospitals."

"Children from foreign countries already come here for surgery. They already compete for organs," Ken said. "In addition as it now stands those foreign children are using our hospital resources as they await a suitable donor organ."

Dr. Sears looked about the table. "Ken makes a good point. This would in fact lessen the strain on our own resources."

"I understand you're proposing that only Saudi children would be treated at the Hakim Medical Center," another board member said. "But if they're successful, wouldn't American families want their children treated there?"

"Couldn't we restrict their licenses to prevent that?" Ken asked.

"I believe so," Dr. Sears said. "We have the authority to regulate the practice of medicine in our state. Limiting them to the care of Saudi children is a stipulation we could impose."

"Dr. Faysal would like an opportunity to come before the Board to present his proposal," Ken said. "Mr. Chairman, I respectfully request we place him on the agenda of our next meeting."

It was several months before the board finally allowed Dr. Faysal to proceed with his plan to purchase and operate a hospital in Puyallup. Their license was restricted to admitting and treating Saudi children awaiting organ transplant surgery.

Gamal Faysal and Ken met at a restaurant in downtown

Seattle to celebrate. By this time they were on a first-name basis. Gamal ordered a bottle of champagne and offered Ken a cigar, and as usual he declined. Soon the pungent odor of fresh cigar smoke permeated the area. A waiter rushed over and placed a smoke air filter on the table. Gamal looked at the device in disbelief.

"I hope this doesn't disturb you," the waiter said, "but with cigar smoke we must consider the comfort of our other guests."

A bluish cloud of smoke swirled above their heads...slowly at first; then in a frenzied rush, the smoke plunged toward them, disappearing into the ravenous contraption that sat as a third guest at their table. Soon the air about them was clear.

"You must get one of those for your home," Ken suggested.

Gamal looked at the device with knitted brows. He reached for an ash tray and extinguished his cigar. He waved for the waiter.

"Yes, sir?"

Gamal held the device in his hand as though it were a dead rat. He handed it to the waiter. "We no longer require this...this thing."

Ken was both puzzled and amused by Gamal's actions. Did he suspect it might have been a recording device? But why? Ken's expression, however, remained impassive. He glanced about the room waiting for Gamal to speak.

Finally, Gamal raised his glass, "Kenneth, this is indeed a milestone. I will be eternally grateful to you."

"I never really believed we'd pull it off. How are the renovations coming along?"

"We have twenty-five rooms, remodeled and converted

for private patients. Laboratory and x-ray services did not require much renovation. The operating suite, however, was not adequate for major surgeries."

"How soon do you expect to start admitting patients?" Ken asked.

"Two, maybe three months at the latest. Now tell me about your research."

"Things are really moving along."

"Yes?"

"This week we've succeeded in preventing tissue-breakdown in a pig heart up to and exceeding twenty-four hours following surgical removal."

"Amazing! If you can replicate that with a human heart...how did you manage such a breakthrough?" Gamal asked.

"The University of Wisconsin has developed a perfusion solution that is now considered the gold standard. But we found although it worked better than anything we tried before, it did not prevent capillary damage. For months Jamael made slight changes in the composition of the solution...we finally hit on a disaccharide additive that protected the endothelial lining of the small blood vessels."

Gamal beamed. "I am so pleased Jamael has proven to be such a valuable and brilliant assistant. You and he have already accomplished much."

"Gamal, this is just the beginning. We're making progress with the hyperbaric process. We place the organs under the equivalent of several atmospheres of pressure. At those pressures, a high concentration of oxygen is maintained in solution. Organs placed in the solution can breathe by absorbing the dissolved oxygen."

"Intriguing," Gamal said.

"There's a delicate balance one must maintain. Oxygen is essential for all life, of course, but can be toxic under high pressure."

"I know you have many technical problems to solve," Gamal said, "but this approach is very exciting. Storage times could expand considerably, might they not?"

"Yes, this technique has the potential of extremely long storage times. Think of it," Ken said, "we might someday stockpile vital organs."

"What of your present technique of rapid freezing? When do you expect to be able to experiment with human organs?"

Ken took a sip of his champagne. "Soon. Very soon. We've gone about as far as necessary with animal organs. Just this week, I submitted a proposal to the Human Subjects Committee."

"Is that a long process?" Gamal asked.

"Research involving human subjects is meticulously scrutinized by the committee. A month or two, maybe longer."

"You must keep me informed of your progress, Kenneth. I'm most supportive of what you're doing. I'll help in any way I can."

On arriving at the hospital one week later, Ken saw fifteen to twenty people carrying placards and marching in front of the hospital's main entrance. He was stunned when he read the signs. "Doctors propose to use your children as guinea pigs." And "Dr. Bernholtz wants to experiment on your children."

CHAPTER THIRTEEN

Ken immediately called the hospital Medical Director. "Stewart, what the hell's going on? Have you seen the picket line?"

"I sure have. My phone's been ringing all morning. Newspaper reporters have been calling about your research proposal. I've no idea how they found out, but they seem know all about your recent proposal to the Human Subjects Committee."

"But no one knew of my proposal except the Human Subjects Committee members."

"Exactly. I talked with the chairman, who was furious. He figures one of his committee members must have leaked the information."

Later that day, a television talk-show producer called Ken. He told him that the show's host, Wally Benedict, wanted him as a guest. He explained they would also invite a guest from a group opposed to the use of human organs for research. They called themselves Americans Against Human Organ Experimentation.

Ken realized he was not likely to change minds of persons with extreme views. But the Wally Benedict Show had a large audience, and he saw an opportunity to inform

Forbidden Harvest

people about the need for organ donors. He agreed to participate.

Ken flew to Washington, D.C. on the day of the show. The television studio, located downtown, looked like an old movie theater. The marquee said in large black letters, The Wally Benedict Show. Tonight's guests: Dr. Kenneth Bernholtz M.D., and William Davidson. Topic: Organ Transplant Surgery.

Despite the tight knot in the pit of his stomach, he pretty much convinced himself not to worry. After all, he was talking about a subject about which he was expert. The others knew very little. He checked his watch. One hour until show time.

Inside the studio, Ken was shown to a small room, where a man who identified himself as the show's director introduced him to an intense young man in a double-breasted suit.

"Dr. Bernholtz, this is Bill Davidson."

They shook hands. Davidson looked as though he had just smelled something very unpleasant. In his lapel was a white button with the red letters, 'A.A.H.O.E.'

The director assured them that Mr. Benedict never tried to embarrass his guests like some show hosts. "Gentlemen, keep your answers to questions directly to the point. No name calling and no obscene language. And no fisticuffs!" He smiled. "Only kidding!"

"Ladies and gentleman, tonight we have with us Dr. Kenneth Bernholtz, MD, Professor of Pathology, Department Chairman at Children's Memorial Hospital and Consulting Professor at the University of Washington School of Medicine. He is a well-known researcher in the area of organ transplant physiology. Our second guest is William Davidson, head of an organization called,

Americans Against Human Organ Experimentation, known by the acronym A.A.H.O.E."

He continued, "Dr. Bernholtz, most of our viewers probably know very little about organ transplant surgery. Could you give us a very quick overview?"

"Yes, I'd be glad to. The procurement of human organs for the purpose of implanting them in another person is now practiced in all advanced countries. Most people first became aware of heart transplant surgery in 1967, when Dr. Christian Barnard, a surgeon in Capetown, South Africa, did the first heart implant in a grocer named Louis Washkansky."

"Yes, I remember that well," Wally said. "I interviewed Dr. Barnard on my show."

Ken went on comfortably, "What people don't realize is that it took years of creative and innovative research to arrive at that point. At Stanford University, Dr. Norman Shumway transplanted hearts into animals. Many surgeons visited his laboratory, among them Dr. Barnard. Other important physicians were Dr. Richard Huffnagel at Peter Bent Brigham Hospital in Boston, who performed the first kidney transplant in 1947. Dr. Denton Cooley was another pioneer, as was Dr. Thomas Starzl who performed liver transplantation and experimented with combinations of drugs to suppress the body's tendency to reject the implants."

Wally Benedict asked, "Where are transplant operations taking place?"

"In the USA many centers are doing transplant surgery. There are over one hundred hospitals with that capability."

"How are these centers regulated?" Wally Benedict prodded.

"In 1984, the procurement of donor organs became so chaotic a congressional committee came up with a uniform policy. In Virginia an organization was formed called 'United Network for Organ Sharing' (U.N.O.S.). It was the first national organ distribution system."

Ken glanced at Bill Davidson, whose fixed expression of distaste had intensified.

"How well does that work?" Wally continued.

"Despite the elaborate network, 50 percent of children awaiting surgery die before ever receiving a donor organ."

"That's a staggering statistic. Why?"

"There are simply not enough donors," Ken said.

Wally leaned forward. "Why?"

"Potential donors are often too sick to be able to give informed consent for the procedure. In fact, the ideal donor is on life support, obviously unable to discuss his or her desires with the family or their doctor."

"I assume the family decides?" Wally asked.

"Yes, in the United States the family decides...but family members are often reluctant to consent, for a variety of reasons. And they often can't agree among themselves."

"So without parental consent donor organs are often not retrieved..."

Sadly, yes. It's extremely painful for most parents. Some parents consider the drive to recruit donors to be more in the doctor's interest than the patient's."

Bill Davidson glared at Martin. "Mr. Benedict, I assume you invited me here for a reason?" he said indignantly.

"Mr. Davidson, I didn't mean to neglect you. I thought Dr. Bernholtz could give our viewing audience..."

"You notice Dr. Bernholtz said that in the United States we require parental consent. That's because in several countries they can remove organs from a deceased child without the approval of mothers and fathers. You see how it works: first they get their foot in the door; then after awhile, they do whatever they please."

"No country in the world has more stringent informed consent procedures than the United States," Ken explained. "As a society we are firmly committed to the idea that the parents acting on the child's behalf have the right to decide medical care and procedures."

"What did you mean when you said that some parents don't trust the doctors?" Wally asked.

Ken stared at the television camera. For the first time that evening he became acutely aware of the presence of millions of viewers awaiting his response. He could feel his shirt, moist with perspiration, cling to his back. He reached for his water glass and took a long drink. "Well, one reason may be the fear that the doctors may not concentrate on saving their child's life, once they agree to organ donation."

"That seems far-fetched to me," Wally said. "What...?"

Bill interrupted, "It's not far-fetched at all. Do you have any idea what an average heart transplant costs?"

"Big bucks, I assume. How much exactly does it cost?" Wally asked.

"It depends," Bill said, "on which organ you're talking about. A heart transplant, for instance, costs more than a hundred-thousand dollars. To keep all those transplant centers going, it takes enormous amounts of money for personnel, equipment, and space. When operations are not being done, there's no income to offset those staggering costs."

Ken shifted in his seat. *Does this crackpot really believe doctors and hospitals are in it for the money? Keep your cool...he's trying to turn this into a debate about costs* when that isn't the real issue.

"Dr. Bernholtz, how do you respond to that?" Wally asked.

"For one thing," Ken answered, "the doctor caring for the potential organ donor is not the same physician who would be performing the transplant operation. In fact, the organ often comes from a different hospital, not where the surgery takes place. The doctor caring for the donor has no financial interest in the process. Second, harvesting surgery doesn't start until the person is declared brain-dead."

"What about the situation where there is no family to fend off the doctors? Who looks out for the patient then?" Bill asked.

"Dr. Bernholtz, Bill asks a very good question."

"I believe Mr. Davidson is confusing the issue of end-of-life decisions regarding interventions by physicians, with the subject of procurement of organs," Ken said. "When a patient doesn't have family or a legal guardian to help the doctor choose an appropriate intervention, hospitals often rely on an ethics committee."

"How do you decide when a person is brain-dead?" Wally asked.

"When an instrument called an electroencephalogram shows absence of brain activity."

"Isn't it true there are many who advocate that people with loss of cortical activity be considered brain-dead?" Bill asked.

"Yes, there are some who advocate that," Ken said. "Persons with cortical death are in a purely vegetative state, similar to an irreversible coma, with no chance to recover higher brain functions."

Bill smiled for the first time on camera. "Now you want

to take organs from people in a coma? You see, that's exactly why our group opposes research with human tissues and organ transplantation. Soon advocates of euthanasia will justify killing infirm people to retrieve their organs. And let me address the issue of deciding when someone is dead. The transplant surgeons came up with this brain-dead business so they could start taking out organs before the person's heart stops. I've seen people they call brain-dead. Their skin is warm, and they have a pulse and heart beat. How can anyone say that person isn't alive? They're helpless... but so is a baby."

"Mr. Davidson, am I to understand that A.A.H.O.E. opposes not only experimentation with human tissues but all organ transplantation surgery?" Wally asked.

"Not all transplant surgery. For example, corneal transplant surgery is a well-established procedure and corneas are simple to harvest. That kind of surgery isn't likely to lead to abuses."

During a commercial break, Wally Benedict leaned over and said, "You guys are doin' great. The phone board is already totally lit up. We should have some interesting questions."

The first call was from a woman in West Virginia.

"Dr. Bernholtz, my son was three years old when he died of a congenital heart problem. My husband is a self-employed taxi driver. We earn too much to qualify for public assistance and not enough to pay high health insurance costs. When the question of a heart transplant came up, the hospital said that without health insurance, I had to come up with $115,000 before they would consider my son for surgery." Her voice broke, and she began to cry. Her husband took the phone. "This operation is for rich people or people on welfare. A family like us is out in the cold."

"What you say is true for many Americans, and it's a national disgrace," Ken said. *"We've failed to come to grips with the fact that millions of Americans are without any form of health insurance. In Seattle, we've established a foundation that's funded from contributions of individuals and businesses. It provides money for families like yours who otherwise couldn't afford the operation. If anyone living in a community without such a foundation would like to write to me, I would be happy to provide you with an article I've written. It tells about how we went about establishing the program."*

"Your address, Dr. Bernholtz?" Wally asked.

"Dr. Kenneth Bernholtz, Children's Memorial Hospital, Seattle, Washington."

"The next caller is from Omaha, Nebraska. Yes, you're on the line."

"Hello, Mr. Benedict, I think your show is great."

"What is your question, sir?"

"I would like to ask Mr. Davidson, what can people like us do to stop this craziness? Just drive through any city in the United States and see the poverty and drugs and all..."

"Sir, get to the question, please," Wally said.

"What I'm saying is we can't afford a hundred centers for organ transplant surgery."

"Fair question," Wally said. *"How do we prioritize the country's needs and decide where the money goes, Mr. Davidson?"*

"I agree with the gentleman, there are great inequities in our system. But that goes along with the free enterprise system that I also believe in. What I don't agree with is the use of human tissues and organs. Abuses are inevitable."

Yes, Ken thought, folks who laud free enterprise are

often adverse to medical care for those without health insurance or the means to pay out-of-pocket medical expenses.

"Dr. Bernholtz, would you like to address that issue?" Wally asked.

"Since we don't have a single-payer system, that question is hypothetical. As things stand now, if money isn't spent in one area, that doesn't make it automatically available for another health-related purpose. There's no mandated lid on total health care spending. Therefore, spending money on expensive high technology procedures doesn't preclude federal, state and local communities from supporting preventive health services."

After Ken and Bill Davidson fielded several more questions, Wally said, "I regret that our time is up. Unfortunately, there are many more callers on the line. I would like to invite our guests to stay for my radio talk show so we might continue this fascinating discussion."

As Ken anticipated, there was no overwhelming sense of having won the debate. There were no right or wrong answers for many of the questions. What he didn't expect was that hundreds of letters arrived, asking for information on how to start up a local foundation to support the cost of surgery for children whose families were uninsured or under-insured. Also, others wrote asking what they would need to do to become organ donors.

Ken called the hospital medical director, requesting additional staff.

"Of course, Ken," Stuart responded. "I'll bring in a couple of temps. Now don't let all this adulation go to your head, my friend."

Ken laughed. "Don't worry, Stuart. I'm not interested in your job."

Ken received requests to speak at universities and colleges throughout the country. He was pleased that he had gotten his message to so many people. But he was eager for things to settle down, so he could get back to his research.

Forbidden Harvest

CHAPTER FOURTEEN

Six weeks after submitting his research proposal to the Human Subjects Committee, Ken met with the Memorial Hospital President, Dr. Jerome Hardy, a medium-sized man with a thick neck and ruddy complexion. Hardy extended his large, strong hand. He led Ken to a sitting area where a couch and two chairs were arranged around a low coffee table.

"Would you care for coffee, Dr. Bernholtz?"

"Yes. Thank you."

Ken noticed a golf putter propped against Dr. Hardy's desk. Since Tom Bradshaw's death Ken had played very little golf. In fact, he stopped going to the club. Some mornings as he hurried to work, the smell of fresh-cut grass would remind him of the game. The manicured greens, the trim fairways, even the sand traps seemed appealing.

"You're a golfer, Dr. Hardy?"

Having arrived at something they had in common, they relaxed a bit, exchanging stories about sand traps and wicked slices off the tee.

Finally, clearing his throat, Dr. Hardy was ready to talk business. He congratulated Ken on his ground-breaking advances in human organ transplantation and his statewide organ-donor procurement program.

"As an affiliate of the University Hospital, we're fortunate to have researchers of your stature on the faculty. It's a travesty that fringe groups are obstructing such important proposals."

Ken smiled. Could Hardy be an ally?

Dr. Hardy sipped his coffee. "I met with the board of trustees yesterday to discuss the building campaign. But we spent most of the time talking about the problems we're having with protesters."

He pointed out that the Memorial Hospital was involved in a multi-million dollar expansion, and the negative press was beginning to curtail donations.

"Dr. Bernholtz, an attorney representing A.A.H.O.E. contacted my office and threatened a court injunction if our committee approves your proposal."

"A court case might resolve the issue," Ken said. "I can't imagine a judge not granting permission."

"Hell, our attorneys tell me they could tie us up in court for years," Dr. Hardy said. "I don't have to tell you how costly that would be. I'm not ordering you, but I believe it would be prudent for you to consider withdrawing your proposal until things quiet down."

Ken was stunned. "That's preposterous. There are researchers working with human tissues at other institutions."

"Unfortunately Children's Hospital is where A.A.H.O.E. has decided to take a stand."

"Even after things settle down, if they ever do," Ken said, "I must still get my proposal past the human subjects committee, and we know someone there must have contacted A.A.H.O.E."

"As you know, each year the Medical Director appoints

new members to the committee as some of the terms expire. Within three years there will be an entirely new membership."

"You're suggesting I sit on my hands for three years? Wait until a new committee's formed?"

"Dr. Bernholtz, if you don't back off, our attorneys tell me that an injunction against your work might compromise other research projects here and at other Seattle Hospitals."

Ken didn't want to be tied up while a court case dragged on. He wished he had a five iron in his hands at that moment. He would send the damn coffee thermos flying. Ken stood and walked to the window. The picketers were purposely demonstrating where they could be seen from Dr. Hardy's executive suite window. He spun around to face Dr. Hardy, who had remained sitting, waiting for Ken's response. Ken knew Hardy could influence the committee chairman and the committee members, some of whom, no doubt, were up for promotion. The smug bastard, he thought, I'm not going to make this easy for him.

Ken knew what would happen if he went ahead and published his latest findings about his success in use of animal organs. Researchers in foreign countries, especially those who do not have to contend with restrictions placed on American researchers, building upon his work, would move ahead with human tissue experimentation. His position in the field would be taken over by others, less skilled, less qualified.

"I will not let the committee off the hook by withdrawing my proposal," Ken said.

Dr. Hardy stiffened. "I'm sorry you feel that way, Dr. Bernholtz. We will see."

One week later, he received a letter from the Committee

chairman, notifying him that after careful deliberation, they had decided it was not in the hospital's best interest to allow Ken to proceed.

That evening Ken had dinner with the Bradshaws. Tom Senior, Lydia, their son Tom, Brenda and Link were seated around the dinner table. The conversation was, as usual, about Bradshaw Industries and who would succeed Tom Senior when he stepped down from the CEO position. He had been diagnosed with lung cancer a year earlier. He appeared to Ken to have lost at least thirty pounds, but despite his weakened condition, he continued to go to work every day. Ken marveled at his stamina. He was obviously determined to get his house in order before he died.

Lydia sat opposite her husband at their large rectangular dining room table. Ken sat next to her. They talked quietly about Tom's condition. Ken was conscious of Tom Sr. staring at them.

"Ken, do you think my wife is still a very attractive woman?" Tom Sr. asked.

Conversation around the table stopped. Ken emitted a nervous laugh. "Well...I..."

Lydia interrupted, "Tom, darling, what a strange question. What is Kenneth to say with the entire Bradshaw family around him?"

Link, nine years old at the time, said, "My friend Mike says he thinks Grandma is real pretty, even if she is old."

Lydia laughed, "Well, a woman always likes to know she has a secret admirer." She turned to Ken. "I'm afraid we're going to have to call the question."

He raised his glass. "Here's to Lydia. I think Link's friend's assessment was right on, except for the last part. I agree. Grandma Bradshaw is real pretty."

Lydia playfully punched Ken's shoulder. "As pretty as you'd expect for a woman admitting to sixty."

The conversation returned to business. Who should assume leadership of T.B.I.? Lydia believed their son, Tom, despite his youth, was well prepared.

"Mother, I'm really into research and development," Tom said. "I'm not sure I want the CEO job."

"If it means more evenings away from home, I'm against it," Brenda insisted.

"Prince Edward became King of England when he was ten years old," Link said. "I'm ten-and-a-half. Plenty old enough to run a company."

"I'll give that serious thought, young man," Tom Senior said. "But my board will accuse me of nepotism if I don't at least pretend to consider other qualified candidates."

Ken was amused and fascinated, but he could add nothing to the conversation. His mind was still on the letter he had received that afternoon from the committee chairman. As was usual at the Bradshaw table serious business comingled with small talk and that wry Bradshaw humor. Ken usually enjoyed the banter, but tonight he resented the self-assurance and optimism that surrounded him.

"Kenneth, what's wrong?" Lydia asked. "You've been very quiet tonight. You've hardly touched your food. Is your fan mail dropping off since your appearance on the Wally Benedict Show?"

It took little encouragement to get him to recount his difficulties with the Human Subjects Committee.

"It's not like I can protect my ideas with patents. We've basically developed a complex process using existing technology. When and if I publish my most recent findings, it'll be right smack dab into the public domain. Researchers *throughout the world will be free to move ahead and profit by those experiments."*

"This Dr. Faysal you've been helping," Lydia asked, "might his government offer you a chance to continue your work?"

Tom Senior added, "Ken, it seems to me you could call your own shots with the Saudis. The King himself awarded you a commendation."

"Yes, Dr. Faysal has hinted that if I were to move to Saudi Arabia, they would provide me with whatever resources I'd require."

"That would be a first. A resident Jewish hero in the Saudi Court," Tom Senior quipped.

Link was building something with his mashed potatoes. He looked up. "Uncle Ken, you moving to Saudi Arabia?"

"No, Link, this is my home, and this is where I'll stay. I'll figure out some way to continue my work right here."

Ken dozed. The journal he had been reading slipped from his hands and fell to the floor. He turned off his bedside lamp, and lay in the dark, unable to dwell on the present. How had he allowed himself to go so far in his involvement with Dr. Faysal? It wasn't one giant leap, but rather feeling like a fly caught in a spider web: at first a pesky annoyance, but progressively being trapped by hundreds of almost invisible filaments.

He recalled that dark day he had sat at his desk holding an envelope marked personal...the return address, the Human Subjects Committee. His hands had trembled as he tore it open. Had they formally rejected his proposal? He was on the brink of a major breakthrough in organ-preservation research. He had devoted his entire career to this area. How could they deny him the right to continue? Even if he had decided to hold off for three more years, there was no guarantee a newly formed committee would approve his research proposal.

He could seek a position at another academic center. But the extremists who thwarted his work at Children's Hospital could still pursue him, wherever he went.

At autopsy, he held in his hands organs that could not be used because he did not have parental approval. It would be a breach of medical ethics to use those organs....but children were dying every day for want of a kidney, liver or heart. What if he took an organ here or there? They were not doing the dead child any good, and if he were to perfect his technique, many more children would have a second chance.

He recalled a conversation he once had with one of the transplant surgeons at the Hakim Medical Center. It was on a day that an eight-year-old girl in renal failure died waiting for a suitable donor. Although the hospital was obtaining some organs from legitimate sources, many children were still succumbing to their illnesses because there were not enough donor organs to meet the demand: the wrong blood type, tissue incompatibility.

"Dr. Bernholtz," the surgeon said, his eyes brimming with tears, "I know you are doing much to help us. I pray your research will soon be successful. I beg you, don't let our children die."

Ken wanted desperately to help, but he'd be risking his entire career by violating what he had always considered a sacred trust. After a lifetime of conformity, could he follow another path? He chose not to let children die.

And now, after three years of using clandestinely obtained cadaver organs, he had made significant advances in tissue preservation. He had transported hearts, kidneys and other organs to the Hakim Medical Center, where they were successfully implanted up to twenty-four hours after harvesting!

He wanted desperately to tell Lydia and Tom just how far he had gone to continue his work, but how could he? They were frantic over Link's worsening condition; they didn't need to concern themselves with his problems. And now, ironically, his godson needed a heart transplant to save his life. They probably had a mere two to three months to search for a heart through legitimate channels...if that were not successful, Ken was determined no matter what it might cost him personally, to get a heart for Link.

Forbidden Harvest

CHAPTER FIFTEEN

Link asked his dad to bring his walkie-talkie radios to the hospital. He hoped he wouldn't ask too many questions, because he didn't want to have to lie. But he and Marty needed the radios to carry out their plan to get her into the morgue during an autopsy.

That evening when his dad visited, Link thought he looked really sad. He rarely joked around like he used to. Link missed his old dad, the one before the car crash, before Link's stupid heart attack.

"Dr. Tupelo said you're feeling a little pokey," his dad said.

"Yeah. Most foods are, like, yuck! Marty says maybe I'm pregnant."

"Sounds like she has some sense of humor."

"She's sort of crazy."

"I'm really glad you have such a good friend here," his father said.

"Me too." Maybe if he met Marty and her mother, his dad wouldn't be so sad about everything.

"Marty's mom brings in a home-made meal once a week. Maybe we could, you know, meet in my room or

Forbidden Harvest

Marty's," Link suggested.

As they spoke Tom flipped through a copy of *Fortune*. Link remembered that the magazine once ran a story about Bradshaw Industries.

Tom said, "Oh? Well...sure. I could bring in some Chinese takeout. You could invite Marty and her mother to join us. Would you like that?"

Link tried not to act too excited. Now he had to make his dad think it was his own idea.

"It's a great idea, Dad, but I'm not sure I can eat Chinese food. Everything tastes the same. Sometimes I close my eyes and try to guess what I'm eating. I can tell sherbet from mashed potatoes. That's about it."

"I'll have a special dinner made up. I'll make sure they don't add any salt. There are other spices that taste good and won't make you swell up like a blowfish."

His dad blew out his cheeks and placed his hands on the sides of his face and fluttered his fingers like fins.

"Dad, that's almost as good as the whale impersonation you used to do in the swimming pool. And remember how mom used to jump off the diving board with her arms and legs bent out to the side, and her cheeks all puffed out?"

His dad smiled and nodded. They were both quiet for a time. Link thought of the everyday things he took for granted. He never figured that his mother wouldn't always be there. He thought of that awful night his mother was killed.

Link awakened suddenly. In the dark he sensed his mother's presence. "Is that you, mom?"

There was no response. He lay back and pulled the covers under his chin. When he was little, his mother had taught him a bedtime prayer. He hadn't said it for a long time, and he wasn't sure he could remember the words. As he said the prayer aloud, it seemed he could hear his mother's voice praying with him.

"Dear Angel, given to me and me alone.

Gather your wings about me as I sleep.

And help me be the best that I can be,

But love me as I am, oh gentle spirit"

Link drifted off to sleep. The sound of voices woke him. He looked at the digital clock on his nightstand; it was three in the morning. He got up and walked to the head of the stairs.

His Uncle Ken was speaking. "I can take the sitter home," he said. "Cindy, would you please wait in my car? I'll be there in a few minutes."

Link heard the front door open and close.

"Lydia, would you like me to stay?"

"No, I want to tell him myself. But come back after you drop Cindy off. I want you in the house tonight."

Link came halfway down the stairs. He was about to say something but stopped.

His grandmother and Uncle Ken hugged. She started to cry. Even his Uncle Ken was crying. They stood, holding each other, and sobbed. Link's heart beat against his chest so hard he could hear it in his ears. He wanted to ask what was wrong, but his throat closed up. He could barely breathe. In the darkened hall, neither of them noticed.

"I'll be back soon," Uncle Ken said.

After he left, she turned toward the stairs. She jumped when she saw Link.

"What's the matter, Grandma? Where're Mom and

Dad?"

Link had not stopped to put on his glasses. Everything was out of focus. He rubbed his eyes.

She walked to Link and lifted him into her arms. He was too heavy for her to carry. They sat on the steps. She held both of Link's hands.

"Your mother and father were in an auto wreck. They were taken to the hospital."

Link studied his grandmother's face in the darkened hall. He didn't recognize his own voice.

"Are they gonna be okay?"

"Your father had to have an operation, but the doctors said he would be all right."

Link stared at her face. His grandmother's eyes were so sad...he couldn't keep looking at her. "What about Mom? Did she get hurt?"

"Your mother was driving. A truck hit their car on her side."

Link stood, jerking away from her. "It's not true, Grandma, it's not true. Don't say it!"

She reached for him, but he turned and ran to his room. He threw himself on the bed, sobbing into his pillow. Soon, she came and sat on the bed next to him.

"She's dead, isn't she?" He still would not look at her.

"Yes, Link, your mother is gone." She placed her hand on his shoulder. "The doctor said she was killed instantly. She didn't suffer."

Link cried harder than ever before. She pressed him against her chest and rocked him back and forth. Once he stopped crying, he couldn't seem to get his breath. It felt as though his throat was swollen. He kept breathing deeper and deeper to get enough air. His head started to spin. His mouth felt numb.

"Just breathe slowly. Don't force it," she murmured softly.

He did what his grandmother said, and pretty soon he could breathe okay. He stayed there a long time in her arms. After awhile, she laid him back in bed and straightened the covers and pulled up a chair. Neither Link nor his grandmother was able to sleep. He sat up with his back pressed against the headboard and his head slumped forward, staring at the patch-work quilt his grandmother had given him.

"How did you find out?"

"The doctor in the emergency room called, and the sitter gave him my number. Your father was already in the operating room when I got there. I didn't know what to do...I called Uncle Ken. After the surgery, we saw your father for just a few minutes in recovery."

"Did you know how the accident happened?" His voice was hoarse, his nose runny from crying.

"A rescue worker said that a tractor trailer had driven across the road. They think maybe the driver fell asleep."

She reached for a box of tissues on the night table. She handed him a few and placed the box on her lap.

"What happened to the truck driver?"

"I don't know, Link, I never asked."

"Grandma, tell me as much as you do know." He blew his nose into a wad of tissues.

"They said that after the truck hit your parents' car, the car crashed through a guard rail and rolled down a hill. The doctor said it was a miracle your father wasn't killed."

Link couldn't stand to think of their car rolling over and over down a hill with both his mother and father inside.

"Did they let you see Mom?"

"Yes," she whispered.

She held out her arms. He came to her, sitting on her lap, leaning against her. He didn't want to ask any more questions. He didn't want to hear how much his mother was hurt. He cried some more and then fell asleep in her embrace.

When Link awakened the next morning, the smell of coffee and bacon made him feel sick. After getting dressed, he went downstairs. People were standing around in small groups, talking quietly. Some were sitting at the dining room table. It seemed as though everyone stopped talking and stared at him when he came into the room. He walked to his grandmother, who was pouring coffee for a lady he recognized. She was Miss Simmons, his dad's private secretary.

"Would you like some breakfast?" Lydia asked.

"I'm not hungry."

"Well, maybe a glass of orange juice?"

"Okay."

He looked around the room. Who are all these people, he thought? He saw his Uncle Ken across the room. He was talking to Aunt Millie and her daughter, Grace. He recognized a few other people, friends of his father and mother, distant cousins.

"I want to go to the hospital to see Dad," Link said to his grandmother.

His Uncle Ken must have heard him. He walked to the table. "I'll take you," *he said.* "We can't stay long because *your dad probably is still in the recovery room."*

On the way to the hospital, Link sat in the front seat of his Uncle Ken's car. Link knew Ken wasn't his real uncle, but that's what the family called him.

His dad's father, Grandpa Bradshaw, and his Uncle Ken sometimes when they played golf took Link along with them. If nobody was behind them, they'd let Link take a few putts.

Link stared out the car window, not seeing anything in particular. He wished he had been in the car with his mom and dad. He would have done something. He could have saved her. God, make it not be true, he thought. Let me wake up and hear my mother calling me.

"What kind of operation did my dad have?"

"Head surgery. There was internal bleeding. They had to operate to remove a blood clot."

Link looked at Uncle Ken. The sun was shining in the car window on Uncle Ken's side. His face, Link thought, with the beard and all, looked like one of those saint pictures they had at school. Light rays were shining off his nose and mouth.

"How come he hit his head? Wasn't he wearing his seat belt?" Link asked.

"They said he was."

"So it didn't work?"

"I have an idea what probably happened," Uncle Ken said. "They told me the car hit a guardrail just before the collision. That would have caused your father to fall against the passenger door. Because his seat was tilted back, he probably came out from under the chest restraint. When the truck hit, he was thrown forward onto the dashboard."

Link looked at his own chest restraint. If he were thrown to his right his head would keep him from slipping from under it. He tilted back his seat. The chest restraint didn't go back with the seat. He could see that Uncle Ken was right.

"Uncle Ken, that's a design flaw."

Kenneth looked at Link and smiled. "I heard your grandfather say that many times."

"Yeah. He always said how he could make things better."

Neither of them spoke for a long time. Finally Link asked, "Did Dad hurt anything else?"

Kenneth glanced over at Link, who was cleaning his glasses. He didn't answer right away.

"It's okay to tell me. I'm not a baby."

"That's right, Link. I remember when you were a baby. That seems like a long time ago. You just started seventh grade, didn't you?" Link didn't answer. Kenneth continued, "I felt very grown up when I was in the seventh grade."

"Did my dad hurt anything else?" Link persisted.

"He injured his right leg. Some tendons and blood vessels were damaged. The bone in his thigh was broken in three places. They said he'll eventually need an operation on his leg."

Link wondered if his dad would have to be in a wheelchair or need crutches. Could he even go to the office? "Will he walk okay?"

"Your dad's only thirty-six. He's young and strong. I'm sure he'll heal like new."

At the hospital, a woman at the patient information desk told them Tom was still in recovery. When they arrived *there, a nurse said they could see him for just a few minutes. Link had once seen an old movie called* The Invisible Man. *His father's head looked like that. There were holes for his eyes, nose and mouth, but everything else was covered with bandages. A tube sticking out of his mouth was attached to some kind of machine. His eyes were closed. There was a metal frame over the bed. Bars and wires held up his right leg. Link noticed metal rods sticking out from both sides of his father's right knee. The rods were connected by wires to a pulley. A stack of weights hung from the pulley. Link's stomach started to hurt; he was glad he hadn't eaten breakfast. He squeezed his father's hand and leaned over the bed.*

"Dad, it's me."

His dad didn't open his eyes but he struggled to free his hands.

"Dr. Bernholtz," the nurse said, "he's been fighting the endotracheal tube. I was just getting ready to remove it. You and the boy may want to step out for a minute."

"Can't we stay?" Link asked.

"Maybe...a few minutes."

She removed the tape holding the breathing tube in place, and slipped the tube out quickly. His father began to cough. The nurse held a plastic basin against his face, but he didn't vomit. He tried to speak. When they couldn't understand what he was saying, his dad made a motion as if he were writing.

"Could you get him a pen and paper?" Uncle Ken said.

The nurse left and soon returned. She placed a pen in Tom's hand. She rolled the food tray over to the bed and placed a sheet of paper on the tray in front of him. She guided his hand to the paper.

He wrote in a large, shaky way. It was barely legible.

He'd written, "I love you."

"I love you too, Dad," Link said as he leaned close to his dad's ear.

He pressed his cheek against his father's chest. He could hear his dad's heart beating fast and strong. He thought of his mother's heart, cold and quiet...he couldn't stop himself from crying.

"He's still groggy from the anesthesia," the nurse said. As she spoke, she placed a plastic tube over Tom's head and inserted two little prongs into his nose. She adjusted a dial on the wall.

"You'll have to go now. You can visit later today when we move him to intensive care."

"Link," Uncle Ken said as they left the recovery room, "I need to stop by the funeral home to make arrangements. Should I drive you home?"

Link had been to the funeral home when his grandfather died. The smell there had made him feel like throwing up. But he couldn't stand being in the house with all those people staring at him.

"I want to go with you."

On the drive there, Link recalled how his mother was always so careful when she picked out stuff for the house. Her favorite color was pink. She liked things simple. His dad always said, "You decide, sweetheart. It all looks good to me."

"Uncle Ken, can I choose my mother's casket?"

He looked at Link and smiled. He had a kind face but now he looked mostly sad. Link pressed closer to him.

"Of course you can," Uncle Ken said. "She would want you to."

Forbidden Harvest

At the funeral home, Link and Uncle Ken sat in a small office. There were no windows, and the desk pretty much filled the room. A tall thin man in a dark suit sat opposite them. Uncle Ken talked with the man about how many cars they wanted, which florist to use, and things like that. Link looked around the room. The white walls were bare except for a gigantic picture of a field of flowers made from tiny pieces of different-colored wood.

Link was ten years old when Grandfather Bradshaw died. The smell at the funeral home was the same as he remembered. Link usually liked the smell of flowers, but here it was too strong, all mushed together. His mother loved flowers. Sometimes when his father had to work late, he'd send flowers with a note saying he'd be home as soon as he could. His mother liked roses and hyacinths the best.

"Yes, let's go select a casket," the funeral director said. "The boy can wait here if he would like?"

"I'm coming too," Link said. He grabbed his Uncle Ken's hand.

They went to a large room filled with caskets, each illuminated by a small overhead spotlight. There were no other lights in the room. Link pulled his arms about his chest. The muscles in his jaw began to shake like when he stayed outside too long in the snow. It was hard to think of his mother in one of those boxes.

He stood next to a plain, reddish-brown casket. He ran his fingers along the pink satin lining. Tears filled his eyes. Damnit, God, he thought. Why did you make this happen! She didn't do anything wrong. She didn't deserve to be killed!

The mortician cleared his throat as he tapped the casket with a diamond ring he wore on his little finger. It made a loud tinny noise.

"This is our least expensive casket," he said. "We use

them to transport the bodies of indigent migrant workers."

The man walked across the room. Around him were caskets made of brass, cherry, and mahogany. "For Mrs. Bradshaw," the funeral director said, "I believe one of these would be more appropriate."

Link remained standing by the casket with the pink lining. The outside is plain, Link thought, but she'll be inside, not outside. He touched the lining. Soft and light.

"I want her to have this one," Link said.

The undertaker shook his head. "Sir, this is hardly a decision a child should be making."

Ken's walked to where Link was standing.

"I agree with you, Link. I'm sure it is the one your mother would have chosen."

On the way back to the house Link asked Uncle Ken, "Dad won't get to come to the church or the cemetery, will he?"

"No. I'm sure he'll be in intensive care for several days, and it'll be a few weeks before he's discharged."

"I asked Mom when Grandpa died why they do all that stuff with the funeral home and the cemetery and all. She said it was a way for everybody to say goodbye to somebody they loved."

Link opened the glove compartment. A light went on. He thought of his dad taking out all that food from the refrigerator and his mom just shaking her head. It was their last night. He wished he had locked the door and not let them go. He closed the glove compartment.

"Yes, people can help each other by just being together and remembering good things about the person," Uncle Ken said.

"But Dad is all alone in the hospital. He won't get to say goodbye."

His Uncle Ken pulled on his beard while he was thinking of what to answer. Link recalled that when someone asked Uncle Ken a question, his reply would sometimes take a long time.

"Link, we can have Father Justine come to the hospital. Maybe we can have a private service in your father's room...in a few days when he's feeling better."

"It's not the same." Link turned his head toward the window. He didn't cry, but his nose felt all twisted up and runny inside. "It's not the same, Uncle Ken."

"Link, we could ask your dad if he would like us to have the church service videotaped."

It seemed far out to tape a funeral. Yet, it was a pretty good idea, Link thought. He recalled seeing reruns of President Kennedy's funeral on television.

"Yeah, he may like that," Link said.

"Let's check with your grandmother. If she likes the idea, we'll do it."

Link told her about Uncle Ken's suggestion that they tape the church service and the ceremony at the cemetery.

"I think that's a good idea," Lydia said, to Link's relief. "If your dad agrees, I'll make the arrangements."

Link smiled at his grandmother. She didn't look that old to him. Sometimes people would joke about her and his mother looking like sisters. His grandmother was a lot like his dad, he thought. She could always make up her mind really quick and be so sure...his mother liked to think things over.

From now on he would have to make decisions without

her. That won't be easy, he thought. With his mother gone and his dad out of commission, for who knows how long, Link would be in charge of the house. He had never been in that position. He would have to mature pretty fast if he was going to pull that off.

"Grandma, Mrs. McAllister goes home after she makes dinner. Will I be alone all night?" Link asked.

She hugged him. "I was planning on moving in with you until your dad is back on his feet. Would that be okay with you, darling?"

"Yeah, Grandma. I'd like that a whole lot."

Tom waved his hand in front of Link's face. "What are you thinking?"

"That the things we remember are just the same if a person is here or not."

"That's true, isn't it?" his dad agreed. "And you know, some of your memories of your mother are yours alone. As close as I was to her, you have private memories that I don't have."

"I know it sounds crazy, but sometimes I used to be jealous of you and Mom."

His dad looked surprised.

"Why was that?"

"Sometimes when I would be up in my room late, I could hear Mom laughing and you saying stuff that I couldn't hear. I wanted to come in your room, like when I was little. But, you know now that I'm older..."

"Don't ever feel you can't come to me anytime. Not ever. I don't care how big you get." Tom grabbed Link and squeezed him extra hard.

Forbidden Harvest

I'm sorry I told him, Link thought. Now he's was going to think about me feeling left out.

Tom picked up a hairbrush that was lying on the bedside table and combed a part right down the middle of Link's head, then brushed the hair to the sides over his ears.

Link laughed. "I look like that Little Rascals kid."

"Ask Marty to find out if she and her mom would like to have dinner with us." He removed an appointment book from his pocket. "Any night next week...as long as it's Thursday!"

Marty stepped from the shower and stood in front of the mirror as she dried off. It seemed like someone else staring back at her. Her arm muscles had melted away following her last chemo, and it made her elbows look like tennis balls. She propped her good leg on the sink as she rubbed it with a towel. It too was half the size it used to be. Damn it, I look like a sandpiper, she thought, but not as cute. She had to hurry not to be late for her physical therapy.

She said half aloud, "The treatments are a real pain in the butt, but heck, it's better than looking like a stick person."

After her therapy session, she hurried to Link's room. As she entered, he was looking at the CompuServe Bulletin Board. His face was all screwed up into one big question mark. He read from the monitor, "Operation Skyhawk soon to be launched. Further instructions to follow." Operation Skyhawk?

She fluttered her arms out like wings. She opened her

eyes wide. "The hawk hovers in the sky, its incredible eyes taking in every detail on the ground. Sound familiar?"

"The Skyhawk is a plane, not a bird. It's a Cessna 172. My grandfather owned one. Took me for a ride once."

"Okay, whatever. But it's named after a hawk, right?"

"That's true. Oh, by the way, I got the walkie-talkies."

He showed her the radios and explained how to operate them. They were smaller than any she had ever seen. You could easily slip one into your pocket. There was a strap so you could wear it on your wrist.

"I've never seen ones like these."

"My dad bought them when we took a trip to Disney World. He had the most fun with them. He went on the mountain tunnel ride five times while my mom and I did other stuff. I'd be waiting in some boring long line, and she would be telling me what she was doing. My mom could've been a stand-up comic. She was always cracking me up."

A nurse came into the room.

"Link, your telemetry signal is going crazy. I need to check the wires."

"Hmm...The wires are okay." She noticed the radios. "That's probably it. Your radios may be on a frequency close to the telemetry signal. Turn them off, and let's see what happens."

When they did, the monitor went back to normal. The nurse then told Link they couldn't use the radios.

"Wait a minute," Link said, "There are two frequency settings. Let's try the other one." He switched to the second frequency, and turned the radios back on. The monitor worked perfectly.

"Little Doc, you're a genius," Marty said.

Link gave her a smug grin. "So what else is new?"

That afternoon, Marty roamed from one end of the hospital to the other. The radios worked well in most places. In x-ray and in the elevators there was too much static. She stood by the door to the morgue. She whispered into the radio.

"Morgue calling. Can you hear me?"

"I can hear you great."

Two days later, Marty told Link she was ready for a dress rehearsal of operation Skyhawk. She wore high-top black sneakers and a navy blue warm-up suit with two zippered pockets. She pulled the radio from one pocket. From the other she removed a flashlight with a magnet on its side.

"Holy cow, I'm getting nervous just talking about it," Link said. "You're going to need a knife to cut a corner off of one of those tiles. You didn't think of that, did you?"

She pulled a small knife from her pocket. "Taa...daa."

"Where'd you get all this stuff?"

"I called my mother. Told her what I needed. Said I had to have it in 24 hours or less."

"Didn't she ask what for?"

"Sure. I told her you and I were putting on a show, and dress rehearsal was today. When she brought the stuff she wanted to know if you asked your doctor's permission."

"What did you tell her?"

"I told her you have an easy part. You just sit there in one place and talk to me. I have to do all the hard stuff. She said she would like to see the show when we're ready."

Marty moved toward the door. "Stick close to your radio. I'm going to the basement to find a place with a ceiling like the one in the morgue."

A few doors from the morgue she noticed a small office whose door had been left open. The lights in the room were turned off. If a person were away they would have locked the door. Maybe the cleaning lady left it open, Marty thought. She flicked on the lights. In the ten-foot square room was a desk, a computer stand, two chairs and a file cabinet. She checked the telephone extension number. She went down the hall to find an in-house phone. She called the hospital operator and told her she was calling extension 156 and not getting an answer. The operator asked her to hold on and soon was back on the line.

"That's Mrs. Fisher's office. She's on vacation and won't be back until next week. Can I give you her supervisor's number?"

"Never mind," Marty said. "I'll call when she's back."

She called Link on her hand radio. "Link, I scouted out an office that'll be empty until next week. I'm going in. Call you later."

She entered the office and locked the door behind her. She cleared the top of the file cabinet and looked around for something sturdy to put on top.

She radioed to Link. "You there, L.D?"

"Wow, I almost fell asleep! What's going on?"

"The filing cabinet's not high enough for me to be able to lift myself into the ceiling space."

"How about putting a waste basket on top?"

She pulled the chair from the desk and looked. There was one of those old-fashioned, metal baskets. She turned it over and stood on it.

"Hey, good idea."

"Be real careful not to tip it over."

She put the basket upside down on top of the cabinet. After several failed tries to lift herself up, Marty stood back to catch her breath and figure out what to do next. She pulled out a file drawer and used it for a step. It still wasn't easy, but she was finally able to hoist herself up. She stood, slid a ceiling tile aside, and poked her head into the space.

"I'm halfway there!"

"You're sure breathing hard."

"Yeah, almost broke my neck. Feels like I climbed Everest."

She turned on her flashlight. She was almost afraid to look. There were pipes, aluminum ducts and wires running all over the place.

"I hope I don't see a rat or something else icky. I'll call back when I get there. Hey! You listening?"

"If I don't say anything, it's because someone comes in my room. Be careful not to put too much weight on those tiles."

After resting a couple of minutes, she adjusted the waste-basket so it was directly under the opening in the ceiling. She carefully placed her good leg on the basket, grabbed the ceiling frame, and pulled herself into the space at hip level. She leaned forward, grasped the wires that held the metal frame, and dragged herself all the way in. Her heart froze as she felt a ceiling tile sag under her weight.

"*Shit!* I'm not sure it's going to hold me up."

"You don't weigh all that much," Link said. "Spread out

your arms and legs."

As she moved forward, she accidentally kicked out a tile. It crashed to the floor.

"What the heck was that?" Link asked. "You okay?"

She was too occupied to respond. She crawled toward the recessed light fixture in the center of the ceiling.

"*Merde*...it's French for shit...this commando crap is harder than I thought. I knocked down one of the tiles. But I'm okay. I'm in the center of the ceiling. I'm going to pry up a tile and cut out a small piece from the corner." She sneezed. She looked around. She whispered, "What if I see a rat?"

"Hit him on the head with your flashlight."

"Sure, Rambo. Wish you were here."

She sneezed again. "This place is really dusty. I'll have to wear a surgical mask next time. And the damn metal framing is sharp. I cut both of my hands already."

Link said something but she could barely hear him.

"Louder, LD."

"There are doctors outside my door," he whispered. "Are you hurt bad?"

"I'm not going to bleed to death or anything."

She pried up the corner of a tile and cut off a small piece. She pressed her eye to the opening.

"Wow."

"Wow what?" Link asked.

"I can see just about the whole room. If I don't kill myself getting down, we're in business."

As she neared the opening she lifted her body, putting too much weight on one knee. The tile buckled and then split, causing her artificial limb to drop partway through.

"Link, my leg is poked through a tile. It hurts when I try to pull it up!"

"Maybe I should come help you."

"If you ask someone to wheel you down here, my butt will be in deep doodoo."

"Your butt and the rest of you are there already."

"Very funny. Any other bright ideas?"

"About your butt?"

"L.D!"

"Okay," Link said. "Maybe you should bust the tile all the way by pressing down on it. Let the pieces fall. If you hang by your arms, your feet should be no more than a few inches from the floor."

"Makes sense. I'll try it." She punched the tile until it split completely and dropped away from her leg. She looked down. The file cabinet and the desk were not directly below her. "I'm gonna have to drop."

She hung from the ceiling frame, hesitating, then let go and tumbled onto the floor. Pieces of ceiling tiles lay scattered about the room.

"You okay?"

"I'm cool, except for a little hemorrhaging. There's a plastic bag in the wastebasket. I'm going to clean up all the small pieces and dump them someplace. I'll hide the big pieces behind the file cabinet."

"Roger that! You heading back?"

"I'll be up in a few minutes. We'll talk about it."

She hurried to Link's room. He was sitting in a chair beside his bed, grinning from ear to ear. She lay on his bed, spreading her arms and legs like a sky diver.

"Holy broccoli, am I out of shape or what?"

"I wish I would have gone with you. You're lucky you didn't get hurt. I was glad the nurse didn't come in. She would've thought I was hooked up to a 900 number."

Marty rolled onto her side, her head propped up on one arm. "What do you know about 900 numbers, LD?"

"Late night TV expose."

"Yeah, right." She sat on the edge of the bed. "We did it, coach, a real piece of teamwork." They slapped both hands together. "Couldn't have done it without you."

She pulled a piece of ceiling tile from her pocket. "Ask your dad to get us a couple of pieces of tile. Tell him we need them for props. Shit, I don't know the right size."

"I'm guessing they're probably two feet square."

"Yeah, that seems about right. Tell him we need two tiles. I want to replace those sections before anyone notices."

"Yeah. I guess that'll work," Link said.

"I'm gonna have to bulk up before I try again."

"You already go to PT every morning."

"I'll ask the therapist to add more upper arm and shoulder stuff. Maybe I can go back to PT in the afternoon."

As she headed for the door of his room Link said, "Holy broccoli?"

She said over her shoulder, "I'm a vegetarian, remember?"

At her next physical therapy session, Marty told her therapist she wanted a second session each day, to help build up her arms and shoulders.

"You training for some kind of commando operation?"

Marty grinned, "You'd be surprised."

Forbidden Harvest

CHAPTER SIXTEEN

The following week Marty, Link, Gladys and Tom had dinner in Link's room. Tom arrived with a large box full of small containers of Chinese takeout. It was seven-thirty, well past the time the hospital served the evening meal. They piled their plates high.

"You two sure don't have sick appetites," Tom said. "Leave a little bit for Mrs. Lopinski and me."

Marty thought her mom looked real pretty. Her eyes seemed sparkly even without any kind of make-up. And her skin had no wrinkles, the only blemish a tiny mole by the corner of her mouth. She was wearing her favorite gold-hoop earrings and a dress Marty had not seen before.

Marty wished she looked more like her mother. Her mother's hair was dark brown, almost black, and it contrasted dramatically with her fair skin. Her eyes were light brown with small golden specks. She had a smaller, more delicate nose than Marty. Will I look like her if I get to grow up? Marty wondered.

Tom learned during the course of the evening that Gladys had attended Barnard College for one year. He knew that it was no easy task getting admitted to one of the *Seven Sisters*. He wanted to learn why she dropped out after her freshman year, but was reluctant to ask. He didn't have to.

Forbidden Harvest

"My liberal arts studies seemed irrelevant," Gladys said, "when television brought the Vietnam War right into the dorm. I wanted to do something...anything to help end the needless bloodshed."

"So you never went back to school?"

"I fell in love very young. Had a child, but enough of my life's story."

"You've raised a remarkable daughter."

"Write that down, Mom...I like remarkable."

"Conspicuously unusual is one way remarkable is defined," Link interjected.

Tom shook his head. "Don't mind him. He reads the dictionary."

"Hey, LD, that wasn't nice!" Marty pretended to be offended.

"Most of the time you're okay," Link said.

Marty noticed Link was pushing his food around his plate, eating very little. He seemed to be breathing hard.

"What's going on, L.D?" she asked.

"I guess I'm not used to eating so late."

"Is this stuff too spicy?" his dad asked.

Link knew his dad had tried really hard to make the dinner special. "It great, Dad, I'm a little sick to my stomach. That's all."

Marty wasn't worried. She felt like that lots of times. She watched Tom and her mother. She realized how long it had been since she had seen her with a man. She and Link had joked about their parents getting to like each other. Marty kicked Link under the table and raised her eyebrows up and down a few times.

Forbidden Harvest

Marty liked seeing her mom and Link's dad talking and laughing. Maybe the dinners could become a regular event.

Link's life at the hospital was frenetic. At times he got so tired he'd doze off while someone was visiting. Early each morning he went to physical therapy, and then hung out with Marty until almost noon. After that he was pretty much wiped out for the rest of the day. His afternoon was filled with well-meaning visitors...the hospital chaplain, nurses checking his vital signs, the lady with the book cart, and other patients just wanting to hangout.

Dr. Boat dropped by two or three times a week to see how he was doing. Link knew "Big Bird" wasn't in charge of his case. Nevertheless he was keeping an eye on Link's care. His grandmother visited him almost every afternoon. She brought him up-to-date on all that was happening in school. He knew more now than if he was still in class. But he missed his friend Mike. Why hadn't he come to see him? His mother worked...he probably had no way to get to the hospital. Maybe Link's grandmother could pick Mike up after school.

Link liked Mount Saint John, even though the nuns were strict and handed out a lot of homework. One of the Sisters coached basketball and could shoot baskets better than any of the kids on the team. The nuns wore regular clothes except for big wooden crosses around their necks.

But the students wore uniforms. The boys wore heavy green pants and white shirts with green ties. When the priest came to visit their class the boys wore green suit jackets. The girls wore long green skirts and white blouses. On the playground some of the girls folded over the top of their skirts so the hem came above their knees. The girls couldn't wear make up until the ninth grade and even then, only a little.

His grandmother told Link that Pat Balsamo was the

first boy in his class to start shaving. Link couldn't believe Pat was sprouting facial hair.

Father Justine visited Link two or three times a week. He was more than six feet tall and kind of skinny. At first Link tensed up; gradually he realized Father was just a regular guy. He told Link that he played basketball in college. One day Father brought video clips of basketball dunks and other awesome shots. Link had a VCR in his room, and they watched it together. The video was advertised on television as a gift if you subscribed to *Sports Illustrated*. He asked Father if he had subscribed. When he said "yes," Link asked him for some old copies, hoping he would bring in the bathing suit issue. Father did bring in a batch, the next visit, but the bathing suit issue wasn't there. Must've kept it for himself, Link thought.

On Sundays Father Justine brought Link Holy Communion and read short passages from the Bible. On his last visit he read from Mark 10:13-16: People were bringing little children to Jesus to have him touch them, but the disciples rebuked them. When Jesus saw this, he was indignant. He said to them, "Let the little children come to me, and do not hinder them, for the kingdom of God belongs to such as these. I tell you the truth...anyone who will not receive the kingdom of God like a little child will never enter it." And he took the children in his arms, put his hands on them and blessed them.

Link had heard that passage before, and it had unsettled him. "I drove my mother crazy always asking 'why, why, why?' It bothers me when Jesus talks about children as though they're mindless. Or maybe the story was about toddlers."

"That parable is probably a metaphor about innocence. But it isn't easy to decide what's metaphor and what's literal," Father Justine agreed. He was silent for a few moments. "I too have problems understanding certain passages. In fact, scholars who spend their entire lives studying the Bible often disagree."

Link was too tired to grapple with the finer points of Bible study. "Yeah. There's lots of ways of looking at things." There were so many things Link found hard to believe. Would Jesus welcome him? Would he be worthy of the Kingdom of God?

"Not yet," Link whispered, as he drifted off to sleep.

After two weeks of intense training, Marty felt she was ready for another rehearsal. She discovered that the basement office she had used before was empty on weekends. In the meantime she had learned the door-lock combination. She met with Link to map their strategy. They drew up a check list and bought fresh batteries for the radios and flashlight. Link reminded her to get leather gloves so she wouldn't cut her hands.

Marty's cough was getting worse. She decided to bring along some strong cough drops. A coughing spell would give her away.

She was concerned that someone might come to Link's room during operation Skyhawk. They decided the best thing to do in that case would be for Link to excuse himself and go to the bathroom. He would then call out and tell the person that he was feeling sick and please come back later.

"The middle of the morning will be the best time for you to do it," Link said. "By then, the doctors'll finish rounds, and the nurse will've already given me my meds. I'll ask Doc Frank if I can have my PT in the afternoon."

"Bettcha I'm in and out of there in less than twenty minutes." Marty ran her fingers through her sparse hair.

"What if the office is locked?"

"No problem, LD, I know the combination of just about every office around there." Marty told him about the cleaning woman who worked in the basement.

"I told her I was bored, and asked if I could just walk around with her and talk. Pretty soon I started bringing in fresh towels and stuff."

"What's her name?"

"She said just call her Annie."

"Won't she get in trouble telling you the combinations?"

Marty gave Link a gentle bop on the head with her fist.

"Geez, I didn't come right out and ask! I watched when she punched it in. I wrote the numbers on the back of my hand soon as I had a chance."

"Didn't she notice?"

"She was too busy talking. She has a bunch of grandkids and shows me pictures. I can't believe she's a grandmother. She looks the same age as my mom."

The second time around, there was one problem. When Marty crawled back to the point where she had entered the ceiling space, she wasn't sure which ceiling tile to remove to get back down. She decided that next time she'd bring a magic marker and put a cross on the top-side of the tile. Except for some minor glitches, she was pleased with her trial run. There were no damaged tiles and no cut fingers. Training pays off! She was ready for the big-time!

"This is really, really cool," Link said afterwards. "And you're not even winded. You know, I still can't figure out why you would want to see an autopsy."

"I'm beginning to wonder myself. I guess just for the fun

of it. This way I don't have to think of chemo and the bad stuff. Who knows, maybe it'll freak me out? I can just see the headlines: 'Hysterical one-legged teenager, trapped in morgue ceiling, fights off would-be rescuers with flashlight.'"

Marty was concerned how soon to sneak into the morgue the next time they announce code 400. She decided to pump her doctor for answers.

The following morning Frank was all smiles.

"The x-ray shows definite shrinkage of the tumor in your chest since your last chemo. The radiologist estimated a twenty percent improvement. And the part of your lung being blocked by enlarged lymph nodes looks much better."

"If it's better, how come I'm coughing worse?" Was he really telling her the truth? She wanted to believe him, but maybe he just didn't want her to worry. She decided she'd look up the report herself.

"The tumor was probably blocking one of your smaller bronchial tubes," he said. "Now that it's open you're releasing a lot of built-up secretions. Respiratory therapy should help."

"You mean the Irish lady who bangs on my chest and makes me blow in that plastic gizmo?"

"Right." Standing behind her, he listened to her breathing. "It sounds a lot better, Marty."

"Doc Frank, can I ask you something about transplant surgery?"

He re-tied her hospital gown. He walked around and sat in the chair alongside her bed. "You writing a book?" he asked.

She smiled. "Just curious."

"Okay, shoot." He removed a packet of index cards from his breast pocket and began looking through them.

"Well, it's kind of an emergency when a donor dies so the organ they're going to donate doesn't rot or something, right? So how do they get the team together quick enough?"

He looked up. "The hospital operator announces 'code 400', which is a signal for everyone on the team to hurry to the operating room."

"Why doesn't she just beep them?"

"Too many people on the team. It would take too long." The doctor put aside his index cards and looked at her curiously.

"Link was telling me that his Uncle Ken is doing some kind of research on organs from donors who die. He does an autopsy right away so he can take biopsies or something?"

"He checks to see if the tissues are still healthy. He can only do it when the family has agreed," Frank explained.

Marty frowned. "I don't understand."

"Well, if somebody agrees to give all their organs, then there are no organs left for Dr. Bernholtz to test. Or if the heart or lungs have been donated, they can't keep up life support."

"I think I get it....But how does he know when they're finished in the operating room? Doesn't the transplant operation take a long time?"

Frank stood, folded his arms and leaned against the side of her bed. "What's this all about, Marty?"

"I just feel like I've got to know, that's all. Because....it could happen to me."

Forbidden Harvest

She felt guilty lying to him. But she knew he couldn't give her permission to watch an autopsy. Something she promised herself and Link she'd accomplish.

"Okay," Frank said. "To answer your question, the operating room nurse lets the paging operator know when the operation is almost complete. That's when the paging operator calls Dr. Bernholtz."

"So *code 400* means the transplant operation is gonna start pretty soon?"

"Right."

"Just one more thing," Marty said. "If they're going to keep the dead person breathing on a respirator, how can they do the autopsy?"

He grinned and shook his head. "You're getting to sound like Little Doc. They open the chest last so they can use the respirator as long as possible. They also have a special type of knife that cauterizes the tissues as they cut. Do you know what *cauterize* means?"

"This is beginning to sound like 'Mr. Rogers' Neighborhood,' Marty said. "Can you spell *cauterize*? C, A, U, T, E, R, I, Z, E."

"Link says you're a little crazy. I'm not going to disagree."

"I know what *cauterize* smells like. Once a doctor cauterized a wart on my foot. I couldn't see what he was doing because I was on my stomach, but it smelled really bad."

"Cautery is an electric current that cooks the tissues. That's what makes the bad smell. It seals off the smaller bleeders. Larger blood vessels have to be clamped."

"Thanks for the good news about my chest. Doc Frank, thanks for the info, and thanks for being my special friend."

Marty went directly to Link's room to tell him everything Frank had said.

"Sounds to me," Link reflected, "like you should get up in the ceiling as soon as they announce code 400. There's no telling how quickly Uncle Ken will get there."

"I've got an idea," she said. "As soon as we hear *code 400* you call your Uncle Ken. Tell him that you have something really important you want to talk with him about. Ask him to come to your room right away. Say it's something about your grandmother."

"I don't know. What would I tell him?"

"You told me he used to be your grandmother's boyfriend before she met your grandfather. I bet he still likes her. So tell him that since your grandfather died and after the car accident and all, you're real worried about her."

"I'd feel dopey saying that. I'll think of something."

CHAPTER SEVENTEEN

Lydia stepped from the shower, grabbed a bath towel, flipped on the exhaust fan and overhead heat lamp. She wrapped a smaller towel around her head. After drying, she stepped on the bathroom scale. I must get back to that wretched spa, she thought. No wonder it's such a struggle to button my slacks.

She could imagine the aerobics instructor shouting, "Tense those abdominal muscles, now crunch, up, down, up, down. Lydia, don't arch your back. Come on, up, down, up, down."

She dried her hair, gently combing from below, as the rush of warm air lifted it from her shoulders. An occasional strand sparkled as it caught the light. She wasn't eager to have her hair turn grey, neither was she panicked by the thought. As she brushed, she pictured Marty, whose hair was dull and thin, her scalp showing through. Children's Hospital was crammed with Martys and Links...precious, irreplaceable children. Was that why Kenneth never married? How many times had he looked into his microscope and seen those hideous cancer cells? His pathology report had the power to shatter a child's future and a parent's dreams.

Did her work seem frivolous to Kenneth? Digging up shards of pottery and other mundane things? She found it

Forbidden Harvest

absorbing, but it wouldn't add a single day to a child's life.

She studied her face in the mirror. It seemed a stranger's. It was more lined than usual. Her eyes looked sad and flat. How eloquently the eyes can speak without sound...can emote without changing their appearance. In their dark recesses, life's emotions can be expressed in some magical way. She looked away, unwilling to admit the desperation and fear she saw.

She thought of Link. How much closer he and she had become since the onset of his illness. Dear God, she thought, let us keep our child. I promise I'll devote myself to working with children. On her visits to see Link, she had seen so many pale, hollow-eyed children, many bald, and others in wheelchairs or struggling to walk with crutches. Very young children with AIDS were especially heartbreaking to see. How can they possibly understand what was happening to them? Kenneth had told her that some were abandoned by their drug-addicted mothers. Left to either languish in the hospital or hopefully find foster parents. Would I be able to care for a stranger's baby? Give it the support and love it deserved?

She decided to stop by the hospital to talk with Kenneth. Signing up heart-donors was proving to be fruitless. Link's doctors had identified four potential donors, but only one was close enough in size to Link to be acceptable; a fourteen-year-old with terminal renal disease. And there were still many children ahead of Link on the waiting list.

She called Ken. "It seems every way we turn we run into a dead end. Where in God's name are all those would-be donors?"

"It's maddening to realize how many there are," Ken said, "and how few actually sign up. It's good to line up outside donors. But patients who are already hospitalized are the main source of organs. The rest are usually children involved in car crashes."

"Are there no other sources?"

"There are occasional stroke patients and children with organ failure. And children with congenital conditions not compatible with life."

"Are the parents asked about organ donation in the Emergency Room?" she asked.

"Most of the time the situation is so emotionally charged, no one brings it up."

"Isn't there anyone on the staff who's responsible to at least ask?"

"We orient all new nursing staff. I describe the donor program. There's a file they can refer to."

"So why isn't it working?"

"The parents are often in a state of shock, and the doctors and staff are working frantically to save the child's life."

"There must be a way to make the system work better," Lydia insisted. But what if it were Link, whose organs they were asked to donate even as he fought for his life? A question Lydia could barely contemplate. Yes, what if it were Link?

Around mid-morning the following day, Ken visited Link, who had just returned to his room from physical therapy.

"Hi, Uncle Ken."

Ken adjusted the nasal prongs that had partially slipped out of Link's nose. He glanced at the oxygen gauge mounted on the wall behind Link's bed. Despite what looked like an adequate flow rate, Link appeared to be working hard to get enough oxygen. Ken picked up a book that sat on Link's bedside table. It was a collection of stories by Arthur Conan Doyle. On the inside cover was an inscription written in a familiar handwriting.

"I hope you enjoy these Sherlock Holmes stories," it read, "as much as I did when I was your age. Love, Grandma."

Ken wondered if Lydia read to Link when she visited him. He asked Link if he would like him to read from the book.

Yes, Uncle Ken. There's a marker where Grandma left off."

Ken hadn't read Sherlock Holmes stories in years and had forgotten how good they were. After a few minutes Link dosed off. Ken closed the book and set it on the night stand. He leaned over and kissed Link before he left.

He went to his office in the morgue. On his desk were a stack of reports waiting to be dictated. As he picked up the microphone, someone knocked.

He went to the door. "Lydia, what a pleasant surprise." He led her to the small office area.

Lydia folded her arms, pressing them tightly against her chest as they walked past the stainless steel table in the center of the room.

"Kenneth, this is a dreadful place." As she sat next to his desk, she looked about the cluttered room and sighed.

"Would you care to hang some of your artwork here?" Ken asked.

"I know you're teasing. But it wouldn't be such a bad idea. This place could use a decorative touch."

Ken stroked his beard and nodded. He stared at Lydia's hands without speaking.

Forbidden Harvest

"Kenneth?"

"Yes, even better, a woman's touch, a wonderful thing."

"Are you reconsidering the virtues of bachelorhood?" she asked.

"I wasn't aware that bachelorhood is necessarily a virtuous state."

Lydia leaned forward, placing her elbows on Ken's desk. She rested her chin in the cup of her hands.

"I've been thinking. You recall our conversation about the Emergency Room as a source of donors. I have an idea."

She asked if she could personally hire someone who would work in the ER from late afternoon until mid-evening. This person could tell the parents about Link and explain the donor program.

"Can you imagine what you might have said, if when Tom was taken to the ER after the car wreck, someone had asked you about organ donation?"

"I would have been furious...you're right...and especially a child. I was thinking of that this morning. Guess it's not a very good idea."

"What might work," Ken suggested, "would be to approach the parents of children admitted from the ER on life support. The person we might hire would have time to establish rapport with the family. If it becomes obvious that the child will not survive; then it would be a more appropriate time to bring up the possibility of organ donation."

"Yes, I can see that," Lydia agreed. "The parents have already faced the worst."

"We'll need to clear hiring someone with the hospital administration. We'd need a sensitive, mature person to approach the parents."

Lydia stood and took a long white coat from a clothes tree in the corner. She put it around her shoulders. "I'm freezing."

"Would you prefer to go to the snack bar? It's just down the hall. The thermostat there is set for the living."

The bar was crowded with employees and visitors.

"There's an empty booth in the corner," Ken said. "I'll get a couple of coffees. Would you care for anything else? Something sweet?"

"No thanks, just coffee."

Ken slipped into the booth with two black coffees. They talked about finding the right person to approach the parents of critically ill or injured patients. He suggested that a graduate student in social work might have the right skills.

"I'll put up a notice on the school's main bulletin board."

"We have so little time," Lydia said. "Let me know as soon as you're able to find someone. I can't believe it's almost three months since Link's been on the waiting list. If Dr. Manning's prediction was right, we've only a few weeks." She bit her lower lip. "God, I'm beginning to sound like the damn doctors." She fought hard to hold back tears. "Didn't one of the consultants talk about a new drug that could sustain Link until we can locate a donor?"

"I checked Link's chart just this afternoon," he said. "They've already started the drug."

"Lord. Let's pray that it helps. Kenneth, there's so much

I want to talk to you about. Can we meet for dinner later?"

He offered to pick her up at seven, but Lydia said she would be at the hospital visiting with Link. They decided to meet at a restaurant. He gave her directions to Pierre's.

After she left, he was unable to concentrate on his work. He couldn't remember when he and Lydia had last gone out to dinner, just the two of them. Was it his imagination or was she acting differently toward him?

As he carried a small bottle of solvent to his microscope, it slipped from his hands. The bottle shattered as it landed on the tile floor. He stood shaking his head, looking at the mess. He really hadn't changed that much through all these years. He was still the same old klutz, especially when it came to Lydia.

Ken was standing in front of Pierre's when Lydia stepped from a cab. She looked around.

"I'm glad I didn't drive, I never could have handled the traffic down here."

"The cuisine is worth the effort."

The name of the restaurant was engraved on a brass plate and below, in smaller letters, *by appointment only.* A brick stairway led to the basement of what looked like an office building. The dining room was no bigger than a large living room. The walls were white stucco. Scattered about the room were several small round tables covered with white tablecloths that hung halfway to the floor. On each table was a narrow vase containing a single rose. Large square, brick-colored ceramic tiles covered the floor. The walls were bare except for several wall-mounted gas-lighted fixtures.

Lydia wore a diamond pendant on a thin gold chain. Her hair looked different somehow. Her skin seemed to glow in the stark whiteness of the dimly lit room.

Forbidden Harvest

"You've done something with your hair."

"Yes. Julian said he was depressed doing it the same old way. He was so pleased with his handiwork."

"He has a right to be pleased. You look stunning."

"If you had exuded all this charm when we first met, I might have run off with you that very night."

"I was a bit clumsy in those days." He laughed. "You know, Tom was everything I wanted to be: handsome, self-confident, great fun to be with. I didn't have a chance once he came along."

"You gave up too easily. I thought maybe you didn't care that much. You know, you never told me you cared for me during the year we dated, before I met Tom."

"I was afraid you wouldn't take me seriously."

"Aren't you going to order me a drink?"

Ken motioned to a waiter.

"Remember the time we chartered a sailing boat?" Ken asked. "Tom insisted he navigate. Then he ran us aground."

"I can remember exactly what he said," Lydia recalled, "'Damn it, Lydia, that reef isn't where it's supposed to be here.'"

We bobbed in the surf for six hours before someone came along and pulled us off, Ken thought. How wonderful it would have been if Ton weren't there. To have had her all to himself!

By the time dinner was complete, and they were drinking coffee, they had both grown very quiet.

He could see her hand tremble as she placed her napkin on the table. It was time to talk about Link.

"Kenneth, I know how much effort you've put in, finding

a heart for Link. Yesterday I spoke with Dr. Cronce. He said that he's been working closely with you. But so far nothing."

"We've searched both locally and nationally for possible donors."

"It's beginning to look hopeless, Kenneth." Her eyes brimmed with tears.

"It's not hopeless. You mustn't say that," Ken pleaded.

"I just can't sit back and watch my grandson slip away. There must be something more we can do."

"It's absolutely maddening to know that we have the ability to make him better," Ken said, "and all we can do is sit and wait and hope that a heart will turn up. There are so many variables and so damn little time."

"What about your method to preserve organs? Wouldn't that help us expand the search?"

"You remember the flap with the hospital Human Subjects Committee? They refused to approve my request to go ahead with experiments using human organs." He wanted desperately to tell her of the organs he was removing without parental permission. But he didn't want to implicate her or raise her hopes.

"You're my dearest friend," she said. She reached out and covered his hand with hers. "I don't mean to burden you. I just don't know where to turn."

Ken's resolve not to tell her the whole truth dissolved the instant she touched his hand.

He was silent a few moments as he gathered his thoughts. "I'm going to tell you something that may shock you, but you must promise not to repeat it."

"My God, what?"

Pierre was hovering about. Ken glanced at his watch. "Let's go to my place; we can talk there."

Lydia sat at a counter in the kitchen, as Ken made a pot of espresso. He started from the very beginning, describing his mounting exasperation over children who were dying for lack of donor organs and the hundreds of autopsies he had performed, where perfectly normal organs were not made available, permission forbidden by grief-stricken parents.

His hand shook, as he poured them both some coffee and sat next to her. She was shocked. He was always so steady, unflappable. She reached out and covered his hand with hers.

"At first I channeled my frustration into building the statewide donor program...but the overall yield was modest. And even when we enlisted suitable donors, it was difficult to get the organs to the children in time." Ken was quiet for a few moments. "When the Human Subjects Committee turned down my proposal....I was so damn close to a break-through I decided to go ahead, without their approval."

"I'm shocked, Kenneth. How could you have kept that a secret?"

He went on to explain his research proposal to do an immediate autopsy on donor bodies to see if the ventilator was maintaining oxygenation of the organs that hadn't been removed.

He reached for the coffee pot and poured them both another cup.

"But how did that help you to continue research with human organs?" Lydia asked.

"Doing the biopsies at those autopsies was a ruse to get

the body to the morgue with the ventilator still functioning and maintaining the tissues in a viable state. I removed whichever organs that hadn't been harvested and subjected them to our cooling process. Next, my assistant transported the organs to the Hakim Medical Center. When a suitable match wasn't available, we used the organs for research."

"All those clandestine goings-on...so unlike you, Kenneth. I'm shocked. But I can certainly understand how you were driven to do what you did."

"It was frustrating at first. Rejection rates were high. But we made adjustments, and the organs began to maintain their integrity for longer periods than any other place in the country. Lydia, my research has been successful beyond my expectations."

"That's marvelous. But how can you share what you've accomplished without bringing the institution down on you?"

"It's not just the hospital I have to worry about. The families denied permission for me to remove those organs."

"My Lord, I hadn't thought of that."

He stood. "Let's sit in the living room," he suggested.

She sat on the couch, holding her cup. He sat close to her.

"How dreadful," she said. "You've had to work in secrecy."

"Lydia, you can't imagine how often I've thought of finding a way to get a heart for Link."

"But wouldn't the surgeons have to know where the heart came from?"

"That's exactly the problem. If I were to falsify a record,

the chances of discovery would be close to one hundred percent."

"How good are the Saudi doctors? Why not transfer Link to the Hakim Medical Center?"

"They're only licensed to care for Saudi children."

"It's so damn frustrating." Her voice shook with emotion. "You're risking everything to help the Saudi children, and we can't do a blessed thing for Link."

She placed her empty cup on a table next to the couch. She moved closer to him. Ken placed his hand on her shoulder. Without speaking, she leaned against him. She put her arms around him and pressed her head to his chest.

"Kenneth, I've treated you so badly all these years."

"You treated me like family. I've treasured our closeness."

She lifted her head, their faces just inches apart.

"I do love you, you know," she whispered.

He looked into her face. He gently touched her hair. They kissed, softly, slowly.

"Lydia, I've loved you from that very first night."

Their love-making started slowly with kissing and caressing. With each kiss, Ken felt as if he was sinking deeper and deeper into a vast space where only they existed.

All the intervening years slipped away. They were young again. Lydia had invited Ken to lunch. She told him that Tom asked her to marry him. But she hadn't made up her mind. She was asking his advice!

"I don't know if I have the energy to spend the rest of

Forbidden Harvest

my life with a human dynamo," Lydia said.

Ken thought to drop to his knees, to tell her how much he loved her and beg her to marry him, not Tom. "Do you love him?" he asked.

"Yes. I do."

Ken reached across the table and grasped her hand. "He's a lucky man. I'm happy for both of you."

After they made love, Ken lay awake. He thought of his boyhood, of the coal furnace in his parent's house. Winter in Vermont was like living in a refrigerator. To save fuel his mother would remind him to "bank the furnace" at bedtime. He would go to the basement and spread ashes over the coals to partially smother the fire. The following morning he would stoke the fire, add coal, and soon the old furnace glowed, spreading its warmth throughout the little house.

He reached over and placed his hand on Lydia's shoulder and ran it lightly along her side to the hollow where her ribs ended and the soft curve of her hip rose. Until this night, he had banked the fire within him. Now a surge of heat flooded his body as he pressed against her.

In the morning he lay in bed looking at Lydia as she slept peacefully beside him. He lightly touched her face. She awakened and smiled at him. "Good morning. Is that fresh coffee I smell?"

"Yes, I got up early to make it."

He fixed toast and scrambled eggs as Lydia dressed. They sat at the kitchen table. "Kenneth, I'm sure you've never realized how many times through the years I imagined how different my life would have been if I had married you. Not that Tom and I weren't happy, we were."

"Well, you're not getting away from me again."

They quietly drank their coffee.

"I don't believe this is a good time to let the children know about us," she said.

"I understand, of course. And I promise I'll do everything in my power to help Link." He reached out and squeezed her hand. "I will find him a heart, I promise."

CHAPTER EIGHTEEN

Marty knew her way around the morgue, but she decided to check her plan again. She opened the door ever so slightly. The room was empty. Once in, she looked over the small office, where there was a desk and a single file cabinet. This was where she would gain access to the ceiling. But the top of the file cabinet was piled high with medical journals, two moldy coffee mugs, and a stack of slide trays. It was also stained with spilled coffee. She would have to clear off that mess. She was concerned that if Dr. Bernholtz came into the office when she was already up in the ceiling, he might notice that his things had been moved. She'd have to think of a way around that.

Later in Link's room, she told him about all the stuff on the file cabinet.

"I have to move that junk or I'll break my neck up there. How do we handle that, Professor Holmes?"

Link pretended he was smoking a pipe, "Dear Dr. Watson, the solution is quite simple. Think, my dear chap, who normally would clean off the top of the cabinet?"

She threw out her stomach and did her best Watson impersonation. "Come, come, Holmes, don't play with me, come out with it."

"What did you say the cleaning lady's name is?" he

asked.

"Annie something."

"Well, what you can do is stack the journals real neat along one side of the file cabinet. Wash out the coffee cups before you go up there,"... He paused a few moments to catch his breath. "Then set the cups on top of the journals. Write a note..."

"Don't tell me anymore. I know. Write a note from Annie saying she hoped he didn't mind her moving his stuff to clean off the cabinet. Little Doc comes through again." She walked over to Link and roughed up his hair.

She noticed Link would often stop talking to catch his breath. They had him hooked up to an intravenous pump. At times he'd reach for the nasal oxygen mask.

"Hey, what's with the intravenous?" she asked.

He said, almost whispering, "My new medicine only works by vein."

"What's it for?"

"It's supposed to make my heart stronger. I hate it. I have to drag this pole with me even when I take a leak."

"Can I still push you around in the wheelchair?"

"Yeah, they can attach the IV bottle to a pole that fits on the back of the chair."

"It's been almost two weeks and no code 400. I can hardly wait," Marty said.

The following day at two in the afternoon the hospital operator announced, "Code 400, code 400."

Marty immediately climbed into her sweat suit, grabbed up the gloves, flashlight, walkie-talkie, knife and marking pencil and took off for the morgue. She called Link.

Forbidden Harvest

"Did you hear the operator announce code 400?"

"Yeah. I already called Uncle Ken. I asked him to come see me right away."

"Great. Try to keep him there at least a half hour, okay?"

Marty cautiously approached the door to the morgue. It wasn't locked. She peeked in, holding the door slightly ajar.

"Drat, some guy's in there fooling around with those instruments," she whispered to Link.

"That's probably Uncle Ken's assistant," Link whispered. "His name's Jamael...I can't remember his last name. You'd better wait."

"He just went back into the next room." She stepped into the morgue and quietly eased the door shut. She rushed to the office area and crouched alongside the desk.

Jamael pushed through the doors with a large cart. On top of the cart was a box the size of an ice chest. It had a bunch of gauges and dials on the outside. He wheeled it against a wall several feet from the autopsy table and covered it with a cloth. He went back through the double doors. Marty heard Link whisper, "Hey...Uncle Ken's coming down the hall. I have to sign off."

She waited several minutes to make sure Jamael didn't return. When he didn't, she cleared off the top of the file cabinet. With him in the next room, walking in and out of the morgue, there was no way she was going to the sink to wash the coffee cups.

She grabbed a pen from the desk and added a post script to the note. "I'll come back to clean the cups and the top of the file cabinet." She laid the note on top of the journals. She removed the wastepaper basket from under

Forbidden Harvest

the desk and placed it upside-down on the cabinet. Then she rolled the desk chair over and climbed from the chair to the top of the cabinet. She carefully stood on the wastepaper basket. As she went from a crouching to a standing position, she raised a section of ceiling tile and slid it to one side.

Just then, Jamael came through the doors. She couldn't do anything but stand there motionless. Because the office partitions went up only half way, if he looked in her direction he'd see her. "God, don't let him look my way," she prayed. She held her breath until she heard him leave.

She pulled herself through the opening and replaced the tile. She was in almost total darkness. She took out the flashlight. Pulling a black marking pen from her pocket, she drew a large cross on the tile she had just replaced.

She kept her radio on standby as she made her way to the center of the ceiling. Using her pocket knife, she pried up one of the tiles and cut off a corner. The light from the morgue shone through. Moving her eye close to the hole, she could see the entire autopsy table and most of the room. Her heart pounded so hard she wondered if someone below could hear.

"Uncle Ken just left," Link said. "Where are you?"

"I'm above the table. I can see perfect. That asshole Jamael keeps running in and out. He damn near caught me."

"What's that noise?"

"He turned on an exhaust fan. Good luck! They can't hear me with that thing going full blast."

Twenty minutes later Ken Bernholtz arrived. He was tying on a face mask as he entered the morgue. Jamael came in from the next room. They stood talking for a few minutes, but she couldn't hear what they were saying.

Then they both left the morgue and went through a pair of double doors into a room that Link had told Marty was Dr. Bernholtz's laboratory. The room was quiet for a long time. Marty began to doze. She was awakened suddenly by a loud knock. Jamael opened the door to the morgue. Two men in white uniforms wheeled in a stretcher. A body was covered with a sheet except for the head. A respirator and oxygen tank sat at the end of the stretcher.

"They're lifting the body onto the table," she whispered. "Uncle Ken just told the attendants to plug in the respirator and to take the portable power packs back to the operating room."

Marty watched as the attendants left. Then Ken removed the sheet from the body.

"The boy's naked. He looks about ten, maybe."

That could be Link's body they're getting ready to cut into. Oh God, I can't do this, she thought. Was I nuts? What was I thinking? She wanted to grab her stuff and run.

"Hey. What's going on?" Link asked.

"I'm not sure this was such a good idea. I'm tired of saying their names. I'll call Jamael, Dr. A, and Dr. Bernholtz Dr. B."

"Okay. Sure."

"Dr. A helped Uncle Ken into a gown and tied it in the back. Then Uncle Ken put on gloves. Dr. A's scrubbing the front of the body with a purple liquid."

What happened next caused Marty to cover the hole. Her mouth became dry. She began to retch. She vomited. "God Almighty, did I ever make a mess."

"You okay?" Link whispered.

"I just threw up lunch. Nobody heard me. Thank God for that exhaust fan. I made a mess. When Dr. B picked up a knife and made a cut from the neck all the way down to below the boy's belly button, I almost passed out. I'm trying to get up the nerve to look again."

By the time she removed her hand, they were working in the boy's abdomen. After a few minutes Marty continued, "Dr. B removed what looks like a kidney. He's bringing it over to a table. He just put it in a big jar that's filled with a yellow liquid. Now Dr. A is carrying the jar to some kind of box. It has a lot of dials and stuff on it. When he lifted the lid a white cloud came out. He put the kidney in the box. Dr. B is working in the belly. He must be tying off blood vessels because there's not so much blood now."

"Did you puke again?" Link asked.

"No, I covered the hole when I saw Dr. A reach for a saw. I can hear them doing something disgusting. I'm not looking. That's for sure!"

"You're not going to watch anymore?" Link asked.

She bit her lip as she uncovered her peep-hole.

"Now they're working in the chest. They put these big gizmos on the ribs to hold the chest open. Geez! His heart is still beating. I don't get it."

She was soaked with perspiration, and the smell of vomit in the confined area was overpowering.

"This is bad as chemo. I gotta puke again."

After a few minutes she was back on the radio.

"Dr. A just turned off the respirator. Uncle Ken is holding something in his hand. It looks like the heart. Now he's carrying it to the table and putting it in another glass jar. He carried the jar to that big chest thing. He's wheeling it into the other room.

"Dr. A's doing the autopsy by himself now. He keeps taking out things and weighing them on the scale and then putting them back. I'm getting a sore neck looking through this darn hole."

"Marty, a nurse is coming to give me medicine. I have to turn off the radio."

Dr. A talked into a microphone suspended from the ceiling. Marty figured it was probably connected to the Dictaphone she noticed on the desk in the morgue office. He was using a foot switch to turn the recorder on and off. He described what he was doing, like the color, size and weight of the organs. He was using scissors to cut off pieces of tissue. He put those in small glass jars.

"The nurse just left. How are things going?" Link asked.

"It seems like I've been up here for hours. I can't wait till they finish. I'm so stiff I don't see how I'll ever be able to climb down."

Jamael picked up a needle and thread and began to sew up the incision.

"Thank God! Looks like he's finishing up."

He scrubbed the body with soap and water, dried it off, and covered it with a sheet. He lifted the body onto a stretcher and rolled it toward the vault. He was out of Marty's visual range but she could hear the vault door slide open and pretty soon she heard the drawer slide shut. He spent another few minutes cleaning up the table and floor. He left the morgue and joined Dr. Bernholtz in the next room. Marty had no idea how long they would be."Link, they're both gone now, but I don't know if I should come down or not. They could come back in here any time."

"I bet they're in there doing experiments. You'd better get out of there. It's almost dinner time. The nurse is going to wonder where you are."

"It sounds pretty shit-simple sitting there in your room, but I'm the one who might get caught." He didn't respond.

"Okay, LD, I'm heading back."

Every part of her body ached as she struggled to crawl down. She lifted the tile part way and listened. The room was quiet except for the sound of the exhaust fan. As she eased herself through the hole, her flashlight fell from her jacket pocket. It hit the filing cabinet and bounced on the floor, shattering the lens. She backed up above the ceiling space and closed the opening. She heard someone come through the doors and figured it was Jamael checking out what had made the noise. After a couple of minutes she heard him leave.

She lowered herself onto the top of the file cabinet and soon was standing on the floor. She picked up a journal and used it to scrape up the broken glass, threw the pieces in the waste-paper basket and slipped it under the desk. She kept an eye on the double doors as she made a dash for the morgue entrance. Safely in the corridor, she walked slowly so as not to attract attention. On the way to her room, she called Link on the walkie-talkie.

"Operation Skyhawk completed! Yours truly is one totally pooped and icked-out Butterfly."

"I hate to tell you this," Link said, "but tonight your mom and my dad are coming to dinner. They should be here in half an hour. I hope you haven't lost your appetite."

CHAPTER NINETEEN

Gladys slipped a lasagna pan from the oven, and as she did, the back of her hand touched the edge of the hot door. She shrieked. The pan crashed to the floor.

The baking dish cracked apart. Lasagna spread like lava over the kitchen tiles. She had only a half-hour before leaving. She promised Marty she was bringing lasagna. She'd have to stop at the Italian deli on her way to the hospital.

She rummaged through her closet for something dignified. Marty had asked her if she had ever worn those hippie clothes in the back. Yes, she had. Gladys loved the muted colors, the sheer, layered long skirts, plain cotton blouses and paisley vests. But for tonight she selected a conservative tailored suit. She referred to it as her interview ensemble. She looked at it for a moment and then returned it to the rack.

As she dressed, she thought about Marty's new chemotherapy treatment. Dr. Gibbs had discussed it with her. She was terrified of making the decision to use an experimental drug, assuming Marty would be willing to go ahead. During the course of her last chemotherapy she had told her mother repeatedly, "Don't let them do this to me again, Mom. Please promise me you won't."

Gladys didn't know who to turn to for advice. The

doctors were biased toward aggressive treatment. Gladys' parents, who lived in Omaha, weren't very helpful. Her mother's usual response was, "I didn't go to medical school. The doctors know what's best."

Gladys thought, well, neither did I, but I'm going to have to live with whatever decision I make. Her own father was convinced that megavitamins were the answer to all problems, including cancer. Maybe Tom can help? After all, he heads up a successful business. His job's all about making good decisions.

Throughout the meal, Marty pushed her food around the plate. She nibbled the garlic toast.

"Thought this was your favorite, sweetheart," Gladys said.

"It's great stuff, but I'm just not hungry. My stomach's queasy."

"Marty was watching a medical show today," Link said. "It was real bloody. It kind of spooked her."

"Yeah," Marty said. "Nothing's less appetizing than blood, guts and gore!"

Gladys sensed that Marty and Link were up to something. All those things Marty had asked her to bring in! Whatever it was, the caper was probably pretty harmless. What trouble can they get into here, she thought. And from the way Marty and Link were exchanging glances, they were obviously having fun.

"Did you watch the same show, Link?" Tom asked.

"No, but Marty used her walkie-talkie and told me about it blow by blow," Link said, grinning from ear to ear.

"The next time I make something special for you, please watch a ball game," Gladys said.

After dinner Tom and Gladys walked toward the

elevator.

"Tom, I'd like to talk with you about a new treatment they're recommending for Marty. Do you have a few minutes?"

"Of course. Let's go to the snack bar. I could use a cup of coffee."

They sat at a booth. Gladys usually drank her coffee black. She took a sip and grimaced.

"Pass the sweet and low, please. This stuff must have been brewed yesterday."

He took a sip. "Maybe last week."

Even when Tom managed a smile, she could still see the sadness in his eyes. She wondered how long it had been since his wife died? And now with Link so desperately ill, why should he give a damn about her problems?

She glanced about the room, crowded mostly with visitors speaking in subdued tones, their expressions concerned, their smiles stiff. This place is depressing, she thought.

She rested an elbow on the table, causing three silver bracelets to slide midway down her forearm.

"I talked with the oncologist today," Gladys said. "She's recommending an experimental drug called EP149."

"What's that?"

"She said it's a whole different class of drug from the other chemotherapy medicines. They've only used it to treat thirty kids so far."

"Marty just had a course of chemo. Why so soon?"

"Dr. Gibbs said since she had a slight response to her recent treatment, she may be especially receptive to the new drug. She said it was like a boxer hitting his opponent again before he could get back up."

She looked at Tom's hands. He wore a plain gold band. He was absent-mindedly twisting the ring as they spoke. His hands appeared strong, steady. She wondered what it would feel like to have him hold her face in those hands. She felt her cheeks grow warm. She could see the sudden concern in Tom's expression.

"I know how sick she's gotten with her regular chemo," he said. "Will this new drug be that bad?"

She took a sip of coffee and immediately reached for another packet of sweetener.

"That's the problem. It's very toxic. There's not that much between the treatment dose and what could kill a person."

"My God. Why would the oncologist recommend such a dangerous drug? Have you talked with Dr. Tupelo?"

"I have. He said even though Marty responded some to her last treatment, the type of cancer she has, once it recurs, is rarely if ever cured. He said at most she might survive...a year or two." She looked away, fighting hard to hold back tears.

"I'm really sorry. I had no idea the prognosis was that bad," Tom said.

Gladys went on to tell him what Dr. Gibbs had said about the medicine, its effectiveness and the risks involved.

"That sounds horrendous. What does Marty want to do?" Tom asked.

"She says she doesn't want chemotherapy, with Link being so sick."

Tom reached across the table and placed his hand over

Gladys'. She turned her hand over. His ring hurt a little as he squeezed.

"You and Marty have to decide what's best for her, regardless of Link's condition."

Gladys fought back tears. She wondered if Tom thinks she was waiting for Link to die, so Marty could go ahead with the chemo.

"Marty wants to spend time with Link, and not be in her room dealing with the side effects of chemo."

"I understand," Tom said. "I got a call from Dr. Cronce," he said, "just before I came to dinner tonight. He wants to meet with me and Lydia in the morning to discuss Link's condition. He said Link's kidneys are beginning to fail. They're considering some kind of temporary operation."

"I'm sorry to bother you, when you have so much to deal with," Gladys said.

"Marty's been a wonderful friend for Link. And she's a girl you can be very proud of. I'm pleased you decided to talk with me. If there is any way I can help, please call me."

Gladys had grown close to Link. She couldn't imagine how desperate Tom must be. "Feel free to call me, too," she said.

CHAPTER TWENTY

It was a crisp spring morning. Clusters of dogwoods bursting with buds and young blossoms promised warm days. Lydia breathed deeply. She stood at her front door as Tom pulled up the drive. Dr. Cronce had said he wanted to discuss something about a temporary surgical procedure. Was he thinking about using an artificial heart? She recalled one of the consultants had said that could buy Link more time.

Buy time? Lydia thought. What a meaningless expression. She can buy damn near anything she wanted....but not a heart for her grandchild. Time is a priceless gift, given freely at birth, and reclaimed without reason or apology.

She buckled into the passenger seat. Tom looked straight ahead, his expression solemn.

"I don't understand exactly what this meeting is about," Lydia said. "Did he tell you any more than what you told me?"

"He said he didn't want to discuss Link's medical condition on the phone."

"I would have pressed him. I'd like to go in knowing in advance what he planned."

"Mother, he's not a business adversary, he's Link's

doctor."

"I asked Kenneth to be there. Do you mind?"

"He's family, Mother. Why even ask?"

She studied Tom's profile. Tom was angry. He had lost Brenda in a terrible crash, and now he might lose his only child. Her heart ached knowing how agonizing the past two years had been for him.

"You know, it's not such a bad thing to get mad once in awhile," she said. "And you're driving too fast. Speed makes me nervous."

He pounded the steering wheel with his fist.

"I'm so damn sick of going to that hospital. And that fat little Dr. Cronce--if I have to watch him polish his glasses one more time! I want to bring Link home." His eyes brimmed with tears. "How I hated those months I spent in the hospital. And now seeing my son languishing in that damn bed!"

The days immediately following the accident had no beginning or end. Constantly in pain, Tom would ring for the nurse at precisely the time he was due for another shot of morphine. Soon he would drift into a vivid dream world where scenes of the crash played and replayed the moment of impact: the tumbling car; flashing police lights; the pulsating image of Brenda clutching the steering wheel. Awakening, he looked about, confused as to where he was. Why were his arms tied? He tried to sit, but the pain in his leg caused him to collapse back in bed. He was only vaguely aware of his family being there, speaking in hushed voices. Why wasn't Brenda with them? He'd shut his eyes tightly to make them go away. This was not his family. Dear God, where were they?

As the need for morphine decreased, Tom began to separate his frightening dream world from what was going on around him.

"Am I going to lose my leg?" he asked the doctor.

The young orthopedic surgeon, surrounded by even younger-looking men and women in white coats, brushed off the question as though he had asked if he could have two eggs for breakfast instead of one.

"You came close, Mr. Bradshaw, damn close. But with a little luck you should be back on your feet in a few months." *He patted Tom's leg and quickly left the room, his young disciples followed at a respectful distance.*

Later that morning, Tom's intern sat beside his bed and explained in detail the series of operations that would be necessary to reconstruct the shattered bone in his right thigh.

"Man, you're going to need intense physical therapy and rehab to get you to walk again."

The combination of the intern's smooth black skin and slight British accent prompted Tom to ask, "You from Jamaica?"

"How'd you guess, man?" *He flashed a brilliant smile.* "Most people think I'm from Sweden."

"You're the only doctor here who sits to talk to me," Tom said. "Did you skip class when they taught you how to make rounds?"

"Actually, it was a whole course. They called 'Schmooze or Cruise'."

"I guess you flunked the course, right?"

Two weeks after the crash, Tom came out of intensive care. He had asked Lydia to bring the videotape to the hospital. He looked at his watch. Kenneth and Link were also on their way. Just then Father Justine came into his room. Damn it, Tom thought, I don't want him around when the family gets here.

"I was in the hospital to bring communion to an elderly parishioner, and thought I'd stop in to say hello."

"Thanks, Father. I could use a spiritual lift today."

Brenda had once told Tom that Father Justine harbored the dream that someday Tom might convert to Catholicism. As a teenager in the late sixties, Tom had been distrustful of organized religions. But his strident anti-establishment sentiment of that era had mellowed, and he had developed a grudging respect for the church's adherence to a moral code that flew in the face of modern humanistic philosophy.

Father Justine pulled a chair alongside the bed.

"I don't mean to be rude, Father, but I've a terrible headache. Could we keep the visit short?"

"Of course Tom, I understand. I have several people to visit yet. So I'll be running along." As he moved toward the door he said, "Give my love to the family."

Tom again checked his watch. As he pulled a newspaper from the bedstand, Link, Kenneth, and Lydia walked into the room. Lydia was wearing a dark dress. She carried a bouquet of roses. She removed some wilting flowers from a vase on the table next to his bed and replaced them with the roses.

Kenneth was carrying a plastic bag that he placed on his lap as he sat in a chair opposite Link. He wore a dark suit and black tie. He glanced at the traction mechanism that suspended Tom's right leg. "I understand they're going to put a prosthesis in your right thigh?"

Tom shrugged.

"You're gonna have a chunk of metal in there?" Link asked.

"No, it's a kind of hard plastic," Tom said. He turned to Kenneth. "Well, did you bring the tape?"

"I have it right here. We can watch whenever you like," Kenneth said.

"You want us here when you do?" Lydia asked.

"Yes, of course, I want you here." Tom crumpled the newspaper and threw it to the floor. "Damn it, Mother, if I hadn't drunk so much that night I would have been driving the car. Maybe things would have turned out different."

Lydia leaned over Tom and brushed back his hair. "It wasn't your fault that truck came across the road. There wasn't enough time to react, whoever was driving."

Tom didn't respond. He pushed her hand away.

Link, who was sitting on the opposite side of the bed, leaned over and placed his arm across Tom and rested his head on his father's chest. Tom lay there passively until Link awkwardly withdrew.

"Let's look at the tape," Tom said, as if he wanted to get it over with.

As Kenneth loaded the cassette and adjusted the controls, Tom looked from Link to Lydia. They seemed afraid to say anything. It made him even more irritable to see how he was affecting them. He wanted his mother to scream at him. He wanted Link to behave like a teenager and say, "screw you" and storm out of the room. Link sat staring at his hands, seemingly scared to look at him. When he did, his lower lip quivered.

"Why are you mad at me? I miss mom just as much as you," Link said.

"It wasn't your fault, that's why. Can't anybody

understand that?"

"Maybe we should do this another time?" Lydia suggested.

Tom cranked up his bed to a full upright position. Kenneth started the tape. Lydia adjusted the blinds.

On tape, Father Justine said the Mass. Most of the service was identical to the Masses Tom had attended with Brenda on special occasions, like Easter and Christmas. The casket sat in the middle aisle of the church; a large floral spray lay on top. After the formal Mass service, Father Justine walked to the center of the altar. He addressed the family and friends of the Bradshaws.

"We have come here today to say our final goodbye to Brenda Bradshaw. Our hearts go out to her family, who must bear her loss the most. Our faith tells us that this is a glorious day. A loved one has gone to her eternal reward. We should rejoice knowing she is no longer suffering.

"Well, my friends, that may be true on a purely intellectual level, but still my heart aches. I'm in despair at the loss of such a young woman. A woman of inner beauty and grace. Her enthusiasm for life made us who knew her happier and better people. And now that life has been taken from us, suddenly, violently. How can we ever comprehend God's reason? If we could change what happened that dark night, we would beg God not to take her from us.

"Jesus, the night before he was crucified, prayed to his father to let him off the hook. 'Take this cup from me, Father,' he pleaded. And who could know better what to expect after death? It is no wonder we cling passionately to those we love."

Tom strained to listen as Father Justine continued to speak, but he could no longer grasp what he was saying. The sounds of screeching brakes and Brenda's final scream *were all he could hear. Tom grasped his head and looked away.*

Kenneth pushed the pause button.

Lydia, who had remained standing beside Tom, touched his hand. "Tom, do you want us to stop the tape?"

"No, just turn the sound down so I can't hear it."

Kenneth muted the sound and continued the tape.

After a few minutes Father Justine walked up to the casket and sprinkled it with holy water. The camera showed the first few pews, where the Bradshaws and Brenda's parents and two sisters sat. Link was between Lydia and Kenneth.

The scene switched to the cemetery. Tom saw Kenneth, Lydia, and Link at the graveside. Father Justine prayed as each family member came up and tossed a single rose on the coffin. The coffin was lowered partially into the ground until the top was at ground level. The scene faded, the tape ended. Kenneth turned off the tape player. Lydia, who had been holding Tom's hand, hugged him. For the first time, Tom began to weep.

Lydia pressed his head against her breasts. He reached around and held her tightly. As he did, he felt excruciating pain in his right thigh. He embraced the pain as well as his mother.

The room had been quiet except for choking sounds as Tom gasped for air between spasmodic sobs. Somehow this signaled the beginning of Tom's recuperation, and of the restoration of them all.

But when Link's heart began to fail, the Bradshaw family was thrust into its present desperation. Driving to the hospital, Lydia remained silent as Tom appeared to be lost in thought. She placed a hand on his shoulder. She wanted desperately to tell Tom about Kenneth's experiments, and the fact that he had been able to preserve a heart for twenty-four hours, still viable for transplant. It pained her to see Tom become more anxious. I must talk with Kenneth as soon as possible, she thought. If Tom knew, it would give him hope, and perhaps he might think of a way to help both Kenneth and Link.

Dr. Cronce looked surprised as he shook Ken's hand. The difference in the two men struck Lydia as almost comical. Ken, over six feet tall, slim, and bearded; Dr. Cronce closer to five feet tall, chubby, and baby-faced. He looked as though he might be a medical student.

"Of course you are aware that Link's condition has been slipping steadily. We're now worried about his kidney function. Blood tests indicate that waste products are present in higher concentrations than normal."

Tom glared at Dr. Cronce. "Why is that? With all the damn meds he's taking. Is there no way to prevent that?"

"The medicine has definitely helped, but it's not enough..."

"Are you suggesting he may need to go on dialysis?" Lydia asked.

"No, not yet. We started a new intravenous medication to help with his cardiac output. That will support kidney function." He looked from Tom to Lydia before continuing. "Maintaining adequate nutritional intake is another problem. Link continues to lose weight. Some of his liver enzymes are elevated. That's adding to his nausea."

Tom stood and began to pace. "What are you trying to tell us? We're going in circles. 'We may have to do this; we may have to do that.' What the hell are you actually going to do?"

Dr. Cronce pushed back his chair and turned to face Tom, who had walked across the room.

"I'm afraid we have no more options as far as medicine is concerned," Dr. Cronce said. "We've pushed up the dosing of all his present medications as high as we dare. The new medicine is helping some but hasn't reversed what's going on."

Tom walked back to the table and sat directly opposite Dr. Cronce.

"Has there been some specific problem that's causing Link to deteriorate so fast?" Tom asked.

"No, we've ruled out other causes and believe it's due to the natural progression of the cardiomyopathy."

"Dr. Cronce," Lydia said. "You told us before that cardiomyopathy is a fancy word for weakening of the heart?"

"Yes, I believe I did say that."

"What you just told us was that the weakening of his heart is due to a weakening of his heart."

"Mother, let's listen to Dr. Cronce."

"I have been listening! It doesn't make any sense to me."

There was a prolonged silence as Lydia waited for Dr. Cronce's response.

Ken broke the silence. "I would say that the heart muscle is weakening because of persistent ischemia." He turned to Lydia, who looked puzzled. "Ischemia is a lack of blood and oxygen being supplied to the heart muscle."

Dr. Cronce reddened. "In my attempt to simplify the explanation, I confused Mrs. Bradshaw."

Lydia spit out the words, "Dr. Cronce, I'm not confused. Please feel free to talk to me as you would any reasonably intelligent person, and let me decide when to simplify."

A deep reddish-purple started above Dr. Cronce's shirt collar. It quickly spread to his entire face. He cleared his throat. "If I might continue...when potential heart transplant recipients are unlikely to survive more than six weeks, they are placed on a special high priority list. It saddens me to say that I and the rest of my colleagues believe Link has reached that point." He paused. As Dr. Cronce continued to speak, Lydia seemed no longer to comprehend what he was saying. Like Tom, she wanted desperately to take Link home and have this nightmare come to an end. Her jaw tightened, catching her lower lip between her front teeth. Blood trickled from her lip. She retrieved a tissue from her purse and blotted her mouth.

"Mother, are you alright?" Tom whispered.

Suddenly Dr. Cronce's words came back into focus. He was explaining, "What I am trying to say is that Link has very high priority status, and we will be contacting every possible source. We've reason to be fairly optimistic about Link's chances of getting a donor now that he'll be moving into this position."

Lydia clutched her purse. She looked down at her hands. She wanted to scream and run from the room.

Tom put his arm around her shoulders. "Will you be okay?"

She wanted to embrace Tom, but was unable to move.

"Mother, would you like Ken to take you home?" Tom asked. "I can stay and talk with Dr. Cronce."

"No, Tom. I want to stay," she whispered.

"Dr. Cronce, is there anything we can do to help?" Tom asked. "We're prepared to pay for additional staff to make the necessary calls to the agencies and hospitals on behalf of Link."

"Dr. Bernholtz has information on the various potential sources," Dr. Cronce said. "If you were to hire such a person he or she could work closely with him. I believe that would be very helpful."

"I've been contacting all the available sources for some time," Ken said. "But additional staff would enable us to keep in daily contact."

"Ken, my administrative assistant at T.B.I. can help," Tom said. "I'll ask her to report to your office in the morning."

The following morning Alison Simmons sat before Ken. She wore a tailored pinstripe suit and a white silk blouse. A pair of reading glasses hung from a chain around her neck. Despite her austere appearance, Tom had told Ken that she was warm and friendly and a marvel on the phone. She was persistent without being pushy.

"Dr. Bernholtz, I'm here at Tom Bradshaw's request. Tell me what to do, and I'll work as long and as hard as necessary."

He pointed to a horizontal file cabinet behind his desk. "Ms. Simmons, in this file drawer are all the possible donor sources within a four-hour access area. Now that Link has been placed on high priority status, you'll need to re-contact all these sources. I have already alerted the National Computer Network."

"I promise you, I will harass the hell out of them, but sweetly."

The woman exuded competence and self-confidence. Ken was pleased with Tom's choice.

"Until I can find you some office space," he said, "you

can work right here. I have an office in the morgue that I can use for now. The extension there is 107. If I'm not there, have the operator page me. I may need to be in and out of here to get files, but otherwise you can have full use of this office."

The day after Marty had seen the autopsy, she sought out Dr. Tupelo. He was sitting at the nurses' station looking through a patient's chart.

She scooted up next to him on a swivel chair. "I heard the code 400 announced yesterday. Did you know the boy who died?"

He looked at her with a puzzled expression.

She realized she wouldn't have known it was a boy. She said, "I heard it was that boy who was hit by a car."

Frank nodded. "He ran into the street to get a ball. There was no way the car could've avoided him."

"Did he die from being run over?"

"No. He died of head injuries."

"Was he already dead when he got to the hospital?"

"He was alive, but he went into a coma. They had to put him on a respirator. His parents agreed to donate one of his kidneys to a boy here who's been on dialysis for a long time."

"It seems really weird to take a kidney out of someone whose heart is still beating."

Marty spun around on the swivel chair. She stopped when her head started to swim.

"You have second thoughts about being an organ donor?"

Forbidden Harvest

"I'm just curious. They're going to be doing it to me someday."

Afterwards, Marty thought about the autopsy. She had seen Dr. Bernholtz take out a kidney and the heart. But the surgeons had already taken out the kidney his parents agreed to donate. Was she seeing things or what? It didn't seem right, she thought, to take extra helpings. She wondered if they'd hollow her out like a chocolate Easter bunny, even though she only wanted Link to have her heart. But she couldn't say anything to Link because it was his Uncle Ken who took the heart. She knew Link liked him a lot. Once Link said he might want to be a doctor who does experiments like his Uncle Ken.

No matter how she tried, Marty couldn't stop wondering why the doctors would take those organs without permission. Then she remembered Link telling her about experiments his Uncle Ken was doing with animals. Maybe he's using them to do experiments. Then she recalled a long time ago seeing a television news story about people picketing in front of Children's Hospital. They said the doctors wanted to use children as guinea pigs.

Maybe Dr. Tupelo was wrong. Maybe the boy's parents gave permission to take out other organs. But how could she find out? That afternoon, Marty couldn't sit still. She made several trips to the nurses' station, asking for Dr. Tupelo. She had to talk with him.

"Marty, I've told you a half-dozen times, he'll be back around four this afternoon. I can ask one of his interns to see you."

"I'll wait."

She was watching *Days of our Lives* on television when Dr. Tupelo came into her room. She pushed the mute button as he parked in a chair next to her bed.

He glanced at the television. "What's your favorite soap?"

"I don't know. Dove, I guess."

"I should have seen that coming."

"I need to ask you some more questions."

"Shoot."

"Doc Frank, after patients die, what happens to their charts?"

"There's a room in the basement where the records are stored. You're sure full of strange questions these days. I would be happy to talk about what's on your mind. You know whatever you tell me is confidential."

"I know. But I can't. Not just now."

Marty called the hospital operator. "Hi, I'm Cindy, one of the volunteer candy stripers. The nurse asked me to get a deceased patient's medical record for a conference. She said it's in the basement, but she didn't know the room number."

"Sure, honey. Let me look it up." She came back on after a few minutes. "I'm sorry it took so long; I had to make a couple of calls. It's room 063. Near where all those photographs are hung."

That's right down from the morgue, Marty thought. She remembered that she had been in there with Annie. The room had smelled musty, and Annie said it was a room she didn't like to work in. She hadn't told Marty why, but it was probably because those were records of kids who had died. Annie may have known some of them.

Marty checked her list of door combinations. There it was-- room 063. That evening, she told the floor nurse she was going to the snack bar. Once in the basement, she went directly to room 063. The corridor was empty. She slipped into the room. The records were filed by the patient identification number. Drat it, she thought. What am I gonna do now?

Then she noticed a computer monitor blinking on a desk in one corner of the room. Using Frank's password, she got into the patient information system and punched in *Lang, David*. His hospital identification number came up on the screen. She went to the files and soon found his chart. It took her a few minutes to locate the organ-donor consent form in the thick medical record. She walked to the copying machine, copied the form, and returned the chart to the file. Just then, she heard someone at the door. She ducked behind a stack of files. She hoped whoever it was wouldn't come down the row she was in.

The files were on a track. In front of the file was something that looked like a steering wheel on a ship. A whole row could be moved in one direction or the other by rotating the wheel. The person was getting closer and closer to where she was hiding. The row she was in began to narrow. As the file rack pressed against her, she screamed.

"Hey! Stop!"

A man peered down the aisle. It was Mr. Foushee, one of the evening-shift orderlies. 'Holy shit, girl! You scared me half to death. What're you doing here?"

Her heart slammed against her chest. "Mr. Foushee, I had something I wanted to copy...I noticed the door was open so I walked in."

"Hey, child, don't fret. I just come to get a chart. Now you carry yourself out of here, and I won't say nothin' to nobody."

"Thanks, Mr. Foushee." She hurried from the room.

Forbidden Harvest

Once in her room, she studied the form. It was signed by Fred and Helen Lang. It said that if their son were to die, they agreed to donate a kidney to a recipient chosen by the hospital authorities. There was no mention of the second kidney or the heart! Yet she saw those organs removed with her own eyes. And by Link's Uncle Ken, one of the top doctors in Seattle. This is radically intense stuff!

"I know this is going to sound really crazy," Marty said as Dr. Tupelo entered her room the following morning, "but I don't know who else to tell."

"I've known something was on your mind." He sat in the chair next to her bed.

"I hid in the space above the ceiling in the morgue, and I watched Dr. Bernholtz do an autopsy on that boy who just died. You know, David Lang."

"Come on, Marty. You don't really expect me to believe you."

She started from the very beginning, how she had decided she wanted to see an autopsy, especially after she agreed to be a heart donor. She told him how she and Link had planned the whole thing. The practice runs, how she had worked out to be strong enough, and how she had been able to talk with Link while she was hiding in the ceiling.

When she got to the vomiting part she embellished it some. She could tell she was knocking him out. He looked really serious.

"What an irresponsible thing to do!" he said. "You could have gotten hurt...I'm surprised that ceiling supported your weight."

"Are you going to turn me in after you said I could tell you anything?"

He shook his head. She continued. "I saw Dr. Bernholtz and his assistant do the autopsy. They took out the other kidney and the boy's heart."

"Marty, they were probably going to perform tests on the organs and then put them back later. Why would they steal organs? They'd have to be used right away to be any good."

"They couldn't put them back, because I saw Dr. Jamael sew the body closed after Dr. Bernholtz put the heart and kidney in a box that looked like a big ice chest. He took it to his laboratory."

"Well, it's possible that the family gave the hospital permission to remove other organs. He probably was running some kind of tests."

There was a book on Marty's bed. She picked it up and removed a folded piece of paper. She handed it to Frank. It was a copy of the donor consent form. He studied it for a few seconds.

"How on earth did you get this?"

"Face it, Frank. I'm clever as hell."

She told him how she had managed to get into the record room in the basement. She left out the fact that Ned Foushee had caught her in the act.

"You could have been confused," Frank said. "You've never seen an autopsy before."

"I swear to God, I saw Dr. Bernholtz hold that boy's heart in his hand. I was so close I could almost have reached out and touched Dr. Bernholtz on the head. If the boy's body is still here you could check for yourself."

"Not possible. The mortician would have picked up the body the same day."

"Couldn't the undertaker tell if some of the organs were

missing?"

"They use a special embalming technique for people who have donated organs. They wouldn't know which organs were removed."

"So there's no way to find out?" Marty asked.

"Dr. Bernholtz never allows students or residents in the morgue when he does an autopsy on a transplant donor," Frank said. "He says he has to work very rapidly, and that learners would distract him."

"I wouldn't want anyone there either, if I was stealing hearts and kidneys," Marty said.

"Marty, don't breathe a word of this to anyone, and please, no more snooping. I'm sure there is some logical explanation. Even raising such a question could hurt Dr. Bernholtz. He's really close to the Bradshaws. Did you know that he's Link's godfather?"

She nodded. Tears filled her eyes. "I'm sorry I ever went up there. I don't want to do anything to hurt Link."

Frank stood. He put an arm around her. She leaned against him. She remembered that once he told her that his mother wanted him to be a dentist.

"I'm glad you didn't become a dentist."

"I'm sure we'll find there's nothing to this," he said. "In the meantime, remember, speak not and snoop not."

"One last question."

"Just one. Now what?"

Her voice suddenly failed her, and words came out in a whisper. "If Dr. Ken could do that...I mean, break the law and all, why couldn't he have just given that heart to Link?"

After leaving Marty's room, Frank went to the residents' room and lay on the lower bunk. He had to think this through. Could the ceiling in the morgue be strong enough to hold her weight, he wondered? Then he recalled the large light over the autopsy table and the heavy scale hanging from a chain. That ceiling had to be stronger than average. Yes, it probably could hold someone as light as Marty.

But a fifteen-year-old seeing an autopsy for the first time might well be confused. On the other hand, if she wasn't confused, the donor permit did show the Langs gave permission for removal of only one kidney. But Marty seemed so sure of what she had seen.

He knew any accusation that proved to be false would certainly ruin his own chances of being chief resident the following year, to say nothing of the impact on his plan to apply for a fellowship in pediatric cardiology.

Dr. Bernholtz might be taking the organs simply for teaching purposes, Frank thought. That's probably it. It's done all the time. He wished he had told Marty that.

Could Dr. Bernholtz be doing experiments on the organs? Everyone knew how the Human Subjects Committee had denied him permission to go ahead with his research.

Could there be any other motive? He had heard of black market organs being sold to the highest bidders. But he couldn't reconcile that with what he knew of Dr. Bernholtz.

He recalled how Dr. Bernholtz had helped the Saudi doctors bring their children to Seattle for transplant surgery. The national press had picked up the story. The effort was a great success. Saudi children were going back to their country with American hearts and other organs. He recalled a special commendation of Dr. Bernholtz by the Saudi royal family. President Bush had commented on national television that programs, such as the one Dr. Bernholtz had initiated in Seattle, do more to cement relations between the United States and our friends abroad than millions of dollars in foreign aid. He referred to it as, "one of those thousand points of light."

Frank sat up suddenly, striking his head on the upper bunk. "Damn!" Could Dr. Bernholtz be passing these organs on to the Saudi doctors?

Frank recalled Ken taking a group of pediatric residents to the Hakim Medical Center. The Saudis treated him like visiting royalty. Ken was bursting with pride as they rounded and met some of the children recovering from transplant surgery. He spoke to some of the children in Arabic.

The older children greeted him by name, obviously coached by the Saudi physicians.

Even if Dr. Bernholtz were operating out of purely altruistic motives, removing organs without parental consent and doing experiments on human tissues without approval of the Human Subjects Committee was unethical. Was it even more than unethical? If they were paying him for the organs, that would be a felony. Frank didn't want to be the one to expose Ken, even assuming he was guilty. But would that constitute a cover-up of what he knew to be a criminal act?

He sat at his computer and looked up Link's labs. The kidney and liver tests were showing signs of continuing loss of normal function. His most recent x-ray showed that the pneumonic process in the left lower lobe wasn't clearing, despite antibiotics. Frank called the infectious disease consultant immediately. He headed for Link's room.

CHAPTER TWENTY-ONE

As Link's condition worsened, he seldom used his computer. The least thing exhausted him. Television, however, was like easing into a sauna. It took no effort. He let plots and characters wash over him, and with the sound muted, the screen was hypnotic. He especially liked black-and-white reruns; the familiar silent images were old friends.

He could see the sadness in everyone's eyes, but nobody talked to him about dying, not even his grandmother or his dad. Father Justine had sometimes, but not lately. The only person who talked about death was Marty. She asked him if he was scared of dying. They talked about what it would be like. Although Marty was also going to Mount Saint John, she wasn't Catholic. She told Link that her mother liked the school for all the reasons Marty hated it. The sisters, even the lay teachers, were really strict, and they zonked you with tons of homework. Link told her about heaven and how only Jesus and His mother Mary had their bodies. "All the rest are spirits." He talked about purgatory and hell.

He told Marty that Father Justine said he would certainly go to heaven and wouldn't have to stop in purgatory even a single minute. And that his mother would be waiting for him.

Forbidden Harvest

"I wish I could be sure like you are," Marty said.

"If they have computers up there, I'll figure out some way to send you a message," Link said.

Frank had stopped by radiology to get a look at Link's chest X-ray. Why wasn't the infection responding to antibiotics? Could he be missing something? Link was asleep when Frank arrived. There were dark hollows beneath his eyes, and his breathing sounded noisy. Frank turned off the television and gently woke him.

"I know your dad will be here soon, so I won't stay too long."

Link's voice was hoarse. Frank could hear the junk in his chest without a stethoscope.

"Grandma was here," Link whispered. "She always likes me to sit up in the chair. She says I'll get weaker staying in bed all day"

Frank helped Link into a sitting position and put a stethoscope to his chest.

"You still have a patch of infection in your left lung. I've asked the infectious disease doctors to see you tonight. I want their opinion about which antibiotics we should try. The one you're taking isn't helping. Tell your dad in case he's here when they come. I called, but couldn't get through to him."

Frank sat in a chair next to Link's bed. "Marty told me about sneaking into the morgue and seeing the autopsy of the boy who was killed in the auto accident."

Link's eyes opened wide. "She did?"

"You must be sure not to tell anyone because she could get in a lot of trouble. This has to be a secret between you, and me, and Marty."

"I should've tried to talk her out of it. But there's no changing her mind. And she needed my help."

Frank wondered how Link could possibly have helped her. "Well, the important thing now is not to breathe a word of this to anyone. Even if someone should ask you directly, tell them you have no idea what they're talking about. I don't like to ask you to lie, but for all you know Marty could have been sitting in her room just play-acting the whole thing. You know what a ham she is."

"No, Doc Frank, it really happened. She was up there in that ceiling in the morgue. I don't mind telling a lie if it's gonna keep her out of trouble."

Throughout the day, Frank continued to think about how he might prove to Marty that she was wrong about Dr. Ken taking the organs illegally. But first he had to convince himself. He checked the date of the kidney harvesting operation on David Lang. Then he asked some nurses at Children's Hospital if they knew nursing staff at the Hakim Medical Center. It turned out that several of the hospital temps had been offered jobs there. He made a list of names, called hospital personnel and asked in which departments they had worked. He learned that one had worked in the operating room at Children's Hospital. She might prove to be helpful.

At the Hakim Medical Center, Tina Carrol was preparing the operating room for surgery. The ward secretary poked her head into the room. "There's someone's on the phone for you, Tina."

Tina picked up the phone at the nurses' station. "Hello, this is Tina Carrol."

"Hi, I'm Frank Tupelo. I'm a resident at Children's Hospital. I understand you worked here as a temp."

Tina remembered Frank. She carried the phone to the

charting area, away from the secretary. Why is he calling me? "Yes, I did. I remember you. I'd say about five ten, dark brown eyes, wavy black hair, olive complexion, and a friendly smile. Am I thinking of the right person?"

"That's close enough, I guess. I'm preparing a report for Dr. Bernholtz, and I need a listing of all transplant surgeries at the Hakim Medical Center over the past month. Would it be possible for you to copy the daily operating-room schedules and fax them to me, here at Children's?"

Tina had often seen Frank during his internship year. Since he was one of the few unattached male residents, more than several of the nurses were interested in him. But he seemed totally involved with his young patients, oblivious of the staff. Yet here he was calling her! The request seemed simple enough. Everyone at the Hakim Medical Center knew of Dr. Bernholtz. She also thought Frank was intriguing. She didn't want to turn him away.

"Dr. Tupelo, we don't have a fax in the OR department. I live in Seattle, and I'd be glad to drop the copies off at Children's Hospital. Are you on duty tonight?"

"I am. That would be terrific. Have the operator page me. I'll meet you in the lobby."

After work, Tina stopped by her apartment to change before going to Children's Hospital. Her white stockings, dowdy uniform, and nursing shoes weren't exactly sexy.

Tina saw Frank as he stepped from the escalator. He looked about the lobby, but obviously didn't recognize her. He was probably expecting someone in a nurse's uniform, not high heels and a snug-fitting black cocktail dress. Soft blond curls bounced against her bare shoulders as she walked toward him. She reached for his hand.

"Hello, Frank."

Forbidden Harvest

His mouth hung slightly ajar as he pumped her hand.

"Here are the OR logs you asked for." She handed him an envelope.

"You're Tina Carrol?"

"I'm crushed. You don't remember me?"

"I don't get to the OR often."

"I'm on my way to a dinner party and was afraid it would be too late if I stopped by afterwards. Please call me if you need any more help. My number's in the envelope."

She smiled and turned to leave; after a few steps she looked back at him and waved. He looked like a deer staring into onrushing high beams.

Once in his room, Frank removed the operating room schedules from the envelope and looked for one dated October 25th, the day David Lang died. If his hunch was correct, these sheets should be helpful. He located the schedule for the day of the autopsy, and found that neither a kidney or heart transplant had been performed. Frank was relieved. He felt mortified that he had mistrusted a respected colleague. Now he could tell Marty that she was mistaken, that Dr. Bernholtz was merely using the organs for teaching purposes. It's strange, he thought, how a tiny seed of doubt can germinate into an elaborate conspiracy theory. He looked at Tina Carrol's phone number. How could he not remember her? She had certainly given him the full, I'd-like-to-get-to-know-you gaze.

Without knowing exactly why, he continued to leaf through the daily schedules. As he glanced at the surgeries performed October 26, the day after the autopsy, he saw listed two transplant operations. A kidney and heart transplant!

He wondered if Dr. Bernholtz might be trying to test his

preservation process. If that were true, it looked as though he had been successful well beyond what was known to be possible. The heart transplant had been done twenty-four hours after the organs had been harvested! Was it a coincidence, or could these be the kidney and heart of poor little David Lang?

He decided to wait for the next organ-harvesting operation and afterwards use ultrasound to check the body for missing organs. He needed solid evidence before he would even consider confronting Dr. Bernholtz. The problem was how to do the ultrasound examination between the time the autopsy was completed and the mortician arrived to pick up the body. With Dr. Bernholtz and his assistants in the next room, it would be too risky to try to do that in the morgue.

He headed for Marty's room. He had to convince her not to tell anyone else about their concerns.

She was sitting on her bed, cross-legged, painting her fingernails a candy-apple red. Music was blasting from a portable cassette player.

"You like Bon Jovi?" Frank shouted as he turned down the volume.

"He's totally radical. Doc Frank, I've been thinking about what you said. Maybe they were just going to use those organs to show medical students. I asked a student. He said the fine print in an autopsy permit gives the pathologist permission to save specimens. You know, like to show to students."

"You didn't tell the student anything about what you saw?"

Marty began to color the toenails on her good leg.

"I promised you I wouldn't tell anyone."

"Good. That's probably exactly what happened. Just to

prove that there's nothing to all of this, the next time they announce a code 400 I'm going to check out the body afterwards. I'm sure I'm not going to find anything missing."

Marty's eyes opened wide. She put aside her nail polish. She went to the door to her room, closed it, and said softly, "So you really think something funny is going on?"

"No, I just want to prove to you and myself that there isn't anything going on."

She pointed above her head. "Why not hide in the ceiling like I did? I can give you pointers."

"Even if I weighed eighty-five pounds, I'd be afraid to try a stunt like that." Frank laughed. "Can you imagine me crashing through the ceiling and landing on top of the autopsy table?"

"Yeah, and Dr. Bernholtz would say, 'How nice of you to drop in.'"

"I'll have to check the body after the autopsy."

"How can you tell after it's zipped up?"

"I'll use ultrasound."

She hoisted herself back onto the bed and resumed applying nail polish. "That's a great idea. But how can you? Dr. Bernholtz and his assistant run in and out of the morgue all the time."

He was reluctant to tell her the specifics, but if he didn't she might continue to snoop. He explained that if code 400 were called late in the evening, or during the night, the mortician would not pick up the body until morning. Nobody would be in the morgue or the laboratory. He could get in with the ultrasound unit and have the place to himself.

"What about during the day?"

He shook his head. There was no halfway with Marty. "That's trickier. I'll find out which undertaker will be picking up the body. I'll ask him to have the hospital operator beep me when he has the body on the loading dock. I'll offer to bring the signed death certificate to him."

"But how can you do anything with him there?"

"I'll arrange to have the operator beep me while I'm talking to him. I'll pretend Dr. Bernholtz's assistant wants me to bring back the body for a bone-marrow biopsy. Then I'll send the mortician off to the snack bar. While he's gone, I'll duck into a room where I'll have the ultrasound machine stashed."

"Awesome! Hey, I can beep you."

"No. Absolutely not."

"Okay, but what if that mortician comes back before you're finished? Maybe I should be in the snack bar. You know, talk to him."

"You stay put, young lady." He tugged at the peak of her baseball cap.

She shrugged. "Okay. You're right. Your plan sounds like something Link..." She broke off in mid-sentence. Her lower lip quivered.

"What is it?"

"I just came from his room. They're moving him to the CCU."

"I know."

Marty's eyes glistened.

"I sat there, running off my mouth as usual. He didn't even open his eyes. He's giving up."

"He's so weak, talking is too much effort. He needs to be in intensive care where they can insert a catheter that measures pressures in the heart chambers. That way they can regulate his fluids better."

"They only let family in there. But I've got to be able to see him."

"Marty, call Link's grandmother. If anyone can get you in there, she can." He reached in his breast pocket and pulled out one of his index cards. "I have Mrs. Bradshaw's phone number right here."

Marty wrote the number on the back of her hand. As soon as Dr. Tupelo left, she called Mrs. Bradshaw. She answered the phone immediately.

"Mrs. Bradshaw, this is Marty. I guess you already know that Link is going back in the CCU?"

"Yes, Link's father called. I was just getting ready to leave for the hospital. It's was thoughtful of you to call."

"They won't let me visit him in the CCU. Could you adopt me or something?"

"I'll see to that as soon as I get to the hospital. It would be fun to have an honorary granddaughter!"

Forbidden Harvest

CHAPTER TWENTY-TWO

As Ken sat at his desk in the morgue, he looked about the room in disgust. He never realized how hard it would be to get suitable space after giving his office to Ms. Simmons. He seldom used the morgue office. It was cluttered with old journals and other junk. The smell of formaldehyde was overpowering. He called hospital housekeeping and asked that they do some heavy-duty cleaning.

He walked to the file cabinet, and as he was about to slide open the top drawer, he noticed that the journals and coffee mugs that had been piled on top were now stacked on the floor. A note signed by Annie was lying on top of the journals. It said that she had moved them to clean the cabinet top. She added a postscript that said she had run out of time and would return to clean it later. He was surprised, because besides emptying his waste basket every day, Annie hardly ever moved anything. She mostly dusted and hauled away papers and magazines he indicated he wanted her to get rid of. He suspected the morgue creeped her out.

When Annie stepped into the morgue with her cleaning supplies, Ken told her he got her note. "I guess you haven't had a chance to finish up."

"Dr. Bernholtz, I don't know what you talkin' about."

Forbidden Harvest

She looked about the office. "Yes, this here room is gonna take the best part of the mornin' to clean up right. By afternoon everything will be like new."

"I have some things I need to do here. Could you come back a little later?"

"Yes, sir. I'll be down the hall. Just come git me."

After she left, he sat at the desk, wondering what the hell was going on. Who wrote that note if Annie hadn't? Had someone been snooping in his office? He looked through the desk drawers and his files. Nothing had been taken that he could tell. He pushed his chair back and looked under the desk. Something caught his eye. It was a sliver of glass. Using a pen-light he could see several other pieces of glass. Something had obviously broken. Had someone removed the rest of the glass, and hadn't thought to look under the desk? Who had been there and what were they looking for? Despite the coolness of the room, he began to perspire.

Why had someone cleared off the top of the cabinet? He looked at the ceiling above the file cabinet. Something about it had caught his eye. A corner of one of the sections was not placed properly in its metal framing. Had someone climbed up there to spy on him?

He dragged a chair over and stood on it. He could see smudges along one edge where someone's dirty hands may have gripped it. Pulling himself onto the top, he raised the ceiling tile and, using his flashlight, looked about the space above the ceiling.

God, something must've died up here, he thought. When he turned off his flashlight he could see rays of light coming through a spot near the center of the ceiling. He looked at the tile he had removed and noticed someone had drawn a large cross on the back surface. After replacing the tile he stepped down from the cabinet to the chair and, as he grasped the back, it tipped over, sending him sprawling.

"Son of a bitch!"

Jamael rushed into the morgue from the adjoining laboratory. He helped Ken to his feet.

Ken thanked him. "They don't make these flimsy damn chairs like they used to."

"Dr. Bernholtz, I was getting ready to go to lunch. Do you think I should remain here in case you have any more need for me?"

"Very funny. I believe I'll manage, thank you."

After Jamael left, Ken walked to the stainless steel table in the center of the room. Above it was a ceiling tile with a small wedge missing. He climbed onto the table and examined the tile. It had not been damaged accidentally. The edges were smooth, as though cut with a knife. Someone had entered the ceiling space to watch him do an autopsy!

Was it just curiosity, or did someone suspect what Ken was up to? It couldn't have been a very large person; those tiles couldn't support much weight. Had the person seen just any autopsy...or did he or she watch the David Lang procedure?

The hospital is full of curious children, he thought. Could a child have observed him without any help? How would he even begin to figure out who the child was? Then he remembered Marty asking if she could see an autopsy. Yes, he thought, that young lady is brash enough to have carried it off, despite her missing leg. He recalled running into Marty and Link near the morgue. Might his godson have been involved?

So many unanswered questions. How would Marty have known when he was going to do an autopsy? How could she get into the locked morgue? Only he and Jamael knew the combination. And of course, Annie.

He found her down the hall. "You can go back now, Annie. Oh, be careful; there's some broken glass under the desk."

"Somebody broke something. I found a bunch of glass in the trash the other day."

"Have you seen anyone hanging around the morgue lately?"

"No, sir, I ain't."

"Do you know a young girl named Marty Lopinski?"

"I sure do. She used to come around a lot just to talk. I figure she must be lonely bein' in the hospital all the time. I sure do like that little girl. I ain't seen her for a few days. I hope nothin' happened to her."

"Oh no, she's just fine. She told me to say hello. That's all."

Ken's regular office, located on the sixth floor in the administrative wing, had an unopposed view of Portage Bay. It was six AM. as Alison Simmons watched a small tugboat struggle to push a massive flat barge, loaded with gravel, toward Lake Union. She felt somewhat like the tiny boat as she tried to manipulate a large, complex, organ-procurement system. She soon learned that it was fruitless to call anyone before nine, so she started at six, calling hospitals and other centers in the east, and gradually worked her way across the time zones. In areas that were beyond or close to the four-hour procurement limit, or where commercial airlines were not readily accessible, she had to line up private carriers. Her worst fear was that even if she were able to find a suitable heart for Link, she might not be able to get it to Children's Hospital in time.

She sat at her desk, several files that listed potential private donors spread out before her. Ken's secretary placed calls from a listing Alison had given her. The logistics of contacting people was frustrating. Over the intercom the secretary said, "Ms. Simmons, I have the hospital operator at Saint Christopher's in San Diego on line three."

"Hello, I'm calling for Dr. Bernholtz in Seattle, and I need to speak with Mrs. Young, your organ procurement coordinator."

"Hold please, I'll connect you." After several rings, the operator asked, "Would you like her voice mail?"

Alison placed her hand over the mouthpiece "If I get one more damn recording...." She removed her hand and said, "Yes, please."

"Ms. Simmons, I have Dr. Collins in Boise on line two."

"Dr. Collins, Alison Simmons here. I spoke with you earlier this week."

"I'm afraid there's not much change in Matthew's condition."

"Dr. Collins, did you receive all the data you requested on Link Bradshaw?"

"Yes, I did. It appears that Matthew would be an entirely suitable donor."

"Link's condition is desperate, Dr. Collins. Please call me immediately when you determine your patient is near death. Do you mind if I call you back in a couple of days to see how things are going?"

"Of course not."

Many of the people she contacted told her that most of

their potential donors were much smaller than Link. Despite his high-priority status, she was beginning to wonder if she would find a heart. Matthew was their best lead. If only Link can hang on long enough. He must, she thought.

Tom and Lydia called her twice a day for a rundown on prospects. Everyone was desperate. Only days remained.

After talking with Link's grandmother, Marty decided to go to the residents' on-call room. A sleepy-looking intern answered the door.

"Dr. Tupelo said it's okay if I use the computer."

"You won't bother me. I had four hits last night. I just hope this is a quiet night." He climbed into the lower bunk and pulled the sheet over his head.

The room smelled of old socks and stale popcorn. It was dark except for the greenish glow that came from the computer screen.

Using Frank's password, she got into a search program called Medline. She fumbled around, trying to remember how he did it. Finally the words on the screen read, *connect, 20201, National Library of Medicine, Bethesda, Maryland.*

She wanted information about the drug Dr. Gibbs had mentioned. A message on the screen asked which database she wanted to search. There was a long list. She chose *Cancerlit*, the same one Frank had shown her. It asked her for the name of the cancer. She typed in *osteosarcoma*. From another list she chose *chemotherapy*. This brought up another menu: *therapy based on disease staging; single drug therapy; multiple drug therapy; and experimental protocols.*

She chose *experimental protocols.* It listed several different numbers. There it was---EP149. There was a long narrative describing the drug, the history of its use, and toxic side effects. It listed the centers and the doctors approved for treatment. Children's Memorial Hospital in Seattle was among the hospitals mentioned: *Local investigator: Dr. Norma Gibbs.*

By this time, the intern was making loud breathing sounds, less like a snore than a kind of gasping. It reminded her of when she was little, and her father would come home drunk. Her parents would fight, and then he'd sleep on the couch. Once, he pushed her mother, and she fell and hurt herself. That night Marty lay awake listening to her father snoring. She prayed to God he would stop breathing. But he didn't. He kept drinking. The arguing and fighting got worse. After he left, he never came around, even for her birthdays. Some father! Her mom hardly ever talked about him, and after awhile, Marty rarely thought about him. Was he still alive? Did he even know she was sick? Did he care?

She leaned forward, trying to concentrate on the screen. In the thirty-two people to whom EP149 had been given, all the patients had metastatic disease and all had a minimum of two courses of conventional therapy. Only six of the thirty-two patients had a favorable response. And only two had a complete remission. That's only about a six-percent chance of being cured. Pretty poor odds, she thought, considering it's such a toxic drug.

There was a box with the word *WARNING* in bold print. It said that the difference between the effective treatment dose and the lethal dose was minimal, and extreme care had to be employed.

Marty again looked at the toxicity information. It described kidney and liver damage, but didn't say that it could hurt the heart. If I die my heart may still be okay for transplant, she thought. Dear God, please make Link be still alive if that happens.

That evening her mother visited, wearing a long, cotton print skirt that came almost to her ankles. She had on a loose- fitting lacy blouse and a necklace made up of tiny sea shells. "You look great tonight, Mom. I always like it when you wear your sixties stuff."

"Most everything I own is sixties, except clothes for the office."

Marty sat on the edge of her bed in the lotus position.

"I've been thinking about that new treatment a lot. Did you know that Dr. Gibbs is one of only six doctors in the whole country approved to use the drug?"

"Oh..."

Marty went on to explain what she had learned.

"Has Dr. Gibbs been talking with you?"

"No, Doc Frank showed me where to get the information."

She could see her mom was upset. She had this habit of biting her cheek and scrunching her eyes when she was trying not to lose her temper.

"What happens to the children who don't respond?" her mom asked.

"That's the bad part. Three children had to go on kidney machines. And three kids died because their livers were shot."

Her mother's face reddened. "Damn it, Marty, Dr. Tupelo shouldn't be filling you up with all that crap without me being here."

"Mom, it didn't really happen like that. He wouldn't go

behind your back."

"It sounds like an awfully dangerous treatment to me...it kills more kids than it cures."

"But all of those kids were going to die without the treatment. The odds are lousy, but it's a chance."

Her mother fell into the upholstered chair alongside Marty's bed. She leaned back, dropped her beaded purse to the floor and closed her eyes.

Marty was about to say something, but decided to give her mom a chance to calm down.

"How is Link doing?" her mother asked, eyes still closed.

Marty wanted to press her mother harder about the experimental drug, but decided she'd better back off. She told her mother that Link had been moved to the CCU.

"But I'll still be able to visit him." She went on to tell her that Link's grandmother fixed it.

She and her mom talked about how much they had enjoyed the weekly dinners with Link and his dad. "Mom, I think you and Link's dad should keep up the tradition and go out to dinner every week on your own."

Gladys stood and put her arms around her daughter. "You're not fat enough to be cupid."

"I think he's real nice, and I've noticed the way he looks at you. I'd go for it."

Her mom smiled and shook her head. Marty leaned toward her. "I want to start that treatment as soon as possible. Dr. Gibbs said now is the best time. I'm not keen on dying, but if I do, I want Link to have my heart. Don't you see? It'll be like part of me will still go on?"

"Damn it, honey, I don't know what's the right thing to do." She stood and squeezed Marty. "But I promise to call

Dr. Gibbs, so the three of us can talk."

"Let's do it as soon as possible." Marty clung to her mother.

Dr. Gibbs' office was in the hospital administrative wing, just down the hall from Dr. Bernholtz. As Marty and Gladys waited for Dr. Gibbs to return from rounds, Marty stood at the window overlooking Portage Bay.

"Wouldn't it be great to live on a houseboat? You could take off whenever you wanted."

Gladys stood behind Marty. She put her arms around her waist. "Not for me, sweetheart. I always get a sinking feeling whenever I'm on a boat."

Marty laughed. "Link would call that a malapropism."

Dr. Gibbs entered her office, a stethoscope poking from a side pocket of her knee-high white doctor coat. She wore thick glasses that made her pale blue eyes look small and round. Her smile only went half way, as though she didn't really didn't mean it.

She sat at her desk, giving them her fifty-percent smile.

"Yes, Mrs. Lopinski, you asked to see me this morning. How can I help you?"

Gladys and Marty sat in chairs opposite Dr. Gibbs. Gladys explained that she was afraid of the experimental treatment, EP149, but that Marty had wanted her to consider it.

"You understand, Mrs. Lopinski, that we must have your written permission?"

Marty was afraid that her mother might change her mind, because she didn't answer Dr. Gibbs right away.

"Yeah, my mom and I talked it over," Marty said. "She's willing to let me go ahead." She turned to her mother. "Right, Mom?"

Her mother nodded. Dr. Gibbs began to explain about her experience with the drug. She told Gladys pretty much what Marty had read on the computer program. Her mother then signed a consent form. Marty knew about the possible liver and kidney damage, but there were a lot of other reactions as well. As Dr. Gibbs described a bunch of bad things, Marty's hands began to get cold and sweaty. The toes of her good foot felt squishy inside her sneaker.

"Honey," her mom asked, "Are you absolutely sure you want to go through with this?"

Marty nodded. But her brain was telling her she had to be crazy to have the treatment. It's like going before a firing squad, and expecting every one of them would miss.

Dr. Gibbs went on to describe the treatment. They would give EP149 intravenously on three consecutive days. Children who responded usually did so within four weeks. The highest risk of toxicity was in the first four to five days. While the drug was being administered, blood tests would be done every eight hours. Baseline tests would be needed. Treatment would start the following Monday.

Before leaving the administrative area, Marty said goodbye to her mother; then walked to Dr. Bernholtz's office. She wanted to talk with Ms. Simmons to see if she was having any luck finding a heart for Link. A secretary sat in an open area near his office door. "I'm a friend of Link Bradshaw. I'd like to talk with Ms. Simmons."

The secretary spoke into an intercom on her desk. "Yes. Go right in."

Marty hadn't seen Alison Simmons before. She was wearing a silk shirt with a button-down collar and a man's tie. She stood and shook Marty's hand.

"I've heard Mr. Bradshaw speak of you. It's nice to finally meet you."

On the desk was a photograph of Link's grandmother, Dr. Bernholtz, and another man she figured was Link's grandfather. They were all smiling and looked really young. Dr. Bernholtz didn't have a beard, but she could tell it was him.

"I heard you found somebody who's the same blood type and about the same age as Link."

"The boy's type O negative. That's compatible with Link's blood type. The boy's desperately sick. Nobody understands how he's able to go on so long. He could end up outliving Link."

Marty sat quietly for a moment. She began to cry. Alison walked over to her and pressed Marty to her chest. Ms. Simmons had soft cushiony breasts. Would she ever have breasts like Ms. Simmons? Marty wondered. She noticed the mess her mascara had made on Ms. Simmons' shirt.

"I'm sorry ..."

"Don't worry about it."

Marty was surprised to see tears in Ms. Simmons' eyes. She was glad this lady was looking for a heart for Link. She wished she had started a whole lot sooner. Why do people get so sick so quickly? That's just not fair.

Forbidden Harvest

CHAPTER TWENTY-THREE

Marty picked up a book Doc Frank had given her. It was about cancer patients, written by a surgeon whose picture was on the book jacket. He had a big smile, a happy face. Marty thought it looked kind of peculiar for the cover of a cancer book. But Dr. Tupelo had said it was really good and had helped some of his other patients. She wondered whose fingers had turned the pages. Was it a boy or girl? Were they still alive? Marty loved the smell of new books. She sniffed it. It didn't smell good. It reminded her of Crystal. Marty met her the last time she was in the hospital. Crystal was waiting for a kidney transplant. How many kids like Crystal had breathed on those pages? Marty closed the book and placed it on the bedside table. Her phone rang.

"Hello, Marty, this is Dr. Bernholtz. There's something I have to talk with you about. Could you come to my office in the morgue this morning?"

Marty's stomach bunched into a tight ball. Holy cow! What does he want to see me for? It's about that autopsy, I know it is. No way she wanted to go there. "The morgue kind of gives me the heebie-jeebies," she said. "Could you come to my room?"

"No, I believe it would be best to meet down here where we won't be interrupted."

She tried to sound calm, but her voice still came out trembly. "I go to physical therapy from nine to ten. I could be there around ten-thirty."

Marty ran down to the nurses' station and asked if anyone had seen Dr. Tupelo. The nurse told her that he had gone to X-ray with a group of doctors. Marty returned to her room. She called the operator and asked her to beep Dr. Tupelo. He called right back.

"Doc Frank, this is Marty. Dr. Bernholtz...he just called. Wants me to come to the morgue to see him. I'm scared. You think he found out somehow? How could he?"

"Hey, slow down. He probably just wants to talk with you about Link."

"Even if he figured out I watched an autopsy, he wouldn't know which one I saw, right?"

"You're getting all worked for no reason. Just wait and see what he wants to talk about."

"Were there any regular autopsies around that time that you know about?"

"Yes, the day before the David Lang autopsy. A four-year-old boy drowned and was brought to the Emergency Room. They did the autopsy that afternoon. In fact, I stopped in and saw part it. I had done CPR on the boy in the Emergency Room."

"What part of the autopsy did you see?" Marty asked.

"He was examining the lungs when I came in."

"Did you say anything?"

"I told him I ran the code on the boy, but that it looked pretty hopeless from the start. Dr. Bernholtz said that from the looks of the lungs there was no chance I could have revived him."

Forbidden Harvest

She could hardly breathe as she thought of that little boy's lungs filling with water as he struggled for air. How must Doc Frank have felt when he couldn't save him?

"Are you still there, Marty?" Frank asked.

"Yeah. Thanks."

The door to the morgue was locked. Marty knocked, but no one answered. She knocked louder and finally Dr. Bernholtz opened it.

"I thought it was you, Marty. Did you forget the combination?"

The way he looked at her, she knew he had figured out that she had watched an autopsy. Maybe he's just guessing. I have to play it cool, she thought.

He led her to his office and pulled out an extra chair.

Her right knee was shaking so bad she was sure he could tell how nervous she was. As she sat, she folded her good leg under her. He must've found out, but how?

"Marty, somebody has been snooping around the morgue. I have reason to believe you might know something."

She tried to sound shocked. "What makes you think that?"

Her mouth was so dry, her lips stuck to her teeth.

"Marty, you're a very clever girl, the way you made friends with Annie so you could learn the combination numbers. And that note was written beforehand, so you must've scouted out the place. And I bet you intended to clean off the top of the cabinet and wash the cups, but you were afraid of being discovered."

Marty lower lip began to quiver. She fought back tears. She was stunned how much he had been able to figure out.

"So you took a pen from my desk and wrote a postscript. You were quite right in thinking I might have noticed that the journals had been moved, so the note was meant to quiet my curiosity. And the way you marked that ceiling tile with magic marker so you could find your way out. Very clever. But you weren't very careful cleaning up the broken glass. My guess is that you probably dropped your flashlight."

She nodded. When she was finally able to speak her voice sounded like someone else's. "I'm really, really sorry, Dr. Bernholtz. You said I couldn't see an autopsy. I wanted to...really bad."

"Why is that?"

"I know someday I'm gonna be on that table. I had to see what it would be like. I didn't mean to hurt anybody. I didn't get to see much, either."

"You certainly didn't come down until every one was gone, so you must have seen the entire autopsy."

"No. When you made that first big cut all the way down the front, and I saw the little boy's insides, I covered the hole with my hand and threw up. And I was afraid to look because I thought it would make me sick again. I took my hand off when I heard Dr. Tupelo's voice. He's my doctor."

Dr. Bernholtz smiled. He leaned back in his chair and kept nodding his head and stroking his beard. His face wasn't so serious anymore. *It really worked, she thought! He thinks I saw a regular autopsy. I'll lay it on extra thick.* "So you saw the rest of the autopsy?"

"Well, I saw you doing something in the boy's chest and showing it to Dr. Tupelo, but it felt like I was going to get sick again so I stopped watching."

He wheeled his chair over to where she was sitting and put a hand on her shoulder. "You shouldn't have come into the morgue without permission, and climbing above those ceiling tiles was very foolish. You could have fallen and injured yourself. Tell me, have you mentioned this to anyone else?"

"Link would be the only person I would tell, but he's been so sick, he doesn't seem to care."

He looked really serious again.

"Well, if I hear you've told anyone I will be forced to report this."

"I swear I won't tell anybody."

Dr. Bernholtz scooted his chair back to his desk. "Marty, I don't want to get you in trouble, but breaking and entering is pretty serious. So this has to be our little secret."

"Sir, my lips are sealed." Holding her hands low so he couldn't see them, she crossed her fingers.

"Good. Very good."

"Dr. Bernholtz, could I ask you something?"

"Of course, Marty. What is it?"

"Have you ever heard of a chemotherapy drug called EP149?"

"That's a code name for an experimental drug. I'm afraid I am not familiar with it."

"I'm supposed to get it next week. I'm excited and kind of scared at the same time. One of every eighteen kids went into remission. But the odds of being killed by the treatment are the same. Maybe I should say goodbye now," Marty said, lowering her head.

"Of course not! Young lady, if anyone can survive that treatment, you will. Now run along and think positive."

Forbidden Harvest

CHAPTER TWENTY-FOUR

Ken sat at his desk, mulling over their conversation. Marty had looked so damn frightened when he confronted her. He tried to convince himself that she had not observed the David Lang autopsy.

Had she lied? If so, how in hell would she know about the other autopsy, about Dr. Tupelo being there? She could have seen both autopsies and was lying about not seeing the second. But why would Marty risk a second snooping expedition?

On the other hand, if she had only seen the David Lang autopsy, she must somehow have found out about the one he had done the previous day.

He suddenly recalled what Annie said about finding broken glass in the wastebasket. Did she empty it every day? If so she might recall which day she had found broken glass. He left his office to talk with her. If broken glass had been in the wastebasket on Thursday, the day of the drowned boy's autopsy, then Marty was telling the truth. He hoped so.

"Hi, Annie. I'm so glad I could find you. I'd like to ask you some questions if I might?"

She looked at him sideways. "Yes, sir, Dr. Bernholtz."

From her reaction he suspected she was afraid she had done something wrong. "Annie, someone broke into my office last week. Do you remember which day it was that you found glass in the wastebasket?"

"It were Friday. I check that basket every day. Usually there ain't nothin' much in it. I remember when I saw that glass because we can't throw glass in with regular trash."

"Are you absolutely certain, Annie?"

"It were ...yes sir, it were Friday last. I remember thinkin' that I don't need all this extra work on Friday.'"

"You're sure, Annie, there was no glass in the basket the day before?"

"No, sir."

Ken was stunned. Marty had lied. Had Dr. Tupelo said something to her about running a code on the boy and also mentioned the autopsy? She could have made up the rest. Or had she confided in him?

Ken called Gamal and arranged to meet him that afternoon. He wondered how Gamal would react to the news that one or more persons have discovered what they were doing. What choice did they have but to stop the transfer of organs and try to cover their tracks? It would be a serious blow to the Hakim Medical Center. They had become overly dependent on him. He had provided them with organs for almost half of their transplant surgeries.

When Ken entered Gamal's office, he came from around his desk and shook Ken's hand. They walked to a sitting area. Stark white, overstuffed armchairs were arranged around a beveled glass coffee table, cut in the shape of Saudi Arabia.

"Would you care for coffee or tea?" Gamal asked.

"Nothing, thank you," Ken responded.

One could not rush Gamal, regardless of the urgency. He asked Ken about his health and inquired about Link and his family.

Ken's eyes glistened. "Link is dying. They've moved him to intensive care. He may not survive more than a week or two."

"My, my, such sad news."

"Lydia and Tom are frantic," Ken said. "We're doing everything we can to find him a heart."

"I'm very sorry for my dear friend. I'll pray daily for your godchild. It seems ironic that you, who have saved the lives of so many of our children, are unable to save one so close to you."

Ken asked about Gamal's family and expressed his pleasure that his wife and children were doing well.

He dreaded telling Gamal that someone may have discovered that he was removing organs without parental consent. Why didn't he cut off the flow of organs a long time ago? God knows how often he thought about it. But there was always one more child who needed a heart or kidney.

"Today I discovered that a patient at the hospital concealed herself in the ceiling of the morgue," Ken said. "She watched me do the autopsy on David Lang. She's a very bright fifteen-year-old. You may have heard me speak of her...Martha Lopinski?"

Gamal's expression displayed neither anger nor fear. He seemed lost in thought.

"Isn't she the child with metastatic bone cancer?" Not waiting for an answer he continued, "And hasn't she consented to be a heart donor for your godson?"

Ken nodded. He told Gamal about the experimental

chemotherapy drug she'd be taking the following week. "It's a desperate attempt to induce a remission."

"I see."

"About a month ago," Ken said, "she asked if I would let her come to the morgue to watch an autopsy. I told her it would be an invasion of privacy, that there was no way I could allow it. Unfortunately, I didn't appreciate how determined she was, and how skilled she was at breaking and entering."

Gamal managed a stiff smile. "But such a young person...would she even have understood....?"

Ken explained how he had traced several clues. "There is no doubt that she had seen that autopsy and must have suspected I didn't have the parents' permission to remove his heart. Otherwise, why would she have made up a story about a previous autopsy?"

He had never seen Gamal perspire. Before speaking, Gamal patted his forehead with a silk handkerchief drawn from his jacket pocket.

"Kenneth, your reasoning and elaboration of this matter is brilliant. I've no doubt your analysis is accurate. But she must have had an accomplice."

"I can't conceive of any adult allowing this one-legged girl to take such enormous risks. She's a close friend of my godson, but as sick as he is, there's nothing he could have done to assist her." Even as he spoke, Ken recalled the phone call from Link, asking him to come to his room. It had come almost immediately after the operator had announced code 400. Could Link have wanted to keep him out of the morgue so Marty would have time to gain access to the ceiling space? Impossible! Surely it must have been a coincidence.

Gamal rose and began to pace, leaning forward, both

hands clasped behind his back.

"Gamal, she's very clever. I'm convinced she could have gained access on her own."

Gamal continued to pace. He spoke without looking at Ken.

"We have gone to great lengths to prevent exposure. It is a pity that in such a noble cause we must be so guarded."

"Gamal, my deepest concern is for the children at your hospital. Exposure will put an end to the flow of organs."

Gamal walked to his desk. He removed a cigar from a canister and lighted it with a gold cigarette lighter. He sat back and inhaled deeply.

He watched the swirls of smoke rise. "You swore the young girl to secrecy, Kenneth, but can we trust her?"

He answered his own question. "Of course not! You cannot trust such a child. What bothers me most is how little time elapsed between when you called her, and the time she arrived in your office. Since she claimed she witnessed a previous autopsy, she had to tell you something very specific about it. What was distinctive was the presence of the pediatric resident. What's his name?"

"Frank Tupelo. He's a second-year resident."

"What do you know of him? We may not be able to trust him either. And he can damage us...more than she."

"He's Marty's doctor. From what I hear he's being considered as chief resident next year. In fact, he may be offered a cardiology fellowship."

"Let us assume," Gamal said, "that she called this Tupelo person and told him what she'd done. Unless she informed him of your unauthorized removal of organs, he would have simply advised her to admit it and ask your forgiveness. This doctor would assume that you would give her a fatherly lecture and send her off. But she comes to you with a concocted story of having observed a previous autopsy. Her story contains details only Dr. Tupelo could have supplied. I suspect the only reason he would do that is because of what she had seen. He most likely believed her to be in danger."

"Danger? Danger from whom? It's inconceivable that anyone might harm her."

Gamal walked to the couch and sat next to Ken.

"Much is at risk here, my friend. We've created great expectations among persons who have generously supported your research. Our reputations are at stake. In Riyadh, I'm considered a national hero, but I would be disgraced if we were exposed. My superiors know nothing of our arrangement. And you, Kenneth, who will trust you or employ you? The young doctor would be correct in fearing that men will do desperate things to protect their life's work, their families, and their friends." His eyes narrowed as he leaned toward Ken. A ripple of fear caused Ken to shudder. Gamal's usual congenial expression was replaced by an uncompromising stare.

"I knew the risks when I started down this path," Ken said. "But there are dozens of children alive today, thanks to what we've accomplished. I'm not ashamed of that."

"You have reason to be proud. We have hurt no one. An organ from a dead child, here and there, is nothing. In many countries consent to donate organs is presumed."

"But not so in America. Here, the right of the parents to decide is highly valued and ingrained," Ken insisted. "I violated that responsibility and trust and so I've got to face the music. You and your family can go back home, where a whole lot of parents thank you for saving their kid's lives."

"I will not give up so easily," Gamal said. He stood and again began to pace. "What do you think Tupelo will do with this information? He has only the word of what a young girl believes she has seen." He stopped pacing and sat close to Ken, their faces inches apart. "This girl has an advanced stage of cancer. Her doctors are resorting to an experimental drug. There's a good chance she will succumb to her disease. If that happens, this doctor will have lost his only witness!"

Ken was stunned. Gamal's remark was a thinly veiled suggestion that they'd be better off if Marty died sooner rather than later. "Dr. Tupelo's interest and curiosity are based entirely on the girl's word. I doubt he'd do anything without more information," Ken said.

"That is exactly my reasoning," Gamal added.

"But we must be extremely cautious. He may figure out that the only place I could use the organs would be here at your hospital. I'd increase security so no one can come in here to look through your records. I'm especially concerned about the children who received the organs from David Lang."

"Yes!" Gamal said, his fist striking the air for emphasis. "We may be able to contain this situation if we can prevent the doctor from gathering evidence. The children who received the organs will be sent back to Riyadh immediately. Their complete medical records will accompany them. Until they are transferred, I'll assign extra security."

"What about the operating room logs? How secure are they?" Ken asked.

"At the end of each month they're sent to the record room for storage."

"In the interim, where are they kept?"

"In the surgical suite...Hmm...I'll check on how secure they are there."

It was Ken's turn to stand. His legs ached from sitting so long in one position. He walked to the window, turned, and sat on the edge of the sill. "The operation logs are obviously incriminating. I'd suggest you handle them carefully."

"You're absolutely right. I shall implement a plan without delay."

Ken walked to the couch, sat back down and opened his briefcase. He hesitated. Should they temporarily cut off the flow of organs? But how could he when the life of a child might be at stake? "I understand you have a boy here on high priority status for a donor heart."

Dr. Faysal moved alongside Ken. "Yes, he's the son of a prominent Saudi family. They are desperate to save this, their youngest and only male child."

He asked Ken if he had brought an up-to-date computer printout of potential organ donors at Children's Hospital.

"Yes...of course," Ken said. He removed the printout from his briefcase. He handed it to Gamal.

Gamal removed reading glasses from his pocket and studied it. "I see there is a compatible donor on this list."

"Unfortunately it's not compatible with Link's blood type." Ken went on to explain that the Zack family had agreed to donation of the child's corneas and had also agreed to an autopsy. "He's been on life support for the past week."

"We must proceed cautiously, Kenneth. This Tupelo may be snooping about."

Although Ken had seen only two security guards on his visits to the Hakim Medical Center, he assumed Gamal employed others to cover nights and weekends.

"I wonder," Ken asked, "if you could spare one of your

security guards to keep an eye on the morgue area while I'm doing the autopsy on Christopher Zack?"

"It will be done."

CHAPTER TWENTY-FIVE

Frank parked in front of the Orient Express, a long, narrow structure separated from the sidewalk by a strip of dandelions and crabgrass. As he climbed the pink-colored cement steps to the main entrance, he felt a sense of guilt, recalling how frightened Tina had sounded when she called and asked to meet there.

He spotted her in the far corner. Despite the anxiety he felt, there was also a twinge of excitement when he saw her. As he approached she smiled. My God, she's beautiful, he thought. How long has it been since he'd been on a date? He slipped into the booth and reached for her hand. She shook it vigorously.

"Yes, I know you're Dr. Tupelo. I met you a couple of days ago."

"Should I step outside and try that again?"

"Just grab a waitress. I'm starved."

"What's up?"

"I have no idea," she said, "but the hospital went crazy today."

"What do you mean?"

Tina glanced about the diner. "The atmosphere at the

Hakim Medical Center is usually relaxed. But today and yesterday they posted security guards all over the place."

Frank waved for a waitress. He turned toward Tina. "Anyone say why?"

"Not exactly. There was a guard at the main entrance checking I.D. badges. I've never seen that before."

He tried to sound reassuring. "It's probably just what they do every so often."

"Could it have something to do with me copying those operating room logs?"

"Why do you think that?" Frank worried about them both getting into trouble over those records. Had she told anyone she had copied them for Dr. Bernholtz?

"My supervisor said she heard there was a security breach. She was told that from now on, the operating room logs had to be kept locked."

A waitress approached their booth. She wore a dark skirt well above her knees and a form-fitting white blouse, its buttons straining to contain her breasts. Her hair was a lusterless blond except at the roots. She pulled a pencil from behind her ear. "Can I get you something to drink while you look over the menu?"

They both ordered a Bud Light. Tina asked for a glass.

When their drinks arrived, Tina over-filled her glass. As the beer started to overflow, she leaned over, sucked up the foam and smiled. There was a bit of foam at the corners of her mouth. Frank laughed. "You about to have a seizure?"

She removed a compact from her purse and blotted her lips with a tissue.

"No, Frank. Italian men always have that effect on me."

Forbidden Harvest

He wondered how the hell he missed her when she worked at Children's Hospital.

"Do you think anyone saw you take the OR logs?"

"I don't think so," Tina said.

"Anyone see you make the copies?"

"No...Wait a minute, one of the doctors came into the copy room as I was leaving."

Frank sipped his beer. He wanted to ask her how long it took to do her hair like that, messy, but in an attractive windswept look. "Did you have to discard any copies?"

She thought for a moment. "I did. I didn't notice the paper orientation was off. The first few copies came out sideways."

"You threw the bad copies in the recycling bin...right?"

"I guess I did." Her eyes widened, "You think somebody saw them?"

He took a long swallow of his beer. He nodded.

"I had no reason to hide what I was doing. You told me that Dr. Bernholtz had asked for those copies," Tina said indignantly. "And what the heck's happened to Miss America?"

Their waitress was a couple of tables from them. Frank waved to get her attention. He didn't want to implicate Tina by telling her the whole story, but she deserved an explanation.

"I'm sorry. I did mislead you about Dr. Bernholtz needing the information."

She jerked her hand toward him and accidentally knocked over her water glass. "Damn it, I knew stepped-up security had something to do with those records."

Forbidden Harvest

He blotted the table with his napkin as she shifted quickly in the booth to avoid the water spilling over the edge.

"You want to sit on the dry side?"

Frank stood as she slipped into the booth on his side. Now this is more like it, he thought as he sat, pressed against her.

The waitress returned for their orders. She winked at Frank. "Sorry to keep you waiting. What'll you have?" Leaning forward, she leaned against Frank's shoulder as she reached to refill Tina's glass.

Neither of them had looked at the menu. "What would you recommend?" Frank asked.

She said the house specialty was their *corpus delecti*...an eight-ounce broiled hamburger with melted cheddar cheese and mushrooms. They both ordered a hamburger and coffee.

After the waitress left, Tina shook her head. "The lady must be after a really big tip." She sipped her beer. "Tell me, why are you so interested in those records?"

He gulped the last of his beer before answering. "Have you ever heard of black-market organs being used in transplant surgery?"

"Of course. I've heard of poor people selling their organs."

"I can't prove anything yet, but it's possible that organs are being taken from deceased children, without the parents' consent. And I suspect they're being sent to the Hakim Medical Center to be used in transplant surgery."

"That would explain why they'd be excited about those logs being copied."

Frank nodded.

"I imagine a wealthy family would be willing to pay anything to save their child," she said.

"And I suspect they're not likely to ask too many questions," Frank added.

Their food arrived, and Frank ate several bites of his hamburger. "I'm famished. You'd better guard your *corpus delecti.*"

"Which one are you referring to?"

Her eyes were the most beautiful blue-green he'd ever seen. He took another bite of his hamburger and smiled. "Right now, the hamburger. But ask me that question again sometime."

They ate in silence for a minute or two as the waitress refilled their coffee cups.

"Let me guess," Tina said. "The organs are coming from none other than the internationally renowned Children's Memorial Hospital in Seattle. The well-known pediatric thoracic surgeon, Dr. Frankenstein, is removing hearts and other organs from cadavers. He resuscitates the organs in his laboratory located in the second basement. His trusted man-servant Igor then transports the organs to the Hakim Medical Center in the dead of night. Another life is saved, and a quarter of a million dollars gets deposited in Dr. Frankenstein's Swiss account."

Even though she was kidding, she was so close to the truth that Frank didn't know how to respond. How could he bring Tina fully into his confidence? He knew virtually nothing about her. He assumed Ken and his accomplice at the Hakim Medical Center were aware that Marty had witnessed an event that might expose their conspiracy. Men in desperate situations do unthinkable things. He was worried about Marty's safety. And of course, he didn't want to put Tina at risk.

"Hello, Frank, are you there?"

The waitress asked about dessert. They ordered two espressos and Italian ice cream. She gathered their dishes and smiled at Frank. "Your lady friend's a little messy."

As she leaned over, Frank noticed a dark mole on the cleavage side of her right breast. He looked directly at it. "You should have that checked."

She smiled. "You a doctor?"

"He's a pediatrician," Tina said. "You outgrew him a long time ago."

As she carried their plates away Frank grinned. "Thanks for rescuing me. You know, that mole could be malignant."

"Sure, and this headache I have is probably a brain tumor." She leaned back and closed her eyes. "Now tell me everything, please."

"Tina, the less you know right now, the better. And don't mention my name to anyone at the Hakim Medical Center. Even if they ask you directly, deny that you've talked with me."

She nodded.

"When I called the other day," he said, "I didn't tell the secretary who I was. Did you mention my name?"

"No. I didn't want to start a bunch of gossip. I'm one of the few single nurses, and I've had enough trouble with the medical staff."

"Tina, the doctor who entered as you left the copy room would at least have noticed it was a nurse who passed him. They are probably checking out all the nurses who might have access to the operating logs." He looked around the diner uneasily.

"I was concerned when I called you," she said, "but now

you're scaring the hell out of me. Shouldn't you notify the police or the FBI?"

"If I'm wrong it could hurt someone I respect a great deal."

"Speaking of Dr. Frank Tupelo?"

"Including me," he continued, "Don't call me at my apartment. Here's my pager number."

He wrote the number on the back of his credit card receipt. "Use a pay phone. Have the operator page me. We should arrange to meet again soon."

She nodded slowly. "I would like that, Frank. Maybe go on a real date when this conspiracy mess blows over."

CHAPTER TWENTY-SIX

Tina sat at a table in the cafeteria at the Hakim Medical Center. As usual, the room was crowded with nurses and other staff. A doctor at the next table smiled. Tina nodded and then looked away. She could sense he was staring. She looked about the room, and noticed one of the guards she had seen at the hospital entrance. He glanced in her direction when she stood and carried her mostly uneaten lunch to a conveyor close to the exit. Turning back she could see that the man was watching her every move.

On the drive home that evening, she kept one eye on her rearview mirror. But no one appeared to be following her.

Her apartment was on the third floor of a six-story brick building. She pulled her car into a parking area underneath. The deserted garage was poorly lighted. She stared into the shadows before leaving her car. As she passed a parked SUV, she noticed someone sitting behind the wheel adjusting his rearview mirror. She looked over her shoulder and watched as the car backed out and headed for the exit.

At the elevator, as she reached to press the button, the doors opened and two men came toward her. She was about to scream when they nodded and walked past. She boarded the elevator and immediately pushed the close-door button.

Tina hurried to her apartment. Startled to see the door slightly ajar, she turned and raced to the stairway; then ran down three flights to the superintendent's apartment. She banged on his door. When he opened it she could hardly speak. "Mr. Polanski...my apartment...it's open. I'm sure that I locked it when I left this morning. I'm afraid to go in."

Mr. Polanski, a brawny man in his late sixties, grabbed a billystick from a hook by the door.

"I'll check it out, Miss Carrol. It was real smart not goin' in there, what with all the kooks running around."

He pushed her apartment door open with his foot, slamming it hard against the wall before stepping inside. Tina waited in the hallway. She could hear him walking about.

He shouted, "Ya better come in here, Miss Carrol."

The floor was covered with clothing, books, and papers that had been emptied from drawers and bookshelves. The bed covers were removed and the mattress had been pulled almost off the bed.

She gasped. "What have they done to my place!" She looked around to see if anything was missing. Her phone and a small television set and VCR she kept in her bedroom were gone. She kept extra cash in a shoe-tree pocket that hung from a closet door. She checked. The money wasn't there! Those guys knew what they were doing, she thought.

"I can't believe they stole my phone!" Tina said.

"I'll call 911 from my office," Polanski said. "They sprung your door lock. I'll get ya a new one. And a deadbolt besides."

Two police officers arrived ten minutes later. They canvassed her apartment and made an inventory of the missing items.

"How much cash would you say was taken?"

"About sixty dollars."

"Looks pretty amateurish," one of the officers said.

"Yeah," the second officer agreed. "Lucky you weren't here when they broke in."

Polanski reentered the room with a tool box and new locks.

Tina drew her arms about her chest. "It's freezing in here!"

"You okay staying here tonight?" one of the officers asked.

"I can't stand the thought of people pawing through all my personal things."

"Miss Carrol, you can use my office phone if you want to call somebody," Polanski suggested.

After the police left, Tina went directly to the superintendent's office. She called Children's Hospital and asked the operator to beep Frank.

"Frank, it's Tina. My apartment was robbed while I was at work. The place looks like it was hit by a tornado."

"I'm so sorry...is anything missing?"

"My phone, my television, a VCR, and some cash. Frank, I'm not so sure someone wasn't trying to make it look like a simple break-in. I'm afraid those goons at the hospital may be onto me. I feel paranoid as hell."

"You may be right. Then again it could have been a coincidence," Frank said.

"I don't believe in coincidences."

"Had you written my name or number anyplace?"

"No."

"I did give you my beeper number."

"I had it in my purse."

"Good."

"No way am I going to work tomorrow."

"They may be more suspicious if you don't show."

"Maybe you're right. But what about tonight?"

"Any family or friend you might stay with?"

"No family in the area. And there's no one I'd feel comfortable calling on such short notice."

"If you'd like, you can stay at my place. I can sleep in the residents' on-call room tonight."

There was a long pause..."What if they follow me there? That may be exactly what they want me to do."

"Damn. You're right. Let me think---where's your car parked?"

"In a garage under the building."

"Can the parking entrance be seen from the apartment's main entrance?"

"No. It's on a side street."

"If whoever broke into your apartment is waiting to follow you, they'd probably be parked on the side street, not at the main entrance."

"That makes sense. Okay. I'll call a cab and head over."

He gave her directions to his apartment.

"Frank, I hate to displace you from your own place. And

don't worry. I won't lay a hand on you."

"Well...okay. If you promise. I'll leave the hospital as soon as I sign out to the on-call resident. My apartment's nearby. I should be there in a few minutes."

Tina returned to her ransacked pad and quickly packed an overnight bag. Polanski was still installing the locks. He insisted he escort her to the cab.

Frank grew increasingly apprehensive as he approached his place. As Marty's doctor, he would have to be high on the list of conspirators. He was somewhat relieved as he entered; things appeared to be exactly as he had left them. He went to his desk, where he had placed the copies of the operating room logs. He pulled open the drawer. The logs were gone. *"Damn it!"* He slammed the drawer shut. And why had they trashed Tina's apartment and not his? His desk must have been the first place they looked. What a knucklehead for keeping them there! He should've stashed the logs at Children's Hospital. There was a knock at the door. He froze.

"Frank, are you there?"

Tina stepped into the room. She dropped her overnight bag to the floor. "Well, it looks like the mysterious *they* didn't break in here."

Frank shook his head and pointed to the desk.

"The copies of the operating room schedules were in that drawer."

She flopped onto a chair. "Shit! Who the hell are these guys?"

"Now they're sure you and I are onto them. I'm afraid we can't stay here tonight," Frank said. "While I'm packing, call a cab. Then see if you can get a reservation at a motel near the airport."

Frank entered the room with an overnight bag. He wondered what Tina might be thinking as he watched her standing by the window, holding the slats of the blinds apart. He had never experienced the kind of fear that gripped him now. Why the hell would they be going to such extremes to identify us, he thought, if they weren't going to follow up in ways he tried not to imagine? Maybe they just want to get our copies of the operating logs so we have no physical evidence? Does Bernholtz even know what the Hakim Medical Center brass was doing?

"The cab's here." Tina grabbed her overnight bag. They hurried from Frank's apartment.

"Take us to the SeaTac Motel on the south side," Tina said.

"That's a good ways off. You got lots of dough in those bags?"

As the taxi pulled from the curb, Frank looked out the rear window. A black BMW across the street made a U-turn and pulled up behind them. The windows were heavily tinted.

"There's a twenty-dollar tip," Frank said, "if you can lose the car behind us."

The driver nodded. He glanced in the rear-view mirror, and then drove slowly through the city streets, as though oblivious they were being followed. Suddenly, he swung around a car in front of them, so that now there was a car between the cab and the BMW. He again drove slowly until they approached an amber traffic light. He stopped. When it turned red he shot across the intersection. Horns blared. The car behind them stopped. The driver of the BMW leaned on his horn, but heavy traffic was already on the move. By the time the light changed, the cab was safely out of sight.

"You've done this before," Tina said.

"Naw. I seen a lot of car chases in the movies and figured out how I would do it when I got the chance. I know this city like the back of my hand. No way some clown in a BMW's gonna keep up with me."

Frank leaned back and closed his eyes. He thought, I'm headed for a motel with a beautiful woman, and my knees are knocking like castanets...but for the wrong reason. He looked at Tina and smiled.

"You must be thinking what I'm thinking," Tina said.

"I doubt that."

"Let's eat," she said. "Then I want the whole damn story, especially the parts you left out."

SeaTac was a typical strip motel, beige paint, parking spaces in front of each unit, a sad little pool. They stepped into a large room, with a sitting area by the door, a queen-sized bed in the center, a kitchenette beyond, and off to the right a bathroom that was clean but stark. The floor was covered by a shag rug of indeterminate color.

"What, only one bed? Tina asked.

"Sorry, this is all they had available."

They talked until two in the morning. Frank told Tina everything he knew, in as much detail as he could recall. When he finished, she shook her head in disbelief. "My Frankenstein theory wasn't far off, after all. Those poor children! I can see how a doctor might begin to convince himself that he, and not the parents, knew what the right thing to do was. If you do prove that Dr. Bernholtz is illegally removing organs, what will happen to him?"

"My guess is that Ken's medical license would be revoked. His reputation as a researcher would be seriously damaged."

"You mentioned that Marty may be in danger. You don't think Dr. Bernholtz would do anything to harm her?"

"God, no. I've known him a long time. You know I went to medical school here at University Hospital. He often conducts Grand Rounds there, although his primary appointment is at Memorial. He's a kind, gentle man. I can't believe he'd be a danger to anyone."

"What about the medical director at the Hakim Medical Center? Do you know Dr. Faysal?" Tina asked.

"I met him once. A group of pediatric residents visited the hospital with Dr. Bernholtz. Dr. Faysal was at his side the entire time. He was extremely gracious, and, I thought, somewhat guarded."

"Guarded? In what way?" she asked.

"It's hard to say exactly. Just a feeling I had about him."

"I rarely see Dr. Faysal at the hospital," Tina said. "Once or twice he showed up at Grand Rounds, but never contributed to the discussion. Maybe he's not a medical doctor."

"He is a physician. Bernholtz introduced him as a pediatric cardiologist. I found out later that Dr. Faysal had originally contacted Bernholtz with the idea of opening a hospital in the Seattle area staffed by Saudi physicians. It's a sure bet Faysal's Ken's accomplice. I doubt his motives are as altruistic. As you said, a family would pay anything to save their child. We have to assume Dr. Faysal might resort to violence to keep the status quo. If that's the case, he must be desperate to find out how many people already know."

"If you really believe that, why in hell did you drag me into this?"

"When I first called you I hoped the records would prove Marty was mistaken, and that would be the end of it."

"Well, now we know better, so why not go to the police? Two break-ins are reason enough to be suspicious."

"I'd rather he turn himself in," Frank said. "That way we

don't have to drag you or Marty into this."

"Well, master sleuth, what next?"

"If he does another autopsy on an organ donor, I've a plan to prove whether he's removing organs without authorization." Frank looked at his watch. "Damn. It's almost time to get up." He grabbed one of the pillows. "You can have the bed. I'll sleep on the floor."

Tina smiled. "My mother will never believe this."

Forbidden Harvest

CHAPTER TWENTY-SEVEN

Gamal Faysal's office was dark except for a desk lamp that cast a greenish glow over the stark white furnishings. He paced, leaning forward, his hands folded behind his back. He stood before a floor-to-ceiling window that looked onto a grassy slope bordered by stately oaks and a scattering of white birch. The darkening sky and a light rain gave the scene the grainy look of an over-enlarged photograph.

How he detested the incessant Seattle rain....day after day without a glimpse of the sun. Were not his current troubles sufficiently oppressive without having to endure grey skies and unbearable humidity?

He was furious with this disruption of his daily routine. Each evening on returning home, his children clung to him. His beautiful wife tended to his every need. And after casting off his Western clothes, he'd dress in finely tailored robes suitable for a prince. Not born into the aristocracy, he nevertheless could now afford to live in a sumptuous style. They brought with them from Saudi Arabia two young servants. One devoted herself entirely to the children, acting as their governess and maid. The other did domestic chores and prepared their meals.

Although he had been expecting a call, he jumped when the phone rang.

"Dr. Faysal, this is Anwar. Dr. Tupelo and the lady left his apartment thirty minutes ago. It was rush hour....I'm sorry to report that we lost them."

"You're professionals. How could they have eluded you?"

"The cab driver was very clever."

"Did you find what you sought in the doctor's apartment?"

"We have them in our possession."

"Good. Good. Bring them to me immediately!"

The following morning, Frank was up at six. As he dressed, he glanced at Tina, still sound asleep. The room was dark except for a night light coming from the bathroom. He went to the bed and gently shook her shoulder. She rolled over onto her back, and then jumped on first seeing him.

"It's me, remember?"

Tina sat up in bed. She was wearing pink flannel pajamas.

Frank smiled. "Those things have feet?"

"I couldn't find a pair with feet in my size."

"I think it would be a good idea if you stayed here today."

"What time is it?" She turned on a bedside lamp.

"Almost seven. I have to leave."

"Go already! See you later." She turned off the lamp.

When she finally woke it was late morning. As she

dressed, she looked about the nondescript room. She regretted not having a magazine or two. She went to the window. The parking area was deserted except for a family two doors from her, loading a mini-van. As the man and woman packed their luggage, their children were in constant motion, circling the vehicle and running up and down the walkway.

Tina headed for the motel office for something to read. A young man behind the check-in counter directed her to a shop not much bigger than a curbside newspaper kiosk. As she browsed through the magazines, a medium-sized man in a rumpled business suit brushed against her.

"Excuse me," he said. "I'm a little impaired before my morning coffee."

"I know what you mean." She turned and picked up a *Seattle Times*.

"Would you care to join me for a cup?" he asked, moving a bit closer to her.

She moved toward a rack of paperbacks. She looked at him over her shoulder.

"Sorry. My husband's waiting for me."

As she approached the lobby with a newspaper, a paperback novel, and a copy of Cosmopolitan, she saw the same man talking with the motel clerk. As she passed, he turned toward her.

"Maybe some other time?" he asked as she passed.

She ignored him. She looked back several times as she hurried to her room.

Once there, she secured the door chain. She tried to calm herself, thinking he was probably your average slob trying to pick up some action. She called the front desk clerk to inquire about room service.

"Sorry, ma'am, we don't have any. There's a Denny's a couple of doors down."

"Any take-out places?

"Sure are." He gave her the phone numbers. She decided to have something delivered later that afternoon.

Each time a car pulled up, Tina went to the window. It's amazing how many people look suspicious when you're all alone and have good reason to believe someone is out to get you. She gathered pillows and propped them against the headboard. She snuggled up with the book. Romance, thank you. No murder mysteries.

After leaving the motel, Frank took a cab to the Space Needle. From there he walked around the block, making sure he wasn't followed. He hailed another cab. "Children's Hospital, please."

That morning, as the pediatric team was finishing rounds, the hospital operator announced code 400. Joel Zack had been in hepatic coma for several days. He was expected to die any moment. Frank wasn't Joel's doctor, but he had been involved in his care when on-call. It saddened him to think that they could do nothing more to save that brave little boy.

He stopped at the nurses' station in the intensive care unit and approached the nursing supervisor. "I heard code 400 announced. I assume Joel Zack died?"

Ms. Rigolotti, referred to by the staff as Ms. Rigormortis, sat as though she were tied to a stake, her shoulders square, her back arched.

"Yes. The poor child. We all loved him. Dr. Hennasay declared him brain dead at 10:15," she informed Frank.

"How incredibly sad. Have you notified the mortician?"

"That's SOP. I told him the surgeons will be harvesting the boy's kidneys, and afterwards do an autopsy, so they shouldn't come to pick up the body before three. I hate it when they get here too early. I can't relax with them pacing up and down the hall, waiting for someone to sign the death certificate."

Frank tried to imagine Ms. Rigolotti in a relaxed posture. "I know. It's always a hassle to get the signature," he said. "I'd be glad to do that."

"Great!" She opened the boy's chart, removed the certificate and handed it to Frank.

"I want to talk with the mortician about coming to one of our pediatric conferences." Frank said. "I'll hand-deliver the death certificate when he gets here." He tucked it in his pocket. "Then I'll hit him up for the conference."

"Beware of doctors bearing gifts." Ms Rigolotti gazed at him over the top of her reading glasses.

"Hi, Doc Frank," Marty said as he entered her room. She held up the book she had been reading. "This is interesting stuff. Dr. Siegel tells some amazing stories about how his patients, you know, eliminate cancer cells. Like imagining the cancer is a block of ice, and they picture themselves at the beach, lying in the sun. The warmth of the sun like penetrates their bodies and melts away the cancer cells."

He was pleased she was reading *Love, Medicine and Miracles*. "Did you get to the part where Dr. Siegel talks about anesthesia?"

"Yeah. He tells how he plays soothing music and won't let anyone say anything negative. He did a study that showed they didn't lose as much blood and got better faster."

"The unconscious mind controls a lot more than most people realize."

"The operator announced code 400. I hope it was nobody I know?" Marty asked.

"A ten-year-old boy. His name is Joel Zack."

She shook her head. "Geez. Only ten. I don't even want to know what he died from." She was sitting in a bedside chair, one foot propped on the bedrail. "When should I meet you at the loading dock?"

"I already told you to stay away from there."

"Yeees Sir!" Marty saluted.

Frank shook his head. She was obviously having fun playing detective. But she had no idea how quickly their plans had begun to unravel.

Marty closed the door to her room and said in a conspiratorial whisper, "Houston, we have a problem! Your plan's cool, but you'll have to re-think it."

"Why so?"

"This morning, on my way to the snack bar I happened to pass the morgue, and I saw a man standing there. And when I passed by an hour later he was still there with his arms crossed."

"What did he look like?" Frank asked.

"He was tall. He had a big head and a jaw like a bulldog. Not the kinda dude to mess with."

That was almost exactly how Tina had described one of Faysal's security guards, Frank recalled. Damnit. That changed everything. "Thanks for that bit of bad news."

"I'll be in my room all afternoon. Keep me posted."

Silas Jones, an undertaker at a local mortuary, parked

his hearse by the loading dock at the basement level. He wore a dark suit, white shirt, and narrow black tie shiny from years of wear. His suit hung from his thin frame as though it were unoccupied. His shoulders were rounded, and he stood with his knees slightly bent. After removing a stretcher from the hearse, he wheeled it to the morgue. Standing alongside the doors was a tall, powerfully-built man whose head seemed too big for his body. The man's eyes narrowed as Silas approached. "I was instructed not to allow anyone in the morgue."

"I'm from the funeral home. They said I should pick up the deceased."

The guard banged on the door. Dr. Bernholtz's assistant held it slightly ajar. When he saw Silas was there, he admitted the stretcher, but motioned for the guard to wait outside.

Zack's body lay on the stainless steel table. Jamael covered him with a sheet and gently lifted him onto the stretcher. The guard walked alongside Silas as they wheeled the stretcher toward the loading bay. Silas shook his head. Who the hell is this guy? He wondered. And people say undertakers are creepy.

"My name's Jones, Silas Jones." He extended his hand.

The guard ignored his outstretched hand. "I must stay with the body until you load it into the hearse."

Silas shrugged. "There's a doctor Tupelo who's supposed to come give me a signed death certificate. I gotta tell him I'm ready to leave."

Silas stepped into a nearby office. He called the hospital operator and asked if she would page Dr. Tupelo.

"I'm at the doors to the loading dock," Silas said. "I understand you have the signed death certificate."

"I sure do. I'll be right there," Frank said.

Frank called the hospital operator. He asked her to beep him in exactly three minutes. "Certainly, Dr. Tupelo. Trying to get out of a meeting?"

"Something like that. It's very important...exactly three minutes."

Silas approached the stretcher. "The doctor said he'd be here pretty quick. We gotta wait."

A few moments later, Frank poked his head from the room where he had stashed a portable ultrasound unit. His stomach churned when he saw the guard standing alongside Silas. Marty was right. He would have to scuttle his plan. But how was he to get the death certificate to the mortician?

"Where's the nearest toilet?" the man asked Silas. "I ain't pissed all day."

Silas pointed down the hall. "Go to the end of this corridor and turn left. You'll see a snack bar. A little ways down you'll see the bathrooms on your right."

"You're gonna stay here until I get back, right?"

"Of course. Go ahead."

As the guard headed for the bathroom, the mortician stood shaking his head. He'd picked up hundreds of bodies, but never before had one been guarded.

As soon as the guard was out of sight, Frank approached the mortician. They shook hands. "Hi, I'm Dr. Tupelo." He looked about. He only had a few minutes to execute his plan.

"Silas Jones, nice to meet you."

"I have the death certificate right here." Frank handed it to Silas.

"It's real nice of you to do this."

"Could I ask you something, Mr. Jones?"

"Sure, Doc."

"I'm in charge of the conferences for our new interns. I'd like you to come talk about what embalming entails. Patients are always asking our doctors about what the undertaker does."

"I can do that. Just gimme a call."

Frank's beeper went off.

"Excuse me." He ducked into the office.

He soon returned. "That was Dr. Bernholtz's assistant. The boy was on an experimental drug and part of the protocol was to do a bone marrow biopsy, which they forgot. I have to take the body back to the morgue. Why don't you go to the snack bar for coffee and meet me back here in fifteen minutes?"

Silas looked at his watch. "Okay. I could use a little caffeine." He headed down the hall, and as he rounded the corner he ran into the security guard.

"Hi. Let me treat you to a cup of coffee. I had to bring the body back to the morgue. They gotta do a biopsy."

The guard looked hesitant, but shrugged and went into the coffee shop with Silas. As they sat at a booth drinking their coffee, a young girl wearing a scrub suit and Braves baseball cap approached their table. She removed her cap before she spoke.

"Excuse me, sirs."

The mortician stared at her. She was obviously a patient. He could see how thin her blond hair was. He was certain she'd had chemo.

"Hi, little lady. What can we do for you?"

"I came down all the way from my room on the fourth floor to get a bottle of lemonade and chips. But I forgot to bring enough money. Could I bum a dollar? If you give me your name and address, I'll mail it to you when I get back to my room."

"How can I refuse a pretty young lady like you?" Silas reached for his wallet.

"Thanks loads." She glanced at the other man and smiled.

The guard's expression didn't change. He looked away.

After getting her drink and chips, she returned to their table. "Okay if I sit with you? I hate to eat alone."

"Sure." He moved over to make room. "You been in the hospital very long?"

"I'm sure you don't have enough time to hear my whole story."

She broke open her bag of chips, using her teeth. She offered them some. "A year ago they found out I had bone cancer. I've been in and out of the hospital a lot." She turned toward the big man. "I've never seen you before." She squinted at his ID badge. "You visiting somebody?"

Again he ignored her and looked at his watch. "We better be getting back."

"You look familiar though," she said to the mortician. "You must've been here before."

"I work for the Whitfield Mortuary. I come here often to pick up bodies." He felt bad as soon as he said it. He figured she must be about the same age as his granddaughter.

"My friend died yesterday," she said. "His name was Joel Zack." She opened her eyes wide. Silas was afraid she was about to cry. "Is that who you came to get?"

The big man groaned, pushing to the edge of the booth. "Let's get out of here. I'm supposed to stay with that body."

Silas reached out and touched Marty's hand. "I'm real sorry your friend died. We have to go now. It was nice talking with you." He glared at the guard. I sure wish it was him I was picking up, Silas thought, instead of this little girl's friend.

Frank wheeled the stretcher to a room close to the loading dock, where he had stashed the portable ultrasound unit. He pulled the sheet from the boy's chest and rubbed on a Vaseline-like lubricant. He passed the ultrasound transducer over the chest. He could not detect the characteristic heart shadows! "Good lord!" he said. He hit a few buttons and produced a copy of the ultrasound image. He now had proof that Bernholtz had removed the boy's heart and, as he already knew, against parental orders.

He wiped off the lubricant. Before he covered the body, he studied Joel's face. There was no hint of the fear and pain he must have endured. He thought of Link and Marty and how bravely they faced their own mortality. Was it so terribly wrong to defile this poor child's body....to take his heart? Let that little part of him live on?

Frank rolled the stretcher back to the corridor to await Silas' return. Moments later he saw him and another man round the corner at the end of the hall. His first instinct was to run, but why? The guard would have no idea what he had done. He walked through the doors leading to the loading dock.

"Who the hell is that?" the guard asked as they approached the stretcher.

"He's the doctor who gave me the death certificate."

The guard lifted the sheet and checked the identification tag on the boy's ankle. He lowered the sheet, exposing Joel's face. "This the same kid you just picked up?"

"Of course it is. What's going on?" Silas asked. "They got body snatchers running around here?"

CHAPTER TWENTY-EIGHT

As Silas and Gamal's security guard loaded Joel's stretcher into the hearse, Frank circled around to the hospital emergency entrance. He passed through the waiting room, crowded with parents, crying babies and older children. Some clung to their mothers, while others romped noisily in the toddler play area.

A young mother called out to him, "Dr. Tupelo!"

He recognized her as someone whose little girl he'd seen the week before. He walked to where she was sitting. She wore cut-off jeans and tennis shoes without socks and a loose- fitting cotton top.

"How is Robin's ear doing?" he asked, relishing the normalcy of his everyday routine in the midst of eluding Faysal's spear-carriers.

The little girl's pony-tail pointed straight up as she buried her head in her mother's lap.

"Her ear doesn't hurt anymore. But she's still running a fever."

He chatted with her briefly; then moved on to the nurses' station. At least Tina's safe, he thought, as he dialed the motel number. He sat with his back to a group of medical students clustered around a computer monitor. He spoke quietly, "Tina, this is Frank."

"Frank! What's going on? I've been waiting all day to hear from you."

"Sorry I couldn't call earlier. Anything unusual happen there?"

"I watched a couple of soaps, read the newspaper---even the obits. Now I'm halfway through a romance novel. The room is like an incubator, and I can't open either of the damn windows. The manager said they're working on them."

Frank imagined Tina propped against the bed headboard, wearing just panties and bra, surrounded by books, magazines and empty chocolate wrappers. He suggested, "Take a cold shower. I'm sure I'll need one by the time I get there."

"What all's happened at the hospital?" Tina asked.

"Joel Zack, the boy on life support, died. He's the boy I told you about. Extraordinary child. The whole place is in mourning."

"That's the downside of working at a children's hospital."

"Dr. Bernholtz always performs an autopsy on children who die while on life-support. It's the ideal time to harvest an organ, and if he's been helping himself to body parts, that would be the best time to do an ultrasound."

"How did you manage that?"

"I'll explain later. I was stunned. There were no heart shadows!"

"My God!"

"Bernholtz obviously removed the heart. I printed the ultrasound image as proof."

"So Marty was right. Frank, I can barely hear you."

"Too many people around."

"Don't put it off, Frank. It's time to go directly to the hospital medical director."

"I'm going to meet with Bernholtz in a few minutes."

"Will you show Dr. Bernholtz the ultrasound print-out?"

"I'm keeping that somewhere safe. One of Faysal's goons saw me with the body after the autopsy. I don't want our only real piece of evidence where they can get their hands on it."

"Be careful, Frank. Chances are that guy's still around."

"I don't think he'd try anything until I leave."

"What if he follows you?"

"I'm not driving my car. I'm leaving from the ER after dark. I'll bum a ride with one of the rescue squad ambulances. Should get to the motel around eight."

"I wouldn't go anywhere near Dr. Bernholtz," she said. "How do you know he hasn't been in on all of this?"

"I'm certain he doesn't have a clue. I believe he took that heart to save some sick little kid at the Hakim Medical Center."

An anxious-looking intern pressed close to Frank. "I need to use the phone. The rest are tied up."

"I'll only be a minute." Frank said. He dialed Ken's office.

"Hello, Dr. Bernholtz here."

"It's Frank Tupelo."

"What is it, Frank?"

"It has to do with the autopsy on the Zack child."

Ken hesitated. When he finally spoke, his voice sounded strained...cautious. "I have to leave soon to catch a plane for London. Can you come to my morgue office?"

"No. I have an unstable patient on three-west. Meet me in the conference room," Frank insisted.

The small, windowless room smelled of stale coffee. Ken entered, glanced at his watch and sat opposite Frank.

"I have very little time, Frank. What's this about?"

Frank ran his fingers through his hair. His hand came to rest at the base of his skull. He massaged his neck muscles, which had grown sore and tense over the past two days. He was about to confront a man he admired and respected. He focused on the blackboard at the far end of the room. Earlier that day someone had drawn a complicated-looking family history. Frank stared at the mass of crisscrossing lines and names. His mouth was too dry to speak.

Ken looked at his watch. "Frank, I told you, time's urgent. I'm preparing to leave for London. What's up?"

Frank looked at the table as he spoke. "Marty told me what she saw at the David Lang autopsy." He looked up at Ken, who leaned back, clasping his hands behind his head.

"She denied that, but I thought she had."

"She was just curious at first. If she had realized then that sometimes organs are removed for teaching purposes, she probably wouldn't have given it a second thought. She somehow retrieved the patient consent form and showed me a copy. There was no permission to remove those organs."

Ken dropped his arms to the table. He leaned forward, resting his head on the palms of his hands. Frank could barely hear him speak.

"You don't understand, Frank..."

"At first I was certain Marty was confused," Frank interrupted. "And I couldn't figure out what you would be doing with those organs. You might be using them to do experiments. Then I recalled your connection with the Hakim Medical Center and suspected that maybe you were sending the organs there."

He told Ken how he had gotten copies of Hakim Hospital's operating-room logs that listed a kidney and heart transplant performed the day after the Michael Lang autopsy.

Ken stood and began pacing. "My God, this is the absolute worst time for this to come to light."

"I still wasn't sure. It could have been a coincidence. But after my apartment was broken into and those records were stolen..."

Ken stopped, his mouth dropped open. "Dr. Faysal is the only one who knows that Marty may have confided in you. He must have been responsible for the break-in. Believe me, Frank, I would never have condoned that..."

"Today a man was guarding the morgue. You must've known that."

"He's one of Gamal's security guards. I wanted him to prevent anymore snooping. I had Marty in mind, not you."

"Despite what Marty told me, I was still hoping I was wrong. After the autopsy today, I did an ultrasound. I printed a copy. It was obvious you removed his heart."

Ken walked around the table and sat next to Frank. He placed a hand on Frank's shoulder. "Frank, in the morning I'm going to London to retrieve a heart for Link. Please don't say anything about this to anyone. I intend to go to the hospital authorities when I return. I promise to tell them everything. But for now, nothing must interfere with picking up that heart."

"But Dr. Manning wouldn't accept a heart from London."

"I told him I was going to go to Cook County Hospital to retrieve the heart of a young boy who is near death. I assured him that I had checked out every detail. And that the heart would be a perfect match for Link. Because Link is barely hanging on, I said I'd call on my way back from Cook County so the transplant team can be ready and waiting in the OR."

"You assumed that he wouldn't take time to check out the source before surgery?"

"Exactly."

Frank realized Ken's decision to retrieve a heart for Link in London would expose the fact that he had perfected a method of organ preservation well beyond what was currently possible. He was intentionally exposing his unauthorized experimentation with human organs in order to save his godchild. Frank reached for Ken's hand.

"I promise I won't say a word to anyone. But Dr. Faysal still scares the hell out of me. Contact him. Demand that he stop harassing us."

"He's most likely just trying to intimidate you. If all goes well, I should be back in two or three days. I'll call him tonight."

"What about the other doctors at the Hakim Medical Center?"

"None of the medical staff know that any of the organs were obtained illegally. To my knowledge, only Dr. Faysal and his security staff are involved."

"The Bradshaws know you're going to London to get a heart?"

"I told Tom and Lydia everything. They know that I plan to go to the hospital medical director after I return. Tom was concerned about how Dr. Faysal might react. His involvement would also be exposed. Tom said he'd call you?"

"I did get a message...I haven't had a chance to return his call."

"Please do," Ken said. "Tom wants to help."

Ken headed for the door. As he hurried down the hall Frank walked alongside him, practically running to keep up with Ken's ostrich-like stride.

Frank thought of Marty, who was starting experimental chemotherapy the next day. She would be thrilled to learn that a heart for Link might soon be on the way, but if she knew, would that influence her decision regarding chemo? He didn't want that to happen.

"Dr. Bernholtz, does Link know?" Frank asked.

"Yes. I was with him when you called."

Frank headed for Link's room. On the way, he thought of what Ken had said. Maybe Faysal was only trying to intimidate them. He hadn't done anything to harm anyone, at least not yet. But Frank wasn't ready to drop his guard.

As he entered Link's room, Frank saw Tom applying a moist cloth to Link's forehead. Link appeared to be asleep.

"Dr. Tupelo, Link is so damn lethargic," Tom said. "Even if I shake him, he opens his eyes for only an instant. I'm staying tonight."

At the foot of the bed was a chart on which the nurses entered vital signs and laboratory results, as well as Link's intake and output. Frank studied the data.

"Kidney waste products are building up. Dialysis should

help."

Frank motioned to Tom to follow him into the corridor. "I just spoke with Dr. Bernholtz. I understand he told you what's been going on?"

"Yes," Tom said, "and I'm worried that Dr. Faysal isn't ready to pack up and head back home."

Frank told Tom about the two break-ins.

"Good God! That bastard...you're going to need protection."

"But we can't call the police. They're investigating the break-ins, but they don't know the whole story," Frank said.

"We don't need to. I'll bring in one of my former employees."

They walked toward a phone at the nurses' station.

"He's a retired cop," Tom said. "He's done private work for the family. I'll ask him to come to the hospital immediately. His name's Nate Chase. I want him to go to the motel with you tonight."

"You think that's necessary?"

"We've nothing to lose by being cautious. Where should he meet you?"

"I have to check on my patients and then sign out to the resident on call. Have him meet me at the ER in forty minutes."

Frank started to leave; then turned. "What do you think is going to happen to Dr. Bernholtz? Will he go to jail?"

"He and I talked about that. Ken knows defending him isn't going to be easy. He thinks, and I agree, that a prosecutor isn't going to believe he wasn't part of the cover-up. We're going to have to prove he wasn't."

Forbidden Harvest

"But when he returns he told me he's going to come clean with the medical director...shouldn't he already have a lawyer?"

"He will. I'm putting him in touch with one."

Tom asked his assistant, Alison, to get the company attorney, Ted Nance, on the phone. "He might've left for the day. Call him at home. Track him down."

Ten minutes later Tom's phone rang. "Tom, this is Ted. What's up?"

Tom explained that he needed a law firm experienced in defending medical malpractice cases. Ted didn't hesitate. "The most celebrated firm is Lee, Davis and Carrington in Nashville. Davis is the star of the group. Their pretrial research is so good that most of their cases are settled out of court."

Tom thanked him and immediately placed a call to the firm. He spoke to Mr. Lee and explained that a prominent physician had allegedly performed medical procedures on deceased children without parental consent, and the organs were reportedly transferred to another institution. Mr. Lee listened attentively and said he would confer with Archibald Davis.

In just a few minutes Mr. Davis was on the line. "Mr. Bradshaw, I'm intrigued by this case and would be happy to be a consultant for your attorney in the areas that involve medical malpractice. This, however, is no ordinary medical malpractice case. It's a felony to trade in human organs. The insurance company that covers this doctor may disclaim any responsibility, because there was clear intent on the part of the physician. The families might bring assault and battery charges for performing unauthorized medical procedures. Mr. Bradshaw, your friend needs the best damn criminal lawyer he can find."

Forbidden Harvest

"But the organs were being used to save the lives of children...hundreds of children."

"That argument might affect how severely the judge decides to punish this individual, but the fact that crimes have been committed is unchanged. I know of an excellent criminal lawyer who also has considerable experience in malpractice cases. Her name is Charlotte Richards. She was a former prosecutor in Dade County, Florida. She's as tough as they come, but can act sweet as your mama."

Tom called Ken. "I spoke with a malpractice lawyer in Nashville. He suggested someone experienced in both malpractice and criminal law...recommended an attorney in Miami. Charlotte Richards. Said she's one of the best."

"I haven't time..."

"I have the lawyer's phone number," Tom said. "At least talk with her. You can meet with her after you return, before you go to Dr. Krandall."

Ken called Charlotte Richards. Her answering machine provided an after-hours emergency number. A woman answered. "Hello, Charlotte Richards speaking."

Ken told her who he was and where he worked. He said he needed an attorney who could meet with him on his return from London, where he was going to harvest a heart for his godchild, who was desperately ill awaiting transplant surgery.

"I plan on going to the hospital medical director..."

"Why?"

He went on to tell her he had removed major body organs from children who had died at Children's Hospital. The parents of the deceased children had not consented to organ donation.

He experimented with some of the organs, he explained, and had sent others to a hospital in Puyallup, Washington, where they were used in transplant operations for children who otherwise would have died.

"You asked the parents, they denied you permission and you went ahead anyway?"

"I never personally ask since I have no clinical relationship with the patient or family. The attending physician or house-staff discuss organ donation and obtain written permission if the parents agree."

"Slow down, doctor, and let me get a chair. My feet are killing me." Moments later she was back on the line. "You did that how many times, doctor?"

"Over one hundred...I'd have to check to give you an exact count."

"Lordy, lordy. Somebody pay you for those organs?"

"Not directly. They did contribute to my research trust fund."

"I assume somebody found out, and that's why you need a lawyer?"

"A teen-aged girl hid in the morgue. She observed an autopsy. Later she told her doctor." Ken went on to explain about Dr. Faysal and the break-ins. He also told her that he intended to go to the hospital medical director to confess. "I've been advised to have an attorney with me when I meet with him."

"Aaaah."

Ken said, "Pardon me?"

"Oh, I was just expressing how good it feels to get my shoes off. You know, as I get older, my feet occupy more of my attention than I would ever have imagined."

Forbidden Harvest

Ken wondered if calling her had been a good idea.

"Don't worry, Dr. Bernholtz, I'm one hell of a lawyer. It's my brain you're hiring, not my feet."

"You come highly recommended. How soon can we meet?"

"I have a court case that should wind down by the end of the week. But why the rush..."

"The fact that I'll be able to successfully preserve a donor organ for up to twenty-four hours will make it clear to the transplant surgeon and the hospital authorities that I have continued my research after I was forbidden to do so."

"I see. So you're knowingly exposing yourself to save you godchild. Are you sure there are no other options?"

"My godchild's on life support. He's not likely to survive if I miss this opportunity."

"Of course you must go. I'll fly to Seattle after your return. Call me. My secretary will let you know my arrival time. Meet me at Sea-Tac. Take a cab. That'll give us time to go over your statement without driving distractions."

"I can do that," Ken said.

"By the way, Dr. Bernholtz, I hope you have plenty of money. This case is going to cost right much."

"Reasonable legal fees should not pose a problem."

"Who said reasonable?"

Ken wasn't sure how to respond. Regardless of the cost, it seemed he had little choice. The effect on his career would be irreparable, regardless of the outcome. But the prospect of a possible jail term was unimaginable. He was prepared to spend all he had to prevent that.

"I have some resources. And also the CEO of Thomas

Bradshaw Industries has promised to help out financially."

Charlotte let out another "aaaah," and Ken assumed she was still massaging her feet.

"Dr. Bernholtz, I'm not looking forward to a flight to Seattle. By the time I arrive, my feet will look like a pair of water-wings. Before our meeting, write in chronological order every detail you can recall, from the very beginning. Don't use a computer, and certainly don't dictate anything to a secretary or recorder. When you return from London, stall the meeting with the medical director, so we can huddle for at least a day or two. And for God's sake, don't do anything stupid like fudging records or destroying evidence. I don't want to clear you of a crime, then have you nailed for obstruction of justice."

CHAPTER TWENTY-NINE

Earlier that day, Razi, one of Gamal's security guards, called the Yellow Cab Company and reported he had left his briefcase in one of their cars. He didn't know the driver's name, but had written down the license number as the cab drove off. He was placed on hold.

"I'm sorry sir, but the driver didn't report finding anything. His name is Marcos Lopez. I can give you his phone number."

Razi looked up Lopez's address in the phone directory. That evening, with a Seattle street map spread on the passenger seat, Razi drove around for an hour before he located the apartment. He pulled up to the five-story building. In the front hall was a battery of mailboxes. Marco's apartment was 512. An out-of-order sign was taped to the elevator doors. Razi headed up the steep, dingy wooden steps. Along the stairway large sections of plaster had come loose, revealing lathe that had been painted the same color as the walls. Graffiti was everywhere. The combination of food odors and the pungent ammonia-like smell of urine permeated the hallway. By the time Razi reached the fifth floor he was nauseated and gasping for breath. Having gotten stuck in rush-hour traffic, he was in a foul mood. He realized that the doctor would soon be leaving the hospital, and he was concerned that he and the woman might move once again, making them harder to trace.

He knocked with authority. A woman answered. She was wearing zebra-striped leotards and a tight-fitting T-shirt cut off to reveal her trim waist. She didn't unlatch the door chain. Razi eyed her appreciatively. "I'm sorry to disturb you, ma'am, but does Mr. Lopez live here?"

She fingered a large pendant earring as she spoke. "What party should I tell him is calling?"

"Yesterday he picked up a couple we suspect of a crime." He poked a badge through the partially-opened door.

She shouted over her shoulder, "Marcos, there's a cop here to see you." She opened the door but didn't invite him into the room.

A short, powerfully-built man wearing jeans and a tank top approached Razi.

"Yeah?"

It was already dusk, and the only light came from the kitchen. Razi looked about the room before he spoke. In the far corner was a television set sitting on a cardboard box. The only other furniture was a recliner and a plastic-covered couch.

"Yesterday," Razi said, "you picked up a man and woman on Thirty-Second and Graham. They were carrying luggage. You remember them?"

Martino bit into an apple and chewed deliberately before answering. Razi waited.

"Sure. The guy gave me a twenty-buck tip." He took another large chunk from the apple.

"Smells like the chicken's burning," the woman said. "I better check."

"They're counterfeiters," Razi said. "We were following them in an unmarked car." He moved closer to Marcos, their faces just inches apart. "I need to know where you took them, and I don't have a lot of time."

Marcos took another bite of his apple.

"Hey, that's funny. I asked them if they had dough in those bags. I'll be damned."

Razi reached out and grabbed Marco's shirt. "If you don't stop eating that apple and tell me where you took them, I'm bringing you in."

"Hey, what the hell's going on?"

Razi tightened his grip. Marcos was barely able to maintain his balance. "Yeah, I remember, it was the Seatac Motor Inn on the south side."

Razi shoved Lopez, causing him to fall. He stood over him, hoping he would give Razi an excuse to sock him.

"Shit, man, what kinda cop are you?"

Razi left the room and raced down the steps two at a time.

He called Dr. Faysal from his car phone.

"Doctor, they went to a motel close to the airport. The Seatac Motor Inn...."

"Excellent. Call Anwar. He's at the hospital. Have him meet you at the motel. Wait for Dr. Tupelo to arrive. He'll lead you to her room...then proceed with our plan."

"You're certain we must do this?" Razi asked.

"They intend to expose us. Too many people would suffer. Especially our sick children. It must be done."

Later that evening, Gamal Faysal sat in his study,

Forbidden Harvest

waiting for Razi to report back to him. Kenneth must not know of his plans to deal with the nurse and Dr. Tupelo. Besides, how was he to prevent Kenneth from going to the authorities?

They had become friends over the past three years. But Kenneth is weak, Gamal thought. He'll never go so far as I to preserve what we've accomplished. The phone rang.

"Hello, Gamal, this is Ken."

"Ah, Kenneth, I was going to call you."

"I'm on a plane headed for London. I've located a compatible donor for my godchild. The donor is near death. I called ahead to Guys Hospital. They will place the child on life support, if necessary."

"But Kenneth, to keep the heart viable you'll have to employ your rapid-cooling technique. You'll be bringing our secret into the open."

"It's no longer a secret. I spoke with Frank Tupelo this afternoon. He knows everything...he even has an ultrasound record that proves I removed the heart from the Zack boy. But he's agreed not to tell anyone until I get back from London."

"Kenneth, I beg you, do not do this."

"It's too late to cover up. And you must not harass Frank or the nurse. Dr. Tupelo told me of the break-ins. I assume your guards were involved?"

Gamal gripped the phone tightly. He did not respond.

"There's no reason the Hakim Medical Center can't continue its work," Ken insisted. "Organs will still be available through legitimate channels. I plan to publish my animal-research findings. Others can duplicate my results with human organs."

"That might take years. In the meantime, what's to

become of the children?"

"It's true. More children who need transplants will die. That's tragic. But in time, many will benefit from the technology we've perfected."

"Kenneth, do what you must. But you're betraying our friendship..."

"Damn it," Ken snapped. "Can't you see...we have no other choice?"

"It's easy for you to say that some children will suffer. These are my country's children who will die. Don't tell me what I should or should not do. I'm committed to do everything in my power to protect those children entrusted to my care. Goodbye, Kenneth. Don't forget the money! Our enterprise has brought much that is good for both of us. That must not end!"

Gamal thought of the friendship that had grown between him and Kenneth. He had broken bread with Gamal's family. He had held Gamal's children on his lap. He and Kenneth had played chess evenings after dinner. An exasperatingly slow and methodical player, Kenneth was nevertheless an impressive tactician. His one serious flaw was that he hesitated too long to move in for check-mate. Kenneth will be an easy adversary, Gamal thought.

Gamal immediately called Dr. Jamael, Kenneth's assistant. "Jamael, are you aware Dr. Bernholtz is at this moment on his way to London to harvest a heart for his godchild?"

"Excuse me for a moment," Jamael said. "I'm staining some slides. I need to rinse this batch or they will be ruined." Soon he was back on the phone. "Yes, Dr. Faysal, you said Dr. Bernholtz went to London?"

"Didn't he tell you?"

"I know he left in great haste, taking with him all the equipment he would need to transport an organ. He said he'd return in two to three days."

"Didn't you think this significant enough to immediately share with me?"

"I was busy. I didn't give it much thought."

"Jamael, if anything were to happen to Kenneth, you must be prepared to take over his work."

Jamael remained silent.

"I learned today that Kenneth intends to betray us on his return from London," Gamal said. "We cannot permit that. The families who have entrusted their children to us will be furious."

"Dr. Bernholtz is a brilliant man. He has taught me well. I never believed it would come to this."

"When I chose you to work with him, I made it clear that you must be prepared to take over his work eventually."

"Yes, but..."

"You have given me your solemn word. Are you prepared to carry on his work as you promised?"

"I am familiar with every phase of his research. Within the year, the hyperbaric process will most likely be perfected. It will allow us to store organs almost indefinitely. I have given you my word, but I'm deeply saddened by what you say."

CHAPTER THIRTY

After signing out to the on-call resident, Frank hurried to the ER. How was it possible that one day he was going about his medical training, taking up the never-ending battle with disease, and suddenly, because of the curiosity of a fifteen-year-old girl, he was caught up in a bizarre organ-snatching scheme? Who would ever have suspected Ken Bernholtz, Link's godfather! Also, would he have dreamed a week ago that at this moment he'd be heading to the ER to meet his bodyguard?

As he walked through the double doors that separated the waiting room from the patient care area, a clerk called out, "Dr. Tupelo, there's a guy said he's supposed to meet you here."

Frank turned and looked about the crowded room. A tall, heavy-set man with a full shock of grey hair and a ruddy complexion stood and walked to Frank. He reached for Frank's hand. "I'm Nate Chase. Tom Bradshaw sent me."

Frank led him to a patient exam room. He closed the door before speaking. "I'm planning to hitch a ride on one of the ambulances. The loading bay isn't visible from the parking area, so anyone watching wouldn't be able to see us board."

Nate, half a head taller than Frank, looked as though he

Forbidden Harvest

could pick him up with one arm. Frank was glad he had been able to come on such short notice.

"Smart idea, Doc," Nate said, "but they may already know where you're staying. They had a couple of days to figure it out. I suggest you have the ambulance drop you off at Dunkin' Donuts down the road. I'll go ahead in my car and meet you there."

"We'll drive to the motel in your car?"

"No, you catch a cab from there. I'll follow you. I'm driving a dark blue Taurus. Where are you going, in case we get separated?"

As Nate spoke, he joined his fingers and, turning them palm-out, cracked several knuckles. His hands looked powerful enough to crack a coconut.

"What?" Frank asked, distracted.

"Where you goin'?"

"We're staying at the Seatac Motor Inn."

"Yeah. I know where that is."

Frank boarded the next ambulance that left the emergency area. He told the driver that his car had broken down, and that someone was meeting him at Dunkin' Donuts.

A few minutes later, Frank stepped from the ambulance and was relieved to see a dark blue Taurus parked out front. The evening was cool, and a misty rain filled the air. He looked at the sky. He could see neither moon nor stars. Just then, another car pulled into the parking area. He glanced at the driver, who stared back at him.

When Frank entered, he saw Nate sitting at the counter. He sat next to him.

"I lost twenty pounds after I left the force," Nate said,

looking straight ahead. "I love those little fat-balls."

Frank ordered two coffees and a dozen doughnuts to go. He glanced around the room, looking for the man he had seen before he entered. Where had he gone?

"There's a pay phone in the parking lot," Nate said. "I'll leave first. I'll call you a cab; then I'll wait in my car. Keep an eye out for the cab; it should be here pretty quick. I'll follow you."

"Are you planning on spending the night" Frank asked.

"Yeah. I'll stay in my car and park where I can see the door to your room. Let me have your motel key. The nurse can let you in."

Frank stepped from the cab, just a few feet from his motel room door. He looked about the parking lot and saw the blue Taurus pull into a space two doors down from his. The late evening air was chilly. The earlier mist had turned into a light rain. He began to relax, knowing that Nate was nearby. He knocked.

"Who is it?"

"It's me, Dr. Frankenstein."

Tina opened the door, not releasing the chain bolt.

"It's okay. I'm alone."

As he stepped into the room, Frank sniffed.

"It smells great in here."

"I was starving. I had some Chinese delivered."

They walked across the room beyond the queen-sized bed to a kitchenette. Tina was bare-footed. She wore jeans and a pink tank top that hung loosely about her waist. Her hair was pulled up into a bushy ponytail that bounced from side to side as she walked. Frank set the box of doughnuts and coffee on the table. He pried off the lid of a Styrofoam cup and took a sip. He reached into the box for a doughnut. Tina looked over his shoulder, peering into the box. She lightly pressed against him.

"Save the jelly doughnut for me. Okay?"

She walked to the microwave, placed the Styrofoam boxes inside and started the timer.

"So what're we supposed to do?" she asked. "Sit here and wait for someone to attack us?"

Frank told her about Nate.

"He followed me to make sure none of Faysal's men show up. He's sitting in his car just a couple of doors from us."

She checked the food in the microwave, and then set the timer for two additional minutes.

"What did Dr. Bernholtz say?" she asked.

Frank reached for the jelly doughnut. She slapped the back of his hand.

"That one's mine, remember?"

She sat next to Frank, took her coffee cup and propped her feet up. "You didn't answer my question."

"Bernholtz was stunned when I told him about the break-ins. He believes Faysal is just trying to scare us."

Tina jumped when the microwave bell went off. She laughed.

"I've been edgy as hell all day. You have no idea how good it is to have you here."

Frank stood and looked toward the door. "Did you hear that?" He watched as the door, restrained by the chain, opened a few inches. Hadn't he latched it securely? He started to move toward the door, and stopped. He watched transfixed, as a pair of steel jaws grasped and snapped the chain.

CHAPTER THIRTY-ONE

The door flew open. Anwar and Razi burst into the room. Anwar held a bolt cutter in one hand and a gun in the other. Razi carried a briefcase. Frank saw Nate come up behind the men.

"Drop that gun," Nate shouted.

Razi dropped the briefcase and reached into his jacket. He froze when Nate pressed a gun against his temple.

"Doc, bring a couple of chairs so your visitors can have a seat," Nate said.

Frank grabbed two chairs and carried them to where the two men stood. Nate ordered the men to sit with their arms raised above their heads.

Anwar was the tall man Frank had seen at the hospital. He turned to Tina, who had ducked behind the table. She stood and grabbed a plastic knife, holding it in her clenched fist.

Nate walked to Razi to search him. "This little man has a mean lookin' toy." He removed a derringer pistol from a shoulder holster. He handed the pistol to Frank.

"Miss Carrol," Nate said, "would you retrieve that briefcase? I'm curious to see what's inside."

As she walked past Razi, he jumped to his feet and

reached his forearm around her neck, pulling her toward him. He placed his other hand behind Tina's head.

"Drop those guns, or I snap this pretty neck."

Frank's hand shook so bad, he didn't trust himself to fire.

Nate slowly lowered his hand and let his gun slip to the floor. "Do like he says, Doc."

"The one under your belt," the man holding Tina said. "Drop it to the floor and kick it over to me."

Tina tried desperately to get Razi's forearm from around her neck. The more she struggled, the harder he pressed. In her right hand she tightened her grip on the plastic knife. She swung her arm over her shoulder. The knife snapped as it struck Razi, opening a wide gash just below his eye. He released his grip on Tina enough to allow her to spin around and slam her right knee into his groin.

Razi pushed her across the room, causing her to crash to the floor. He lunged for Nate's gun. Nate fell directly on him, grabbing his outstretched hand as he pressed Razi's head to the floor.

In the meantime, Anwar reached for the gun Frank had dropped. As Anwar grasped the gun, Frank kicked it from his hand. It careened across the floor and landed close to where Tina sat, clutching her throat. Her nose was bleeding. Anwar propelled himself toward the gun, sliding on his belly as he reached for it. But Tina got to the gun first. She held it in both hands.

When the gun went off, it sounded like a cannon in the small room. The bullet smashed into the carpeting, missing Anwar's hand by inches. He rose into a crouching position, holding his hands above his head. He inched closer to Tina. She pointed the gun at his head and screamed, "Don't come any closer. I won't miss next time!"

In the meantime Nate had subdued Razi and retrieved his gun. He shouted to Anwar, "You lay next to your friend here."

Frank felt lightheaded. His knees shook as he walked toward the open door. The carpeting close to the door was soaked with rain. He grabbed the briefcase, closed the door and walked to the bed where Tina sat, rubbing her neck. The gun she had fired lay on the bed between them. Frank gently held Tina's swollen nose and applied slight pressure. "I don't think it's broken."

"It's my neck. That animal damn near crushed my trachea."

Frank opened the briefcase. Tina reached in and removed two multiple-dose vials. She read the labels. "It's morphine. It must have come from a hospital or pharmacy. I don't get it."

Frank removed the rest of the items and laid them on the bed. There was rope, strips of cloth, a tourniquet, disposable gloves, syringes, needles, packets of alcohol, sponges, a screwdriver and a door-chain mechanism.

"Looks like our friends here were going to treat you and the lady to a little party," Nate said. "Doc, tie their hands behind their backs; they were nice enough to bring the rope."

Frank cinched the rope around Razi's wrist. He then tied Anwar's hands. "What do we do with them now?" Frank asked.

"I know what I'd like to do." He rolled them onto their backs. Nate stared at them menacingly. "I'll call the police. Tell'm I made a citizen's arrest as these jokers were breaking into your room. Armed robbery, possession of drugs...that'll put'em away for a while."

Nate placed his gun in his shoulder holster and scooped

up the other gun from the bed. He placed it under his belt.

"That was a hell of a move," Frank said to Tina.

"In nurse's training there were a bunch of rapes on campus. I took a course in self-defense."

"Taught you how to handle a gun?" Nate asked.

"I've never even held one before."

Nate laughed. "I never would've guessed it. You sure scared the living bejesus out of him."

Minutes later, two patrol cars with sirens screeching pulled to the door of the motel. Nate described what had happened. One of the older officers recognized him. "Thought you retired. You can't keep your nose out of it, can you?" He looked at the dinette table. "You must've smelled the doughnuts."

An officer took statements from Tina and Frank, while a second officer placed Anwar's and Razi's guns in plastic bags. They took snapshots of the contents of the briefcase. It was two hours before the police told them they could leave.

"Their boss, whoever he is, is playing for keeps," Nate said as they walked to his car. "Mr. Bradshaw asked me to take you to his place tonight. Wants me to stay until Dr. Bernholtz gets back from London." He looked from Frank to Tina. "That okay with you?"

"I need to be at the hospital by seven," Frank said. He turned to Tina. "Maybe Nate should drive you to the airport for a flight to Baltimore. Isn't that where you said your parents live?"

"I'm not dragging my parents into this. I'll stay at Tom's tonight and go with you to the hospital in the morning." She bumped Nate in the chest with her fist. "I don't want to get too far away from this guy."

On the way, Nate called Tom. "Mr. Bradshaw, two guys showed up at the motel. They were armed and dangerous. They're in the hands of the police right now. I'll tell you more about it when I get there."

"God Almighty!" Tom said. "Frank and Tina okay?"

"Yeah, they're fine. See you in a half hour."

The rain by now was coming down in earnest. Nate adjusted his rear-view mirror. "Hey, you guys okay back there?"

"Yeah. I guess. I still can't believe what just happened," Frank said.

"We'd of been in a jam if your lady hadn't made a move."

Tina leaned back. "Everything was so fast, it doesn't seem real."

"And just a couple of hours ago I about convinced myself this whole mess was beginning to be resolved," Frank said.

The Bradshaw property was surrounded by six-feet-high wrought-iron fencing. Nate pulled up to an entrance gate. He pressed a button on a speaker phone mounted on a post on the driver's side.

"Yes, who is it?" a male voice asked.

"It's me, Nate. Mr. Bradshaw's expecting me."

"Yes, sir."

The gate slowly swung open and closed behind them as they drove up a tree-lined drive. The house had the appearance of an Italian villa, with a plain facade of beige stucco and large shuttered windows.

Tina looked wide-eyed at Frank. "Tom's place?"

"The estate belonged to Lydia and Tom Sr.," Nate interjected. "After Brenda died, he and Link moved in here. A year later Lydia moved into a condo downtown."

Lydia met them at the door. She embraced Frank.

"Dr. Tupelo, thank God you're okay." She turned to Nate and shook his hand. "You've come through again for us, Nate. I wish Tom's dad could be here to thank you."

Tom joined them in the vestibule. Frank introduced Tina to Lydia and Tom. An elderly gentleman wearing a blue blazer and black bow tie reached for their luggage.

"Albert, please take their bags to the guestrooms," Tom said. "We'll not bother you anymore this evening, thank you."

Tom led them past a formal sitting area into his study. The walls were lined with books on hand-rubbed walnut shelving. There were several upholstered chairs arranged in front of a stone fireplace. "Make yourselves comfortable. Can I get you something to drink?"

"I could use something stiff," Frank said.

"How about some Deanston single-malt Scotch on ice?" Tom asked.

"Sure, thanks."

"And you, Tina?" Tom asked.

"I'll have some of the same. Maybe it'll stop my insides from shaking."

"Nate, the usual?"

"Yes, sir. A couple of fingers of Jim Beam. No ice."

Frank put an arm around Tina. "I know what you mean. I feel as though I've been on a vibrating bed for a couple of hours."

"I hope you plan on staying here until Ken returns," Lydia said.

"I agree. Faysal's desperate," Tom said as he mixed their drinks. "There's no telling what he'll try next."

"Mr. Bradshaw..." Frank said.

"Let's drop the formalities," Tom suggested.

"Marty's starting her new course of chemo tomorrow. I need to be there," Frank said

"We really appreciate everything you've done for Link," Lydia said. "And Marty."

"Link sleeps most of the time," Frank said, "but I try to say encouraging things to him. I believe he's aware of what's happening around him."

Tom smiled as he handed Frank a drink. "Link not only has a good doctor, but a wonderful friend."

Lydia leaned forward. "Now, Nate, tell me from the beginning what happened tonight."

As Nate reached the point where the two men approached the motel room door, Tina interrupted, "I only left the room for ten minutes all day. How on earth did they figure out where I was?"

Nate cracked his knuckles. "Well, if I was trying to find you I'd look up that cabby who brought you there. They followed you awhile before you lost them. They must've gotten the license number. After that, it would be easy to find out who he was."

"So they just parked by the motel entrance and waited for me to arrive," Frank commented.

Nate continued telling how one of the men grabbed Tina and practically strangled her.

"Good heavens," Lydia gasped.

"It was dumb to walk between you and that monster. I realized too late that you meant for me to circle behind him."

Nate told how Tina immobilized one of the men, picked up a gun and subdued the second man. He then went on to tell them of the contents of the briefcase. "I figure they were going to shoot up these nice young people with that morphine and try to make it look like they died partying."

"But what about the cut door chain?" Tom asked.

"There was a screwdriver and chain bolt lock in the briefcase. They might have gone into one of the other motel rooms to check out the door locks. They pretty much had all day to lay out their plans. They must've figured that the chain might be latched and brought along a replacement, just in case."

"Dr. Faysal must be a madman," Lydia said. "And to think how Ken trusted him!"

"This changes everything," Tom said. "Uncle Ken may be in real danger. Mother, I'm flying to London the first flight I can get out of here. I want to be with Ken. Faysal may move against him while he's still in London, or when he arrives back here."

"Tom, Link's desperately ill. Shouldn't you be here with him?" Lydia asked.

"Mother...if we don't get that heart..."

"Of course you're right," Lydia said.

Tom stood. "I'm going to pack a bag. Mother, please call British Airways. They fly non-stop to Heathrow." He looked at his watch. "Their red-eye leaves at 10:55. I've flown it before. Get me on that plane." He turned to leave the room. "And call Uncle Ken. Tell him what happened at the motel and ask him to be careful as hell."

Lydia hurried from the room. She returned a few minutes later. She stood before the fireplace, her arms folded across her chest. "Thank God I was able to get Tom on the flight. Our company jet couldn't have been mobilized that fast. Not for a transatlantic flight. Tom'll be on his way in less than an hour."

"That's pretty amazing," Tina said.

"Has Dr. Bernholtz arrived in London?" Frank asked.

"He will soon. I spoke to Dr. Shellbourne. He's the boy's doctor. He said the boy has been placed on life support. Poor child. Doesn't it seem cruel to be wishing for the child to die sooner rather than later?"

"Tom had been planning to stay with Link tonight," Lydia continued. "I'm going to the hospital. Frank, wouldn't it be a good idea for someone to stay with Marty?"

Frank nodded. "I'll call her mother. I've been concerned about Marty. She's been depressed about Link's condition. She's just not her perky self lately. And she's ambivalent about this new chemotherapy."

"That poor girl," Lydia said. "Let me know if for some reason Gladys can't stay. I'll get a private-duty nurse." Lydia left to get ready to go to the hospital.

Frank stood. "I'd better call Marty's mother."

Frank returned to the den and sat next to Tina. He gently touched her damaged nose. "I'm really sorry about that."

"Do you think the injury makes my face more interesting?"

"My mom would like it. You look more Italian."

Nate stood. "I'm gonna pass out for a few hours. What

time did you say you had to be at the hospital?"

"By seven," Frank said. He turned to Tina and took her hand in his...if he could only go back and start over. It was thoughtless to have dragged her into this mess. But if he hadn't....

Tina leaned her head on his shoulder. "It's just too much. With all this going on...and those two children so desperately ill." She began to cry.

Lydia had stopped back to say goodnight before leaving. She walked to the couch and crouched in front of Tina. She reached for her hands. "You two were almost killed tonight. My God, I'd be hysterical if it had happened to me! You need to get some rest. Let me show you to your room."

Tina kissed Frank goodnight. She and Lydia went upstairs.

Nate stood there awkwardly. "That's a hell of a lady friend you got there, Doc."

Frank felt his cheek where she had kissed him. "I just met her a few days ago. I'm surprised she's not furious."

"Holding hands and kissing doesn't look furious to me," Nate said. "Stabbing that guy in the face...that was furious."

Frank slept fitfully. He awoke at five, dressed, and went downstairs to the kitchen. He sat at a marble-top counter and removed a stack of index cards from his pocket. On each card was a patient's name and ID number. The cards were filled with shorthand notes about test results and scheduled procedures. Soon his team would be rounding with the chief resident and the attending physician. The interns would be pre-rounding on their patients in about an hour. They had to be ready to present their patients later on team rounds. The major diagnostic tests scheduled for the day would be reviewed to make sure the patients were adequately prepared. Frank would visit all his sicker patients before rounds. He also needed to catch up on any new admissions. He checked his watch. It was time to wake Nate and Tina. At the hospital, Frank got Tina a scrub suit. "Did you bring the beeper?"

"It's right here." She searched in her purse. "Damn it, where is it?" She removed several items. "Here it is."

"Make sure it's turned on, so I can find you."

Frank got Nate a long white coat and told him not to say too much, but to stay at his side. Frank introduced Nate to the other doctors as someone in private practice, rounding with him to learn whatever he could. The attending physician conducting rounds assumed Frank was referring to the practice of pediatric medicine. He shook Nate's hand, then proceeded to ignore him.

Following rounds, Frank checked Link's laboratory test results from the previous night. "His labs are back up to where they were before the dialysis. He'll need daily dialysis if we're going to keep him from slipping into a coma."

"Sounds pretty bad," Nate said. "Poor little guy."

"It totally wipes him out. Let's stop by his room."

Lydia was at Link's bedside when Frank and Nate entered. Link's eyes were closed. Was he asleep, Frank wondered?

"Hi, Link," Frank whispered, "I've got somebody here you know."

Link slowly opened his eyes and looked toward Frank. "Hi." His voice was hoarse. He looked at Nate..."Mr. Chase? You going to medical school or something?"

Nate's eyes glistened. "Hey, big guy, I hear you're

hanging in there."

"I already told Link about Uncle Ken going to London to get a heart," Lydia said. "And that he should be on his way back today or tomorrow."

Link dozed off. Frank talked directly into his ear in a quiet, soothing voice. "Link, you've got to keep being strong. With that new heart, before you know it, you and I can shoot baskets. If I can whip myself into shape, we can play a little one-on-one as soon as you're out of the hospital. I have to go now, but I'll stop back later. You want me to set your computer on the bed?"

Link nodded. Frank cranked the bed higher and set the computer on Link's lap. He raised the screen and booted, using Link's password to get into the Compuserve bulletin board. He scrolled *browse* until he saw a message signed *Madam Butterfly*. He reached over, took Link's glasses from the bedside table, and carefully put them on. Link struggled to read Marty's message.

"Marty's starting that new chemo..."

"I know," Frank said. "She told me to have you say a prayer for her."

Frank leaned over and read the message. *"Hey, Little Doc, chemo starts late this afternoon. I'll send you one more message before I check into the Puke-More Cafe. When I finish chemo in a week, I want to come see you in the recovery room with a new heart. Madam Butterfly."*

After Frank and Nate left, Lydia asked, "Link darling, would you like Marty and her mother to have lunch up here?"

"Yeah, that would be okay." He looked away from his grandmother. He whispered, "But I can't eat anything."

Gladys and Marty arrived at noon. Lydia had sent for

sandwiches, sodas and ice cream. Link was being fed intravenously, but he did manage to swallow a spoonful of chocolate chip ice cream.

Marty wasn't wearing any mascara or lipstick. Her eyes seemed flat, frightened. Gladys had stayed at the hospital all night and had not had a chance to shower or change. Lydia gave Gladys a hug and kissed Marty on the cheek.

"I don't know what's going on with my mom," Marty said. "She won't let me out of her sight. She's totally creeping me out."

Lydia was bursting to tell Marty and Gladys that Kenneth would soon be on his way with a heart for Link, but Frank had asked her not to.

"Your mother's worried about the chemo," Lydia said. "It's got us all on edge."

"Well, I have to talk with Dr. Tupelo this afternoon, and I want to see him alone, okay?"

"Of course you can," Gladys said, trying to sound upbeat.

After that exchange, Marty seemed to relax. She went to Link and roughed up his hair. "Hey LD, I'm saving up for that Hawaii trip." She did a little hula swivel at the bedside.

"The Puke-More Cafe, you make me laugh." Link looked at his grandmother. "Grandma, when is Dad coming?"

Lydia looked at Gladys and Marty; they both had the same question in their eyes. Coming from where? What could she tell him? She couldn't say he'd gone to London.

"He'll be here just as soon as he can."

Link closed his eyes and was soon asleep.

"Sometimes I come by to talk, and he just lies there and doesn't say anything," Marty said. "Like he's drugged out."

"The doctors said it's because of his kidneys," Lydia said. "Waste products build up in the blood."

"You look as though you could use a little sleep too, Mrs. Bradshaw," Gladys said. "In fact, we all could."

"I have to talk with Dr. Tupelo this afternoon, remember?" Marty said, as she and her mother walked to her room.

"Changing your mind about the chemo?"

"It's not that. I gotta ask him something."

At the nurses' station, Gladys approached the ward secretary. "Please page Dr. Tupelo and ask him to come to Marty's room as soon as possible."

"Patients are not supposed to page a doctor. He usually makes afternoon rounds at 4:00."

"I'm certain Dr. Tupelo won't mind. Just do it, please."

The woman shrugged and picked up the phone.

Frank and Nate Chase arrived at Marty's room thirty minutes later. Gladys was sitting at her bedside.

"She wants to talk with you," Gladys said. "I'll go to the lounge. Let me know when you're through."

After she left, Frank introduced Nate without explaining who he was.

"Doc Frank, can he leave us for awhile?"

"No offense taken, sweetie," Nate said.

Once they were alone, Frank pulled a chair to her bedside. Marty was sitting on the edge of the bed with her good right leg tucked under her. He waited for her to speak.

"Well, this is my big day, and I'm sitting on my leg so you won't see how much it's shaking. I'm scared poopless, and I just need to know everything they're going do to me."

"Fire away."

"Does the regular chemo team do all the usual stuff to get me ready? You know....figure out the dose and all?" As she spoke, she flopped onto her back, staring at the ceiling.

"Dr. Gibbs and her assistant will come by. Because it's a research drug, they have to follow very strict procedures. Two people have to check the dose before it's started."

"Will they be using one of those special pumps they used before?" She continued to avoid looking into his eyes.

Frank stood and leaned over her. "Marty, look at me. What the heck's with you?"

When their eyes met, her pupils were so widely dilated there was a mere sliver of color. Her facial expression was frozen as though it were a mask. He could sense the fear and isolation she must be feeling. He reached for her hand. "Marty, you don't have to do this."

Her eyes filled with tears. "It just seems no matter which way I turn, I see something real scary looking back at me. Even if it works, the damn cancer's coming back. It always does!"

Frank knew she was right. At best the treatment might give her a year, maybe two. But he mustn't rob her of hope. "This is a new kind of chemo. There have been some promising results."

"Tell me about the pump," she said, turning her face away.

"It's similar to ordinary pumps, but it's designed to deliver medicine extremely accurately. The protocol calls for them to calibrate the pump before each use. They may be doing that right now."

She pulled her hand from his and ran the fingers of both hands through her hair. "I know. Dr. Gibbs said they have to give it at the exact right speed."

"There's a strict routine. Her assistant will calculate the dose, and then Dr. Gibbs will do the math and double-check it. Dr. Gibbs will personally program the pump and start the medicine. The chemo nurse will check back every half-hour until it's all given."

Marty closed her eyes.

Perspiration covered her neck and face. He had never seen her like this. "You know it's not too late to change your mind," he said a second time.

She opened her eyes but didn't look directly at him. "It's not that," she said. "I'm afraid they're going to mess up. What if the machine starts to pump too fast and the chemo nurse doesn't come by for another thirty minutes?"

"Once it's programmed, and the rate changes for any reason, an alarm goes off. The floor nurse would come immediately to check the pump."

"But I've had pumps like that before. They sound off all the time."

"Most pumps are designed to go off if a little air is in the IV line. The nurse usually checks the line to make sure there isn't enough to do any harm. If not, they just reset it."

Marty sat up. She managed a tepid smile. "Thanks for answering all my stupid questions."

"I'll tell your mom we're finished talking. I'm on-call tonight. I'll stop by later."

As he started to leave, she called after him. "Doc Frank..."

He turned as he reached the doorway. "Yes?"

"Sorry I've been such a pain in the butt. I really do appreciate everything you've done. Love ya." She threw him a kiss.

CHAPTER THIRTY-TWO

Because of the bulk and weight of the equipment Ken needed to process and store the donor heart, he had constructed a collapsible luggage cart that resembled a baby carriage. Right after landing at Heathrow Airport, Ken phoned Dr. Shellbourne at Guys Hospital to tell him he was on his way.

Ken was grateful for the boxcar-sized cab that pulled to the curb. The driver helped him load the carriage into the back. Ken checked his watch. It was 11:30 AM. British time.

"I need to get to Guys Hospital as fast as possible."

"No problem, mate. That's how I like to go."

Ken regretted having asked the cabby to hurry. The speedometer read 160 kilometers. He leaned back, making a rough conversion. Almost a hundred miles per hour!

As the cab pulled in front of the hospital, Dr. Shellbourne was outside. He told Ken they expected the Moore boy would not make it through the night.

"His parents have signed the consent forms. The surgical team is fully prepared for the heart-harvesting operation. As soon as he's declared brain dead, the operation will begin."

"If he should die in the night, how quickly can you

assemble the surgical team?"

"The surgeons and nursing support staff are staying at the hospital tonight," Dr. Shellbourne said. "Everyone is extremely excited about being part of this."

As they spoke, Dr. Shellbourne grabbed Ken's luggage while Ken loaded the organ-storage canister on the carrier and proceeded to wheel it into the hospital's main entrance.

"You understand this is a special situation," Ken said. "The recipient's family is aware this is an experimental approach. I appreciate your promise to keep the information from the press until after I return to Seattle. In making the announcement, I'll give your team full recognition."

They brought the organ-storage canister to the surgical suite where Ken carefully scrubbed the equipment's exterior. He plugged it into an electrical outlet.

"We have to keep the batteries fully charged, so they'll be ready for the return trip," Ken explained.

Dr. Shellbourne brought Ken to the doctors' lounge. "There's tea and coffee here, and cream in the fridge. It you rummage though the cupboard you'll find a dish of scones and biscuits. Please help yourself. Oh, by the way, there was a call from Mrs. Bradshaw. She asked that you phone her."

As Ken dialed, he prayed that it wasn't bad news. God, after all Link had been through, Ken thought, don't let him slip away just when he was about to retrieve a heart.

Lydia answered the phone. When he heard her strained voice, a wave of fear swept through him.

"How's Link?"

"About the same, but he's requiring more frequent

dialysis."

Ken told her that Christopher Moore was on life support and his death was imminent. "I expect to be heading back within twenty-four hours."

"Dr. Faysal is a lunatic." She went on to tell him of the attack at the motel where Tina and Frank had gone to hide out.

Ken was appalled. "I called Faysal on my way here and told him not to harass them. Christ! What a monstrous and senseless thing to do. I said I would come clean on my return."

"That's exactly why Tom's concerned. Dr. Faysal might try to attack you while you're in London," Lydia said. "Tom's on his way to join you. He should arrive in about twelve hours."

"Tina and Frank must have been terrified."

"They'll be just fine. Nate's not letting them out of his sight. I've asked Tom to bring in the British police. There's no reason to take any chances."

Tom arrived at Guys Hospital late that evening. He and Ken sat at a table in the doctors' lounge. Tom looked as though he hadn't slept in days. Ken recalled how Tom had slipped into a state of despair after Brenda's death. He had that same anguished look in his eyes.

"Uncle Ken, you and I haven't had a chance to talk about how all this got started. I do remember three or four years ago, how frustrated you were about not being able to go ahead with your research."

"It's a long story, Tom." Ken tugged at his beard. "It's hard to know where to begin."

Forbidden Harvest

The room was comfortably furnished. The coffee they used was packaged in small bags, like tea. The aroma alone was enough to keep him awake.

There were four captain's chairs around a small table. Tom kicked off his shoes and massaged his toes.

Ken leaned back in his chair, staring at the ceiling. "The damn ceiling...harboring an inquisitive girl at just the wrong time," Ken lamented. "Who would have thought it would set in motion all that has happened since that day!"

"But things would have unraveled once you decided to come to London to retrieve a donor heart for Link."

"That's true. I accepted the fact that once Link's surgeons learned where the heart really came from...not Chicago, but London...they'd realize it had remained viable for an unprecedented twenty-four hours. They would surmise, and rightly so, that when I was denied the chance to replicate my animal experiments with human organs, I had gone ahead without the Human Subjects Committee's approval...and must be removing organs from deceased children without the parents' permission."

"But sending organs to the Hakim Medical Center was a whole other issue. What was behind that decision?"

"Once I started to use cadaver organs for my experiments, Faysal asked if I would consider providing his hospital with donor organs."

"But why did you confide in him?" Tom asked as he poured himself a second cup of coffee.

"The Saudi hospital was getting donors through legitimate channels but not enough for all the children waiting for transplants. Their surgical staff was desperate. It was heartbreaking to see those children die, knowing I had it in my power to save them."

"Why didn't you say anything to us? I know my dad

would've offered to help."

"I couldn't involve your family. Your dad was very sick."

They remained silent, lost in thought. Tom spoke first.

"I don't understand how you can use cadaver organs. Don't the tissues break down rapidly after death?"

"You're right. To get around that, I came up with a research study that the Human Subjects Committee approved. In essence, I proposed to validate the effectiveness of continued life-support measures during the critical time between the declaration of brain death and the completion of the harvesting operation."

Tom looked puzzled. "You lost me, Ken."

"For example, after harvesting, say the corneas, or a kidney, the surgeons would leave the life-support apparatus intact and send the body to the morgue."

"And that's when you helped yourself to whatever organs were left?"

Ken nodded. He walked to the counter and grabbed the coffee thermos. He refilled their mugs. "I took samples to determine if the tissues were still well oxygenated up to an hour after brain death had been declared. But while I had the body in the morgue, I also removed organs to send to the Hakim Medical Center. If they didn't have an immediate need for an organ, we used it for our experiments."

"Wouldn't all of the organs have been harvested by the transplant surgeons?" Tom asked.

"Families often decide to limit donation to specific organs."

"Your assistant had to know what was going on," Tom suggested.

"Yes. But I told Jamael that I had special permission from some parents to remove organs and tissues at autopsy to use in our research."

Tom looked incredulous. "No one's going to believe that."

"I doubt Jamael did. He knew how much the Saudi doctors depended on the organs we sent them. He's a decent man, who chose to look the other way."

"You two have dug yourselves into one hell of a hole."

"You're right. I couldn't publish my findings since the hospital had denied me permission to proceed with the research. With my quick-freeze method, I was able to preserve human organs four to six times as long as anyone else, yet my only outlet was the Hakim Medical Center. I was totally boxed in. I came to realize that success with our hyperbaric research would be my only way out."

"I don't understand; you said you couldn't share your results because you didn't have permission to do the experiments on human organs."

"With the hyperbaric method we've only worked with laboratory animals," Ken said. "We've done that so we'd be in a position to publish our findings."

"Didn't my dad lend you an engineer to help develop the hardware for your project?"

"He did. He was excited by its potential. Storing organs under several atmospheres of pressure has the potential of preserving them almost indefinitely."

"Imagine," Tom said, "being able to stockpile organs. Kids like Link could have transplant surgery when they need it."

"It's very exciting, Tom. Within a year we may have had that method developed well enough to publish our findings."

"But if you're exposed now, would anyone publish your work?"

"I'm hoping to get a preliminary report on the hyperbaric method in the medical journals as soon as possible."

Ken noticed the deep lines in Tom's forehead, the set of his jaw, and tightness about his mouth that hadn't been there before Brenda's death and Link's illness. Where had the little boy gone who had sat on his lap and tugged at his beard?

"You're going to need one hell of a lawyer," Tom said. "Have you called Charlotte Richards?"

"I did. But all I care about now is getting a heart for Link." Ken stood. "I'm going to find Dr. Shellbourne. See what's happening."

Ken handed Tom a packet of airline schedules. "Check these out. Once we've gotten the donor heart, we must move as quickly as possible."

Ken and Tom stayed at Guys Hospital that night. They lay in bunk beds in the doctors' on-call room. Every few minutes a beeper went off. It reminded Ken of his internship at Massachusetts General. As a young sleep-deprived intern, he had slept through the noise. But now, he stared into the darkness, too wide awake.

Christopher Moore didn't die that night. So Ken and Tom could do nothing but maintain their death watch, hour after hour.

CHAPTER THIRTY-THREE

Late that afternoon, at Children's Memorial Hospital, Marty lay motionless in her bed, drenched in perspiration, staring at the ceiling. After her conversation with Frank, she knew how to reprogram the pump to deliver what would be a deadly dose of chemotherapy. Closing her eyes, she was transported to the hours and days after her last chemo....her stomach had rejected the poisonous drugs in an unrelenting, fruitless effort to regurgitate what it couldn't. The powerful spasms of her abdominal muscles made her head feel it would explode and her eyes feel as if they would burst. Eventually she'd collapse, totally spent, only to erupt again and again in an unending cycle of unbearable retching and pain.

"Never, never, never again," she had begged her mother in the days following the ordeal. Even if she went into remission, how long would it last? Cancer would come back. Like always. "Never again," she whispered. Sitting up in bed, she reached out and pulled the IV pole toward her.

Frank picked up Link's medical record at the nurses' station and headed to his room. The early morning bustle had subsided, and a sleepy grey light flooded the corridor. Frank stopped at the door. His breath caught as he anticipated the familiar odor of renal failure. He approached Link's bedside and gently shook his shoulder. No response. Frank grasped his hand.

"Link, you're going make it. You have to hang on. There're a lot of us pulling for you. Uncle Ken called from London. He'll heading back here with a new heart any minute."

Link's leg jerked and his eyelids quivered, but he remained asleep. Frank noticed that his laptop computer was sitting on the bedside table, its screen in the upright position. It was blank except for a green light, indicating the computer was in operation. A nurse came into the room.

"He dozed off while he was on the computer," she said. "I set it over there. I was afraid to mess with the keyboard."

Frank hit the space bar, and the screen lit up. Marty usually left Link a message in the late afternoon, for the following morning when Link checked the bulletin board. Maybe Link was getting ready to leave her a message. He tried to wake Link to see if he wanted to tell her something, but he wasn't responsive. Frank asked the nurse to draw blood for stat blood gases and electrolytes and to call Link's intern.

"Tell her to review Link's intake and output over the past three days and to beep me as soon as possible."

Frank scrolled the screen of Link's laptop. The words *Madam Butterfly* flashed by. He went back a screen.

"Dear Link, this afternoon they'll be starting my chemotherapy with EP149. This whole hospital scene has been a bummer. Without you and Doc Frank and my mom, I guess I would have quit trying a long time ago. You have a great mind. Someday you could be a scientist like your Uncle Ken. But whatever you do, I want you to have a chance to grow up. I figure us having the same blood type

and all...God must've meant me to be part of your life. I read once about a mother who died giving birth. It was real sad but she was still sort of alive in the new baby. I guess that sounds kind of crazy. But if you have my heart, Link, I'll still be alive in a way....Even if this chemo were to help me it would only be for a short time. I'm sick of being sick, pretending everything is a big joke. Yesterday I went to see my other friend, who's dying from some kind of weird blood cancer. When she turned and looked at me, it was my face I saw. By the time you read this, you'll be recovering from the operation. Feel your pulse, Link. That will be me talking to you. Forever, Madam Butterfly."

Frank was stunned. He called the nurses' station closest to Marty's room. "Have they started the chemotherapy on Marty yet?"

"Yes. Her mother just stepped out for a few minutes. She told me not to allow anyone in the room."

Frank raced down the hall. He checked out the elevators. Two were on the first floor, one the eighth. He ran to the stairway and down three flights of stairs, and then dashed past the startled staff as he headed from the south to the west wing of the hospital. He passed a woman...it was Gladys. He stopped.

"Who's with Marty?" he asked.

"She begged me to get her some ice cream before the nausea kicks in. I asked the nurse to keep an eye on her until I got back."

"I'll take her the ice cream. I need to talk with her alone."

As Frank raced toward Marty's room, he recalled all the questions she had asked about the special pump used to infuse the drug. If she had watched the chemo technician, she may have figured out how to re-program it. Why hadn't he realized that sooner? He stopped briefly at the nurses' station.

"Has the infusion-pump alarm sounded?" he asked.

"Yes, about fifteen minutes ago. I checked. It was going in at the rate it was programmed for. I couldn't see anything else the matter with it. So I figured, false alarm. Is something wrong, Dr. Tupelo?"

"Page the chemo technician and have her come to Marty's room immediately."

"Dr. Tupelo, what the hell's going on?" Gladys asked as she caught up with Frank.

"I'll tell you as soon as I have had a chance to talk with Marty." He ran ahead to her room. She was lying with her eyes closed. Frank immediately went to the infusion pump and turned it off. The alarm sounded.

"Marty, look at me." He stood beside her bed and laid his hand gently on her shoulder.

She turned toward him, tears streaming down her cheeks. "Damn it! How'd you find out?"

"I saw your last message to Link, and then I remembered your questions about the pump. The chemo tech will be here in a few minutes, so I'll have to talk fast. Dr. Bernholtz will soon be on his way back from London with a heart for Link. Sometime in the morning he'll probably be having his transplant operation. Marty, you have to understand it's not a question of who should live, you or Link. Both your lives are precious."

She sat up in bed, her face inches from his. "Why didn't anyone tell me about Uncle Ken getting a heart? You must've known."

The chemotherapy technician walked in and immediately checked the infusion pump. "Why did you turn it off?" she asked. "Has Marty changed her mind?"

"I'm afraid Marty was fooling around with the programming buttons. I cut it off until you could take a look at it."

The technician was clearly startled. She checked the programming. "Good heavens! It's set for double the rate." Her face reddened. "I don't believe this. Marty, we're not playing games here. This is a powerful drug. I told you how important it was to get exactly the right dose."

Gladys, who had been standing by the door, rushed to Marty's side. She squeezed her daughter tightly. "Sweetheart, you are so special and wonderful. Don't even think of doing anything like that! I know this new drug is going to help you, I just know it." They clung tightly to each other.

"I screwed up, Mom. I didn't want to hurt you."

The chemo technician left, taking with her the infusion pump and intravenous solutions. Gladys and Frank sat beside Marty's bed. Marty pulled herself into a sitting position and reached for her Braves baseball cap.

"Mom, all day I was petrified thinking about the chemo, thinking it was all going to be for nothing. And I keep seeing myself in Cindy's bed with all those tubes. I was doing it as much for me as for Link."

Gladys was in a daze. She looked over at the bedside table where Frank had set the dish of ice cream. "Your ice cream's melted."

Marty laughed. Frank managed a weak smile but he felt like a fist as big as Nate's had punched him in the gut.

"Mom, you're the greatest. Pass me the glop and look in the top drawer; I keep a bunch of straws in there."

Marty turned to Frank. "You should've told me; you always told me everything." She started to cry. "And what's going to happen to Dr. Bernholtz after he gets back with the heart for Link?"

Gladys asked Frank, "What's this all about? What kind of trouble could Dr. Bernholtz be in?"

Frank was uncertain how much to tell Gladys. "It's extremely complicated and sensitive. I promised Dr. Bernholtz I wouldn't discuss with anyone what's happened until after he returns."

Gladys looked from Frank to Marty. "I'm confused. How does Marty know?"

"I'll tell you later," Marty said. "It's all my fault."

"That's not true," Frank said. "Dr. Bernholtz said he'll tell the medical director everything."

Marty sat up suddenly. "Do you think they'll put him in jail? I wish I'd never seen that freakin' autopsy."

"You saw an autopsy?" Gladys asked. "Dr. Tupelo, you let her see an autopsy? She's a child! What on earth were you thinking?"

"Mom, he didn't know. Nobody knew. I snuck into the morgue. I saw Dr. Bernholtz remove organs he didn't have permission to take out. I told Doc Frank. I should've kept my big mouth shut."

Gladys patted Marty. "You should have. You screwed up. Deal with it!"

"Yeah, I've heard that one before. It's your favorite *mantra!*" No one spoke for half a minute as Gladys rubbed Marty's back.

"I'd better get going. I have to meet with Dr. Cronce. See you in the AM., Madame Butterfly," Frank said.

Marty looked over her mother's shoulder. Her face was wet with tears. "Not if I see you first!"

As Frank hurried down the corridor, he remembered he

had not heard back from the intern about Link's lab results. He beeped her.

"I'm sorry, Frank," the intern said, "the attending happened by while I was with Link, and he wanted me to update him. Dr. Cronce just left. Link's fluid intake has pretty well kept up with his urinary output, but his electrolytes and blood gases indicate he's acidotic. Dr. Cronce believes fluid loss due to increased respiratory rate has probably made the difference. He suggested we correct it cautiously, because his cardiac compensation is so tenuous. He's worried that if Link doesn't get a transplant in the next day or two, we may have to use an artificial heart. He asked me to start Link on heparin in case we have to use the bridge device on short notice."

Frank realized the situation had become desperate. Dr. Cronce was preparing to use a device which transplant surgeons had little experience or success using in children. We can't take that chance, Frank thought, not when we're so close to getting Link a heart. He decided to call his cardiology attending to explore possible medical options. That might buy them enough time to convince Dr. Cronce to postpone using an artificial heart.

"Be sure you draw baseline coagulation studies," Frank said to the intern. "I'll be right there. We can go over the protocol together."

Lydia had gone home to shower and get a few hours of sleep before returning to the hospital. She barely got into bed when the phone rang. She was terrified. After several rings, she reached for the receiver.

"This is Dr. Cronce. I understand Tom is out of town. I'm sorry to call so late..."

"Has something happened to Link?"

"I've just examined him. We're having difficulty keeping fluid from building in his lungs and getting enough blood to pump through his kidneys. Do you recall me talking with you about the bridge device?"

"Yes."

"There's very little experience using it in children. But we're rapidly approaching the point where that may be our only recourse. We're starting a blood thinner tonight in preparation for attaching the pump tomorrow. We'll use it only if the situation becomes desperate. I've prepared a consent form. Can you come by first thing in the morning?"

"I'll come in right now."

"That's not necessary. Get some sleep and come around eight."

Lydia decided she would call Tom right away to discuss her signing permission to use an artificial heart. Not that they had much choice. She decided to return to the hospital just as soon as she spoke with Tom.

It was mid-morning of their second day at Guys Hospital. Ken and Tom could do nothing but wait. Earlier Tom had called Scotland Yard and reported that Dr. Bernholtz had received death threats from a group opposed to human organ transplantation. He asked for police protection, especially for the trip to the airport. He said Dr. Bernholtz was retrieving a heart for his godson, who was desperately ill. They had to get back to Seattle as soon as possible. A British police officer came and checked Tom's and Ken's passports and other identification. The police discussed transportation options to insure Tom's and Ken's safety on their return to the United States.

At eleven o'clock that morning, Dr. Shellbourne paged Ken. "The boy has just been declared brain dead.

Everything's ready. We should harvest the heart within the hour."

The time it took to perform the surgery seemed a lifetime to Tom. He gazed out of a third-story window in the surgical waiting area. It overlooked a curved drive that led to the emergency entrance. A car careened up the drive and came to a screeching halt at the doors to the ER. A man sprang from the car and helped a woman from the passenger side. He could hear nothing but could see that the woman was pregnant. Two attendants came through the doors with a wheelchair. They whisked her into the ER. Tom recalled the night Link was born. Things started with a bang when Brenda's water ruptured and labor pains came on suddenly, with great force. Brenda was serene as he rushed about frantically...

He came running into the kitchen with a towel. He slipped on the amniotic fluid that covered the floor tiles and swerved to avoid hitting her.

"You okay?" she asked.

"I'm having a brain cramp...what should I do?"

She slipped off her soaked panties. "The bag I packed is by the front door. Bring it here." She bent over, taking short rapid breaths until the pain subsided.

Tom returned and set the bag on the table. Brenda opened it, removed a fresh pair of panties and slipped them on. She grasped her abdomen. "Here comes another one. God, they're strong!"

"That was only a couple of minutes. How come the pains are so close? We'd better get you to the hospital."

"Call my doctor. Her number is by the phone. Tell her my water broke, and the pains are strong and close."

By the time he was off the phone, Brenda was in the

middle of another contraction. She clutched her abdomen. Her face reddened.

"My God. Don't push...breathe, honey, breathe," Tom said.

"I can't help it. I have the urge to push. The baby's head must be really low. What did my doctor say?"

"I got her answering service. She's already at the hospital with another delivery."

Tom grabbed Brenda's overnight bag. He took her arm.

On the drive to the hospital her contractions continued every two minutes. Brenda struggled desperately not to push. Rapid short breaths definitely helped. But the pain in her pelvis was almost unbearable, as the time between pains grew shorter and shorter.

"Dear God, keep him in my belly until we get there!" Brenda prayed. "Tom, my mother's first baby delivered an hour after her water broke!"

"Don't tell me that." Tom pressed the accelerator to the floor.

"Tom, don't speed!"

It was too late. The wail of a police siren grew louder and louder.

"Where the hell you think you're going, Mister?" the officer asked.

"My wife's going to have our baby right here in the car if we don't get to the St. Joe's Hospital..."

Brenda pleaded, "Please hurry...my baby's coming..."

"Wouldn't be the first time. Follow me! I'll get you there!"

Two attendants and Brenda's doctor were at the ER

entrance. They lifted Brenda onto a stretcher, whisked her to the maternity suite and directly into the delivery room.

"She's fully dilated. I'm going to give her a caudal nerve block," her obstetrician announced.

A half-hour later, the doctor placed their baby in Brenda's outstretched arms. His tiny hands grasped her breast, his mouth searching for the nipple. Tom mesmerized, blissfully speechless. Brenda looked up, her eyes filled with tears of joy. "Oh Tom, isn't he perfect...isn't he beautiful..."

Link was beautiful, but he wasn't perfect. He was born with a congenital heart anomaly his mother would never know about. If only she were with him now, here in London, waiting.

Kenneth tapped Tom's shoulder. "You're awfully quiet."

Tom turned. There were tears in his eyes. "I was thinking of the night Link was born."

As Tom and Ken wheeled the canister containing the donor heart to the hospital emergency department, Tom filled Ken in on arrangements for their return trip.

"I was able to commandeer three first-class seats on a British Airways flight to JFK," He checked his watch. "Leaves in forty-five minutes."

"Great. How'd you manage that?" Ken asked.

"I offered the passengers a deal they couldn't refuse."

"And I thought I was the godfather! What about JFK?" Ken asked.

"It took more bumping, and a lot more money. We'll have to hustle. We have less than an hour between the time we land and our connecting flight to Seattle."

As they approached an ambulance, ready and waiting to transport them to Heathrow, Kenneth asked Tom if he had arranged for a police escort. "Faysal's enraged. What if he hired someone to intercept us?"

"Don't worry, Ken. I've got that covered." Tom tried to sound confident. After all, he had the heart. He was determined to insure its safe delivery.

CHAPTER THIRTY-FOUR

The ambulance, lights flashing and sirens blaring, departed from the hospital. But Tom and Kenneth weren't inside. They went instead to the roof where they boarded a helicopter. When they reached the airport, they were met by two police officers, who stayed with Ken and Tom until they were safely aboard British Airlines Flight 493.

Ken studied Tom's profile as he rested his head on the seat cushion next to him. He looked so much like his dad, except for the cowlick of sand-colored hair that arched stubbornly over his forehead. It had been Tom's idea to send a decoy ambulance to the airport. Just like something Tom Sr. would have done, Ken reflected. He himself would never have thought of that.

The canister containing the heart for Link was strapped into the seat between them. For the time being, they were safe. The stewardess offered them champagne, but they weren't ready to celebrate. Considering Link's weakened condition, both Tom and Ken knew how delicate the surgery would be. They can't lose him now, Ken thought. It was as close to a prayer as he could manage.

Ken used the on-board phone to call Lydia. He looked at his watch...it would be around three in the morning in Seattle. After several rings he hung up. Was Lydia staying with Link? He dialed Children's Hospital and asked to be connected to Link's room. When she came on the line, Ken hardly recognized her voice. "Lydia?"

"Kenneth, darling, I'm so glad to hear from you. Where are you?"

"I'm on my way to JFK with Tom. How's Link?"

"He's desperately ill. I'm afraid to ask about the heart."

"Yes, we have a heart...." His voice broke.

"Oh, thank God."

Ken handed the phone to Tom. "Mother, we're arriving at JFK in less than six hours. We'll take a direct flight to Seattle on British Airlines, Flight 2271. It's scheduled to land at Sea-Tac around ten AM., your time. Ken will call Dr. Cronce to prepare Link for surgery and to have the hospital helicopter meet us at Sea-Tac. I've already arranged for airport transportation to the heliport."

"Tom, slow down. My head is spinning. Let me get something to write on."

She was soon back on the line, "Yes, Tom?"

Tom repeated what he had told her. "Mother, by the time we arrive at Children's Hospital, Link will be in the operating room being prepped for surgery. There is no way anybody can stop us now."

"I won't relax until I see you and Kenneth," Lydia said.

"Call Nate and have him meet us at the airport here in Seattle, just in case."

Lydia had him repeat the flight number and time of arrival. "I'll call Nate right away. I can't believe you're on the way with a heart. Tom, darling, do be careful."

Lydia returned to Link's room, shaking his shoulders gently to awaken him. He stared at Lydia, wide-eyed, as though he didn't recognize her. "Link, it's Grandma."

"Did they operate already?" He looked down at his chest. He felt it with his free hand.

"Link, your dad and Uncle Ken are on their way here with a donor heart. You'll have the operation today."

"But I thought they already did the operation." His eyes filled with tears. "Now they gotta do it again."

"Oh, sweetheart, that was a dream. You haven't been operated yet. I'll ask Uncle Ken to stay with you during the surgery. He'll make sure they do everything just right."

She had spent that and the previous night at the hospital. It would be a long day ahead. She needed to freshen up.

"Link, I have to run home. I'll be back in about an hour." She leaned over and kissed him. "You rest now."

Lydia called the hospital operator from her car phone. She told the operator that she had to speak with Dr. Tupelo immediately. She knew that he had stayed somewhere in the hospital that night.

The phone in the residents' call room rang several times.

"Hello, Dr. Tupelo."

"Frank, this is Lydia Bradshaw. Tom and Kenneth are on their way back from Guys Hospital. They have a heart for Link."

"That's fantastic news. Does Link know?"

"Yes, I told him just a few minutes ago. I must talk with Nate as soon as possible. Do you know how I can find him?"

"He's right here." He awakened Nate.

Lydia told Nate that Tom wanted him to meet them at Sea-Tac, just in case Faysal had any more surprises. She gave him the arrival time and flight number.

CHAPTER THIRTY-FIVE

Dr. Faysal sat in his opulent office at the Hakim Medical Center, awaiting a call from Tito, who had tapped Lydia's car phone. He would soon know the when and where of Kenneth's return from London. He certainly had time to leave the country, but once exposed he could not return to his home. His government would face international embarrassment. He'd lose his status in the kingdom, and the Prince, who supported him, would claim he had dishonored his deceased son's name.

Kenneth didn't know of the hundreds of thousands of dollars Gamal was charging the families of organ recipients. Not only for the organs he was getting from Kenneth, but also for those obtained from legitimate sources. Gamal had grown wealthy over the past three years. He could easily take his family to Switzerland and enjoy a comfortable life. But the prestige of his present position, and the recognition he had earned in the Saudi capital, were even more important.

In a matter of hours, Kenneth would go to the authorities at Children's Hospital. Gamal felt an intense hatred for Kenneth, whom he had trusted, and who was now about to betray him. The fact that Kenneth was willing to expose himself to censure, Gamal considered the act of a weak man. Gamal's security guards had bungled his first efforts to contain the problem, but he, Gamal Faysal, was not ready to give up.

He called his travel agent, asking her to book him on the earliest possible flight to Zurich. He then went through his files, seeking correspondence from Kenneth that contained incriminating references to the families of children who received organs. He retrieved and shredded all of the stored operating-room logs that documented forbidden surgeries.

The travel agent called back. She said he could be on a plane to JFK in two hours, and a connecting flight to London was available with a short layover in New York. He had multiple options for direct flights between London and Zurich. He said he'd contact her about travel plans for his family in a day or two.

He walked to a wall safe, retrieving his passport and twenty thousand dollars in cash. He sat at his desk, intending to place an international call to a banker in Europe. He started to reach for the phone, and then changed his mind. Phone records are retrievable, he thought. He would do it later at the airport.

Gamal called Kasib Salemi, the associate medical director at the Hakim Medical Center, asking him to come immediately to his office.

Kasib sat in a chair opposite Dr. Faysal.

"I must leave for Riyadh in one hour. I've a personal emergency that demands I do so," Gamal said. "Might I impose upon you to drive me to the airport?"

Kasib, a pleasant-looking, middle-aged man with more hair allocated to his eyebrows than on the top of his head, looked about Gamal's office. Gamal followed his gaze. A drawer in the file cabinet Gamal normally kept locked was slightly ajar. A shredder next to his desk was overflowing. Gamal was irritated by Kasib's smug expression.

Forbidden Harvest

Although Gamal had never brought Kasib into his confidence, he suspected that Kasib may have observed enough to be suspicious. On one occasion, Gamal caught Kasib looking at a letter Gamal had left on the desk in his office. A child's parent discussed a large cash payment in the correspondence. Afterwards, Gamal carefully re-read the letter. It was fortunately couched in hypothetical terms.

"Certainly, Dr. Faysal. I'll meet you in front of the hospital in exactly one hour. Would you like to stop at your home for luggage?"

"No. I'll send for what I need."

Gamal opened his desk drawer and removed a small box. He handed it across the desk to Amin.

"Here is a key to my mailbox at the Puyallup post office. Check the box daily. I'm expecting an important document. Forward it to me immediately at this address." He handed a slip of paper to Kasib.

"I would be pleased to do so," Kasib said. "Most pleased."

After Kasib left, Gamal called Delta Airlines and asked if they had any flights from JFK arriving later that morning. "Yes sir, there is a Delta Airlines Fight 339 landing at 11:05."

Gamal called the airline escort service. "Hello, this is Dr. Bernholtz. I had arranged to have you meet me on the arrival of my British Airways Flight 2271. I'm transporting a donor organ to Children's Hospital. I arranged for a shuttle to take me to the heliport."

"Let me check that, Dr. Bernholtz." After several seconds the voice returned. "Yes, Doctor, we are all set to pick you up. The flight's expected to arrive as scheduled at 10:08."

"Unfortunately we had to make a last-minute change of plans. I'll be arriving an hour later on Delta Flight 339 at 11:05 AM."

"That's no problem. We'll meet you at the Delta gate. Would you like me to notify the heliport dispatcher?"

"I've already called them. And thank you for your understanding and kindness."

On Gamal's desk was a private phone. He jumped when it rang.

"Yes, Tito, I've been waiting for your call. Anwar and Razi have been arrested."

"When? How?" Tito asked.

"I can't explain now. But there is still time to save our enterprise. You and Faris must prevent Dr. Bernholtz from destroying everything we have created."

"Yes, doctor. I will do whatever you ask," Tito responded

Gamal quickly reviewed his plan with Tito. He told him that he had reserved a flight for both him and Faris. "You must bring a suitcase so as not to look suspicious."

Nate arrived at Sea-Tac at 9:45 AM. He had only fifteen minutes before Ken's and Tom's expected arrival. He called the transport service to confirm that they were meeting Dr. Bernholtz, arriving on British Airways Flight 2271.

"Sir, Dr. Bernholtz called and said he was arriving on Delta Flight 339 at 11:05 AM."

Nate thanked her and hung up. Was Tom Bradshaw setting up another decoy? Or had Faysal made the call to get rid of the people who were going to pick them up? Nate went to the British Airways ticket counter. He asked,

Forbidden Harvest

"Is it possible for me to call someone on Flight 2271?"

"No, sir, I'm sorry, there is no way to call the aircraft once it has taken off."

Nate checked the overhead monitors. Flight 2271 from JFK was arriving at Gate 157; he hurried there. He had not brought a gun. He knew he couldn't get it past airport security without up-to-date police credentials. At the gate he asked if a Dr. Bernholtz was aboard.

"I'm sorry sir. We can't divulge that information."

Nate flashed his old police badge. "It's very important that I know, Ma'am."

"I have no authority to share that information. The flight will be arriving any minute."

"Yeah. Thanks a lot, lady."

After speaking with Dr. Faysal, Tito and Faris quickly packed and headed for the airport. On the way they stopped at a pharmacy and bought a walker.

At the curbside luggage-loading area for British Airways, Tito stepped from a taxi. He helped Faris out of the cab, unfolded the walker, and slowly approached the entrance to the terminal. Tito said to a porter standing nearby, "My companion has a heart condition. We called for transportation to the British Airways ticketing area."

"Yes, sir. Should be here soon."

Tito helped Faris aboard a shuttle. The young driver placed the walker and their bags in a rear compartment.

As the shuttle moved through the terminal, Faris leaned forward. "I'm gonna be sick. I have to go to the bathroom."

Tito urged the driver. "You must hurry."

"There's a bathroom up ahead," the driver said.

As Tito helped Faris off the shuttle, Faris dropped to his knees, covering his mouth as though he was about to vomit. "Could you please help me?" Tito asked.

"Yeah. Sure."

Tito and the driver struggled to support Faris.

"Let's take him to the handicapped stall," Tito said.

There were two men in the bathroom standing at urinals, a third leaning over the sink, turned and watched as they carried Faris into a stall, closing the door behind them.

Tito pointed his gun at the startled driver. He whispered, "Don't make a sound. Strip down to your underwear."

Tito undressed and changed into the driver's clothes, tugging at the shirt sleeves. He grabbed the driver's ID badge, took a passport-sized photograph from his pocket and placed it over the photograph on the shuttle driver's badge using double-sided adhesive.

They gagged the driver, sat him on the toilet seat, and tied his hands behind his back. They looped a rope around the plumbing fixture and tied his feet around the toilet bowl.

"What if someone discovers him before we get the hell out of the airport?" Tito whispered.

Ferris struck the man a powerful blow with the butt of his gun. "He ain't coming to for a long time."

Tito stepped from the toilet stall and calmly walked to the shuttle. Faris remained in the stall, waiting until the bathroom was empty. He then ducked under the door.

Faris removed a suitcase from the shuttle. He placed it in front of the rear fender in order to shield Tito, who used a putty-like substance to attach two guns to the under-surface of the fender. They boarded the shuttle, and Tito drove to Gate 157.

As they approached the metal detector archway, Tito asked a security guard to help him with his passenger. Faris hunched forward. The walker looked like a toy under his massive frame. They led him to the archway. The security guard folded the walker and passed it through the X-ray conveyer along with the suitcase. Then Tito and Faris walked through the archway. Tito circled back to get the shuttle. A security guard casually inspected the shuttle battery compartment and looked around the seats.

One of them said to Tito, "You new here?"

"Yeah. First day." He was careful not to let the security guard get a good look at his ID badge.

After driving the shuttle through the checkpoint, Tito helped Faris aboard and retrieved the baggage and walker. They continued on toward Gate 157 and pulled into the first empty gate section, where they retrieved their semi-automatic pistols from under the fender of the shuttle.

As Nate sat at Gate 157, he scanned the area. The flight was due to arrive. There were several people standing by the door the incoming passengers would enter. The place was noisy with the rumble of excited voices as adults and children milled about, jockeying for position along both sides of the door. There were uniformed guides carrying signs from local hotels with the names of individual passengers. Others stood at a window overlooking the tarmac. They watched as the accordion-like walkway snuggled up against the side of the plane.

A dispatcher stood at the gate, preparing to direct passengers. Nate approached him. "A friend of mine is arriving on this flight. He'll need a ride to the heliport."

The man shrugged. "The lady behind the desk can help you with that."

A shuttle pulled into the gate area.

"Hey, there's a shuttle," the dispatcher said. "Maybe your friend called ahead. If not, he may be able to hitch a ride."

Nate moved close to the shuttle. There was a large man sitting in the back seat. He studied the driver. He looked strange somehow, but Nate couldn't figure out why. Then he noticed that the man's cap was perched a little too high on his head. His shirt sleeves were a bit short. He was wearing an identification badge. Nate was too far away to see if the face on the badge matched that of the driver. He again looked at the man sitting in the rear of the shuttle. He was tall, heavy-set, wearing a wide-brimmed hat pulled down so far, his face was barely visible. Nate noticed a bulge under the man's left upper arm. So this is Faysal's little reception party, Nate thought. He wondered how they had commandeered the shuttle. And how could they have gotten past airport security with weapons? Nate was certain they were armed, but doubted they would try anything in the crowded terminal. He assumed that they would make their move on the way to the heliport. There had been a story in the papers the day after he apprehended Anwar and Razi at the motel. Would they recognize him? He approached the driver. As he got closer he tried to get a better look at his ID badge. The driver stroked his chin, covering the badge with his arm. There was no hint in the driver's expression that suggested he recognized Nate, or saw him as a threat.

"Excuse me, sir," Nate said to the driver. "I have to get

to the heliport right away, and the dispatcher said I might hitch a ride with you."

"I can't take no extra passengers," Tito said. "Ask the desk to call another shuttle."

Passengers began to emerge. Nate edged closer to the driver. He could now see the picture on the identification badge. It was the man's photograph, but the size of the head was out of proportion to that of the badge. Yeah, these are Faysal's guys, Nate was certain.

"I can't wait," Nate told Tito. "I'll miss my connection." He reached for his wallet. As he did, the man in back placed his hand inside his jacket. "Come on. Squeeze me in, and I'll be real grateful." Nate held out two twenty-dollar bills.

"Get out of my face, Mister." Tito pushed Nate away.

Nate moved toward the roped-off area, ducked under and walked down the ramp toward the plane.

"Sir, you can't go in there," the dispatcher shouted.

Nate ignored him. Disembarking passengers streamed past him. There was no sign of Tom or Dr. Bernholtz. Had they actually changed their flight plans? Assuming those two clowns sitting out front were Faysal's men, Tom's plan had worked. Then Nate saw Tom at the end of the ramp.

"Mister, is this your shuttle sitting out here?" Nate shouted to Tom. "I need to hitch a ride to the heliport. Whataya say?"

As Tom approached, Nate moved toward him and whispered, "Two of Faysal's men are on the shuttle...they're armed. When I say 'now baby,' we jump them. You take care of the driver. I'll handle the big guy."

Tom, pretending he didn't know who Nate was, pushed him, causing him to stagger. Tom approached the driver of the shuttle. "What's going on here?" He pointed to Nate.

"Who the hell is this guy?"

The dispatcher walked to the shuttle. "Can I be of any help, gentlemen?"

"I arranged for a private shuttle to take Dr. Bernholtz to the heliport. This man here is insisting he come along."

"Well, if it's so damn private," Nate said, "what's that guy doing riding in the back?"

Faris put down his newspaper and stood. He looked to be well over six feet tall, his height exaggerated as he stood above them. Nate guessed the man weighed well over two hundred. He had a massive forehead and a prominent jaw. He took off his hat and smiled. "I'm not looking for any trouble. I just want a ride to the heliport. Anybody have a problem with that?"

Tom threw up his hands. "Hell, there's plenty of room for everybody. I'll go get Dr. Bernholtz. Be right back."

As Ken and Tom approached, Tito stepped from the shuttle to help them load the stainless steel box that contained the donor heart. As they were doing so, a golf-cart-sized vehicle pulled up. Two airport security guards approached the dispatcher.

"I think things have pretty much been resolved," the dispatcher said. He pointed to Tom. "This gentleman and Dr. Bernholtz have agreed to allow the man in the shuttle and this man," he said, pointing to Nate, "to share his shuttle."

"I'm Dr. Bernholtz." Ken said. "I'm delivering a donor heart to Children's Hospital." He pointed to Tom. "This is Mr. Bradshaw. The heart is for his son." He pointed to Nate. "And Mr. Bradshaw hired this man to insure my safety. An extremist group has threatened my life. I don't feel safe riding with that man in the shuttle."

The security guards exchanged glances, obviously

puzzled. "We were told you and Mr. Bradshaw would be arriving on a later flight. I need to see identification."

Ken showed him his driver's license. The man smiled. "Yes, Dr. Bernholtz, now I recall seeing you on television."

Tom pulled out his wallet. He showed the officer his driver's license. Nate nodded his head and moved toward Faris. Tom moved closer to Tito.

Nate screamed, "Now, baby." He lunged toward Faris. He grasped Faris' right arm as he reached for his gun. At the same instant, Tom tackled Tito, hitting him forcefully across the knees, slamming him to the floor, his head hitting with such force he was momentarily stunned. Tom quickly reached inside Tito's jacket and felt the butt of a gun. He removed the gun and handed it the one of the startled airport security guards. He ripped off Tito's identification badge and handed it to the security guard. "This guy is not an airport employee!"

Faris pulled Nate into the air and began punching him in the face. Between blows, he tried to reach his gun. Nate clutched desperately to Faris' arm. They fell against the back of the shuttle and tumbled onto the floor. The man's gun fell from his shoulder holster, landing close to where Kenneth was standing. As Faris reached for it, Ken stomped on his hand.

One of the security guards forced the barrel of his gun into the side of Faris' neck. The other subdued Tito. Both men were handcuffed.

Nate vigorously shook Ken's hand.

"Welcome home, Dr. Bernholtz." He turned and slapped Tom on the back. "Nice work, Tom."

"We have to get to Children's Hospital as soon as possible," Tom said. "Can one of you drive us to the heliport?"

Tom, Ken, and Nate boarded the shuttle. A security officer jumped into the driver's seat. With the horn blaring, they raced through the terminal.

"Hellofa tackle, Tom." Nate grinned. "Your high school football coach would be proud of you."

"Yeah, considering I played second string."

As soon as they boarded the helicopter, the pilot called the hospital. "We have Dr. Bernholtz and the heart aboard. We'll touch down in twenty minutes."

CHAPTER THIRTY-SIX

"Dr. Bernholtz," the pilot said, "I called the dispatcher at Children's Hospital. They're on alert."

"Great," Ken said. "Tom, call Children's. Have an OR nurse meet us at the helipad. And page Dr. Manning. He'll need to prep Link and assemble the transplant team immediately."

"Come up here, Mr. Bradshaw," the pilot said. "You can use my radio."

As Tom placed the calls, Ken began the complicated process of preparing the heart. He had to circulate within its chambers a liquid programmed to raise the heart's temperature to a predetermined level. He opened a compartment on the top of the canister which controlled miniaturized, battery-operated pumps used to circulate liquids through the heart's chambers.

Delicate sensors embedded in the heart muscle displayed continuous temperature readings. In order to prevent crystallization in the tissues, the thawing had to proceed with meticulous care. Every five seconds, the monitor displayed both the desired temperature and the actual temperature of the heart muscle. Ken had to make minute adjustments when the difference was more than one three-hundredths of a degree Celsius.

The process took twenty minutes. He slipped on a pair of sterile gloves and removed the heart from the pump apparatus. He placed it in a smaller stainless steel container.

"Dr. Bernholtz, we're approaching the hospital," the pilot said. "We should be on the ground in five minutes."

Ken looked out of window as they hovered above the helipad.

"Link should already be in the operating room," Ken said to Tom. He could sense Tom's anxiety. It was similar to his own.

Ken watched as the helicopter eased onto the large white cross of the heliport. Months of painful, exasperating searching had come to an end. Link still had many hazards to face, but Ken had gotten him a heart. He had given Link a chance.

"Tom, you won't have to go to the waiting area to see Lydia," Ken said. "She's right there." How lovely she looked, even with little sleep and unbearable tension.

Tom pressed his face against the window. Lydia was standing as close to the landing site as the attendants would allow. She waved at them with one hand while she attempted unsuccessfully to hold down her dress as the chopper-generated wind swirled about her.

They stepped from the helicopter. Lydia rushed to Tom. They embraced. Ken transferred the canister carrier to the deck of the heliport. Conversation was impossible over the roar of the engine. A nurse helped Ken load the carrier onto a stretcher.

"Dr. Bernholtz," she shouted, "I was told to escort you directly to thoracic surgery. The transplant team's already there."

They moved swiftly to an elevator. Tom, Lydia, Ken and

the nurse crowded in.

No one spoke. Lydia placed her hand on Ken's and squeezed. Their eyes met. "Thank God. Thank God. You've done it," she whispered finally.

They exited and hurried toward the surgical suite. After years of walking those halls, every part of the hospital was familiar to Ken, but now his surroundings seemed strange, unreal. Was this really happening? Had he done everything right? He'd gone through the thawing-out procedure dozens of times on organs he'd delivered to the Hakim Medical Center.

Suddenly there they were, at the doors to the operating room.

"Lydia, Tom, you'll need to go to the waiting area. I have to change my clothes before I can enter the OR."

Five minutes later, Ken, fully scrubbed, masked and gowned, stepped into the OR. The nurse had removed the English boy's heart from the canister and placed it in a steel basin alongside the operating table. The assembled surgical team stood aside as nurses draped Link's body. Two technicians prepared the bypass pump, while another adjusted the cooling mattress. And at the center of the swirl of activity lay Link, his eyes wide, frightened, taking in everything around him. He turned toward Ken as he approached the head of the table, but looked away. Ken was just another of the small army of masked strangers surrounding him.

"This is your Uncle Ken. I'm going to be right here during the operation." He leaned close to Link. "Soon one of the doctors will give you an injection that'll make you go to sleep. I'm going to check out everything."

Link turned to face Ken. He managed a weak smile. The anesthetist injected methohexital into Link's IV. He was asleep in seconds.

When the anesthetist indicated that Link was ready, Dr. Manning and his surgical assistants made the initial skin incision. Within minutes Link's sternum was divided. Assistants applied retractors to separate his ribs. They incised and spread the pericardium, fully exposing Link's heart. Ken was shocked. It looked twice normal size.

Ken recalled holding Link at his baptismal ceremony. Link hadn't appreciated the cold water that Father Justine poured over his head. He screamed with vigor, and his little heart had thumped as Ken pressed him against his own chest. Now, almost thirteen years later, Ken stood by as Dr. Manning prepared to remove that very heart. Ken was drenched in perspiration. What if he had miscalculated the freezing and thawing process? They would be replacing Link's own heart with one that was in even worse condition. It would be Ken's fault, no one else's. They had trusted him completely; now self-doubt was making his own heart race. He tried to concentrate on what the surgeons were doing, but hundreds of paired temperature readings were flashing before his eyes. What if he had missed a significant difference in temperature? His body swayed. He spread his legs to brace himself.

A nurse standing next to Ken asked, "Are you going to be alright, Dr. Bernholtz?"

"I'm okay. Would you mind wiping my face, please?"

The surgeons clamped off the main vessels going to and from Link's heart. Then they attached the tubing from the bypass pump. It circulated a solution that diluted Link's blood to less than half the normal concentration. They injected potassium chloride and other electrolytes that caused Link's heart to stop beating.

Once artificial circulation was established, Dr. Manning made the final incisions to separate the heart from the great vessels. A small portion of the upper chamber of the heart was left. This was the area that contained specialized nerve tissue that generates the electrical impulses needed to innervate the new heart.

After making certain there were no bleeders in the operative site, Dr. Manning removed the donor heart from the steel basin. Then he began the arduous task of sewing Link's major arteries and veins to those of the implanted heart. Every suture had to be placed with meticulous care. Dr. Manning was sweating profusely; one of the scrub nurses frequently wiped his brow to prevent perspiration from contaminating the surgical field.

Wires, connected to an external pacemaker, were attached to the surface of the heart muscle. When the clamps were removed and the new heart allowed to take over, there was absolute quiet in the operating room. Link's new heart did not begin to beat.

Marty and her mother sat in a lounge down the hall from her room. A man sitting on a couch in one corner had fallen asleep. He had been watching a wrestling match. Marty walked over and turned off the television. She began to pace. Gladys sat at a table drinking coffee.

"It's taking so long," Marty said. "Something's gone wrong. I just know it."

"Sit down for God's sake, you're making me nervous," Gladys snapped.

"It should've been over by now. You remember what Doc Frank told us?"

Marty plopped next to her mother. She laid her head on her mother's shoulder and began to cry. Gladys gently rocked her.

"I don't know what I'll do if Link doesn't make it," Marty whispered.

"He's got too many people praying for him not to....that didn't sound right, but you know what I meant."

"What if that heart doesn't work, and they already took out Link's own heart?" Marty said.

"It's going to turn out okay. You'll see."

In the operating room, Dr. Manning reached into Link's chest and gently massaged the new heart.

"You're getting good perfusion," the anesthetist said, "but there's significant ischemia."

Dr. Manning stopped massaging the heart to see if it would continue on its own. The monitor picked up electrical activity, but the new heart refused to beat. Ken's own heart raced. Perspiration stung his eyes. A suffocating quiet blanketed the room. Dr. Manning once again massaged the heart. He continued for a full three minutes. When he stopped, there was a slight pause, and then the heart began to beat erratically.

"He's in v-fib!" the anesthetist shouted.

Dr. Manning nodded to an assistant, who immediately applied electrodes directly to the heart muscle.

"Stand clear!" Dr. Manning shouted.

The defibrillator fired. Link's new heart began to beat at a rapid but regular rate. There were no shouts of *bravo* from the surgeons or nurses, but the tension that had gripped the room suddenly vanished. The surgeons seemed to stand taller. Even with masks in place, it was obvious that everyone was smiling. The anesthetist leaned over the cloth barrier that separated his work area from the surgeons.

Forbidden Harvest

"Fantastic, Dr. Manning. His vital signs are great."

Ken was totally exhausted. Knowing how anxious Tom and Lydia must be, he decided to speak with them without waiting for Dr. Manning to oversee the final stages of the operation.

As he entered the patient waiting area, Tom and Lydia stood and rushed toward him. The room was empty except for a frightened-looking couple who sat off by themselves. Ken's broad smile told Tom and Lydia what they wanted to know. Tom pumped his hand. Ken embraced Lydia, lifting her off her feet. He spoke over her shoulder.

"The new heart was a little stubborn at first, but it's working great now. His vital signs look good. They'll let you see him briefly in the thoracic surgery intensive care unit. He's been lying on an ice blanket for hours. Don't be shocked by how cold he'll feel. That's absolutely normal."

Ken continued, "Dr. Manning should be out soon. I need to call the Hakim Medical Center. I'll stop by to see you later." He hurried from the waiting area.

From his office, Ken called Gamal's private number. Kasib came on line.

"Yes, Dr. Bernholtz?"

"It's urgent that I speak with Dr. Faysal."

"He left for Riyadh early this morning. I have reason to believe he'll not return for some time."

"Did he tell you why he left? Did he give you a phone number where I could reach him?"

"He said it was a personal matter. He will call in a few days with further instructions."

Ken gripped the phone tightly. A flash of anger surged through him. He doubted Gamal would return to Riyadh.

But wherever he went, he'd escape punishment in the US. Ken was left to face the consequences alone.

"I assume his family left with him?" Ken asked.

"No. They didn't leave until this afternoon. I drove them to the airport."

Ken hung up and sat silently for a few minutes. Gamal must have realized it was all over, so the only plausible motive for the attack at the airport was revenge. It saddened Ken that Gamal could be driven by such blind hatred. He had misjudged the man completely. What a damn fool he'd been!

Ken called his research assistant.

"Dr. Shaheed here."

"Jamael, I just learned that Dr. Faysal has left for Riyadh."

"I know nothing of Dr. Faysal leaving for Riyadh. Dr. Bernholtz, I am so relieved to hear you. I was afraid he intended somehow to prevent you returning from London. I was frantic, but I had no idea how to contact you. He said you intended to betray us if you were permitted to return."

Ken went on to explain to Jamael how a child had observed an autopsy and told her doctor about it "She saw us remove organs from David Lang. The doctor gathered evidence and has threatened to report me to the hospital authorities. I talked him into waiting until after I returned with a donor heart for my godson."

"Thank God you were able to find a heart. When will they operate?" Jamael asked.

"He's already had the surgery. He's doing okay so far."

"God be praised. I am so pleased for you and the young boy." Jamael was silent for a moment. "What of our work? Will we be forced to abandon it?"

Forbidden Harvest

"After what's happened, there's no way we'll get permission to continue with human organs. Some other researcher will probably profit from our efforts. That's just the way it is. But we've made great progress, especially with the hyperbaric technique. You'll have to continue with animal organs. There's no other choice."

"I agree about good progress. I am very excited about our prospects," Jamael said.

There was a long silence. Then Ken said, "I want to meet with you some time tomorrow to go over what I intend to tell the medical director. Jamael, I'm sorry how things have turned out."

"I understand your position. I promise to tell the truth about what you and I have done," Jamael said. "But I will claim total ignorance of any involvement with the Hakim Medical Center. I made a solemn promise not to implicate Dr. Faysal when he chose me for this position."

"Damnit, Jamael. He could have warned you. He could have taken you with him. Why protect him?"

"It is not for me to judge his motives. I assume full responsibility for my actions. I'll not go back on my word."

"Jamael, I'm going to do everything possible to convince the director that you weren't part of the conspiracy. If he believes me, you may still be able to continue our work on the hyperbaric project."

Ken called Frank Tupelo. He asked if he and Tina would meet with him in the doctors' conference room next to the thoracic surgery area.

Ken was the first to arrive. The room had a rectangular table in its center, a blackboard against one wall, and opposite, a refrigerator and coffee maker. While waiting for the others, he brewed a fresh pot. He thought of Link, who by now was probably in the recovery room. It had been such a close call. If the heart had arrived even a day later, they would have had to use the bridge device to sustain him. He looked up as Frank and Tina entered.

"I've asked Tom and Lydia to join us," Ken said, "but I wanted to speak to you and Tina first. Faysal's security agents have been arrested at the airport. Faysal himself has left the country."

Tina and Frank raised both hands above their heads and slapped them together.

"The coffee smells great," Tina said, "but what we need is a bottle of champagne."

Ken sat at the table. He closed his eyes, rubbing them vigorously. "I hate to sound morose, but there's so much that can go wrong. The next few days'll be critical for Link. And Marty still has a hellish road ahead."

"Link's a fighter," Frank said. "We're not losing him now. Not after all he's been through."

Tina sat opposite Ken. "Dr. Bernholtz, how did the other two agents get arrested?"

Frank answered for Ken, who seemed lost in thought. "Nate told me what happened at the airport. The other agents tried to ambush Tom and Ken. I'll fill you in later."

"It must have been terrifying to think they might prevent you from delivering that child's heart," Tina said.

Ken walked over to get more coffee. No one spoke until he sat at the table. "All I could think about was that I had to get the heart to the hospital, no matter what. I'm not a violent person. But at that moment I felt a savage hatred." He looked at his hands. They were not stained with blood. But he had known for an instant what it was like to hate enough to kill.

Forbidden Harvest

Tom and Lydia walked into the room. Ken stood as Lydia rushed to embrace him. "We just saw Link in the SICU," Lydia said, as she clung to Ken. "I'm glad you warned me. But I was still shocked when I saw him. His face was so swollen, he was barely recognizable. The poor baby. My irreplaceable grandson! It was heart-breaking to see him in that condition." She held back tears.

"I know he looks bad," Ken said. "That's to be expected after what he's been through. But his vital signs are strong. The new heart is doing its job," he assured her.

When they finally separated, Tom shook Ken's hand vigorously.

"No words can express my gratitude for what you've done for Link."

"Or mine," Ken said, "for all your help in making this possible."

"I'm still concerned about Faysal. I won't be satisfied until he's behind bars," Tom said.

Ken nodded. "They have to catch him first. I called the Hakim Medical Center a few minutes ago. Faysal left for Riyadh early this morning."

"The police will eventually run him down," Lydia said. "I'm happy just to hear he's gone."

Lydia turned to Frank and hugged him, kissing him on the cheek. "Frank, you've been marvelous through all of this. We're so grateful."

"I can't wait to tell Marty," Frank said. He turned toward Tina. "Marty and her mother are waiting to hear about Link's operation. You want to come along?"

"I'd love to. You know, I still haven't met Marty or her mother."

Tom left for the SICU to see if they'd let him sit with

Link. Lydia and Ken were alone in the room. Ken pulled her tightly against him.

"This is going to be messy, darling," he said.

"My God, Kenneth, what are you about to do to me?"

Ken blushed.

"Kiss me," she said. "Stop talking nonsense."

As they clung to each other, he had that same sinking feeling he experienced the night in his apartment. It seemed impossible to stand.

"I love you," she said. "I'll be beside you every inch of the way."

He held her close, but he felt too exhausted to respond.

"I just wish you would wait until Link's recovered from the surgery before you go to the medical director. Now that Dr. Faysal has left and his agents have been arrested, there isn't the same urgency. Is there? In fact, why tell anyone?"

"When they learn that the donor heart came from London, everything will unravel. If Frank doesn't come forward he'd be incriminating himself and everyone else. Who knows? Maybe even you and Tom. I can't let that happen."

"Tom and I are committed to helping you get the best lawyers available," Lydia said. "Tom said you should have a lawyer with you when you go to see the medical director. Please, Kenneth, talk with Tom before you go into that office. Don't go alone."

CHAPTER THIRTY-SEVEN

"Let's take the stairs." Frank hadn't been alone with Tina since the night at the Seatac Motor Inn. It seemed a lifetime ago. On the first landing he stopped and put his arms around her waist.

"I've been thinking of our night together and what a perfect gentleman I was." He touched her hair gently, pressing it against the side of her face. "Your hair's so springy. I've wanted to do that since the first time I saw you."

"I've thought a lot about that night."

They kissed. She drew Frank towards her. "When I saw you as an intern, I imagined getting to know you. Just not the way it happened." She ran her fingers through his hair. "I've wanted to do that since I first saw you."

Someone entered the stairwell at a lower level. The door banged and footsteps started up the stairs toward them. Frank groaned. They separated and continued up the stairs, holding hands until they arrived on Marty's floor. But not before Tina carefully wiped her lipstick off Frank's face.

Marty was standing by the window, her back to the door. She spun around. "Hey, Doc Frank, any news?"

"The operation was over a half hour ago. Link's in the SICU. He's doing great."

"Faan...tastic." She shouted. "Mom, did you hear that?" Marty threw her arms around Frank.

The strength of her embrace surprised him. "I have someone here I want you to meet. Marty, this is my friend, Tina Carrol."

Marty reached for Tina's hand. "Hi, and this is my mom." She pointed to Gladys, who had just stepped out of Marty's bathroom. "She looks great now. You should have seen her when she went in."

"That's enough, young lady," Gladys said, smiling.

"You hear what he said about Link?"

"I did. That's wonderful news."

Marty hugged her mother and then turned toward Dr. Tupelo. "Link's new heart is working okay?" Marty asked.

"For now, yes. But a new heart can fail in the days and weeks after surgery."

"Hey, don't be such a wet blanket," Tina said. "Link's doing great. He'll probably continue to do well."

Marty leaned forward. "Are you a doctor or something?"

"I'm a nurse. I've assisted at transplant surgeries."

"You hear that, Mom? She knows what she's talking about. Link's gonna be okay."

"When is he really out of danger?" Gladys asked, looking from Tina to Frank.

"The first week is pretty much the biggest hurdle," Frank said. "After that, the risk of rejection becomes a factor. Drugs can help prevent that, but they do create problems."

"Like what?" Marty asked, wide-eyed.

"They suppress the immune system. Link will be very susceptible to infection. He'll be in strict isolation for the first two to three weeks. For a time they'll have to do heart biopsies to make sure the muscle stays healthy."

"Yuck. A heart biopsy? How do they do that?"

"It sounds worse than it actually is." He explained the procedure to her. "A very tiny piece of tissue is removed. The pathologist examines it to see if there are changes indicating rejection."

"The new heart is just the beginning, isn't it?" Gladys asked.

"How long do you think he'll in the hospital?" Marty wanted to know.

"About six weeks."

"Geez. That's a long time."

Frank walked up to Marty and tugged on the brim of her baseball cap. "It's just precautionary."

"But I can't see him when he's in isolation. Make sure he keeps checking the bulletin board."

Frank nodded. "Marty, what did you and your mom decide about chemo?"

Marty turned to her mother.

"Marty wanted to go ahead with it as soon as we were sure Link would be okay." She looked at Marty. "Honey, from what Dr. Tupelo says, we can tell Dr. Gibbs to get things ready for this coming week."

"Yuck, yuck, yuck! Doc Frank, can't you hypnotize me or something? I've been reading this book you gave me--it's great stuff. Just the thought of more chemo makes me want to puke."

Tina picked up the book. "Marty, I trained at New Haven Children's Hospital, where Dr. Siegel was on the staff."

"I didn't know that," Frank said. "You continue to amaze me."

Tina reached out and touched Marty's hand. "I worked with him in a children's cancer support group. I helped some of the children with imaging."

"I knew you trained at Yale," Frank said, "but I had no idea you worked under Dr. Siegel."

"If you would like, Marty, I'd be glad to talk with you before your chemo."

Marty looked at her mother. "What do you think, Mom?"

"Yes, of course," Gladys said. Her face showed relief.

"Good. I'll stop by tomorrow. Frank, could I bum a ride to my apartment?" Tina asked.

"I'm due to round with my team in ten minutes. Sorry! Another time for sure."

"I'd be glad to give you a lift," Gladys was gathering her purse and overnight bag. "I'm going to stop by the surgery waiting area to see Lydia and Tom. Why don't you stay and visit with Marty? I'll call you when I'm ready."

After Gladys left, Marty said, "I think my mom is getting the hots for Mr. Bradshaw. I haven't seen her fuss that long over her hair for ages."

"You have a pretty mama," Tina said.

"Yeah, for an old lady. You Doc Frank's girlfriend or something?"

"I fit into the 'or something' category. We really only just met. But I used to work here and he sort of caught my eye. He sure was all medical business. I could've worn a clown suit and done cartwheels, and he wouldn't have noticed."

"Well, you have his attention now. I'm an expert on how people look at each other."

They laughed. Tina sat in a chair beside the bed. "I have a book about imaging and other techniques. I'll bring it by tomorrow if you'd like. It takes over where Dr. Siegel's book leaves off."

"That'd be great."

"I don't know anything about the type of chemotherapy you'll be getting..."

"It's called EP149. You can look it up on Medline under Cancerlit."

Tina looked puzzled. "Dr. Tupelo told you about the drug?"

"No. I looked it up myself. I used one of the hospital computers."

The phone rang. "It's my mom. She's waiting in the lobby."

"What time should I come by?" Tina asked. "For the imaging session, I mean."

"I'm a morning zombie. How about right after lunch?"

"I'll be here at one. In the meantime, re-read Dr. Siegel's chapter on imaging. See what's most helpful right now."

After his mother and Ken left the waiting room, Tom stayed to speak with Dr. Manning, who had remained in surgery, even after Link had been transferred to the recovery room. Ken told Tom that it was Dr. Manning's custom to hold a debriefing of the entire surgical staff after transplant surgery in order to discuss how things went, and how they might improve their function as a team. It was quite a unique practice. Ken respected Dr. Manning for being so open and ready to consider each person's input.

Ken and Lydia returned to the surgery waiting area after having briefly visited Link in the recovery room. Dr. Manning arrived moments later. He looked exhausted, but obviously pleased. Tom had never seen him smile so broadly. Tom pumped his hand vigorously.

"I'm so glad you're all three here," Dr. Manning said.

He described what they should expect over the coming days and weeks. The procedure had gone well, he explained, but Link had lost the equivalent of three units of blood, which they had already begun to replace. They of course had anticipated he would need transfusions after surgery, and over the past weeks had withdrawn and stored several units of Link's own blood. He talked about the drugs they would use to suppress rejection, the side effects, and the precautions they'd have to take to prevent infection.

He went on to outline how they would treat and monitor Link during the first several days after surgery. "Link will be exhausted most of the time and won't be very responsive to visitors." He emphasized that family should not feel hurt or unimportant. He told them he would talk to them about other procedures if and when the need arose.

Tom again pumped Dr. Manning's hand.

Lydia rose and hugged the doctor. "Thank you so much for all you've done for Link."

"Thank you, Ken," Dr. Manning said, "for coming up with a donor when you did. We couldn't have waited a day longer."

Tom was breathless with joy. He and his mother embraced. "Mother, I can't describe it...it's like the feeling I had after Link was born."

Late that afternoon, Tom called Alison Simmons as he drove to his office. He asked her to locate Nate, and for both of them to meet him in his office as soon as possible. As he pushed through the large glass doors at TBI's main entrance, he thought of those dark days following the auto accident and Brenda's loss, when an impenetrable gloom had clouded his brain, and how Alison was indispensible in assisting the interim CEO in running TBI's day-to-day operations.

As he entered his office, Nate and Alison stood to greet him. He embraced Alison. "Thanks so much. Ken told me it was you who located the donor in London."

"He gave me the info I needed. All I did was harass a few people. I'm so happy for you and Link."

Tom motioned toward a conference table. "Nate, you did a great job at the airport."

"Couldn't a done it without you. You damn near knocked that guy's kneecaps off."

Tom leaned forward. "I'm after another set of kneecaps."

"You wannna nail Faysal!"

Tom nodded. "I spoke with Ken before leaving the hospital. The associate director at the Hakim Medical Center told him Faysal left for Riyadh this morning. He took him to the American Airlines terminal. He said Gamal kept checking his watch like he was afraid he was gonna miss his flight."

Forbidden Harvest

"Would a guy skipping town tell anyone where he's headed?" Alison asked.

Tom slammed his fist into the palm of his hand. "That's exactly what I was thinking. Dr. Salemi said he dropped Faysal off at the terminal at nine-thirty," Tom added.

Alison walked to the phone. "I'll call the airline."

She hit the conference-call button and dialed. A recorded message informed her all operators were busy. Maurice Ravel's *Bolero* played in an endless loop. She turned down the volume.

When customer service came on line, Alison asked, "I must leave Seattle for Riyadh tomorrow morning. I need to get there fast. I prefer first class but will accept coach if necessary."

"Let me check...hmm, there's a non-stop to JFK that leaves every morning at 10:55, arriving at JFK at 7:06PM. I can get you a seat in first class..."

"Great... And from there?" Alison said.

As they waited, Tom asked Nate, "What are our chances of getting the police to pick him up at Kennedy?"

"We don't have enough time to get a warrant," Nate said. "But I can ask a buddy of mine at headquarters to send out an APB on him."

"Ma'am?" a male voice said over the speaker phone. "There would be a four-hour layover from JFK to Heathrow. But if you fly from JFK to Boston there's only a one-hour delay."

"And from London to Riyadh?"

"There's a three-hour layover with American Airlines. Your best option is with British Airways. You'll have to check with them. Do you want me to book your flight from Seattle to JFK and on to Boston and London?"

Forbidden Harvest

"I'll get back to you within the hour," Alison said.

"Don't wait too long. You have the last first class seat from Boston to London. When you call back, ask for operator 7751."

Alison hung up and sat at the conference table with Nate and Tom.

"We're not sure where he's headed from London, but that doesn't really matter," Tom said. He asked Nate, "What's an APB?"

"It's a police all points bulletin."

"But they can't make an arrest without a warrant..."

Nate stood and cracked his knuckles. "They can hold him for twenty-four hours. My friend at headquarters owes me. I'll tell him this guy may skip the country. But I'll have to get a warrant by tomorrow."

"What're our chances of getting one?" Tom asked.

"I think we have enough grounds," Nate said.

"And if we don't?"

"Faysal walks."

"We can't allow that." Tom scowled. They were too close to miss now.

Nate looked at his watch. "If he made that flight this morning, he'll land at Kennedy in less than three hours. It's gonna be close." He stood and strode for the door.

CHAPTER THIRTY-EIGHT

At police headquarters, Nate entered a cluttered room. There were several computer monitors scattered throughout. Two desks on the opposite side of the room were covered with manila folders. Nate smiled as he reached for Tim's hand. Nate and Tim's dad had been police buddies from way back. Tim was only a kid when his dad was killed trying to settle a domestic dispute. Tim had grown to look just like his dad: blond, fair-skinned, freckled.

"Hi, thanks for hangin' around," Nate said.

He had briefly explained the situation to him over the phone. Tim had expressed reservations about sending out a message on the APB.

"Even if you locate him," Tim said, "if the magistrate doesn't issue a warrant, there's no way they can hold him."

Nate looked about the room. "Where's your fax machine? A doctor at the Hakim Medical Center said he'd fax a mug shot of Faysal."

Tim opened a folder on his desk. "We already got it. It's not very good. Looks like a photocopy."

Nate studied the photo. "Funny...it's not how I pictured him."

Tim handed Nate the message he had prepared.

Dr. Gamal Faysal, foreign national, Saudi Arabia, suspected attempted homicides, extortion and selling of human organs. May be armed, approach with caution.

Description: Stout, five feet eight inches tall, dark complexion, trim beard, dark hair and brown eyes. Last seen wearing a dark brown suit, white shirt with buttoned-down collar and a brownish-green paisley tie.

He is expected to arrive at JFK on flight 2781 at 9:00 PM this evening. FORMAL WARRANT TO FOLLOW.

"Looks okay," Nate said. "How soon after you send it can I call the airport police?"

Tim scanned the photograph. He grinned. "It's already out there, buddy."

Later that day Nate called Tom and told him that the airport police had met flight 2781 on its arrival at JFK. Faysal wasn't aboard. Tom, sitting at a computer in his study, was furious. "I should've guessed he'd do something like this. Of course! It's what he did!"

"Yeah, this guy is really beginning to piss me off. We can still grab him when he arrives, wherever the hell he's going. We just gotta figure out where."

"Hold on, Nate, I can check airline schedules on my computer." A few minutes later he was back on the line. "Lord, he can go just about any place from Boston."

"I'm gonna call the doctor who took over Faysal's job. What's his name?"

"Dr. Salemi," Tom said

"Yeah, Salemi, that's him. I figure that when he drove Faysal's family to the airport, maybe his wife might let something slip."

"Good idea. Let me know what you find out. If we don't catch him at the airport, we may never get our hands on him."

"I'll get right on it, Mr. Bradshaw."

"I'm running out to the hospital to see Link. Give me a call if you hear anything. I'll let Ken know what's going on."

Tom sat at Link's bedside, clothed in an ankle-length hospital gown, latex gloves, face mask, paper slippers over his shoes, and a surgical cap. Link lay in an oxygen tent. A wire from his upper chest was connected to a cardiac monitor and pacemaker. They had already removed the airway, but Link could only speak in a whisper because of swelling of his vocal cords. He was getting small doses of morphine intravenously, and that combined with the lingering effects of the anesthesia made him sleep most of the time.

Tom unzipped the tent, just enough to get his hand inside. He squeezed Link's shoulder. Link opened his eyes. He said something, but Tom couldn't make it out. As he leaned closer, Link tried to speak, but still couldn't be heard over the noise of the bubbling oxygen and suction pumps at the foot of his bed.

"It's okay son, just rest. Dr. Tupelo says you're doing great."

Tom felt an agonizing fear that Link's body would reject the new heart. What if the drugs didn't work? What if there had been a mistake in testing for blood and tissue factors?

Tom checked his watch. Two-thirty AM. He left Link's room and tossed his gown and gloves in a receptacle. As he turned to leave the thoracic intensive care unit, he collided with someone. Nate grabbed him by the shoulders, "Sorry,

Forbidden Harvest

Mr. Bradshaw. I called you at home but Edward said you were still at the hospital."

Tom searched Nate's face for a clue to what had happened. "You get hold of Salemi?"

"Yeah. He was real helpful."

"Let's go to the waiting room," Tom said. "They've got a coffee pot there."

They sat in the family waiting area, drinking coffee. "So you figure Faysal's on a plane headed for Madrid...how'd you track him down?" Tom asked.

"Salemi told me that when he took Faysal's family to the airport, one of the kids asked his mother if they could go see a bullfight. He says she motioned for the boy to be quiet."

"You figured they went to Spain?"

"Right...or maybe Mexico. But then Salemi remembers a couple of days before Dr. Faysal left, somebody called on Gamal's private line. Gamal was in the bathroom, so Salemi answered the phone and this guy says he wants to talk to Ramond Kareem to tell him his passport pictures were ready."

"Ramond Kareem?" Tom asked.

"I figured Faysal's planning to leave the country with a phony passport."

"You called the airline?"

"Yeah. There was a direct flight from Boston to Madrid."

"And Faysal was aboard?"

"No, Faysal wasn't." Nate grinned. "But this guy Kareem sure was!"

"How much time do we have before he lands in

Madrid?"

"About six hours."

The following morning as Ken prepared to leave for the airport to pick up Charlotte Richards, he received a call from Tom, who updated him on the search for Faysal.

"Can they arrest him without some kind of physical evidence?" Ken asked.

"Nate's going before a magistrate to get a warrant. I doubt they'll even let him enter the country. He was using a forged passport," Tom said.

As Ken waited at the gate area, he wondered if he would be able to pick Charlotte Richards out of the disembarking passengers. As the stream thinned, a middle-aged woman in a knee-length, full skirt and baggy turtle neck sweater approached him. She carried an oversized shoulder purse and a large sports bag. She had a pleasant, round face and dark hair streaked with gray. She broke into a broad smile as she approached him.

"Dr. Bernholtz? Charlotte Richards here." He recognized her voice immediately. They shook hands. "This is all the luggage I have. I don't trust them with my stuff."

They left the terminal and hailed a cab. As soon as they were settled in the rear, she prepared to read Ken's statement. She removed reading glasses and a yellow marker from her purse. As she read, she high-lighted sections. "I want to go through this entire thing one time so I don't keep asking dumb questions. After I'm finished, I'll go back over the marked areas."

Every so often she uttered, "Shit on toast," a variety of profanities and some novel combinations of four-letter words. Ken noticed the cab driver adjust his rear view mirror to get a better look at his passenger. Charlotte remained totally absorbed in the document, oblivious of him or the driver. After reading the entire statement, she suggested they go to Ken's home, so they would not be disturbed. As the cab pulled into the driveway, she stuffed the twenty-page statement into her handbag. "Holy Mother of All the Saints in Heaven, you have dug yourself one hell-of-a deep hole."

Once inside, she kicked off her shoes and sat at the dining room table.

Ken grinned. "Please make yourself at home, Ms. Richards. Can I get you something to drink?"

"If you want me to feel at home, please call me Charlotte and I presume you'd settle for Ken?"

"Of course. Are you a coffee drinker?"

"Yes, please. Caffeinated with a generous amount of cream and a pinch of sugar."

"There's ham and sharp cheddar in the refrigerator," he said as he made her coffee. "There's mayonnaise, mustard and pickles in the door section. There are Kaiser Rolls in the box on the sideboard. Please help yourself."

She opened the refrigerator door. "My God! A bachelor fridge without primitive life forms. I'm impressed."

She carried a platter of sandwiches to the dining area, munching on one as she sat at the table. "What do you see as the best possible outcome from all of this?"

"Number one...not going to jail." He sat at the table opposite Charlotte.

"Any word on Faysal's whereabouts?"

"Nate tracked Dr. Faysal down. He should be arriving in Madrid soon. The Spanish authorities have been alerted. The police are waiting to pick him up."

Charlotte had just taken a bite of sandwich. She tried to swallow and talk at the same time. She coughed. Ken handed her a glass of water. When she was finally able to speak, she said, "My Lord! You waited until I had a mouthfull of food to tell me that?" she asked. "Do they have a warrant? On what grounds?"

"He was using a forged passport." He went on to explain what Tom had told him about Nate trying to get a magistrate in New York to issue a warrant.

"This really puts us in limbo, depending on what he tells them about you."

"What do you think he'll say?"

"I'm sure he'll deny he had anything to do with those attacks. But unless the men arrested at the motel and the airport say they acted on their own, he'll be indicted for conspiracy to commit murder."

"You think he'll implicate me?"

"Implicate in what? He's sure not going to bring up anything about illegally obtained organs. And how would the police know anything about that?"

"After I come forward they'll know."

She ate several bites from her sandwich before answering. "Your statement gives the police a motive for why Gamal would attack you." She sniffed in the direction of the kitchen. "The coffee smells great. Think it's done?"

As he left the room, she picked up his statement, and began to read.

She called out to him, "When Gamal first approached you and you agreed to help him get his doctors licensed to work in the State of Washington, did he at any point suggest they pay you for that?"

"No, he didn't. Well...not exactly."

"What the hell does that mean?"

"He didn't offer me money to intercede for him, but he did say that he and his people would be willing to support my research. I made it clear to him that none of the money would be for my personal use."

"What were your motives?"

He re-entered the room with the coffee and cream and sugar. He placed them on the table.

"I knew from personal experience the tragedy of seeing children die while awaiting surgery. Almost half of the children die for lack of a donor. I was committed to do better."

"At that point there was no mention of supplying him with body parts?" Charlotte took a healthy bite of her sandwich. "Was there?" she asked.

"Absolutely not. Only after Children's Memorial Hospital refused to allow me to replicate my research using human organs did I decide to go ahead without authorization. I did it to save lives despite the risk. I know that sounds awfully damned pious, but it was the way I felt."

"You placed yourself above the law. That wasn't pious. It was reckless."

He glared at her, but knew she was right.

"Tell me about the trust fund you established to support your research."

"I solicited organizations to contribute to the fund. Money from those sources as well as from the Saudi families or Dr. Faysal was deposited to that account. A hospital administrator manages the fund. She's authorized to approve issuing payments for expenses directly related to my research. My secretary sends her the bills and payroll data, and the hospital administrator issues the checks.

We've kept meticulous records."

"Did you ever have the account audited?"

"No."

"We're going to have to bring in an auditor to do that. Had it ever occurred to you that your secretary, or the hospital administrator, or a bank trustee might have been dipping into the account?"

"I guess not."

"What's the average balance in the account?"

"Around eight hundred thousand."

Charlotte whistled. She scribbled notes on a yellow pad as they spoke. "You had much more to gain personally by having them support your research than by buying expensive cars or whatever. One could maintain that you were part of a scheme to pay you for influencing the Medical Board in getting the Saudi doctors licensed. And later supplying them with organs they used in transplant surgery. Any half-baked prosecutor will hammer away at that."

He couldn't understand why she was attacking him. "Damnit. You're not the prosecutor. You're my defense attorney."

"Unless I think exactly like a prosecutor we're going to walk in that court room with our butts hanging out....What kind of paper-work did you send along with the organs that went to the Hakim Medical Center?"

Ken walked to the refrigerator and poured himself a glass of milk. He returned to the table and sat opposite her. "I sent an Organ Transfer summary. It contained information about the donor, such as cause of death, other diagnoses, relevant X-ray reports and laboratory tests. It also contained a statement that signed autopsy permit and organ donor consent forms were in the patient's medical record at Children's Hospital."

"But the actual consent form wasn't sent?"

"Of course not," he snapped. "If I had, it would've been obvious that I didn't have parental consent."

"Loosen up, Ken...I'm on your side, remember?"

"I guess I'm a bit over-sensitive these days."

She removed her glasses and leaned toward him. "I know you are basically a good person. But you did some very dishonest and foolish things. You're going to have to come to grips with that."

"I guess...it's difficult..."

Charlotte put down her pencil and gave him a hard look. "By saying that a signed donor permit form was at Children's Hospital, you were technically telling the truth, but you were implying you had consent."

"Yes, one could infer that..."

"Conclude is more like it. The prosecutor will eat you alive on that point. Don't you see? You created an ambiguous documentation statement for the sole purpose of deceiving the doctors at the Hakim Medical Center."

"Are you saying it's impossible to defend my position?"

"No. People have been caught with the proverbial smoking gun and still have gotten off. It's not impossible. But we're going to have to win this one on some technicality."

"Are you sure you still want to defend me?"

"Are you kidding? I love this case. Now let's get back to work." She reached for another sandwich and returned to Ken's written statement.

"Regarding the staff physicians at the Hakim Medical Center, I believe we can make a case for the fact that there was no reason to question their medical director on this matter."

Ken was beginning to feel better about this lady. "Do you think we'll be prepared to meet with the medical director of Children's Hospital in the morning?"

"We may still be working on the statement by morning. Make another pot of coffee, and let's start in on a barebones version of your statement."

Ken asked if Charlotte had arranged for a place to stay. She said her secretary had reserved a room for two nights at a hotel close to Children's Hospital.

"I'm famished, Ken. Do you have anything besides ham and cheese? I'd rather not take the time to go out for dinner."

"I can have some Chinese delivered."

"Sounds great. Order roast duck, two egg rolls, egg drop soup, and steamed rice for me. And tell them not to forget the fortune cookies and chopsticks."

It was after nine o'clock when the food arrived.

"Let's keep on working," Charlotte said. "We can eat as we go along."

They concentrated on the statement until three in the morning. Charlotte wanted to include an estimate of the number of autopsies in which organs were harvested without permission. Ken told her he kept a log of all autopsies done at Children's Hospital. In the log he inserted a column marked *research protocol*. When that column was marked with a plus sign, it meant at a particular autopsy he had harvested organs without parental consent. It would be a simple matter for him to check the log in the morning. Charlotte suggested they include that list with their statement for the medical director.

"Any idea what that total number might be?"

"I checked fairly recently. We'd done one hundred twenty-eight autopsies up to that time. Twenty organs were kept for experimental purposes and the rest were sent to the Hakim Medical Center."

Charlotte waved her pair of chopsticks, holding a piece of roast duck, in the air. "Premeditated, carefully planned and executed flaunting of parental rights and disregard of medical ethical standards. God almighty! I would love to prosecute this case."

CHAPTER THIRTY-NINE

Frank stopped by Marty's room before leaving the hospital. He wasn't wearing his doctor clothes. She thought he looked cool.

"Gotta a date with Tina?" she asked.

He looked at his watch. "Yes. And the lady was supposed to meet me here. You can come along, if I can sneak you out of the hospital."

Marty laughed. She knew he was kidding. She was in her usual uniform, scrubs, mascara, lipstick, and Braves baseball cap. She made like she was holding a baseball bat. "You going for a blooper over the second baseman's head? Or swinging for extra bases?"

"It's been so long since I've been on a date, I might just bunt."

"Hi, Marty," Tina said, as she entered.

She looked awesome, Marty thought. Doc Frank had that apple-pie look for sure.

"I've a few loose ends to clear up before I leave," Frank said to Tina. "I'll call you in a half hour. Okay?"

Tina suggested they get right to work on the imaging. She read a passage from a chapter in the book. She told

Marty she had to use her own imagination to visualize the cancer cells in her lung.

"Yeah. I've been thinking about it. I picture the cells like tiny globs with little hooks and sticky slime on the outside, and they keep trying to catch the nice normal cells as they pass by. Because they have all those hooks and slime, they stick to each other and form this pulsating blob."

"I can picture that," Tina said. "How are you getting rid of them?"

"I don't know. I can't think of a way right now."

"Marty, it doesn't have to be complicated, or even realistic. Imagine you could do anything you want to rid your body of those cancer cells."

"This isn't going to work. I can't do it." Marty closed her eyes. "I just see that glob getting bigger and bigger, and I can't stop it."

Tina took Marty's hand. "Forget about the cells for now."

Marty nodded.

"What do you do when something swells up? Did your upper leg swell after the amputation?"

"Yeah, they wrapped bandages around the stump to keep it from swelling."

"Well..."

Marty opened her eyes. "Hmm...Sure, that's it. These white blood cells, thousands of them, squeeze out a thin thread like they were spiders. Then they race around the outside of those cancer cells. And pretty soon, the glob of cells looks like a giant ball of thread."

"Good, then what?"

"Then the white cells sit on the surface of the ball and

drill tiny holes into it. They shoot in the EP149. Then smoke comes out of the holes, and the ball begins to get smaller and crinkly like a prune."

"I can just see it happening," Tina said. "What will you do next?"

"Thousands of white cells begin running around the ball again, and make the fine threads like before...but now the ball is much smaller."

"The tumor is getting smaller; you're winning."

"Then they drill more holes and shoot in more EP149. And there're a lot of bubbly and gurgly noises coming from inside, and pretty soon the ball shrinks even smaller."

"I wouldn't want to be one of those cancer cells," Tina said. "You have them on the run."

Tina continued to encourage Marty to let her imagination help her visualize, in her own special way, how the medicine and her body defenses were going to destroy the cancer cells.

After Tina left, Marty leaned back in bed, feeling totally worn out. It was like she had actually done all those things they had talked about. For the first time, she felt as though she was in control of her cancer. She looked forward to her next session with Tina.

CHAPTER FORTY

The following morning, Charlotte and Ken sat in the office of the medical director, on the eighth floor of the hospital administrative wing. Stuart Krandell had assumed leadership of Children's Hospital medical staff at the time Ken was having his problems with the Human Subjects Research Committee. Ken introduced Charlotte Richards.

"This must be serious business, Ken. Perhaps I should have a lawyer to represent me."

"Dr. Krandell, my client, Dr. Bernholtz, has prepared a written statement describing his research activities over the past four years." She reached into her briefcase and handed him the statement. They had boiled the original twenty-page statement down to five. "It probably would be best if you read through the entire statement before we discuss its contents."

It took Stuart ten minutes to read Ken's statement. When he finished, he removed his glasses and leaned forward over the pages. Propping his elbows on the desk, he supported his head with the fingers of both hands.

Without looking up, he said, "This is the most extraordinary thing I've ever read." Gazing at Ken he continued, "Knowing you as I do, Ken, as a friend and colleague for so many years, I find this quite shocking. You've not only done irreparable damage to your own reputation as a researcher, your actions will cause others to question the integrity of this institution. I have no choice but to suspend you from the medical staff, effective immediately."

Ken was not prepared for the shame and humiliation he felt hearing those words from Stuart. He wanted to say he was sorry, but that wouldn't be true...So many children were dying for want of a donor while perfectly viable organs were available. Any guilt he may have felt was overshadowed by his exhilaration whenever he visited the Hakim Medical Center. He looked at Charlotte, who shook her head as if sensing he was about to say something rash, impulsive.

"I'll have to meet with the hospital attorneys and the executive committee to determine further action," Stuart added. "I'll also have to report to the State Board of Medical Examiners that you have engaged in activities that seriously violate hospital policy and ethical standards. I'll advise them that we are suspending you from your present position and other medical staff activities. I'm truly sorry, Ken. At some level I can understand your frustration. But you went far beyond a rational professional response. My God. You risked everything.....A lifetime of distinguished work."

Ken, who had always valued his colleagues' respect, felt the weight of what this would cost him. Could he ever regain the respect of the medical staff?

"I regret any negative effect this will have on the institution and you personally. My statement makes it quite clear that no one else in the hospital or at the university had any knowledge of my activities."

"Dr. Krandell," Charlotte asked, "will you report this to the police?"

"I don't believe this is a criminal matter. Our attorneys

will have to help me make that judgment."

"Would you inform us if you do so decide?" she asked.

"Yes, of course, Ms. Richards. I'll also get legal counsel to see if we have to notify those families.

"One final issue. Ken, you say in your statement that your assistant, Dr. Shaheed, was not informed of the fact that some of the organs were removed without parental consent. But he certainly knew you were using human organs in your research, and it was commonly known that you didn't have institutional approval. I've serious reservations about his innocence."

"Dr. Shaheed comes from a culture that is not likely to question persons in authority," Charlotte said. "Dr. Bernholtz told Dr. Shaheed he'd made special arrangements with some families to use organs for research purposes. Dr. Shaheed accepted that explanation and never questioned him again. I have spoken with Dr. Shaheed, and he has asked me to represent him."

"I want to believe what you say," Dr. Krandell said. "But for now, I'll order him not to perform or assist at any autopsies."

Tina called Marty's mother and told her about a local psychologist, Dr. Skinner, who practiced hypnotherapy. Gladys agreed to have him visit Marty at the hospital. The very next day he stopped by.

He was about six feet tall, had dark curly hair, long sideburns and a big mustache. He had dreamy, deep set, brown eyes. He told Marty that not everyone is necessarily an appropriate subject for hypnosis, and he would have to do some simple tests to see if she would be a good candidate. In one of the tests, he had her hold her arm out and asked her to close her eyes. He told her that her arm was beginning to feel very heavy, and no matter how hard she tried it was beginning to slowly lower toward her lap. Her arm began to drop.

Dr. Skinner told Marty that he believed she would do well with hypnosis. He taught her self-induction. He used suggestion to associate the EP149 treatment with feelings of well-being. The symptoms of nausea and pain were visualized as a stairway. On those stairs, she saw herself climbing to higher levels of health and relaxation. Amazingly she began to look forward to the chemotherapy treatments so she could try out all she had learned from Tina and Dr. Skinner.

On the second day after the heart transplant surgery, Frank visited Link. He was still in the cardio-thoracic intensive care unit in strict isolation. Frank scrubbed and put on a cap, a mask, shoe covers, a gown and gloves. Link's new heart was working well. He was still hooked up to several machines. Two tubes came from his chest and were attached to bottles on the floor next to his bed. One drained the space between the heart and the bag-like structure that surrounds it, the pericardium. The other tube drained his chest cavity. They maintained a constant suction by means of a small pump. A wire was attached to the surface of the heart that passed to an electrode connecting to monitors in his room and at the nurses' station. Another catheter passed through a large vein in his neck and into the heart to measure pressures within the chambers.

"I feel like an octopus," Link said. "When are they going to take these tubes out of me?"

"The chest tubes usually stay in about a week," Frank said. "It depends on how much drainage you have. The catheter that goes into your heart will remain until the surgical and medical teams decide things are stable. Could be just a few days."

"I can't move around much. It hurts when I try to roll on my side."

An incentive spirometer sat at the bedside. It was used to measure how well Link was filling his lungs. The respiratory therapist had left it there. Link was told to take a deep breath, blow it all out; then place the mouthpiece in his mouth and suck in as deep a breath as possible. A small ball rose in a plastic tube that was calibrated in cubic milliliters. Frank reached for the spirometer.

"Show me what you can do, Link."

"It's hard, because my chest hurts. And it makes me cough. I really hurt when I cough."

"It'll help if you keep a pillow handy to hold against your chest whenever you have to cough."

"I do. But it still hurts."

"Just do the best you can." He handed the instrument to Link, who took a deep breath, let it all out, and then sucked in as much as he could. The ball rose to the four hundred mark.

"You're going to have to try to increase how high the ball goes. Maybe when I see you tomorrow you'll be up around six hundred. I know it's not easy, but you've got to try. I'll check your chart and make sure they're giving you enough pain medicine."

Frank looked toward the bedside table, where Link's computer was set up. "Marty's anxious to hear from you. You know, she's starting her chemo in a couple of days."

"I like hearing from her, but everything tires me out. I'm sure sick of just lying here on my back." He turned his head away from Frank to conceal the tears that filled his eyes. "I just wish I would go to sleep and wake up all better."

"How about this...You tell me what to say and I'll log onto Compuserve and type in your message, okay?"

"Tell her by the time she finishes the chemo I expect to be out of isolation, and she can come to see me. Tell her when we both get better I want to take her to see a Mariners' home game. Tell her my dad has box seats on the first baseline. Maybe her mom could come, too."

After leaving Link's room, Frank called Marty and asked her to be sure to check the Compuserve Bulletin Board for messages.

Marty immediately went to the residents' on-call room. She had been coming there every day for so long, the house staff thought nothing of her letting herself in and using the computer. She read Link's message and left him one which would be the last before her chemotherapy, which was due to start the next day.

Dear Little Doc, I'm not in the habit of bringing my mother with me on dates. I've been working with Tina and a psychologist and feel ready to take on this dumb cancer. No way I'm getting cheated out of a box seat at the first baseline. See you after chemo. Love ya, Madame Butterfly.

CHAPTER FORTY-ONE

Dr. Stuart Krandell called an emergency meeting of the hospital administrative director, Broderic Manson, and Alan Gilbert, the hospital attorney. Broderic was wearing a Harbor Towne polo shirt and J. Crew chinos. Stuart suspected he had been headed for the golf links when his secretary called. He would not be in a good mood.

Stuart asked them to read through Ken's statement. As they read, he leaned back in his desk chair, contemplating their reaction and his next move.

"How could this happen? How in hell could this have happened?" Broderic asked.

"This is astonishing," Alan said. "He's one of the most distinguished members of our medical staff."

"We need to decide where to go with this," Stuart said, leaning forward, flipping his copy of Ken's statement onto his desk. "I met with Ken and his attorney, a woman named Charlotte Richards, earlier this morning. Alan, have you heard of her?"

"I have. She has a quite a reputation as a malpractice lawyer, and an outstanding record as prosecutor in Dade County, Florida. When Bush came into office, her name was on the short list for a top job in the Justice Department."

"I don't really care about his goddamn lawyer," Broderic said. "What's our liability? Do we have exposure here? We're talking over one hundred families sharpening their knives. They're going to blame us for having inadequate safeguards."

"If there's anything in the medical record," Alan said, "that should have made us suspicious of wrongdoing, and we failed to detect or act on that, then we would have to assume a degree of liability. We especially have to check the records of the children who had organs removed without parental consent. I'd be curious to see if the autopsy consent form or the organ donor permit were in any way altered."

Stuart rose and walked around his desk. "I'll have the record room clerk pull those charts immediately. For now, this mustn't go beyond the three of us. Call home. It's going to be a hell-of-a long day. I'll make sure there's plenty of pizza and coffee on hand.

"Tomorrow," Stuart continued, "I'll convene a meeting of the executive committee. But I intend to learn the extent of our liability before going in there. If those records show any hanky-panky, it'll bring into question our entire internal auditing program. That's been the centerpiece of my tenure as medical director."

That afternoon and late into evening, Stuart, Alan and Broderic combed through the medical records of the deceased children Ken Bernholtz had autopsied. The charts were thick, and there was often more than one volume for a single patient. They were startled to find laboratory and X-ray reports in the wrong charts. Almost half of the charts they reviewed contained at least one misfiled report. Stuart was appalled. They removed a total of fifty such reports in the one hundred and thirty charts they had reviewed.

"I'm glad we took the time to do this," Stuart said. "I'd hate to think of Charlotte the Terrible discovering these errors."

But not a single chart contained any evidence that Ken Bernholtz had altered the record in any way.

"I wonder what kind of documentation he sent to the Hakim Medical Center." Broderic asked. "I don't recall him mentioning that in his statement."

"He did say he sent an Organ Transfer Summary," Len said.

"As far as I can see," Stuart said, "it looks as though he was guilty of malpractice one hundred plus times and also guilty of a breach of hospital policy regarding research without approval of the Human Subjects Committee. Alan, are we obliged to notify each family that organs have been removed from their deceased child without their consent?"

"There's a tort referred to as 'wrongful concealment'. If one is aware of an act that causes injury, or otherwise wrongs another, that person is required to come forward. However, Bernholtz certainly didn't injure the families, and they can't claim emotional trauma, since none of them knew what had been done. It's an interesting legal question."

Alan continued, "There are certainly incidents where parents have been awarded payments when physicians performed surgical procedures on living children without parental consent. In one such case we had here several years ago, a child who, through a mix-up, was circumcised when the parents had not approved."

Broderic sighed, looked at his watch and munched a piece of cold pepperoni pizza. "Shit. It's almost midnight! I could sure use a drink."

"In the present situation," Alan said, "an unauthorized

procedure on a dead child cannot do harm to the child. I'll check to see if a pathologist has ever been sued for performing an autopsy without written permission."

"But that's not the situation here. He did have permission to perform the autopsies. What he didn't have was permission to help himself to the children's organs."

Broderic used his fingernail to remove a tomato seed from between his molars. "I'm confused. Do we or don't we have to notify the families?" he asked.

"I don't know," Alan responded, raising his hands.

"That question obviously needs to be researched," Stuart said. "I have an additional concern that may be far more serious. Could those families sue the hospital because we benefited indirectly from the sale of organs? You remember, Ken said he received money from both the Hakim Medical Center and individual Saudis who were grateful for having received a donor organ. The gifts went into a research fund administered by our personnel. Money in such funds belongs to the hospital, not the individual doing the research. Was the hospital administration negligent in not monitoring the source of the monies flowing into its coffers?"

"If the money going into that fund," Alan answered, "were judged to be actual payment for organs that would be a felony. As you examine this situation from all angles, it becomes more and more complex."

"The money business bothers me a lot," Stuart said. "After I met with Ken this morning, I pulled an article I had read by a professor at the University of Texas. It was in reference to selling organs. He quoted a law stating that to acquire, receive, or transfer organs for 'valuable consideration' is a federal crime. Transferring money into a research trust fund might be construed as valuable consideration."

"You're right," Alan said. "The money Dr. Bernholtz received is potentially a much more serious issue, since it moves us from a malpractice civil action to a criminal act. I believe we should recommend to the executive committee that we immediately hire a law firm."

"Good God. I just thought of Ken's personal files," Stuart said. "They may contain correspondence between him and Dr. Faysal. I'll notify him immediately not to remove any computer or hard-copy files from his office."

After having left Stuart earlier that day, Ken and Charlotte went directly to Ken's office. Ken asked his secretary to tell anyone who called that he'd be unavailable until tomorrow.

Charlotte asked about his file management system. He explained that it was routine for his secretary to purge computer correspondence that was more than one year old. She kept a hard copy, however. Ken scanned his computer files for the past year, while Charlotte Richards studied hard copies of prior years.

Charlotte wore baggy, navy-blue slacks and a loose-fitting flowered silk blouse with an open collar and long sleeves. She sat in a chair beside Ken's desk, a pile of folders in her lap, her feet propped on the desk. Ken sat at the desk, inches away from Charlotte's orthopedic shoes. She was reading a letter in which he had thanked a Saudi family for their contribution and also inquired about the health of their little boy, who had returned to Riyadh.

"What happened to the records of children who had received illegally obtained organs and later returned home?" Charlotte asked.

"Faysal sent all their records with them on their return to Saudi Arabia. It was almost as though they had never been at Hakim Medical Center."

"But aren't hospitals required by the Joint Commission to maintain complete records on all admissions?" Charlotte asked.

"Yes. I see what you're driving at. The missing medical records smell of a cover-up."

Charlotte nodded. "You got it, baby. When Gamal sent you money after delivering a donor organ, did he send a note along with the check?" Charlotte asked.

"There was a form letter stating that the money was a gift from a Saudi family, who wished to remain anonymous. It went on to say that since Dr. Bernholtz was unwilling to accept any personal gifts, money was being donated to the Children's Hospital Organ Transplant Research Fund."

"There was no mention of any particular child?" Charlotte asked.

"No."

"But if the donations were anonymous, how did you get the names of the fifty-five families you sent thank-you notes to?"

"Those individuals wrote me directly, thanking me for all I had done for their child. The note usually said that they hoped their contribution would further my research. But they never mentioned any specific sum."

"Ken, for a smart man you sure did some dumb things. Any prosecutor worth his or her salt is going to be dissecting your correspondence. Those fifty-five letters will stand out like a pimple on the ass of a Playboy centerfold. They'll contend that you sold organs; then laundered the money in your research account. Furthermore, since those monies represented remuneration for services rendered, that might well affect the tax-exempt status of your research fund. Lordy...do you have any other bombshells lying around your office?"

"Looks pretty damn dismal, doesn't it?"

"I need to know everything they know. Only then can I build your defense. For now we need to get these files back to where they were. After that, let's get something to eat. I'm starved. Could you drive me to my hotel?"

He looked at his watch. It was three in the afternoon. They hadn't eaten since breakfast. "Glad to. What time is your return flight?"

"Not until seven thirty tonight. We have time for a leisurely early dinner and a chance to plan our next move. And don't look so damn morose. Your chance of having to do time is less than fifty-fifty."

"That's a cheerful thought," Ken said.

"Hey, I was only kidding." She grabbed her jacket. "Let me treat you to a hearty meal and a couple of bottles of fine wine."

"You don't have to do that..."

"It's part of my per-diem. Yours truly and a rich CEO will eventually pick up the tab."

CHAPTER FORTY-TWO

The following day Stuart convened an emergency meeting of the hospital Executive Committee, consisting of the major department heads and key administrative personnel. The committee chairman, Dr. Tony Beyers, called the meeting to order. He informed the group that Dr. Krandell had to discuss an urgent medical staff problem. Stuart handed out numbered copies of Ken's statement.

"After the meeting I'll collect these," Dr. Beyers said. "We can't discuss what goes on here with anyone. I'll give you time to read the statement, then take your questions."

Predictably, there was an explosion of disbelief. Dr. Manning, head of thoracic surgery, exclaimed, "My patient has a heart that survived close to twenty-four hours before implantation. This is an incredible breakthrough!"

"We're not here to review the progress of Dr. Bernholtz's research," Dr. Beyers said. "This was medical malpractice on an unprecedented scale...going on right under our noses for more than three years."

Stuart was prepared to endure Tony Beyers' righteous indignation. Tony had lobbied vigorously for the job of medical director, but he had been passed up by Stuart.

"We've reviewed the records of the children involved,"

Stuart said. "There was nothing to suggest anything unusual."

Tony Beyers looked about the room. "Then we have one hell of a systems problem, gentleman."

"I can see maybe once or twice," the Chair of Medicine said grimly. "But getting away with it over a hundred times...We're going to look really bad."

"The hospital may have considerable exposure here," Alan Gilbert added.

"I'd say our entire ass is waving in the breeze," Tony Beyers said.

"Where the hell do we go from here?" Broderic asked.

"I'm more interested in how in God's name we got where we are," Tony Beyers asked.

"Ken's been a respected member of this hospital staff for over twenty years," Dr. Manning said. "He's had a brilliant research career. What could possibly have motivated him to do this?"

"Screw his motivation," Tony said. "We should revoke his malpractice coverage."

"That'd be premature," Stuart said. "I've already suspended him from official staff activities. As of this morning, he will not be allowed into his office without our hospital attorney in attendance. I've informed his assistant, Dr. Shaheed, that he is not to perform any autopsies until his role in this matter has been clarified. In the meantime, pathologists at University Hospital have agreed to do any autopsies we may require."

Following the executive committee meeting, Dr. Manning carefully went through Link's medical record. Ken had told him that he had harvested Link's heart at Cook County Hospital, in Chicago. He had taken Ken's word that

Forbidden Harvest

the donor heart was in excellent condition and in every way compatible. He also assured him that routine tests, including hepatitis and HIV, were all negative. Since the surgical team was already in the operating room when the heart arrived, Dr. Manning had not checked Ken's paperwork.

As he feared, there was no documentation in the chart. Dr. Manning called Cook County. After being bounced from one call center to another, he finally learned that no child named Christopher Moore was registered in the hospital at the time Kenneth supposedly had picked up the donor heart. Since he knew Ken so well, Dr. Manning had deviated from his usual practice of double-checking the donor source. He wondered if anyone would think that he might have been in collusion with Ken. In any event, he would be publicly embarrassed if the matter came to trial.

During rounds the following morning, Dr. Manning announced that he wanted to do a heart biopsy on Link Bradshaw. He asked Dr. Tupelo to discuss the biopsy with the boy and call Tom Bradshaw to sign for the procedure.

"Link. I reviewed your liver and kidney function tests as well as your chest films and cardiac enzymes...everything's coming along really well," Dr. Tupelo said.

"I don't feel so good. I'm sick of all these tubes. And what about the catheter? Why can't that come out?"

"We're taking it out today."

"And the chest tubes?"

"There's still some drainage. They'll need to stay in maybe another couple of days. Link, do you remember reading about heart muscle biopsies in the packet I gave you before surgery?"

"Sort of...sounds scary."

"I know," Frank said. He went on to explain the procedure. "They take a tiny bite of heart muscle and examine the tissue for signs of rejection."

"Will it hurt?" Link asked.

"It's painless except for the initial insertion of the catheter."

"Just the idea of someone taking a bite of my heart. I mean that dead kid's heart that I have in me...it's really weird."

Frank knew that Link, like all transplant recipients, had to learn to accept the organ both physically and emotionally. "That boy who died, wherever he is, would be happy to know he saved your life."

"Yeah. But I feel guilty. When Uncle Ken first told me about him, I prayed that he would die so I could get his heart."

"The boy was near death long before your Uncle Ken even knew about him. You've got to fight really hard to make sure the gift the boy gave you counts for something," Frank said. He told Link that a heart biopsy would have to be done about once a week for the first month; then once a month for six months.

Link's eyes filled with tears. "That's a lot of bites. Am I gonna have to stay in the hospital all that time?"

"The procedure can be done in day-op. You'll be there maybe a couple of hours."

Frank called Tom Bradshaw to report on Link's condition. He informed him of the biopsy and received Tom's permission. All he had to do was come to sign the consent form.

"Why so soon?" Tom asked. "Is there something wrong?"

"When to do the first biopsy is Dr. Manning's decision. He's being extra cautious, because now he knows the donor organ didn't come from Chicago...that Kenneth had lied to him."

CHAPTER FORTY-THREE

That evening, Frank had a fellow resident cover him for a couple of hours so he could take Tina to his favorite Italian restaurant. He wanted to be with her, to have her full attention. Is it just sex hormones, or some other invisible force that brings two people together? Maybe he should talk with Tina about it? No, she'd laugh and say she knows all that.

"Lots of cars," Tina said as they pulled into a parking spot. "The food's either good, or cheap, or both."

As they entered the restaurant, Frank said, "You smell even better than the food. What're you wearing?"

"Never ask. It's part of my mystique."

A young man, with the fresh, self-confident look of a college student, smiled as he poured them tall glasses of water. "Your waitress will be here shortly." He leaned over and lit two small candles in the center of the table, and as he did, Frank noticed the boy's eyes rested ever so briefly on Tina's cleavage. He'd be back often to fill their glasses, Frank thought.

"I love the vases of fresh gladiolus," Tina said. "You've eaten here before. What's good?"

"My favorite is the eggplant parmesan."

Tina crinkled her nose. "I'll pass on that."

"The angel-hair Alfredo with scallops is great. Their chef salad is good, too."

Tina talked about job-hunting. She had interviewed for a position as operating room nurse at Children's Hospital. They practically hired her on the spot, but said they had to check references. She was to return the next day for another interview. "They're going to ask me why I left the Hakim Medical Center, and they'll probably call there for a reference. I haven't decided what I'll tell them."

"Not the whole truth. That's for sure."

"Hasn't Bernholtz already gone to the hospital authorities?"

"Yes, but I doubt if anyone in personnel would be aware of your part in all of that. Ken's lawyer said to wait for the hospital to make the next move."

"It's a long drive to Puyallup," she said. "I could say I wanted a job closer to home."

"That doesn't explain why you left so suddenly. Why not tell them you were being harassed by someone on the staff?"

"That'll send up red flares." She sipped her ice water. "I don't know. I'll just say I left for personal reasons and leave it at that."

The waitress arrived with their salads and a half-carafe of red wine. After she left, Frank said, "I like the harassment idea better. In fact, I feel like harassing you right now."

She smiled. "It doesn't qualify as harassment, when the harassed has all but seduced the harasser."

"I see what you mean. That dress you're wearing has raised my temperature to the boiling point of olive oil."

"I was wondering if you'd notice. Speaking of olive oil, this salad's wonderful."

They ate quietly for awhile. Tina broke the silence.

"What about Link's surgeons? Do you think they already know the heart came from London instead of Chicago?"

"Dr. Manning's on the executive committee. He has to know! This morning he decided to do a heart biopsy on Link sooner than usual. I suspect he's worried about heart-muscle damage, because of the length of time between organ removal and implantation."

"He has reason to worry....I'm going to see Marty tomorrow," she said. "How's she handling the chemo?"

"Today's her third day. We've had to give her very little anti-emetic meds. You and the psychologist did a great job getting her ready."

Tina's eyes glistened. "She's an extraordinary girl. I've enjoyed working with her. Lord, I hope she makes it!"

When their food finally arrived, Tina said, "Frank, I can't eat this much! You'll have to help me." She struggled to keep the spaghetti on her fork. "I'm seriously impaired when it comes to spaghetti. I usually cut it up."

"The secret's not to pick up so much. If you twirl your fork around in a spoon like this, it works better. An occasional slurp's okay."

When Tina laughed her nose crinkled and deep dimples formed at the corners of her mouth. Frank looked at his watch. Damn! He was due back at the hospital in forty minutes.

Later that evening, Tina visited Marty. Gladys was sitting at Marty's bedside studying some of her course notes from school.

Forbidden Harvest

"Tina, I'm glad you stopped by. Marty's handling the chemo so much better with visualization. I believe we owe it to you."

Marty, who was dozing, awakened, rubbing her eyes. "Hey, Tina, thanks for coming by. This EP149 isn't as bad as I thought."

Tina leaned over and hugged Marty. "Only one more day of the chemo left. You've just about got it licked."

"I've been tying up those cancer cells and zapping them every chance I get. I feel like it's going to work. I really do. Hey...have you heard how Link's doing?"

"I just had dinner with Dr. Tupelo. He said Link's new heart is working just fine. They're already cutting back on some medicines."

"Mom, there's no phone in Link's room. Do you think maybe he could use his walkie-talkie radio?"

"What a good idea," Gladys said. She asked Tina, "Would that be a problem?"

"The main thing would be to clean off the radio so there's no chance of infection," Tina said. "I can't think of any other reason why he can't use one." She walked to the phone and asked the operator to page Dr. Tupelo.

Frank was soon on the line. He said sure, why not? Then he added, "Let's hope we're not in for another Operation Skyhawk."

CHAPTER FORTY-FOUR

After driving Charlotte Richards to the airport, Ken called Lydia. He knew she would be eager to hear how things had gone with the hospital medical director. Lydia invited Ken to dinner. She told him that Tom and Gladys were also coming.

"It was Tom's idea...he wanted to celebrate Link's new heart and Marty doing so well with chemo."

"I'd love to come," Ken said

"I called Pierre's and made reservations for four. I took the liberty of ordering for everyone."

Ken would rather have spent a quiet evening alone with Lydia, but there was good reason to celebrate.

"I'm stopping by to see Link," Lydia said. "Meet me at the restaurant at six. Tom and Gladys'll be there around seven. That'll give us some time alone."

That afternoon, Gladys had told Marty she would not be by later that evening because she was going to dinner with Link's dad, his grandmother, and Dr. Bernholtz. Marty couldn't wait to call Link on the walkie-talkie.

"Hi, Little Doc. Operation Cupid has been successfully launched and will reach orbit tonight around seven. Your dad and my mom are going to dinner. Your grandma and

Uncle Ken are going too."

"Holy cow, it worked! But that sounds like a big crowd for cupid-type stuff."

"If your grandma approves, we've got it made. Hey, your voice sounds human today."

"Yeah. My throat feels a lot better."

"How did you con your dad?" Marty asked.

"I told him that your mom said she missed those dinners we had before I got so sick. He said he'd call her. He said he already invited grandma and Uncle Ken to come help him celebrate."

"Good work. I've only one more day of chemo, LD In a couple of days I'll be coming around, looking for you to be out of isolation."

"You know, it's real strange when I feel my heart beat and think that it was somebody else's just a week ago. Last night I dreamed of this kid. He said it was his heart I got. He started crying and said he wanted it back. I was trying to run away from him, but my legs were heavy and I couldn't. All of a sudden he was on top of me, trying to tear off the bandages. I woke up. The nurse was changing my dressings."

"That boy was already dead before they ever took his heart," Marty said.

"Don't tell anyone about my dream. I read where some people need to see a psychiatrist because they can't get used to having somebody else's heart inside them. Promise you won't tell anyone if I tell you things."

"Naturally I promise. Good night, Link. Love you lots."

"Me too."

Ken arrived at Pierre's at precisely six o'clock. There

were several tables filled with dinner guests. Pierre looked frazzled. "I understood you would arrive at seven, Dr. Bernholtz."

"The other guests will be here then. Mrs. Bradshaw and I planned to come earlier. Is there no table available?"

"There is a small table in the corner." He pointed to the opposite end of the room. "Can I bring you something to drink while you wait?"

As he sipped a martini, Ken thought of Lydia. Would he ever measure up to Tom Sr.? Or would he have to settle for permanent runner-up? Since the night they'd made love, he hadn't once gone to sleep without reliving the feeling of her in his arms. All of his senses were totally focused. He would never forget the scent of her body...the sound of her voice as she whispered to him...the feel of her skin, its softness and the sweet taste as his lips kissed her. As Lydia approached the table, he blushed as he stood to help her into a chair.

"Thinking naughty thoughts, Kenneth?" she asked.

She looked radiant. Her hair, usually swept back, now rested on her shoulders. Her deep blue eyes had an intensity and directness that always made his knees feel a little weak. He reached for her hand and raised it to his lips.

"Aside from trying to figure out how to stay out of jail, I have thought only of what a marvelous life we are going to have together. You're still a young woman..."

"I'm sixty, although I don't feel like it. Kenneth, I want to hear all about what happened today." She looked at her watch. "Don't leave out anything. We have plenty of time."

"Has Tom heard anything more from Nate about Faysal's arrest?" he asked.

"Unless Faysal's agents incriminate him in the motel break-in and the attack at the airport, all they can pin on him is entering Spain with a forged passport."

"So how does he explain slipping out of the country with a phony passport?"

"Tom thinks Faysal will claim that he was fearful for his own safety."

"It's all getting too damn convoluted," Ken said. "A police officer is coming by in the morning to get a statement from me about what happened at the airport. He'll probably ask me what I believe was the motive for the attack."

"Do you think Stu Krandell has already gone to the police?" she asked.

"He shared my written confession with other hospital administrators and the executive committee. It could have been any number of people." Ken emptied his glass, enjoying the wave of warmth that spread from the base of his tongue to his stomach.

"What will you tell them as to why you were attacked?"

"Charlotte advised me to just explain what happened and not speculate about a possible motive."

Shortly after seven, Tom and Gladys arrived. Tom ordered champagne. He proposed a toast. "Here's to the speedy recovery of Link and Marty, the two greatest kids ever."

Talk got around to Ken's legal fees. Although his salary was modest, over the years he had accumulated TBI common stock, usually when the price dipped or when Tom Bradshaw Sr. seemed especially buoyant about the company's prospects.

"What's happening with the company, Tom?"

As Tom brought him up-to-date, Ken found himself mostly listening to the conversation between Lydia and

Gladys. Her parents were living in Atlanta. Her mother worked as a private-duty practical nurse; her dad was disabled following a workplace accident. Her grandmother, who was eighty-two, lived with them. Gladys' younger brother was married and had two small children. They lived in Marietta, Georgia.

Gladys said she hoped someday to teach English at a Community College. She needed an additional fifteen credit hours to earn her bachelor's degree. "I'll need a master's to teach at the college level, so I have a lot more schooling to look forward to."

"What of Marty's father?" Lydia asked.

Gladys was nineteen when she met Cleve at a Vietnam War protest rally. They fell in love. "Marty was born a year later," she said softly. "He wasn't ready to be a father. He only worked enough to earn money for drugs and alcohol. By the time Marty was seven, life with Cleve became unbearable. Marty and I went to live with my parents."

Lydia patted Gladys' arm. "How awful that must have been...the drinking and drugs."

"At first he sent her birthday cards, but eventually even that stopped." She hadn't heard from him in more than five years.

"You ladies are pretty darn serious," Tom said.

"Just woman talk," Lydia said. "Kenneth, isn't Pierre an absolute genius? I've always been a menace in the kitchen. If Tom hadn't had a nanny he would have starved."

"Mom, you're too modest. You fixed great breakfasts, and your homemade ice cream was the best."

As small talk wound down, Tom started to revisit Ken's legal problems.

"I really don't know what'll happen next," Ken said. "I

called Charlotte earlier this evening. She said she was sure it would take the hospital attorneys a day or two to determine their next steps."

Ken finished his martini. "This was supposed to be a celebration, remember? I've retained a high-priced lawyer to come up with the strategy."

****

Link felt better with each passing day. He could tell Dr. Tupelo and his dad were really happy over the progress he was making. He tried not to complain when his dad was there. He was still having scary dreams, but Marty was the only one who knew.

They did another heart muscle biopsy, and he didn't mind much this time. Marty looked up the results on the computer and told him about it before Doc Frank did. But he pretended he didn't already know.

The greatest thing was getting rid of those tubes, though it hurt a lot when they pulled them out. One of them got stuck, and when the intern pulled hard, he stretched the rubber. The part of the tube in his chest came out like a slingshot. A blood clot shot out with it and glommed onto the ceiling. And when they pulled out the wires that had been sewed to his heart, it felt just like something in his chest was tearing. He didn't tell his dad or grandmother any of that. He liked to confide in Marty, though, because she always made jokes. Like when she stood on his bed and tried to scrape that blood clot from the ceiling. She said if Grandma Bradshaw were to see it she would have a conniption fit.

"I've heard that expression before, but don't know what it means exactly. Is it physical or psychological?"

"I don't know, but I think it's about the worse thing a

person can have."

Link was happy that he could use the bathroom and give up the bedside commode. It seemed as though every time he sat on it, a nurse would come in the room and ask if everything was okay. Marty said there was a little button in the seat that turned on a light at the nurses' station. He thought she was kidding, but just to go along he asked, "How come?"

"They have to write on your chart every time you make a brownie."

Now that he was out of isolation, Link no longer felt like an extra-terrestrial. And he couldn't believe how well Marty was doing with her chemo. Marty said she looked up her kidney and liver tests, and even though she didn't know what the numbers meant, they were within the normal range. She said Doc Frank told her it would take a few weeks to see if the chemo really helped. When Link told Father Justine, he said he would say special prayers for her. Link figured Father Justine must have a lot of influence up there, because he prayed a lot for him, and look how well he was doing.

Pretty soon it was time for Marty to leave the hospital. Link didn't blame her for being excited, but he was a little jealous.

"Seems strange to be thinking about school and stuff," she said, "after all I've been through at the hospital. It sounds kind of crazy, but I'm going to miss this stupid place." She promised to stop by to see him when she came back for clinic visits.

"How often do you need to be checked?"

"Dr. Gibbs said she wants to see me once a week. She never fools around like Doc Frank, and she isn't nearly as sexy. But I like her okay."

Link took off his glasses and crossed his eyes. "You think I'm sexy?"

"Little Doc, you definitely send off all sorts of male vibrations." She cupped her hands close to his face. "Yes, I'm definitely picking up *airmones*."

"You mean pheronomes?"

"Whatever. You got plenty to spare." She leaned over and hugged him carefully; then planted a kiss directly on his lips. He put his arms around her and squeezed tightly. It hurt a little because his chest was still pretty sore. He could feel her small breasts pressed against him. His friend Mike said that if you didn't open your mouth, it was like kissing your sister. He pressed his tongue between her lips. They were warm and tasted like strawberries. His tongue came up against her teeth. She pulled her head away, and with their faces just inches apart, she smiled, shaking her head from side to side. "LD, you have even more airmones than I thought."

"A week's a long time when you're in the hospital," he said. "How about calling me a couple of times in between?"

Link watched her walk down the hall. He put his fingers to his lips. He put his glasses back on so he could see her better. He would've sworn she wiggled her butt just before she disappeared around the corner. He shook his head and said half out loud, "Madame Butterfly, you are hot!"

He was sure things would never be the same between him and Marty. She'll go back to school where a person could drown in all the airmones that were flying around, he thought. She'll meet some older guy, a senior, even a college freshman. She'll forget about me. Same as Jennifer.

He was also having second thoughts about Operation Cupid. That would seem really far-out...if their parents got together someday she could be his step-sister.

Frank arranged a meeting with Dr Manning and Dr. Gibbs to discuss how he might explain Marty's and Link's prognosis to their parents. Tina, who worked closely with Marty both before and after her chemotherapy, sat in.

In a darkened room in the radiology department, they viewed Marty's CT scan after her most recent chemotherapy. Dr. Gibbs pointed to the location of the metastatic lesion in Marty's left lung.

"It's gone from a centimeter and a half to just a few millimeters. Quite remarkable."

"But she's still not cured. How long might she remain in remission?" Frank asked.

"With standard chemo, she'd have less than a fifty percent chance of surviving five years. But with EP149, it's impossible to predict," Dr. Gibbs responded. "We're in uncharted territory."

Frank turned to Dr. Manning. "I know you're optimistic about Link's near-term prognosis."

He nodded. "He's past immediate post-transplant problems. If he tolerates and responds to the drugs we're giving him to suppress his immune system, his new heart could last into his late teens. But after that, he'll almost certainly need a second transplant."

Frank shook his head. "Those poor kids."

Tina gave Frank's head a gentle tap. "Hey, this is no time for doom and gloom. I'm thrilled about how well Link and Marty are doing right now. And who knows what breakthroughs we might see over the next few years?"

Forbidden Harvest

CHAPTER FORTY-FIVE

Charlotte Richards was on the phone as her secretary entered her office with a thermos of coffee and a special-delivery letter from the medical director at Children's Hospital. Her desk was covered with stacks of file folders and loose papers. The rest of the room was sparsely and inexpensively furnished. An exercise bike stood in one corner, positioned to afford her a thirteenth-story view of downtown Miami. Charlotte swung both feet onto her desk and settled into her high-backed chair. She experienced a ripple of excitement as she began to read.

Her predictions had proved to be correct. The hospital authorities notified the families whose children had organs removed without specific consent. Dr. Krandell included a copy of the letter he had sent to them.

Dear Mr. and Mrs. ---------,

On ----------- you agreed to the organ donor program. When your child was declared brain dead our surgical organ-harvesting team removed the --------- as you specified beforehand.

Following the harvesting of the ---------, an autopsy, to which you also consented, was performed on ----------. The pathologist, on his own initiative, beyond doing a standard autopsy, removed one or more organs to be used in transplant surgery at another hospital. The hospital authorities had no prior knowledge of this until the pathologist came forward with that information. Disciplinary action has been taken. He has been suspended from our staff, and the State Board of Medical Examiners has been notified.

In some instances, the organs were used by the pathologist in experiments to develop a process that would preserve the viability of retrieved organs. We deeply regret that the pathologist involved did not obtain your permission prior to harvesting those organs. I invite you to come to see me if you want to discuss this matter.

Sincerely,

Stuart Krandell, M.D.
Medical Director
Children's Memorial Hospital

Charlotte immediately called the hospital attorney, Alan Filbert, who she assumed had composed the letter.

"God Almighty! Who in hell dreamed up that insensitive piece of crap you sent out to the parents?" Charlotte didn't wait for him to respond. "You're a children's hospital, for Christ sakes! Can't you show a little compassion?"

"I wrote the letter which, I might add, Dr. Krandell signed off on. Our goal was to sound matter-of-fact, in the hope that it might discourage litigation."

"In my opinion it's likely to inspire, not discourage, lawsuits. What kind of response have you received?" Charlotte asked.

"Of the 128 families who had received the notification, very few called..."

"Of course they didn't. They were busy tracking down a lawyer," Charlotte interrupted.

Forbidden Harvest

"We've heard from several attorneys. I expect more."

She wanted to ask Alan what kinds of issues the attorneys were raising, but was certain he would not divulge that information. She would find out soon enough. For now her major concern was a possible felony charge.

She called the medical director, Dr. Krandell, and asked if the hospital's malpractice insurance carrier had made a decision as to whether they would cover Ken. He explained that the hospital was self-insured, so the decision, an internal one, hadn't yet been made.

"Dr. Krandell, since many of the patients may have the same lawyers, wouldn't a class action suit be easier all the way around?"

"Yes, we've discussed that. We've already contacted the lawyers, suggesting they consider joining other attorneys in such a suit. Since there's no question of Dr. Bernholtz's liability, it's more a matter of limiting the hospital's losses."

Charlotte immediately called Ken. She told him about the discussion with the hospital attorney and medical director.

"I assume the press hasn't gotten wind of this yet," Charlotte said. "Enjoy the here and now, Ken, things are gonna hotten up very soon. If you hear from reporters, tell them you've been advised not to comment. Refer them to me. If the police contact you, call me posthaste."

Although Ken was barred from going to his hospital office, the morgue or to his laboratory, no one thought to cancel his password. On his home computer he remained in daily contact with Jamael, who was preparing data for publication about the use of their rapid-freezing technique, using non-human organs, to extend viability from four hours to twenty-four hours. It was the identical procedure he had used to keep Link's new heart viable on its trip from London to Seattle.

He could have submitted those initial results with non-human organs earlier, but decided not to when the human subjects committee had not permitted him to replicate his results with human organs. Nevertheless he had been eager to share his findings with the medical community and submit them before the story of his separate, clandestine activities became public.

He had kept meticulous records. He had enough data to support a work-in-progress report for publication. Jamael downloaded records to Ken's home computer. Ken was up through the night organizing the report, making editorial changes. By morning, the paper was ready for submission to *The American Journal of Pathology*.

Once that was done, he and Jamael turned their full attention to the hyperbaric project. They were close to a solution. During the time the organ was stored under high pressure, they were able to keep the tissues viable by infusing it with a solution saturated with oxygen. But they hadn't as yet solved the decompression problem.

Storing the organs under high pressure had solved the oxygenation problem. But tissue damage was occurring during the decompression phase. They must find a way to prevent that.

The powers that be could forbid his work at Children's Hospital, Ken reflected. But they couldn't control his drive and determination that no child in need of a transplant should languish and die while awaiting a donor organ. He was close to accomplishing that dream. He would find a way. He must.

CHAPTER FORTY-SIX

The highlights of Frank Tupelo's day were his visits with Link, who was now a month post-op, doing better than anyone thought possible. Out of the CCU, fully detached from all monitoring devices, he could walk around the nursing floor without restriction.

"I was checking your most recent labs and biopsy results," Frank said. "Everything's looking good. Dr. Cronce decided to stop one of your medicines beginning tomorrow."

"It's great not to have things sticking in me. Which medicine are they stopping?"

"The diuretic. Since we reduced your steroid dose, you're handling fluids okay."

"Doc Frank, you notice anything different about me?" Link tilted his head back and moved his face closer to Frank.

Frank looked at him carefully. "I'll be darned. You're growing a mustache."

"Yeah, and look at my legs." He was sitting on the edge of his bed. He threw one leg up onto the bed and pulled up his pajamas.

"How about that! You went into puberty right under my

very nose."

"Dr. Cronce said the prednisone's doing it."

"The medicine probably did contribute, but you were on the verge of a major hormone spurt."

"Marty put her hands near my head, like this." Link held his hands alongside his temples. "She said she could feel my *airmones*. I guess she was right."

"This place is kind of dull without her," Frank said. He had a vision of her swaying down the hall, calling out to everyone she knew.

"Yeah. She was just here. Did you see her?"

Frank nodded. "I almost didn't recognize her in her school uniform. She looks great with that new blond hair down to her shoulders."

"She's going to summer school so she can be in the eleventh grade in the fall. You know, she's still kind of crazy; she took off her wig and made me try it on. She said I looked pretty good with long hair. Her father was a hippie, you know?"

"Sounds like her. You think you'll be ready to go into ninth grade?"

"My dad said he's getting me a tutor. I hope I can catch up."

"Speaking of home, you may be out of here in a couple of weeks."

They exchanged high-fives. Link stood and walked to the window. Frank followed, standing behind Link as they gazed at a patch of blue sky.

"Why do I have to stay that long?" Link asked.

"It mostly depends on how well you tolerate increased activity. The physical therapist will be working with you.

Forbidden Harvest

We'll be monitoring how well your new heart holds up."

Link turned to face Frank. "That doesn't mean more catheters and stuff?"

"We'll be using simple measures, like blood pressure and pulse response to exercise."

"Could I go home in a week if I do well?"

"That's up to Dr. Cronce...bet you miss your friends."

"Yeah. But Grandma has been great about keeping me up on what's been happening. She talks to my buddy Mike and my homeroom teacher. She tells me stuff I wouldn't know even if I was there."

Ken settled into his favorite living room chair with the evening paper. It had been two weeks since Faysal's arrest. And except for a cryptic notice in the newspaper, the story seemed to have gone unnoticed.

Therefore, he was shocked to see pictures of himself, Tom, the four captured agents, and Dr. Faysal on the front page of *The Seattle Evening Sun*. He had no idea how the newspaper had gotten information contained in the statement he had given to Stuart Krandell. However, the article did not mention the attack on Tina and Frank at the Seatac Motor Inn. It appeared the reporter or his source was revealing only partial information, for whatever reason. Kenneth's phone rang.

"Ken, have you seen the *Sun*?" Tom asked.

"I was just reading it."

"How the hell do you suppose that happened? I want Link kept out of this."

"I have no idea," Ken said. "I need to call Charlotte. In the meantime, we need to call Nate, Lydia, Gladys, Frank, and Tina. Reporters are bound to be after them. Tell them to say that they have been advised not to comment; the case is under litigation."

"Sure thing. I'll also talk to Link and Marty," Tom said.

Ken phoned Charlotte. She didn't sound surprised.

"It's only a matter of time before the police contact you again. The reporters will harass the hell out of you. Be polite, but don't tell them a damn thing. They may go after the children. Make sure both Link and Marty do not discuss their connection to this with anyone. If there's the slightest discrepancy between versions of what happened, the press will pick our bones...Ken, who is the canary?"

"I can't believe Stuart would have leaked the information. It had to be someone on the executive board," Ken asserted.

"Either that or someone in the DA's office."

"I almost wish we'd have gone directly to the police. Wouldn't it be better than waiting for them to serve me a warrant?"

"We'd be admitting that you may have committed a crime. Faysal is in custody already. They have your statement about the attack at the airport. But illicit organs are another whole angle. We should hear from the prosecutor's office soon. Let's sit tight and wait to see what charges they bring."

After hanging up, Ken turned on his television to a local news channel. They showed the same photographs of him and Tom that were in the newspaper, repeating the details. A TV reporter was doing a live interview.

"This is Angela Scott, reporting to you from the Hakim Medical Center in Puyallup, Washington. Standing beside me is the hospital medical director....Dr. Salemi, have you read the story in *The Seattle Evening Sun*?"

"Yes, I have."

"Were you aware that Dr. Bernholtz and Dr. Faysal were using illegally obtained human organs for transplant surgery at your hospital?"

"I am shocked, as is my entire medical staff."

"Did Dr. Faysal say why he left so suddenly?"

"He said it was an urgent personal matter."

"Has he been in contact with you since he left?"

"No."

The television image faded.

"This is Barry Walker. I am with the medical director of Children's Memorial Hospital in Seattle," the reporter said, looking into the camera.

"Dr. Krandell, you are, of course, aware of the conspiracy between Dr. Bernholtz and Dr. Faysal. When did you first learn of this?"

"About four weeks ago. Dr. Bernholtz informed me of what he and Dr. Faysal had been doing for the past three years."

"Why do you suppose Dr. Bernholtz chose to confess at that time?"

"He had just returned from England, where he had permission to harvest a donor heart for a patient at Children's Hospital. The child was desperately ill, and there were no donor hearts available within a four-hour access area."

"What is the significance of the four-hour restriction?"

"With present technology, we require that the time between removal of a donor heart and implanting it cannot exceed four hours. Dr. Bernholtz, for several years, has been working with animal organs. Unknown to us, he was also working with human cadaver organs. Through his experimentation, he has apparently extended the time an organ can be kept in a viable state. By harvesting the heart in London, Dr. Bernholtz was aware that hospital authorities would know that he was using an unapproved technology."

"So he knowingly exposed himself to get a donor heart for one of the children here?"

"That is correct."

"Was the transplant surgery a success?"

"The young boy is doing remarkably well. He'll be ready to be discharged any day now."

"So, really, Dr. Bernholtz saved his life."

Over the next several days, Ken and the two hospitals were constantly in the news. As more information hit the streets, the news media shifted into high gear. Pictures of Faysal's captured guards were widely published and shown on television. The Saudi prince, who financed the purchase of the Hakim Medical Center, was interviewed in Riyadh. He vehemently denied any involvement of Saudi officials. He was angered that the hospital, named in honor of his deceased son, was being brought into disrepute.

Somehow a *Sun* reporter had learned that Marty Lopinski had witnessed an autopsy, during which organs had been removed.

"How do you suppose they learned of Marty?" Tom asked Ken.

"I did tell Dr. Faysal. He may have told the police, although I can't imagine why he would have."

"It might have been part of a plea bargain," Tom

suggested.

When it became known that the boy at Children's Hospital who had received the heart was the son and grandchild of a prominent Seattle industrialist, media pundits speculated that Dr. Bernholtz may have been providing forbidden cadaver organs for children of the wealthy. And that would include the Saudi children as well.

Four days later, Ken received a call from the office of the county prosecutor, Gianni Rubino. Ken immediately got Charlotte on the phone.

"I've heard of Rubino. He's had a number of prosecutions of prominent individuals. He's going to be tough, Ken. What did he say?"

"He asked if I could clear up some questions regarding the attempted ambush at the airport. And yes, they did have some concerns about the unauthorized removal of organs from Children's Hospital. He said that Dr. Faysal, was telling authorities in Madrid he had no knowledge organs from Children's Hospital were illegally harvested. Mr. Rubino wants to meet with us tomorrow."

"I'll leave for Seattle later this evening."

The following morning Ken and Charlotte sat in the office of Gianni Rubino. Ken had felt an increasing sense of foreboding as he entered the ornate building with its stately pillars and marble floors. He sat opposite Mr. Rubino, his shirt moist with perspiration.

Gianni introduced Ken and Charlotte to his assistant, Roger Kley. Kley nodded. Gianni's black hair was combed straight back, covering the upper part of his ears. He had a classic Roman nose that dominated his pale face. He moistened his thin lips frequently as he spoke.

He apologized for the appearance of his office. It looked and smelled like a movie theater after the last Saturday night showing. Gianni thanked Ken for his cooperation with the officers who had questioned him about the attack at the Seattle Airport. Regarding the attackers he told Kenneth that in addition to his written statements, the prosecutor's office would expect him to testify when their case came to trial.

He said he could find nothing to directly incriminate Dr. Faysal. Charlotte pointed out that even if her client could recall his conversations verbatim, it would be Ken's word against Dr. Faysal's.

"Dr. Bernholtz," Gianni continued, "we realize that a class action suit is being brought against you and Children's Hospital for unauthorized removal of organs at autopsy. That, of course, is a civil, not a criminal, offense and does not concern the office of the prosecutor. However, there is a federal statute prohibiting the transfer of human organs for valuable consideration. Are you aware of that statute, Dr. Bernholtz?"

"Yes."

Gianni flipped through Ken's statement. "It says here that each time you delivered an organ to the Hakim Medical Center, a contribution was made to a private research endowment trust fund established at Children's Hospital. You state that each deposit represented a gift from a grateful Saudi family, in appreciation of your efforts to procure a life-saving heart, or kidney, or whatever."

"That's correct."

"Who approached the family about the gift, and who recommended how much money would adequately reflect the family's appreciation?"

"Dr. Faysal told the families that I could not accept money or gifts. Most were eager to show their gratitude, so Dr. Faysal suggested they make a contribution to my fund at Children's. He explained that the money was used to finance research on improved organ harvesting techniques. And that was true."

"Do you know the exact words Dr. Faysal used?" Gianni asked.

Charlotte answered. "Dr. Faysal told him in only a very general way what he had said to the families, and Dr. Bernholtz's statement reflects that."

"Dr. Bernholtz, we have searched Dr. Faysal's files. We can find no correspondence with Saudi families in which donations to your research fund were discussed. Can you explain that?"

Again Charlotte answered. "Dr. Faysal most likely destroyed those records, or took them with him. We understand he shredded a number of files before he left."

Gianni glared at Charlotte. "Dr. Bernholtz, why have your attorney answer these simple questions?"

"Mr. Rubino," Charlotte said, "your questions may be simple, but we are not. I have sat where you are sitting, and I know a fishing expedition when I see one. My client is facing numerous malpractice claims. My sole purpose here is to explain the facts of the case in a straightforward manner, so you do not decide to launch an unnecessary criminal investigation."

Gianni picked up a pencil and examined the point carefully. He placed it in an electric sharpener that sat on a horizontal file behind his desk. The shrill whine of the motor was the only sound in the room. He removed the pencil and stared at his handiwork. He looked at Kenneth and smiled. "Dr. Bernholtz, my office isn't going to rest until we uncover the full truth. You can be assured that if you are guilty, I will come after you with all the power I can muster."

"There is no evidence that my client has broken the

law," Charlotte said.

"We shall see." Gianni slowly rotated his chair in order to face Ken directly. He leaned back, thrusting his chin forward. "Dr. Bernholtz, do you consider the research you have done in the area of organ transplantation to be important?"

"Yes. Why else would I pursue it?"

"In that case, I assume you value being able to continue?"

"I'm committed to my work. I hope it'll be of value to others."

"Dr. Bernholtz, we've audited your trust fund at Children's Hospital and found deposits in excess of a million dollars over the past three years. Most of that money came from Dr. Faysal and checks drawn on Saudi banks. We are seriously concerned that in exchange for illegally obtained organs, you had at your disposal large sums of money to further your personal research efforts."

"Mr. Rubino," Charlotte responded, "I am sure you are aware that funds in the research trust are the property of the Children's Hospital. Dr. Bernholtz has been officially authorized by the hospital to use those funds to support his research. Every nickel of that money has been meticulously accounted for. It is common for faculty to support research through grants, bequests, or other gifts. I hope you do not seriously believe you can build a case against Dr. Bernholtz based on such convoluted and questionable logic."

"Ms. Richards, how can we be sure that some Saudi family members did not in fact write checks for much larger amounts to Dr. Bernholtz, and that those checks were deposited in some foreign bank?"

Charlotte stood and leaned forward, placing both hands

on his desk. "That is gross speculation, and you damn well know it. We stand on the written statement you have before you. You may end up getting a lot of publicity from these types of theatrics, but I'll not allow you to railroad my client to further personal ambitions."

Kenneth noticed his faint smile, as Gianni attempted to look impassive. He was obviously enjoying this interchange with the well-known and much feared former Dade County district attorney.

"Ms. Richards, a Grand Jury may have to decide if what I say is theatrics or the unraveling of a sophisticated scam that has bilked anguished parents of millions of dollars.

Gianni continued, "And there is also the matter of Dr. Faysal's agents planning to eliminate the young doctor and nurse at the Seatac Motor Inn. It was Dr. Bernholtz who told Dr. Faysal of their involvement. One has only Dr. Bernholtz's word that he knew nothing of the plot. At the present time, the agents will neither confirm nor deny his or Dr. Faysal's involvement. We are prepared to offer them a plea bargain if they cooperate with us. I sincerely hope the doctor is telling the truth. But have no doubt, the truth will prevail." He turned to his associate. "Roger, is there anything you want to ask Dr. Bernholtz or Ms. Richards?"

Roger Kley had been examining his fingernails during the entire meeting. His face had a pudgy unhealthy look. The index and middle fingers of his right hand were heavily stained. Ken wondered what his lungs must look like.

Roger stood, slipping his nail clippers into his pocket. In the lap portion of the front of his trousers, a series of horizontal accordion-like folds suggested to Ken the man did not spend a lot of money on dry-cleaning.

"You have a computer at home, Dr. Bernholtz?"

"Yes, I do quite a bit of my work at home."

"You ever communicate with Dr. Faysal by computer?"

"He never learned to use a computer. We spoke on his unlisted private telephone."

Roger flexed his knees slightly as he tugged at the crotch of his trousers. "You mind if our computer guy checks your home and office computers?"

Ken looked at Charlotte. She shrugged. He said, "Not at all."

Gianni Rubino rose and walked to a window. With his back to them he said, "That will be all, for now. Thank you for coming."

Charlotte rolled her eyes as she looked at Ken. She grabbed his arm. "Let's get out of here."

As they left the prosecutor's office they were approached by five or six reporters. Microphones and a TV camera were thrust into their faces. Charlotte and Ken hurried to his car, refusing to answer questions. A TV anchor shouted, "Did you steal organs to save your godson and other rich kids?" To his dismay, Ken realized the press must know about Link and his family. Even though Tom used to play golf with the publisher, he knew that wouldn't stop the news stories.

Charlotte told Kenneth she suspected that someone in the prosecutor's office was leaking information to the press. She was sure Kenneth would be indicted soon.

"I'll cancel all my other appointments and remain in Seattle," she said. "Gianni Rubino will leak just enough information about the trust fund to stimulate intense interest in the trial."

Ken groaned and stared out of the car window. What a mess he had created, he thought. The humiliation of a trial and possible conviction was no longer a matter of speculation. He had to call Lydia. He must prepare her for the worst.

Ken told Lydia of the meeting in the prosecutor's office. "Charlotte thinks Rubino is cooperating with the press to enhance his own position. She's sure the prosecutor will bring the matter before the Grand Jury soon."

"Why wouldn't he just issue a warrant?"

"The Grand Jury decides if there's enough evidence to issue a warrant. If it does find probable cause, and if the court returns a true bill of indictment, charging me with a crime, the court issues an order for arrest."

"You sound like a lawyer. How do you know all that?"

Kenneth laughed. "I'm not sure I understand it either. I'm just repeating what Charlotte told me."

"Kenneth, this is dreadful for the children. The newspaper reporters and photographers have been following them and embarrassing the children in front of their friends. Tom says if this continues he'll send Nate to protect them from reporters. Some of the children at school are teasing Link about his godfather. They say, 'Don't mess with Bradshaw, or the Godfather will get you.'"

"I'm mortified that your family has to go through this," Ken said.

"Link wouldn't be alive today if you hadn't done what you did," Lydia said. "Believe me, it's a small price for us to pay."

Paul Edinger, a middle-aged plump man with twenty years of experience on the bench, was appointed Assignment Judge for the Grand Jury. He instructed the jurors.

"Ladies and gentlemen: you are to consider evidence as

presented by the prosecutor, and determine if there is probable cause to proceed with a criminal prosecution. If it is unclear whether known evidence is exculpatory, a prosecutor should err on the side of disclosure. You may request additional witnesses if you believe their testimony will help resolve questions you may have.

"The U.S. Supreme Court, in *United States v. Sokolow*, determined that 'probable cause requires a fair probability that contraband or evidence of a crime will be found.'

"The defendant is not obligated to establish proof of innocence; rather the prosecutor must present evidence that establishes a fair probability of guilt."

Gianni Rubino stood and addressed the jurors. He wore a hand-tailored, three-button, brown pinstripe suit and a red silk tie with matching pocket handkerchief. He looked as though he had stepped out of *Esquire*. He smiled, not speaking until he had made eye contact with each jury member.

"Ladies and gentleman, the State of Washington, King County jurisdiction, through the office of the county prosecutor, does hereby accuse Dr. Kenneth Bernholtz of criminal acts spanning a period in excess of three years."

His assistant, Roger Kley, handed each juror a copy of the signed five-page confession Ken Bernholtz had given to Stuart Krandell and later shared with the prosecutor's office.

Rubino read a copy of the statement aloud, pausing frequently while making frequent eye contact with the jurors. He enumerated the counts against Dr. Kenneth Bernholtz:

"One...The accused illegally procured human organs for the purpose of selling those organs for exorbitant fees.

"Two...The accused established Research Endowment

Trust Fund #14763 at the First Union Bank of Seattle for the purpose of laundering large sums of money that were used exclusively by Dr. Bernholtz in the furtherance of his conspiratorial acts.

"Three...Strong circumstantial evidence suggests that the accused Dr. Kenneth Bernholtz and his co-conspirator Dr. Gamal Faysal may have been guilty of planning to murder, by lethal overdose of a narcotic drug, two persons whom they believed were about to expose them.

"Four...By funneling funds that actually represented the payment for organs into a tax-free trust fund, Dr. Kenneth Bernholtz was guilty of fraud and possible tax evasion.

"Five...By his own admission Dr. Bernholtz called Dr. Gamal Faysal and warned him that he intended to confess what he had done, and suggested that Dr. Faysal return to Saudi Arabia in order to escape arrest. This constituted aiding and abetting a criminal in the avoidance of prosecution."

Gianni went on to point out that in Kenneth's written statement, he had admitted to most of the activities listed in the State's indictment. Mr. Rubino then re-read Ken's five-page confession to the jury.

"Ladies and gentlemen, the State could rest here and would have presented sufficient cause to proceed with prosecution. But there is more. There is much more. I would like at this time to call witnesses, whose testimony will further substantiate the prosecution's case."

Mr. Rubino called several witnesses. The funeral director, who picked up David Lang's body, testified that he had seen a man guarding the entrance to Dr. Bernholtz's morgue. The guard told the mortician that he was there at Dr. Bernholtz's request.

Mr. Rubino showed the mortician a photograph of one of Faysal's agents, who had been arrested at the Seatac

Motor Inn.

Silas Jones said, "Yeah, that's him. There's no mistaking that face."

Mr. Rubino later brought to the stand the police officers who apprehended the two armed men after they had broken into Frank's and Tina's motel room. He went on to point out that both Dr. Tupelo and the young woman, Tina Carrol, had learned of the conspiracy between Dr. Bernholtz and Dr. Faysal.

"They represented a threat of exposure," Gianni said at the conclusion of the officer's testimony. "Remember, one of the men who broke into the motel was seen at the hospital, as requested by Dr. Bernholtz."

Gianni Rubino walked to a desk where Roger Kley was seated. Roger pushed a stack of manila folders toward him. Gianni opened one. He was silent as he appeared to be reading the document. He waved the folder in the air.

"Ladies and gentleman, this is one of dozens of letters Dr. Bernholtz wrote to Saudi families, thanking them for their contributions and asking about their children, who had transplants. Clearly a *quid pro quo*, money for organs."

Pounding his fist against the folders, he said, "These alone are sufficient cause for us to proceed." He strode to the jury box. He stood, silent for a few moments. "No, there is more. There is more."

He walked to the desk again and picked up a document. He licked his lips. "I have here an affidavit signed by the parent of a child who received a donor heart from Dr. Bernholtz. At the time of the operation, a check for ten thousand dollars was deposited in the research endowment trust fund."

Gianni read from the affidavit. "After Dr. Bernholtz provided a donor heart for my child, I gave to Dr. Gamal

Faysal a check for five hundred thousand dollars."

He paused for a full thirty seconds. There was absolute quiet in the courtroom.

"Are we to swallow the very unlikely proposition that the person who planned this scam received a relative pittance in a research fund, whereas his co-conspirator pocketed half a million dollars?"

The jury was out a mere thirty minutes. They decided to proceed with criminal prosecution. An order for Ken's arrest was issued, and bail was set at four hundred thousand dollars. A trial date was set for December tenth in King County District Court.

Link rolled onto his side so he could see his clock, but he couldn't make out the time. He scrunched his eyes almost shut but still couldn't tell. He sat on the side of his bed as he put on his glasses. It was 3:00 AM. Something had awakened him. Had his dad gotten up early again?

A leafless oak tree by Link's bedroom window swayed in the moaning wind. A bright moon cast the tree's shadow across the floor and up the wall opposite his bed. He shivered as he slipped on a pair of jeans.

He went to his dad's room. The door was ajar, the room was empty. After going to the kitchen for a glass of milk, he headed for his dad's study. The TV was on, but the screen was just a bunch of snow. Link checked the VCR. His dad had been looking at the tape of his mother's funeral. He turned off the television. He walked to the chair where his dad was sleeping. Link started to wake him, and then changed his mind. He returned to his room and got a blanket and took it to the study. He covered his dad. He went back to bed, but he couldn't sleep. Everybody was worried about Uncle Ken, but his dad just wasn't the same as he used to be. Link decided to talk with his grandmother. Maybe she could figure out how to help.

At school, Link was glad to be doing things with his friend Mike. Even Jennifer acted glad to see him, and they sometimes hung out during recess. She seemed like a kid compared to Marty.

He and Marty talked on the phone two or three times a week.

"Hey, my spies tell me you're smoozing with your old squeeze."

"We just talk and fool around...you know."

"You're breaking my heart, lover-boy. I guess I'll just have to drown myself in theatre!"

Marty kept Link informed about school, the drama club and a school play in which she had a part as one of the witches in *Dark of the Moon*. She promised to get him a front-row seat for opening night. He threatened to stick out his tongue and make her laugh.

Link tried to keep on top of what was happening with his Uncle Ken. With the help of the newspapers and his grandmother, he was pretty well informed. He and Marty talked about what they might do.

"It drives me nuts to think your godfather might go to jail because of me," Marty said. "If I hadn't seen that autopsy...."

"They would have found out after he came back from London," Link interrupted. "It's just as much my fault."

"We gotta help," Marty said. "There has to be a way. Damnit, Link. You're smart. Think of something."

"I sort of have an idea."

"You gonna tell me or what?"

"My dad, Uncle Ken and Charlotte had a meeting at my house. I heard her tell them that she had a list of prosecution witnesses. She said that you aren't on it."

"I know. Your dad called my mom. It kind of makes sense. Your Uncle Ken admitted he stole organs...what I saw doesn't matter."

"She also told my dad that Dr. Faysal's assistant isn't being called to testify."

"Hey! Maybe Dr. Salemi told them something they didn't want to hear."

"That's what I'm thinking. I talked to my dad. He said Charlotte was already planning on going to the Hakim Medical Center to talk with Dr. Salemi. But she told my dad the prosecution calls the witnesses during a Grand Jury hearing, not the defense."

"That doesn't seem fair," Marty said.

"To me neither."

"I'd love to go. You think Charlotte would let me?"

"I don't know. What would you do?"

"Snoop around. I'm a hellofa snooper."

"Yeah, that's for sure. You want me to ask her?"

"No. Give me her number. You don't as yet have my powers of persuasion."

CHAPTER FORTY-SEVEN

A week after the Grand Jury hearing, Lydia called Tom. "There's something I must talk to you about. Can you come for dinner?"

His immediate suspicion was that she was going to tell him that she had known of Uncle Ken's involvement with Faysal long before anyone else. Had Ken confided in her? Was she afraid she might be called as a witness? He knew how desperate she had been to find a heart for Link.

"Of course, Mother. I've a board meeting at six. I can be there by eight-thirty."

His mother was animated and radiant at dinner, but after the small talk wound down, she grew quiet, almost shy as she glanced at him.

"Mother, you said on the phone..."

"Let's have our coffee in the living room. You go on in, Tom. I'll be right there."

A few minutes later she came and sat next to him on the couch. She placed a tray on the coffee table and poured cups for Tom and herself. "I bought some cheesecake today. It's chocolate, your favorite."

"What's wrong, Mother? You're not yourself tonight."

She leaned back and ran her fingers through her hair, sweeping it back off her shoulders. Tom had noticed lately she was styling it differently. He remembered seeing old pictures of her with her hair down. He wasn't sure he liked this new look.

"You know, Tom, before I met your father, Kenneth and I were close friends. I was very fond of him, but he was so reserved back then. I didn't understand. I thought maybe he didn't care that much."

"He's still pretty damn reserved. But he has come through for us. I'd do anything to help him."

"Kenneth has asked me to marry him."

Tom seemed to have lost control of his facial muscles. He had no idea his mother and Uncle Ken were more than very old and dear friends. Although it was more than two years since his father's death, it never occurred to Tom that his mother would remarry. How long had this been going on? "When...I mean, how could you even think about that right now? Ken might even go to jail."

She placed her hand on his knee. She searched his face before she spoke. "I love Kenneth. If he's acquitted, we want to marry right away. If he has to go to prison, I'll wait."

"Mom...it just seems so...so sudden."

"Sudden? We've known each other forty years. Do you remember that night at dinner when your father was so sick, and he asked Kenneth if he thought I was attractive?"

"I do. You blushed like a schoolgirl."

"I saw the way your father looked at him as we talked. He was very fond of Kenneth, too. I believe he was giving us permission to be together after he was gone."

Tom could not as yet bring himself to smile. It seemed

Ken had been part of his life forever...but not like this. "Mother, I have the greatest respect and admiration for him, and if that's what you and he want..."

Lydia hugged Tom. "Nobody will ever replace your father in our hearts, but we have to make room for the living."

Tom realized his mother was also talking about him. "I'm sure you're right, Mother. I want to open up too, but I just can't. Dad did everything a person can do in life. He had time to prepare for dying. Brenda had her whole life ahead of her. I just can't accept her being gone."

"I understand; you need more time. Maybe you should think about talking with someone to help you work through this."

"I don't need some damn shrink! I can handle this myself."

"Link told me you don't play around with him like you used to. And that sometimes you get up in the night and watch the funeral video." Lydia's voice was firm, almost shrill. "Tom, it's time to erase that tape. Don't shortchange Link. He's been through the same trauma as you."

He wanted to throw the cheesecake through a window and storm out of the room. Instead he squeezed his coffee cup so hard the handle cracked. The cup dropped into his lap, soaking his trousers. He jumped to his feet.

"Oh, Tom, did you burn yourself?"

"I'm okay...I'm sorry. I'm not as resilient you, Mother."

Lydia was on her knees, using her napkin to blot up the spilled coffee. She stood and placed her hands around Tom's waist. "Yes, you are, Tom. You're just like your father. You have to be in control. But you can't control everything. Get help, Tom. Please, for Link's sake if not your own."

CHAPTER FORTY-EIGHT

It was standard operating procedure for Charlotte Richards, either formally or informally, to interview prosecution witnesses. She had copies of some of their depositions. Those not on the list were of greater interest to her. That included the new medical director, Dr. Salemi, as well as the doctors and nurses at the Hakim Medical Center. Why wasn't he being called to testify? Dr. Salemi was, after all, the one person who had worked most closely with Dr. Faysal.

Charlotte was curled up on a side-chair in the Seattle Omni Hotel, reading depositions. Her phone rang.

"Charlotte Richards here."

"Hi, Miss Richards. This is Marty Lopinski. You know, Link Bradshaw's friend."

"Marty! I'm glad you called."

"I was wondering if you could give me a part-time job."

"My office is in Florida. That's quite a commute."

"I mean here. You know, like a special investigator."

"You interested in the law?" Charlotte removed her reading glasses and walked to the kitchenette, where a pot of coffee was brewing.

"Maybe. I still have to finish high school. I heard you're going to the Hakim Medical Center on Friday."

"Now how did you hear that?" Charlotte asked, although she had a pretty good idea.

"It's a big hospital. You could use a little help."

"What about school?"

"It's a teacher work-day," Marty responded.

Charlotte laughed. "I bet! Hmm. You're fifteen..."

"I just turned sixteen."

"Well...you meet the age requirement. I'd have to get your mother's permission."

"She already said it's okay."

"You don't mind minimum wage?"

"No. But I want time-and-a-half for overtime."

"It's settled. Three dollars and eighty cents an hour, portal to portal."

The following Friday, Charlotte pulled up in front of Gladys' and Marty's apartment. She was driving a rented red convertible BMW. When she honked, Marty came through the front door and hurried toward the car.

Charlotte was wearing a floppy-brimmed ruffia hat, paisley scarf and aviator-style sunglasses. At first Marty wasn't sure it was Charlotte, whom she had never seen. This was not what she had imagined.

Marty was wearing white slacks, a button-down white shirt, knit tie and blue blazer. Her blond hair was tied back in a pony-tail.

"You look very professional," Charlotte said as Marty settled into the bucket seat beside her. "Anyone would take you for at least seventeen."

"Would you roll down the roof and drive past my school?" Marty asked.

"I think not."

"Please!"

"Not with you playing hooky. I'd be arrested for contributing to the delinquency of a minor."

"At least roll down the roof. I never rode in a convertible my whole life."

"Okay. On the way back, weather permitting."

At a meeting in Dr. Kasib Salemi's office, Charlotte introduced Marty as a special assistant. They sat opposite Dr. Salemi in upholstered side chairs. The three exchanged small talk about the drive from Seattle and the traffic before getting down to business.

Charlotte asked Dr. Salemi how the District Attorney had located families of the children who had received illegally- obtained organs.

"Ms. Richards, it was very simple to trace. Mr. Rubino gave me dates when the organs were transported to us from Children's Hospital. Apparently, he got that information directly from Dr. Bernholtz. The transplant surgery had to be performed within twenty-four hours, so we reviewed the hospital census for that time frame. We went to the record room to locate the charts of all the children in the hospital that day. If a child's medical record could not be located, it was logical to assume those were the children who had received a forbidden organ. Once we had the names of the children in question, we called the hospital in Riyadh and requested follow-up on their condition. That seemed perfectly appropriate. We also asked for names and phone numbers of the parents. It took us three or four days to gather the information I assume his staff contacted the families."

Charlotte nodded. She jotted down some notes. She noticed Marty looking intensely about the room, as though committing to memory every detail of Dr. Faysal's former office.

"Mrs. Richards, we have cooperated fully with the police. We have sick children who need organ transplants. It's my responsibility to do all I can to ensure that organs continue to arrive through legitimate channels."

"But the prosecutor has not asked you to testify."

"No."

Charlotte stood and walked to the office window. She turned toward Dr. Salemi. "Would you consider testifying for the defense?" she asked.

"If you believe I might be of help to Dr. Bernholtz."

"Dr. Bernholtz came to the Hakim Medical Center on many occasions. Was there ever anything that happened that might make you believe Dr. Faysal was not being straightforward with Dr. Bernholtz, especially regarding the gifts to his research trust fund?" Charlotte persisted, gazing into his eyes. Her intensity caught him off-guard.

He was silent for several moments. He shifted gears. "Mrs. Richards, would you care for some coffee or tea?"

"Coffee would be wonderful."

He asked, "Miss Lopinski, would you care for a soft drink?"

"A Coke or Pepsi if you have any."

He spoke with his secretary over the intercom, and then sat at his desk. His forehead was moist. "I am most uncomfortable to discuss this. You see, I am very fond of Dr. Bernholtz. Our entire staff felt him to be a man of integrity and compassion. Whenever he came here, he spent time with the children. He took the trouble to learn some Arabic words, so he could converse with them. He often brought them presents. This was in stark contrast to Dr. Faysal. The only time he fussed over the children was when Dr. Bernholtz was here. At other times Dr. Faysal appeared to be interested only in the financial health of the hospital, not its little patients."

Charlotte smiled. "That's why I'm committed to defending Dr. Bernholtz. What is it you know that might help?"

"Several hours after Faysal left, he called me. I could hear aircraft noise in the background. He sounded very disturbed. He reminded me to check his mailbox daily. He asked that after receiving a special document, I should turn in the key to the post office and ask them to forward any future mail to the address he had given me"

"Was there anything in his post office box?"

"Two days after he left, a letter arrived...no return address. It was post-marked Dusseldorf, Germany. Later that day I forwarded the letter as he had requested. And as he instructed, I gave his key to the post office, also his forwarding address."

Charlotte's eyes narrowed. "Weren't you curious about the contents of this 'special document'?"

"It was a dilemma," he admitted. "At that time there was no criminal investigation. But I long suspected some of the organs from Children's Hospital were illegally obtained."

"Why?" Charlotte demanded.

"The documentation was unusual. There was no organ-donor consent form. Just a transfer summary signed by Dr. Bernholtz. Also, Dr. Faysal had hired four security guards. They all were paid by him, reporting directly to him. That was most unusual in our administrative structure."

"You had reason to be concerned," Charlotte said.

"I suspected Dr. Faysal insisted that large sums of money be donated by Saudi families whose children we cared for. I had no physical evidence, however..."

"I wish you had turned the letter over to me. I could have obtained a court order to examine its contents," Charlotte said.

"That had not occurred to me. Besides, I had not yet met you."

Marty raised her hand.

"Yes, Miss Lopinski?" Salemi asked.

"Anything you tell us will be kept in strict confidence. Even if you opened that letter, our mouths would be sealed, Dr. Salelmi." Marty squeezed her lips for emphasis.

Charlotte smiled. "I am here representing Dr. Bernholtz. I'm searching for any information that will aid in his defense."

He removed a handkerchief from his pocket and wiped his brow. He cleared his throat.

Charlotte was certain he had read the letter, but pressing him might be counter-productive. She leaned forward and remained silent.

After a few moments, he said softly, "I made copies, resealed the envelope and forwarded the original to Dr. Faysal. I gave a copy to Mr. Rubino."

Marty jumped to her feet. "You gave the prosecutor a copy!"

He nodded. "Yes. And I kept a copy."

Salemi's secretary entered, carrying a tray with coffee, a can of coke and a bowl of chocolate-chip cookies. She placed them on the table and left.

The doctor walked to the wall safe and removed a folder. He handed it to Charlotte.

As she studied the contents of the folder, Marty read over her shoulder. The letter was written on plain paper without a letterhead. It was titled, "Quarterly Report." There was no salutation and no account number. Several deposits were listed, the dates and the banks on which they were drawn. The deposits ranged from two hundred and fifty thousand to five hundred thousand dollars. Most were transfers from numbered bank accounts. Others were drawn on banks in Riyadh. There were an equal number of withdrawals of from ten to fifteen thousand dollars written to the Children's Memorial Hospital Research Fund..."

"Holy Moley!" Marty exclaimed. "The Grand Jury should have seen this stuff. It was Dr. Faysal who was making out like a bandit."

Charlotte nodded. "You were saying, Dr. Salemi?"

"The name 'Mr. Hans Schuller' is printed at the bottom, but there is no signature."

"I suspect that's a code name of an officer in a Swiss bank," Charlotte said.

"But the post mark?" Salemi asked.

"It's not uncommon for statements from Swiss Banks to be postmarked from another country." Charlotte removed her glasses and chewed absent-mindedly on the ear piece. "Dr. Salemi, even if we could identify the bank in question, they wouldn't reveal the identity of the account owner."

"Never?" Dr. Salemi leaned forward. "Even in a criminal investigation?"

"The Swiss Secrecy Act of 1934 spells out very specific circumstances in which a bank must open an account to investigators. They aren't really concerned with civil suits, like malpractice. Also, in Switzerland, parental consent isn't required for harvesting body organs, and the transfer of human organs for cash isn't criminal. Dr. Faysal's Swiss bank account would be virtually impenetrable. He picked his banker well."

"But now that he has been arrested, would they not release the information?" Kasib was perplexed.

"Not unless he's convicted of a serious crime. But there's still the problem of locating the bank. In a numbered account, just the bank manager is aware of the owner's identity."

Kasib's shoulders drooped. "Then the statement you hold in your hands may be our only evidence?"

"I believe so. Was anyone else in the room with you when you gave these statements to Mr. Rubino?"

"A Mr. Kley accompanied him to the hospital, but he was off interviewing the operating room supervisor at that time...I believe these records strongly suggest that Dr. Bernholtz did not personally profit from Dr. Faysal's extortion scheme."

Marty noticed the large shredder next to Dr. Salemi's desk. "Dr. Salemi, can I ask you something?"

He smiled. "Of course, Ms. Lopinski."

"What happens to the stuff you shred...I mean, the stuff Dr. Faysal shredded?"

"Normally files would have been compacted and discarded. But in this instance I gathered them into a bag...I didn't trust Dr. Faysal...I believed the material might be of some help in understanding what he was up to. I can give it to you if it will be helpful."

Charlotte broke out into a broad smile. She and Marty hi-fived each other "Pardon the language, Doctor, but you are a jewel," Charlotte said.

He looked stunned. "Oh no, Ms. Richards, I am a not a Jew, I am Muslim!"

Late that afternoon, Charlotte and Marty headed back to Seattle, a copy of the letter from Hans Schuller tucked in the lawyer's briefcase and the bag of shredded files packed safely in the trunk of the car. Deep in thought, exhilarated by her talk with Dr. Salemi, Charlotte did not realize that she was driving 75 mph. in a 60 mph. zone. When she saw blinking lights behind her, she glanced at her speedometer. "Damn! This'll cost me." She removed her sunglasses and put on bifocals.

Marty laughed. She turned down the car radio that had been blaring Indigo Girls' *Closer to Fine.*

The officer asked to see Charlotte's driver's license and car registration. He studied them. "The troopers in Florida must be kept pretty busy if all the grandmothers down there drive like you."

"Yeah, Grandma. He's right!" Marty agreed.

Charlotte bit her lip to keep from laughing. "I'm sorry, officer. I had no idea I was going that fast. If you're ever in Florida and need a lawyer, look me up."

She handed him her business card.

"Hey, how about that. Thought you looked familiar. You're that doctor's lawyer....Your picture's been in the papers."

"Tell me, what do you think of the prosecutor?"

The officer looked around. "Off the record?"

Charlotte nodded.

"Rubino would send his mother to jail to get his picture in the papers. A lot of the force is rootin' for you." He put away his ticket pad and smiled. "Now take the lead out of your shoe and kick ass in court."

As they got back on the road, Marty turned up the volume on the radio. She undid her pony tail and let her hair fly in the breeze. She pumped her arm as though she had just run a mile in less than four minutes. "This is seriously cool stuff. I can't wait to tell Link."

"Keep it quiet for now. Remember, you promised our lips are sealed."

After dropping off Marty, Charlotte called Kenneth. "I have some startling news. Can we meet somewhere for dinner?"

"Lydia and I have a reservation at La Boheme. Why don't you join us?"

"I'm in need of a major infusion of calories," Charlotte informed the waiter. "What do you have on your menu that's low in fat and served in outrageous portions?"

"Any of our pasta dishes. One perhaps with a light marinara sauce?"

When dinner arrived, Charlotte proceeded to attack her food with skill and determination. All the while she carried on an animated conversation with Lydia.

"I love museums," Charlotte said. "Tell me about your work."

"That's a wonderful invitation. Are you sure you have enough time?" Lydia asked.

"As long as the food doesn't run out, I have plenty of time."

"I worked as curator of the Seattle Museum of Natural History for several years until my husband developed lung cancer. I quit work to spend more time with him. After he passed away, I went back to work part-time. Right now we're restoring artifacts from an early Indian village excavated on the Olympic Peninsula. You may have read about the dig. It was headed up by one of Leakey's former students, Dr. Donald Glowa."

Charlotte interrupted her eating. "Yes, wasn't there something about it in the *National Geographic* a couple of years ago?"

Lydia's eyes lit up. "That's right. When I read the article I called Dr. Glowa. I had studied the tribes of the northwest for my Master's thesis. He invited me to be a consultant on his dig. I felt like a child discovering buried treasure. We're re-creating the entire village in a new section of the museum. They've added over 6,000 square feet to accommodate all the structures."

"When I retire from the law," Charlotte said, "I'd like to study anthropology. To dig up and piece together how people lived...that would be fantastic."

"Please, wait until after you piece together my life," Kenneth quipped. They resisted talking about the case until the espresso arrived.

"Seattle has the best espresso around," Charlotte said. "It's worth flying here from Miami just to get a good cup of coffee."

"Kenneth, if you and Charlotte need to talk business, I can take a cab home," Lydia suggested.

"Nonsense," Charlotte said. "He can drive you home first; then he and I can chew the fat at my hotel."

Once there in the hotel bar, Kenneth declined dessert. Charlotte ordered pecan pie with a scoop of vanilla ice cream. They both had more coffee.

Smiling like the cat that caught the canary, Charlotte

reached into her purse. She handed him the copy of the bank statement from Hans Schuller. He read in silence. His face reddened. "How did you get your hands on this? God! To think how piously Gamal spoke about our noble work of saving the lives of his dear Saudi children. That phony bastard! How could I have been so damn gullible?"

Charlotte told him of her interview with Dr. Salemi. "Kenneth, Gianni Rubino had a copy of this letter in his possession prior to convening the Grand Jury."

"I don't understand. It's obvious from this that Dr. Faysal extorted unconscionable amounts of money from desperate Saudi families. There's nothing here to indicate even a penny came to me personally."

"Precisely. And if he had in his hands exculpatory evidence, he was obliged to present it to the Grand Jury."

"What kind of evidence?" Kenneth asked.

"Evidence that would prove your innocence."

"It's not exactly that, is it?"

"No, but it's damn close. The fact that Dr. Salemi has not been formally asked to be a witness for the prosecution makes me suspect that Mr. Rubino has no intention of acknowledging the existence of that statement."

"Wouldn't he want to use those in the prosecution of Dr. Faysal?"

"He has sworn affidavits from the Saudis who paid off Faysal. He doesn't need those statements. And he correctly concluded that they would weaken his case against you."

Charlotte motioned a waiter to bring more coffee.

"I'm totally confused," Ken said. "Are you saying the bank statement is not really all that helpful?"

"I believe it points strongly to your innocence, when you combine this evidence with the fact that it was *you* who decided to come forward. And it was Dr. Faysal's accomplices who attacked you at the airport."

"I'm confused. You argue both sides of this debate eloquently."

Charlotte laughed. "Kenneth, that's the way lawyers are trained. I just have more natural ability than most."

Charlotte requested a conference with Judge Edinger and Gianni Rubino, in order to discuss new evidence. When Marty learned of the meeting through her fine-tuned grapevine, she called Charlotte.

"Can I attend? Or do I need a law degree or something?"

"You're one of my assistants. Your middle-school diploma will do just fine. But this time you are strictly an observer. If you want to speak, just whisper in my ear."

They met in the judge's chambers, a cluttered room with ornately-festooned walls and a terrazzo floor. Several tight-skinned, padded leather chairs were arranged around a low table. Charlotte studied Gianni, who sat facing away from her. There had been no real greeting, no handshake, just a slight nod. The judge, who had come in from the courtroom, was wearing his formal robes. He looked at Charlotte expectantly.

She introduced Marty. The judge looked incredulous.

"Isn't this the young lady who blew the whistle on your client?"

"Yes, Your Honor. She has very special skills. And one day she will make a fine attorney."

Marty whispered in Charlotte's ear. "You're

embarrassing me."

"Your Honor," Charlotte said, "I've recently discovered that the prosecution had in its possession a bank statement that would have cast serious doubt Dr. Bernholtz had received monies other than what went into his trust fund."

She went on to say she believed this evidence supported Dr. Bernholtz's contention he did not personally benefit from the transfer of organs to the Hakim Medical Center.

Gianni Rubino smiled. "Your Honor, what she's referring to is not admissible. The State is attempting to assess the authenticity of the bank statement the defense is referring to. We have an unsigned letter from an unknown individual in Dusseldorf, Germany, written on plain stationary without letterhead, and no return address. It listed deposits into Dr. Faysal's account. We've contacted banks in Dusseldorf; none know of a Mr. Hans Schuller." Gianni waved his hand as though dismissing this so-called new evidence. He continued, "Even if these documents prove authentic, they tell us nothing about Dr. Bernholtz's part in the extortion scheme."

"Your honor," Charlotte said, "we have checked the dates of those deposits, and they all follow dates on which a donor organ was received at Hakim Medical Center. It suggests a motive as to why Dr. Faysal would strike out against Dr. Bernholtz..."

"I understand two of Dr. Faysal's security guards did attack Dr. Bernholtz at the airport," Judge Edinger interjected.

"Even if we could prove that Dr. Faysal was responsible for the assault," Gianni protested, "the fact is that he and Dr. Bernholtz were co-conspirators in a scheme to sell organs."

Charlotte handed Judge Edinger a copy of the letter from the mysterious Hans Schuller. "Your Honor, even though this evidence, which Dr. Salemi had given to Mr. Rubino, would not be admissible in a criminal trial, it would be admissible in a Grand Jury hearing."

Gianni stood. "But Your Honor..."

"Be seated, Mr. Rubino." The judge continued to read the material Charlotte had given him.

Marty whispered, "I like this guy."

After studying the letter for several minutes, Judge Edinger announced that he would hold a formal pre-trial hearing to consider the new evidence. The judge added, "Then I'll determine whether the Grand Jury should be reconvened to revisit its decision."

CHAPTER FORTY-NINE

The United States District Court of Seattle, Washington, on December 3, 1991, held a pretrial hearing in one of the building's small courtrooms. In attendance were Lydia, Tom, Link, Marty, several of Ken's colleagues from Children's hospital, and a group of newspaper reporters.

Gianni Rubino and Roger Kley sat at a table to the judge's right. Ken and Charlotte sat at another table to the judge's left.

As Charlotte anticipated, Gianni maintained that he had no way to confirm the authenticity of the bank statement. Who was Hans Schuller? Which bank did he represent?

The defense presented only one witness, Dr. Kasib Salemi, who had replaced Dr. Gamal Faysal as medical director of the Hakim Medical Center. He testified that Dr. Faysal had called him and requested that he check his post-office box daily for mail and forward it immediately to Riyadh. Kasib said he had opened the letter before forwarding it. He also said he had given a copy of the letter to prosecutor Gianni Rubino prior to the Grand Jury hearing.

The judge asked Dr. Salemi why he had opened the letter in clear violation of the law and Dr. Faysal's right to privacy.

"I had reason to suspect that Dr. Faysal had been extorting large sums of money from Saudi families. I had seen correspondence that mentioned cash donations to the Hakim Medical Center. And yet, these monies never found their way into the hospital records."

"I object," Gianni protested. "Dr. Salelmi's testimony is mere hearsay and not admissible."

"Overruled." The judge asked the witness, "Dr. Salemi, surely Dr. Faysal would not leave such correspondence lying about his office?"

"Dr. Faysal kept a locked file there. I was curious and concerned. The locks were not impossible to overcome. I read several letters in which specific sums of money were requested." Kasib turned to Ken. He continued, "None of the letters said anything about Dr. Bernholtz receiving money."

During cross-examination, Gianni asked if the witness realized it was a federal crime to open someone else's mail.

"I was suspicious because of the letters I had seen and of the very tight security in which he maintained his correspondence with Saudi families. I suspected that the letter might contain incriminating evidence that would help the investigation."

"What you accomplished, Dr. Salemi, was to render this evidence inadmissible in a criminal trial," Gianni said. "And where are those letters? We have gone through Dr. Faysal's files and found no such letters. We have only your word that they ever existed."

"Your Honor," Charlotte said, "Mr. Rubino knows full well that Dr. Faysal shredded a large amount of material before he left the country."

"Again, we have only Dr. Salemi's word that materials

were indeed shredded," Gianni protested.

Dr. Salemi turned toward the judge. "Sir, may I speak to that?"

"Yes, you may, Doctor," Edinger responded.

"Normally shredded material would have been compacted and discarded. However, I suspected this particular material might constitute important evidence. I gathered it up in a plastic bag. I gave the bag to Ms. Richards' assistant, Miss Martha Lopinski."

Marty reached under the table where she sat alongside Charlotte. She pulled up a bulging white plastic bag, walked to where Gianni was sitting, and deposited it on the table before him.

Gianni jumped to his feet, "The contents of this trash bag can, by no stretch of the imagination, be considered evidence. This theatrical ploy is beneath the dignity of this court."

Judge Edinger leaned forward. "Mr. Rubino, what is below the dignity of this court is your withholding possible exculpatory evidence from the Grand Jury."

"I considered the letter from Hans Schuller, as I have already said, does not constitute real evidence. Certainly it is not exculpatory."

"Your Honor, the Grand Jury should be allowed to consider this evidence," Charlotte proposed. "I trust Mr. Rubino recalls that in the United States v. Calandra, in 1974, the Supreme Court ruled that illegally-obtained evidence is admissible in a Grand Jury hearing."

"I object, Your Honor. Although the evidence may be technically admissible, there is no way to authenticate its contents."

Charlotte made a Motion that the Grand Jury be

reconvened to reconsider its decision as to whether her client had committed a crime.

"I object, your Honor," Gianni said. "Must the State present to the Grand Jury evidence it believes to be fraudulent?"

"It is true that the prosecution did not break any laws by withholding this evidence," Edinger responded, "if it were deemed not possible to authenticate. In addition, the prosecution is not under any obligation to present potentially exculpatory evidence to a Grand Jury."

"Exactly, Your Honor." Gianni smiled and sat. His assistant slapped him on the back. He looked pleased. But his smile was not to linger.

Judge Edinger continued. "On the other hand, a man who has had an impeccable medical career and is recognized as a brilliant researcher stands to go to prison, if the people find there is probable cause to suspect he broke the law. I believe the prosecution acted precipitously in bringing Dr. Bernholtz before the Grand Jury. Dr. Salemi's testimony and the bank statement do support the defense's assertion that Dr. Bernholtz received no money, other than relatively modest amounts that went into his research fund."

Judge Edinger went on to discuss each of the counts brought against Dr. Bernholtz. He reminded the court that it was the amount of the checks written by the Saudi parents that had a pivotal impact on the Grand Jury decision. And that the bank statements clearly show most of the money went into, and remained, in Dr. Faysal's account. "That information makes it quite plausible that Dr. Faysal would have struck out against Dr. Bernholtz, when he thought his lucrative enterprise might soon collapse. It was Dr. Faysal who had much to lose if Dr. Bernholtz were to confess their actions. It was Dr. Faysal who was banking hundreds of thousands of dollars, extorted from the families of the children at the Hakim Medical Center."

Judge Edinger looked directly at the jury. "It appears that Dr. Bernholtz's only motive in sending organs to the Center was to save lives," he said. "That is what he has said repeatedly, and there has not been a single shred of evidence presented by the prosecution to indicate otherwise. This court does not condone Dr. Bernholtz's actions. He was aware of acceptable research behavior. When his proposal to use human organs for research was rejected, he went ahead anyway, clearly choosing to breach medical ethical standards. He must be accountable. However, a civil suit is already in place."

The judge looked directly at Kenneth. "Considering all the evidence before us, I do not see probable cause that Dr. Bernholtz has committed a crime."

Some in the court began to applaud and cheer. As the noise level reached a crescendo, the judge slammed his gavel. The sound reverberated throughout the room. There was instant quiet. Judge Edinger looked about the hushed courtroom.

"Although I do not find probable cause," the judge said, "it is the Grand Jury that must make that decision."

He stood, gathering some papers. "Dr. Bernholtz, who has already been suspended from his position at Children's Hospital, is released on his own recognizance until the Grand Jury reconvenes. Good day, ladies and gentlemen." He left the courtroom.

Ken broke into a broad grin and hugged Charlotte. Several reporters rushed toward them. Court guards surrounded them and ushered them from the room. Lydia, Tom, Link, Frank, Tina, and Gladys followed Charlotte, Marty, and Ken to a room adjacent to the courtroom. The celebration lasted several minutes until everyone was

Forbidden Harvest

hugged and kissed. Afterwards they went to Tom's home, where the celebration went on into the night.

One month later, the Grand Jury rescinded its previous decision. Kenneth was free of criminal prosecution. But Dr. Kasib Salemi, whose testimony had turned the tide in Kenneth's favor, was not so fortunate. A federal prosecutor issued a warrant for his arrest for invasion of privacy. The Saudi government intervened, requesting permission for Dr. Salemi to return home and for his prosecution to be handled by Saudi authorities. Charlotte Richards represented Dr. Salemi. She argued that his sole intention was to turn over to the police what he thought was incriminating evidence in a criminal investigation. She did not deny that her client was guilty of invasion of privacy, but she entered a Prayer for Judgment, arguing successfully that punishment be limited to deportation.

Soon afterwards, Tom had a dinner party to which he invited Kenneth, Lydia, Gladys, Marty, Frank and Tina. He looked about the table and proposed a toast. "Here's to the wonderful outcome of the Grand Jury hearing." Everyone clinked champagne glasses, even Link and Marty, whose glasses were filled with ginger ale.

"If we were in France, they'd at least give us wine," Marty whispered to Link.

Link proposed a toast: "Here's to my Uncle Ken, who got me a heart in the nick of time!" There was a second round of clinking glasses.

Ken stood and raised his glass: "And here's to Charlotte Richards, without whose help I would not be here tonight!"

Marty said to Link, "You sure this is ginger ale? I'm getting a little high."

Frank heard what Marty had said. "Young lady, your baseline is close to high."

Forbidden Harvest

"Anything new on the civil suit?" Tom asked Ken.

"The negotiations reached an impasse. The court recommended binding arbitration. In fact the negotiator called two days ago. He's ready to offer four thousand dollars per claimant. That's a total award of three hundred and forty thousand dollars. He said the hospital offered to pick up fifty-percent of the settlement."

"What did you tell him?" Lydia asked.

"It's as good a deal as we're likely to get. I told him to settle."

"You know, I'm willing to help," Tom said.

"Thanks, Tom. But I can manage. Between my TBI stock and the equity in my home I've got Charlotte and the settlement covered."

"After all you've done for Link, Kenneth, let us contribute," Lydia pleaded.

Ken looked across the table at Link. "Seeing Link sitting here this healthy is payment enough."

One week after the malpractice settlement, Wally Benedict devoted one hour of his talk show to review the Ken Bernholtz story. Ken had been invited to participate, but declined. He did, however, watch the program on television.

Benedict introduced his guests: "We have with us tonight Monica Bloom, single parent of a deceased child, who had a heart and kidney removed by Dr. Bernholtz against this mother's specific wishes; Harry Schwartz, investigative reporter for *The Washington Observer*; a Harvard law professor, Dale Cavenaugh; and Jeff Collins, M.D., former president of the American Medical Association."

Wally said, "Many people believe Dr. Bernholtz got off too easily. What do you think, Mrs. Bloom?"

"I'm furious the way he has managed to come out relatively unscathed. I attended the malpractice hearings. Most other parents felt exactly as I do." Her voice shook. "The hospital asked if I wanted our son, Jimmie, to be an organ donor. He suffered so much in his last days that I was appalled by the thought of them doing anything more to him. Dr. Bernholtz violated me as well as Jimmie."

Wally leaned toward her. He asked softly, "Do you have other children?"

"No. Jimmie was my only child." She started to cry.

"That doctor deserves a hell of a lot more than a slap on the wrist," Harry Schwartz interjected. "I believe the Grand Jury got it right the first time. He hired a big-time lawyer. She proved that we have the best damned judicial system money can buy!"

"Dr. Collins," Wally asked, "Do you believe that what turned out to be a modest financial settlement was punishment enough for Dr. Bernholtz's three-year breach of trust? And his flaunting of hospital rules governing research with human organs?"

"Remember," Dr. Collins responded, "he was thrown off the staff of Children's Hospital, and the Washington Board of Medical Examiners revoked his license for five years. Under the circumstance no other state will consider issuing him a license for at least that length of time."

"Big deal," Harry said. "I've been doing some snooping. Learned the Saudis offered him a job. Probably packing his bags as we speak. Probably end up with a hefty pay raise!"

"You know, he was on my show three years ago, after protestors kicked up a fuss about his proposal to experiment with human organs. I want to play a clip from that show. I had just asked Dr. Bernholtz about parental consent. This was his response...."

"No country in the world has more stringent informed consent procedures than the United States. As a society we are firmly committed to the idea that the parents, acting on their child's behalf, have the right to decide medical care and procedures."

"Damn hypocrite!" Monica blurted. "And he never met with the families, never told us he was sorry. Not once!"

"Dr. Cavenaugh," Wally asked, "from a legal..."

Ken switched off the TV. He couldn't stand to watch. Of all the labels that had been applied to his actions, that of hypocrite stung the most.

On top of public humiliation, the worst punishment professionally was that his past and future research would be tainted by his malpractice conviction. Researchers at several transplant centers across the country were interviewed by print, radio and television reporters, and voiced shock and outrage concerning revelations of Dr. Bernholtz's disregard for ethical standards and medical research protocols. Experts they spoke to doubted medical journals would publish his work.

Ken's phone rang. Charlotte had advised him to get an unlisted number. It must be family. He picked up the receiver.

"I assume you're watching the Wally Benedict Show?" Tom asked.

"I turned it off. Couldn't stand it any longer..."

"I wonder how that SOB found out about the Saudi offer."

"I don't care, Tom. Seeing that mother cry..."

Forbidden Harvest

"Think of the families of the children you saved," Tom pleaded.

"I should've met with the families after the suit was settled. But Charlotte didn't believe it would be wise. She was concerned the meeting might get out of control, turn ugly. That I might even have been in danger. I wish I hadn't taken her advice! I should have given them a chance to vent their anger, express their feelings. Tell them I was truly sorry to have caused them pain. I can't retrieve that opportunity. And if the other mothers and fathers are convinced, as Mrs. Bloom is, that I'm a hypocrite, they'll never believe anything I say."

In the months that followed, Dr. Shaheed applied for and received permission from the Human Subjects Committee to extend his experiments with human organs. There were demonstrations outside Children's Hospital, and again threats of injunctions. But this time, the hospital, embarrassed by charges of intimidation and repression of academic freedom, was supportive of the proposal. Jamael applied for and received a grant from the National Institute of Health to duplicate his and Ken's hyperbaric experiments.

Tina perfected Frank's lasagna recipe. She was ready to prepare it for Frank's parents, who were visiting from New Jersey. Frank's dad took seconds.

"Frankie," his dad said, "this is just like your mother used to make."

"It is wonderful, Tina," Frank's mother said. "But who has the time to make it the old way?" She turned to her husband. "Have a third helping, sweetheart. You're going to have to settle for Antonio's frozen lasagna when we get back home."

"Mom, Dad, I have some good news. I've been offered a position as a pediatric cardiology fellow at Children's Hospital."

"Don't they have fellowships in New Jersey or New York? I was hoping you'd be closer to home," his mother said.

"Mrs. Tupelo," Tina said, "the fellowship at Children's Hospital in Seattle is highly competitive. It's quite a distinction to be accepted."

"How's the pay?" his dad asked. "So far, all work and low pay."

"A lot more than I'm making now," Frank said, grinning at Tina. His father was true to form.

"Good. Take the job. Buy a place with an extra bedroom. Maybe we'll move to Seattle. I'm tired of the lousy weather in the Garden State."

Frank and Tina exchanged glances. It wasn't yet time to discuss their future plans.

Link's life was getting back to a more or less normal routine. He still couldn't take regular gym, but he was getting to like swimming and planned on going out for the aquatic team. He and Mike shot baskets almost every day after school. Mike, Link and his dad went to see the Mariners play whenever they were in town. At times Marty also came. Link was worried about his dad. He was some better, but far from his old playful self. Grandma Bradshaw made sure his dad was involved on a regular basis in social events with family and friends. He must have known she was playing therapist, doing what she thought was best for him.

Marty looked and felt pretty good. Three months after

her discharge from the hospital, her blond hair had returned to almost its original length and fullness. One day, as Marty sat at a window brushing out her ponytail, her mother came into the room and stood beside her. Marty reached around her mother's waist and pressed her close. "Mom, do you believe in miracles?"

"I do now."

Now that her school play was over, Marty began working with Tina in her imaging class for children with cancer. In the fall, she would start her senior year. She told her mother she wanted to study psychology, or acting or maybe law in college. Something exciting, for sure.

Despite expectations, Ken was devastated by the decision of the medical staff at Children's Hospital to censure him and revoke his staff privileges for an indefinite period. Their action was unprecedented, compounded by the Washington State Board of Medical Examiners' decision to withdraw his license to practice medicine for a period of five years, subject to review.

Kenneth recalled that three years ago, after the Human Subjects Committee had rejected his proposal, Dr. Faysal's superiors in Riyadh suggested Kenneth consider moving to Saudi Arabia. They said, "Here in Riyadh, you would be welcomed and given the resources necessary to pursue this vital research."

That was a very generous and tempting offer. But he was determined to find some way to continue his work in Seattle. However, Ken's decision to forge ahead without institutional or parental permission had ended dismally. The Saudi offer now was his only foreseeable option. But would they still be interested?

He got in touch with the research division at Alfaisal University College of Medicine in Riyadh. He was invited to travel to Saudi Arabia to make a presentation before their research council. He was interviewed by numerous department heads.

Several weeks later, he received a letter from the University, offering him the opportunity to establish a division of organ transplantation research at the medical school. The offer included a three-year contract, a more than adequate salary, and a generous budget for equipment and personnel. He told them he needed a few days to decide.

Letter in hand, he called Lydia and invited her to Pierre's. After dinner, Ken ordered Remy Martin Cognac and for Lydia, her favorite, a glass of Bailey's Irish Cream. He was silent as he swirled the pungent brown liquid in an oversized brandy snifter.

"Must I pry it out of you, Kenneth?

He reached into his breast pocket and handed her the letter. After reading it she looked up. "My! That's quite an offer. You'll be able to coax Jamael to join you! And the perks are not too shabby."

"Do you think I should accept?" he asked.

"You can't just mope around here with nothing to do. It'll give you a chance to continue your work."

"I can't ask you to leave Link and Tom."

She grasped his hand. "It won't be easy, darling. Tom and Link do need me here. Tom will soon plunge fully back into running TBI. Link and I have grown even closer. I need him as much as he needs me. I wouldn't consider a permanent move, but don't look so glum. I can come to stay for extended visits. And who knows what will happen after three years? If your research progresses, and I'm certain it will, any number of medical schools will be clamoring to get you."

Six months after his acquittal, Ken and Lydia were married. Following the ceremony at Tom's house, they walked through a corridor of well-wishers.

"You know what I'm thinking, Dad?" Link asked.

Marty whispered to Link, "You're wondering what two old fogies are going to do on their wedding night?"

"I was wondering what I should call him. Uncle Ken? Godfather? Grandpa?"

Tom smiled. "For me, he's Uncle Ken forever."

"Don't worry about it, guys," Marty said, "You have a choice. For me, he's just Dr. Bernholtz. Of course that's pretty good."

Tom watched as their car drove off. Of course he wished them well. Ever since Brenda's accident, Lydia had been Link's surrogate mother. And now, besides her life with Ken, she would resume her work at the museum. Tom dreaded the eventuality of her not being as involved as she had been. He looked at Link, smiling, talking with Marty. He should be deliriously happy over Link's recovery. But fear held sway over joy. He prayed to Brenda...help me, darling...help me be the father our son deserves.

In their departing car, Lydia looked through the rear window as family and friends receded into the distance. During the wedding ceremony, as Tom handed Kenneth the ring, despite his smile, she could sense his underlying sadness. That symbolic gesture represented yet another loss for Tom.

She had talked him into accepting the leadership position at TBI. She now regretted that. He had made the move from research and development reluctantly, in order to comply with hers and his dad's dream he would someday take over the company. And like his dad he never did anything halfway, always first to arrive and last to leave. She was now convinced that he must step down as CEO and return to R & D, an area he dearly loved. The move would be good for him and Link. After she and Kenneth returned from their honeymoon, she would insist, only because she knew that was really what Tom wanted. So much has happened, Lydia thought; the car crash; Brenda's death; Tom's months of emotional and physical pain; and the desperate battle to save Link. It was now time to build a life filled with joyful memories. She turned to her husband.

"This is the beginning of a new and wonderful time for us all," Lydia said, resting her head gently on his shoulder.

"I'm certain you'll make it happen," Ken said. "Or as Link would say, 'Roger that!'"

Made in the USA
Middletown, DE
08 February 2018